# Can I
# Give My
# Husband
# Back?

BOOKS BY KRISTEN BAILEY

*Has Anyone Seen My Sex Life?*

# Can I Give My Husband Back?

KRISTEN BAILEY

Bookouture

Published by Bookouture in 2020

An imprint of Storyfire Ltd.
Carmelite House
50 Victoria Embankment
London EC4Y 0DZ

www.bookouture.com

ISBN: 978-1-83888-239-6
eBook ISBN: 978-1-83888-238-9

This book is a work of fiction. Names, characters, businesses,
organizations, places and events other than those clearly in the
public domain, are either the product of the author's imagination
or are used fictitiously. Any resemblance to actual persons, living or
dead, events or locales is entirely coincidental.

*For Lauren and Barry.*
*The happiest divorced couple I know.*

# Prologue

250 days after I told Simon our marriage was over

*What are you wearing?*

*I went black. A dress with ruffled arms. And my black jacket and black shoes.*

*Has someone died? Will you be performing a flamenco for the gentleman?*

*Well, I'm not wearing a shroud. It's classic.*

*Did you wax?*

*I had a tidy. He may not want to sleep with me.*

*He will.*

*God, what if he does?*

*Do you remember how to do it?*

*I hate you.*

*Love you sis. Have fun x*


Hi. Wow. So good to meet you… Hello. I'm Emma. How are you? You look great… Evening Phil!… Phil? You're here, so am I!… Greetings!… It's great to finally connect.

*Connect?* This isn't a LinkedIn date. Why am I rehearsing this in my head like a script? Who does this? I've spoken with this man on the phone and via WhatsApp and it was totally fine and he was lovely. No one on this planet would say the word 'Greetings' unless they were an alien come from another galaxy.

How do I smile? Like full teeth? It'll look like I'm trying to eat him… No teeth. But then I'll look smug and insincere.

*Adjust your tits. Make sure they're facing forwards. Show a bit of bra.* I'd clearly gone to the wrong sister for advice on this one. Lucy, the youngest, who was still single and well-versed in the world of dating.

Does this mean my boobs are not always facing forward? Where are they looking?

To educate me about modern dating, Lucy had walked me around a lingerie floor to teach me about tangas and hipster thongs. Only old, boring people buy cotton multipack minis, she said. And she introduced me to terms like 'ghosting', which I'm glad is nothing to do with sex. I literally thought I'd have to walk around with a bed sheet on my head.

*Oh my days, I should leave.* Is that bad form? Where the hell are my words? I have words. I'm well-spoken. I can do this. I'll be natural and it'll be great and it's a drink, that's all it is. In a bar that serves artisan burgers made out of halloumi and beetroot, and where the chips come in tiny silver pails like one would serve sugared almonds at a wedding.

I had sugared almonds at my wedding. I had a wedding. I was the bride. The sugared almonds were not a good idea. I hadn't accounted for the number of elderly relatives and Simon's Uncle Brian fractured a denture and sent us the bill. Why am I thinking about that? Why Simon? Why now? Get out of my head, you donkey. Think about something else. That girl at the bar is obviously not wearing knickers with that dress, is she? Is that hygienic? I am at an age now where I don a panty liner most days... I guess she doesn't... And when did men stop wearing socks? Again, hygiene. When I was at medical school, I once had to lance a nasty blister that had come from a pair of badly fitting moccasins. And there are different expectations of beauty these days. Eyebrows now have pride of place and teeth are whiter. Shockingly dayglo. People are young too. I don't feel young. I feel like a second-hand car in this showroom. Do I cross my legs? That's always been classy. I don't want to sit here with my legs akimbo. That would send Phil the wrong message. How about knees together? Like royalty? I adjust my tits like Lucy said.

'Emma?'

'Howdy, Phil.'

*Howdy?*

He laughs. Did he see the boob jiggle? He goes in to kiss me on the cheek but we do a strange dance of not knowing what the other is intending so he kisses my ear and I bend into his body like I'm trying to shoulder barge him. I am not quite sure what to think. I smile. I show teeth. He is as advertised and real and his height is as described.

'Can I get you a drink?'

'I have a drink. But I could have another one, I guess?'

He'll think I'm an alcoholic.

'Maybe just a soft drink? To go with my wine?' I say.

'Or another glass of wine?'

'Why not? I'll have a glass of the Picpoul. A small glass.' My fingers suggest I want a shot-sized glass.

He laughs. 'No worries. Have a seat, I'll be back.'

As soon as his back is turned, I reach for my phone to SOS Lucy.

*I've forgotten how to talk to men. This is horrific.*

*Do you need me to do the emergency call?*

*No. I said howdy.*

*Like a cowboy?*

*Like a bloody cowboy.*

*Why are you texting me? Where is he?*

*He's at the bar. I think he's wearing skinny jeans.*

*Men do that now. Can you see the outline of his cock?*

*Why do you have to go there?*

*What were his eyes like? Did he have the look of a serial killer?*

*He looks normal. What do serial killers look like?*

*They usually look normal too until they have drugged you and shoved you in a van. Look out for white vans outside with no number plates.*

*I hate you. I could be kidnapped and killed for my body parts. Look after my girls. Make sure Si doesn't ruin them.*

*Two things: Don't mention that man's name to me. And you're too old to be kidnapped. Your organs would be a hard sell. Again, I hate you.*

I spy him at the bar. Christ alive, he's not wearing socks. I can't bring that up, can I? I have a moment to think about what his feet might look like, sweating away in his suede loafers. I can't judge. I might be wearing things he's not keen on either. He might not like black, too morose. He may not like my face, which would be worse. He said he was 'well-built' which I fear is code for hiding a hint of a dad bod but I can hardly talk. I've had kids, parts of me are stretched and doughy. I can't be fussy. I can't find excuses to not be out here because I'm scared. I have to get myself back on the horse. But not literally because I'm not riding anything tonight. I only had a tidy, after all. He returns to the table. For some reason, I stand to greet him. Again.

'Thanks, can I pay you back?'

He looks at me quizzically. 'Or buy the next round?'

Lord, I am out of practice.

'I could.'

I point to his seat, almost telling him to sit.

'You look as nervous as me.'

My body relaxes a smidge. 'I'm not usually this socially inept.'

'You're fine. You're great,' he replies.

'I'm great?'

'Like, you're here and you… look nice?'

'So do you?'

He laughs. His hair is very still, in that it's been styled and sits in the one position. I want to say like a Lego man. There's a silence and a pause so we take large sips of our drinks.

'I saw you texting someone before. Was that to tell them you hadn't been kidnapped?'

I laugh in a high fake tone. 'Maybe?'

'I've been told to do the same at 10 p.m.'

'How could I kidnap you?'

'Easily done. You could have catfished me.'

'Is that a sex thing?' I ask.

He chokes on a bit of his wine.

'No… it's when people pretend to be someone they aren't.'

I just mentioned sex in front of this man. I didn't need to wear blusher today. He is gracious in the face of my embarrassment.

'I didn't know what it was either until my daughter showed me an MTV show about it,' he carries on.

I laugh.

'Your eldest is ten, yes?' I ask.

'Well remembered. Her name is Jessie.'

We'd shared some details of our lives before our date and I liked his honesty and pride when he spoke about his kids. We found out that we both had children, and we were taking tentative steps back into dating after a long time away. If sod all came of it, I felt like I was drinking with an ally, that we'd have tales to tell and advice to swap.

'Bradley is eight and the rugby player and your youngest is Miles and he is five,' I say.

'Is that your doctor brain talking?'

'I remember things.'

'You have two girls, seven and five,' he replies.

'Iris and Violet.'

I study his face. Not offensive or strikingly good-looking but I like the sincerity in his smile.

'The floral thing…' he prompts.

My ex-husband, Simon's idea. Iris was an aunt who had died; then another popped out and he said their names should match and I didn't fight it which was probably the theme of our marriage. I'm glad I'm not saying these thoughts aloud.

'Just seemed nice. They were both born in spring.' My reply, however, is a bit dull. I may as well have just said I like flowers. But then that would sound like I was expecting him to bring flowers. I expected nothing. Lucy said she once had a date bring her a gift bag filled with lubricant and condoms.

'Did you want to order food?' he asks.

'I'm good. I ate before I came out.'

I'm not sure if that's rude or not. But it's true – and if I eat anything else I'll bloat. Will he think that I was rude for eating before? But then how would I have drunk anything and not fallen over?

'I had some pasta,' I decide to add.

He nods. 'I had a sandwich. Prawn.'

He likes prawns. I like prawns. This should be a match made in heaven. He launches into a short description of his journey home from work and how he had to get Bradley to rugby training but realised he forgot about food so had to stop at a Tesco Metro for sandwiches. I want to talk to him about meal deals. That's not sexy talk, is it? It's not good to comment on how Walkers and Kettle Chips are not savoury snack equivalents. Lucy has me second guessing how interesting I actually am. *Whatever you do, don't talk about your doctor shit, avoid Brexit and any opinion you may have about global warming.* What else is there to talk about? I pretend to be interested in Phil's son not liking his southern fried chicken wrap.

'But then I always left it to Stacey to look after the food thing which I know is completely sexist...'

And there it is. How long did that take? Eleven minutes in and an ex has been mentioned. I was good. I bit my tongue and didn't say his name out loud but here's Stacey, she's on this date now. Apart from the fact Phil looks sensible, has some silver fox action going on and has sailing as a pastime (maritime = man of the sea = dependable), the one thing we have in common is that we are freshly divorced. I hated that term. Fresh is the word you use to describe fish. Dead fish who've been caught and are still edible. And it means that one day, if I'm left out long enough, I'll rot to death and start to smell.

'But then Miles totally had a meltdown, so you know what? I just let him go crazy on the crisps,' he carried on.

My ex liked crisps. He liked cheesy snack foods – which remained a mystery to me – and he used to do that thing at the end where he'd lick each of his fingers to get the last of the flavour off. I take a large gulp of wine, like it might keep the words down.

'Sometimes, needs must,' I reply.

He smiles. 'So, when was the last time you were on a date?'

'2003.' It wasn't even a date really. It was a university bar so it was a drunken free-for-all where people coupled up and I ended up with Si who charmed me with his floppy hair and excellent teeth. Back then he had a thing for brightly coloured jeans and Hackett rugby tops. I snogged him in the bar. We had lacklustre, first time drunken sex back in his student bedroom.

'Been a while then?' he says with a grin.

'I've forgotten all my words today. I'm normally far more interesting. I guess I'm just…'

'Crapping yourself?'

'Pretty much. I mean, not actually.'

I'm not sure why I needed to clarify that fact. I think to that girl at university. Back then, I could go out without a bra and survived on youth, one pound shots and hope. Now I look down at my glass and just hope that it was rinsed properly.

'2008,' he says. 'We went to see *Iron Man*. She ate a whole bag of Maltesers.'

'She?'

'Stacey.' Twice now. 'We had Jessie six months after that and then got married.'

'I got engaged around then.'

But neither of us points to it being serendipitous or the stars aligning. He's mentioned his wife twice now and this wasn't what today was supposed to be about. But it appears that the shackles are still on. This was too soon. It's 8.46 p.m. I stand up.

'I'm just going to powder my nose.'

He looks a little worried he's said the wrong thing. How long does one wait before they go for a wee in a date? Will he think I'm escaping?

'I drank a lot of water before. I have a small bladder,' I explain.

'Oh.'

Too much information. I grab my handbag and then worry that it looks like I don't trust him around my personal belongings. I follow arrows posted around the bar and find the toilets. Inside a group of girls are applying lipstick and chatting around a sink. They wear varying degrees of animal print and shiny leggings. I go into a cubicle, lower the seat and sit down. I take a deep breath. I don't need to wee. I'm a surgeon so I've trained my bladder well. Instead, I refer back to Lucy.

*I'm in the loo.*

*Is it bad?*

*It's fine. He's mentioned his ex twice though.*

*Have you mentioned Si?*

*No.*

*Good girl.*

*I don't like these knickers you bought me.*

*Are they chafing your flaps?*

*For want of a better expression. I told him I was going to powder my nose.*

*Why did you say that?*

*Better than saying I was going for a wee.*

*Also makes you sound like a coke user.*

*Shit.*

*Exactly, don't take too long or he'll think you're having a dump.*

I flush the toilet and emerge. The girls are having a conversation about where they're going after this. I'm going to bed, girls. Maybe with a podcast and a cup of jasmine tea. I'm not brave when it comes to how I look. I've had the same brown bob for twenty odd years, I use brown eyeshadow on my brown eyes and the same Rimmel Heather Shimmer lipstick that I discovered in my late teens. Maybe Lucy is right. I'm boring. Is my face boring? Maybe I should smile. I practise in the mirror but a girl who's taken extraordinary care with her eyeliner catches me in the act and there's a small moment where I think she might start a fight.

'I love your handbag,' she tells me.

'Thanks. I like your… face. I mean, your make-up is extraordinary.' I wave my hand around like I'm drawing on my cheeks. The girl and all her friends look at me. I think that's my cue to leave. When I re-enter the bar, he's texting on his phone.

'Did you think I'd escaped out of a bathroom window?'

He laughs. 'I did worry.'

'Still here.' I take my seat.

'I was texting my brother.'

I smile, taking my phone out of my bag. 'My sister.'

'He suggested this bloody look tonight. Who doesn't wear socks? I'm going to get blisters the size of saucers. And I'm sorry about the jeans.'

'They're fine.'

'They're tight.'

I laugh. 'I was told not to wear black.'

'Nothing wrong with black. It's classic,' he replies.

'Which is exactly what I said.'

Things are warming up. Words are flowing. We can thank wine and interfering siblings for that.

'What's your brother's name?'

'Peter, Pete. Your sister?'

'Lucy, she's the youngest.'

'Of how many?'

'Five.'

'Five?'

'All girls. My mother had her work cut out, that's for sure.'

'Where are you in the birth order?'

'I'm number two.' I just referred to myself as a poo, didn't I? 'Meg, Me, Beth, Grace and Lucy.'

'Are you all doctors?'

'Christ no, we have a journalist, a doctor, a lawyer, a teacher and Lucy who currently lives with me. At the weekends she dresses up as Disney characters and does kids' parties. She's the fun one.'

'You're fun too,' he says, eyes sparkling.

'To a lesser degree, perhaps. So it's just you and Pete?'

'Yup, he lives in Wimbledon.'

'Is he good at tennis?' Oh my crap, that was a terrible joke. I'm lucky he laughs back.

'He's actually Pete Sampras.'

'Is he?'

'No.' He's still chuckling for which I'm very very grateful. 'We work together in IT, run the company together.'

He gets his wallet out to retrieve a business card. I take one out of politeness. It's then I see it. It's a photo in his wallet of a woman. Do people really do that? Wallet pictures? I thought we kept these things on our phones these days. He catches me looking.

'I'm sorry. You didn't need to see that.'

I shrug my shoulders. 'I still keep my wedding ring in my coin purse.'

He looks relieved. 'For when you have no change and need to pawn it in for parking?'

'Exactly.' I look down at the ridge in my finger where that ring used to sit.

'It's just still very new, eh?' he says.

I say something next that I shouldn't. 'Did you want to talk about it?'

We'd said very little via text, other than that we'd both had our hearts broken. We didn't divulge, instead swapping vagaries about each other's lives. I knew he liked white wine and seafood pasta. There was the strong maritime leaning in his pastimes. He knew how to spell which was always a winner. All of this but I didn't know what his wife had done.

'Zumba instructor. Such a bloody cliché. She left me for a Polish Zumba instructor called Val.'

'I'm sorry.'

'Not your fault.' He's pensive. I'm not sure whether to make light and talk about Zumba being a mildly ridiculous fitness pursuit.

'Her loss?'

'Mine really.'

I pause. He still loves her, he still misses her. He thinks this is his fault. 'How so?'

'Maybe it was something I did or didn't do? I'm still figuring that out... Maybe I wasn't a good enough husband? Maybe I allowed things to go stale?'

'Or maybe she's not a very nice person?'

I know I've overstepped as soon as the words leave my mouth.

'She *is* a nice person.'

'I'm sorry, that was out of turn. I don't know her and it was unfair to comment.'

He's still quiet. I feel the need to respond.

'My husband cheated on me several times during my marriage. Several is an understatement. The end came when my mother dislocated a thumb punching his face on Christmas day.'

It's a good story but you can tell that he doesn't want to engage in a competition of who's had their heart broken the worst.

'I found him in our bed,' he continues. 'I'd gone home after the school run as I'd forgotten my phone. Lycra all over my bedroom floor.'

'I'm sorry,' I reply.

'You keep saying that…'

'I was talking about the Lycra.'

That didn't raise the smile I thought it would.

'And the look she gave me. You'd think she'd be scared or ashamed but it was like I'd interrupted her, like she was glad I'd found out.'

She sounds like a complete bitch but I've learnt not to say that out loud. And then something happens that I don't expect. Geez, Phil. I know it hurts but please please please, don't cry. I'm at a loss at what to do so I put my hand in his. The tears roll down the curve of his cheeks in the shape of sideburns. Sideburn tears. They drip on to the table. I pass him a tissue from my handbag.

'Well, this is good. Pete told me three things: don't talk about Brexit, don't talk about Stacey, don't cry.'

'We can move on to Brexit, if that would help?'

He laughs, snot dribbling out of his nose.

'I think I'm out of tears. Simon bled me dry.' Grief has moved to anger. We are obviously at different stages of the process.

'Simon?'

'Simon. My ex-husband. You're allowed to call him a wanker if you want.'

'Wanker.'

It took me years to admit that much.

'This is too soon, wasn't it?' Phil says. 'Pete just thought I could meet up with someone and shag it out of my system.'

My eyes widen at the revelation. Was this just a polite, precursory drink before sex? In a small way I'm glad he thought I was shaggable, unless that's not the case now he's met me. Maybe he cried to get out of the sex. I don't even want to sleep with a man who still carries a picture of his ex-wife in his wallet. I don't want to have sex tonight to help him get over her.

'I think this was too soon. For you at least,' I eventually reply.

'Maybe in a few months' time.'

'Maybe when you're ready to take that photo out of your wallet.'

'Can I buy you another drink? To say sorry for crying and being a shit date?'

'Hell, why not? I'll take some olives too.'

*Luce, you still up?*

*I hope you're texting me from a taxi because you're going back to his.*

*I'm texting from an Uber. I am alone.*

*Second date?*

*He cried.*

*Because you're so boring?*

*Piss off. He's not over his wife.*

*Oh.*

*I would have been shagging him and he would have been thinking about her and cried on top of me and I'd have died of the shame.*

*I'm sad Ems, this one had potential. I liked the seaman thing he had going on.*

*Except I didn't see his semen.*

*Did you just make a joke about cum? I may be having a positive influence on you.*

*Are the girls OK?*

*Yup. Was it a complete car crash then?*

*In parts. I gave him details of my mediation team. He also fixes laptops if we ever need him.*

*Romantic…*

*He also bought me olives and chips.*

*Big spender. Did he at least try and feel you up?*

*No.*

*Then he's a loser. You're smoking hot.*

*You normally say differently.*

*I don't mean it really. I love you Ems x x x x*

*Love you too.*

*If you want some sex, I have an old uni mate who'd shag you. He lives in Brixton.*

*Lovely. No.*

*You're so boring.*

*Back in 5. Put the kettle on.*

# Chapter One

## 624 days since my mother broke Simon's nose

'This is a drop off zone only!'

Ever since we gave Hetty Michaels a hi-vis vest, it's transformed this woman into some power-hungry traffic-calming Nazi. I watch as she dictates the parking law to a man in a four-by-four who has no problems parking up, removing a child from its car seat and strolling into school.

'Move your car, please!'

'Make me. What are you going to do, write me a ticket?' he replies.

The parents of St Catherine's stop in their tracks. I don't know this man but I like how he's standing his ground so Hetty will go back to raffle ticket selling where she belongs.

'This is in the interests of safety for the children!' Hetty's voice rises to a high shrill.

I look at the time in the car. I have half an hour to watch but also navigate this bedlam, still confused that we can send people into space and cure smallpox but can't seem to remedy the drop off and parking situation at these school gates. Their disagreement attracts a crowd, and the school caretaker, who chuckles to himself as he sweeps the autumn leaves off the pathway.

'Why is Mrs Michaels screaming like that?' asks Iris from the back of the car.

'It's a parking thing… Who is that man?' I ask.

Iris peers over to inspect. 'He's Giles' dad.'

'Do we like Giles?'

'Not unless we like boys who pee down slides. He stood at the top, peed down it like a waterfall. The boy is feral,' Iris says, strong judgement in her tones.

'Good use of the word feral, Potato,' I say.

'What's feral? asks Violet.

'It means he was brought up in the jungle,' replies Iris.

The nearest woodland is the park down the road but I am too stressed to correct her. Giles' dad has held up the drop-off process and Hetty is waving her arms around in some manic semaphore trying to sort the ensuing chaos.

'Why do you still call me Potato?' asks Iris.

I spy her face in the rear-view mirror. It fits her round face and blonde locks, like a little golden new potato.

'It just stuck. People have all sorts of nicknames.'

'But not food ones…'

'Honey. Sugar… all the foods,' I tell her.

'I once heard Granny call Daddy an effing melon once, that's food,' adds Violet.

I'm half relieved that's the worst name she's heard her father be called but also that she substituted what my mum most likely prefaced the melon part with. I sigh. I have to do this, don't I?

'That was wrong of Granny. Daddy is not a melon.'

Their little eyes peer at me through the mirror. I did the right thing there. But their father is the worst sort of lying evil shitmelon there is. Don't let your face show what you think, I silently tell myself. Focus on something else, like this line of cars that refuses to shift, the woman on her Dutch cargo bike who swerves around everyone smugly, the gaggles of mums gossiping while their little ones swing off the school fencing.

There's a strange mix of parents at this place. I was educated in a south London state school so I remember book bags and sweatshirts and an array of faces and families representative of the city we lived in. Here there are more au pairs, bigger cars, the jeans fit better and people carry impressive tans from their last weekend break in Antibes. The kids here are suited up too: the PE kit is the size of a small weekender bag, and we put them in blazers and ties and burgundy V-neck jumpers in the vague hope that sartorial smarts will increase the size of their brains. A child walks past me with a cello case, another with a hockey stick. It's a different land, one which my socialist parents don't forgive me for and which my sisters constantly tease me about, but the girls are happy. They thrive, they know little snippets of Mandarin, even if they share a class with a Constantine and an Ophelia.

A knock at my window calls me to attention. I wind it down.

'Are you Violet's mum?' a mother asks.

'I am.'

'It's about Pippa's riding party this Saturday at the riding stables.'

Like I say, different land.

'I thought we RSVPed to that?'

'Yes, you did but we have to change the food options as one of the partygoers is allergic to nuts so I'm making everyone aware and we need to let the guests know that they can't bring any nuts on the day.'

'Have you explained this to the horses?'

She laughs but obviously doesn't get the joke. I wasn't going to send my daughter to a party with a packet of cashews but I nod politely.

'And just gift vouchers for gifts please. Smiggle, if you can.'

Again, I nod, biting my tongue at the presumptuousness. I suddenly panic. We haven't entered the realms of pony riding just yet. Do I have to buy jodhpurs and boots? If I don't, will my daughter be the odd one out? But Pippa's mum saunters off before I have the chance to ask.

'Do I have to go to that party, Mummy?' asks Violet.

'Well, we've already replied. Did you not want to go?'

'I'll go if I *have* to.'

I don't have time to answer, edging the car forward to a vacant space.

'Love you. Aunty Lucy is picking you up today.'

'On the bus? Yes!' they chirp in unison.

Turns out a comfy car with heated seats and a hi-tech music system is nothing compared to the adventure of going on the bus with Aunty Lucy and sitting next to a drunk who sings Boney M. and smells of armpit. They collect their assorted bags and clamber out of the car.

'Bye Mummy! We'll see you after work!'

But they won't. I'll get back home too late and arrive in time to kiss their sleepy foreheads. It always hurts my heart a smidge but they'll be with Aunty Lucy who'll stop at the corner shop to let them buy sweets and overpriced magazines. I wave them off. Meanwhile, Giles' dad is back. This could be entertaining but I have twenty minutes to get home and collect my thoughts. I pull out in front of an angry Mercedes driver who rolls their eyes at me. Oh, piss off – you're wearing sunglasses and a baseball cap in September, you tool. Do I start a fight? No, I have to save my fight for Simon.

I distract myself by turning on the radio. Avoid the North Circular, lots of rain and phone in the next time you hear Ed Sheeran. Why? Can I win Ed Sheeran? That would rile my ex-husband – *look! I've replaced you with a superior being. He can play guitar and doesn't even need a band.* I could give him the spare room and Lucy could bunk in with me.

Simon, Simon, Simon. Why has he called this meeting? His lawyer called on Friday to arrange it. He went with some cutthroat family law firm that always spoke to me in patronising tones. *We know you're a busy lady so we'd be happy to come to you.* It was code for Simon wanting to be in our family home again and check out what I had changed or whether another man was living there. However, although intrusive, it was also convenient. If they were lucky, they'd get to sit down, maybe a glass of water.

When I arrive, George, my lawyer, is waiting for me outside the house.

'You should have rung the bell, George. Lucy should be in.'

'I did. There was no answer.'

*Please still don't be asleep, Luce.* I put the key in the door and let us both in.

'LUCE! ARE YOU UP?!'

'I'M ON THE BOG!'

George smiles at me and wipes his feet on the mat. Lovely George. When I was first going through the process of divorce, my sister Grace put me in touch with George. *Will he help my fight*, I'd asked her, *and ensure I get access to my girls and sort my finances out accordingly?* I wanted fire and brimstone when I took Simon on. I wanted him to feel pure fear, literally soil himself when he met my legal team. Grace responded by sending me George. He is lovely and punctual but as he stands in my hallway, crumbs pepper his shirt and the slightest smear of what looks like marmalade paints his lips. He has a mop of curly hair, a fifty-something paunch and there are pattern combinations going on with the shirt, tie and socks that aren't easy on the eye. It looks like he could be made entirely out of bread and a mature cheddar. Reliable, was what Grace had said. He will get the job done. You don't want drama, you want steely calm and someone who'll know every law and loophole in the book. George knows this. He doesn't know how to keep a sandwich in his mouth but he's a bloody good lawyer.

'Can I get you a coffee, George? Just make your way into the living room.'

'I'm fine, Emma. I've never been here before – you have a lovely home.'

I smile. Like I say, lovely. It was our family home – we chose Richmond because it was south of the Thames, had good transport links into London and was near our families. It's a three-storey townhouse with minimal garden space but it has high ceilings and stairs leading to the front door that reminded me of a New York City brownstone. We bought it when I was pregnant with Violet. I want to say this out loud but my mind is racing. Is this meeting about the house? Simon had tried to get us to sell it, split the asset and start again, but I refused to uproot the girls. He didn't suffer; he bought himself a flat in Kew, near the famous gardens and fifteen minutes away from me. Five hundred million miles away on Mars would have been better but kids dictated he stayed close.

George senses my nervous paranoia. 'You look very worried, Emma. I'm sure it's just formalities today so a more relaxed meeting is ideal.'

'I don't put anything past Simon these days.'

'Which is why it's good I'm here.'

George gets a handkerchief from his breast pocket, wipes his mouth and blows his nose. The problem is I played the game of divorce too safely. I went with reliability – old man George who knew the law and who could get the forms signed and through the courts as quickly as possible. Simon went in the opposite direction with a lawyer called Cat De Vere. You can imagine the girl that goes with that name. She's young and likes a designer suit with barely-there sheer tights and a skyscraper heel. I'm under no illusion that Simon has probably stuck his appendage in her too.

'Maybe make yourself a cup of tea, something to relax?' George suggests.

'I've had three coffees already today. Any more and the caffeine will make me foam at the mouth.'

He snorts with laughter. The doorbell rings. I'm going to have to answer this, aren't I?

'Take a seat, George.'

Breathe. Cleansing breaths through the nose and out slowly through the mouth. I head to the hallway and see their heads behind the glass. Don't cry. Don't kick them down the stairs. He's the father of your children. Civility, always.

'Morning,' I say, opening the door.

'Emma.'

Simon Chadwick. He stands there in a grey pinstripe suit. He's always had good hair – he spends an age in the bathroom styling it. He even had his own hairdryer. The strong jawline, that supreme confidence he exudes. It was once so attractive. Now, I want to slap it. Hard. With a brick.

Cat holds out a hand. I shake it. I went with traditional work-wear: a simple shirt over a black cigarette leg trouser. She looks like the eighties ate her up and spat her back out again. That's some slick hair and a strong shoulder. She stands on my doorstep expecting to be invited in; I'm pretty sure that's what you traditionally have to do with vampires. Simon doesn't wait though, stepping over the threshold. He doesn't burst into flames, which disappoints me. Instead he takes a cursory glance around the hallway.

'You got a new mirror?'

'I did.'

I changed most of the interior when he left. That stupid tartan green wallpaper he loved in the kitchen was the first to go, I got a new bed, and in some manic post-divorce moment, I went a tad crazy with florals, palms and bird prints which my mother said made my house look like Club Tropicana. His eyes scan through to the kitchen. He barely looks at me.

'Come through to the living room,' I say.

Simon puts a hand to Cat's back to direct her through – and annoy me, no doubt. When we enter, George stands up. He's already got his files and pens laid out on the coffee table. Simon's eyes glance upon a photo on the mantle. He looks at me briefly but before he can say anything, Cat launches into a speech as she opens her attaché. Simon takes a seat next to her in his usual way, manspreading so his knee is unfeasibly close to her thigh. I perch myself a good sofa cushion's length away from George.

'So, we'll keep this brief as I know our clients are busy and expected at work today. We basically want to discuss the current custody arrangements.' She gets out her file and I feel a ball of emotion in my throat.

This is one thing that Simon rarely brings up because what we have in place was fair and we both want our girls to come out of this unscathed. I always thought this was mutual. If he wants more access then the gloves will come off, the claws out like bloody Wolverine. Cat pretends to scan a document in front of her. George sits poised, his paunch resting on the top of his legs, shirt buttons straining to reveal a vest underneath. I hear footsteps on the stairs. *No, no, no.*

'I thought I smelt something. I thought there was a problem with your pipework, Ems.'

'Lucy.'

Cat and Simon look mildly confused.

'This is Lucy, she's my youngest sister and she lives here,' I explain.

Simon gives her a look like one would a stray cat. It's not far from the truth but Lucy has been a godsend with childcare and saved me a ton of money. She can't cook or clean and she uses all my shampoo but she also brought some light to the house when grey clouds threatened to consume it.

'I do. My sister needed help fumigating the place after Simon left,' says Lucy. She eyeballs my ex-husband with her yoga pants get up and tousled blonde hair bundled on top of her head.

All my sisters collectively hate Simon but Lucy's anger seems to burn the strongest. On that Christmas Day two years ago, she was the one who'd caught him receiving a photo of a nurse's bits, grabbed his phone and threw it out of a first-floor window. She could have very easily killed him that day but I am glad that she'd probably had too much sherry so didn't have the clarity of thought to go to the kitchen and find a carving knife. Lucy goes over to shake some hands but leaves Simon out, obviously. She scans Cat up and down.

'I was about to make tea,' she says in pointed tones. 'Who wants tea?'

Simon doesn't look sure about accepting drinks off this sister.

Cat puts a hand up. 'I'll take a glass of water, please.'

The rest of us decline and Lucy disappears into the kitchen, still in my line of sight. She stands behind the door with her middle finger up at Simon and doing a strange angry dance. George watches her curiously. Cat looks ready to continue. I sit with bated breath. Don't make this about our girls, I silently beg.

'So yes, custody. The current arrangement sees you have your girls during the week on Mondays, Tuesdays and Thursdays, my client has them on Wednesdays and Fridays and you take turns to have them every other weekend.'

I nod cautiously.

George intervenes. 'This is correct. Is your client proposing something different?

'My client has recently taken on a promotion at work and his elderly mother will look after some childcare, so he's just looking at his timetable and wondering if he could have Tuesdays in place of the Wednesdays.'

I frown. Simon's mother, Linda, is hardly frail. She's civil with me but Simon has brainwashed her into thinking that his indiscretions were down to addiction problems beyond his control thus meaning I was breaking my marriage vows. A better wife would have stuck by him.

'I've agreed to sit on a board that's supporting some research projects. It supplements my income and will bring great kudos to the hospital,' Simon says.

I don't need to know that but it's not unlike Simon to brag.

'I think that should be fine. If it's just a switch of days then I don't think it will impact the girls too much. Iris has gymnastics Tuesday so you'll need to factor that in.'

Lucy re-enters the room with a glass of water. She retrieves a coaster and places it on the table. There is foam at the top of the glass which sets off alarm bells.

'Lucy, we're talking about switching days a little in the week as Simon has a new job.'

'Is he the new mayor of Wankerville?' she mutters under her breath, as she perches next to me. I can't laugh. George obviously heard and a broad smile fills his face.

'Well, I can fit the girls around my schedule, no problem,' she says.

'Still unemployed then, Luce?' Simon retorts. Oh, Simon don't prod an angry cat.

'She works weekends mostly and is studying so helps me in the week,' I say in her defence. 'Beth, my mum, my dad, everyone pitches in.'

'A true family affair.' Lucy puts a hand to my shoulder.

Simon whispers something to Cat and she smiles.

George is quick to react. 'An informal meeting should mean we're able to speak plainly in front of each other. If your client has something to say then to whisper is just bad manners.' If Lucy could high five George now, she would.

'My client has highlighted Miss Callaghan's suitability in looking after the children,' Cat replies. 'If she's to continue in such a capacity then he'd ask that she is qualified with at least a child first aid qualification as a minimum.'

Lucy stares him out. If looks could kill, this one would impale him to the walls through his eyeballs.

'Every au pair we've ever had in this house, Emma, was aptly qualified,' Simon adds.

'Usually at sucking your penis,' I reply.

I hold his gaze. Lucy inhales deeply and giggles. George and Cat don't look too bothered. I expect being party to some martial tête-à-tête is part of their job description. Simon glares at me and then glances at the photo behind me.

'Lucy is family,' I reply. 'She's not an au pair and is as qualified as your "elderly" mother at looking after our girls. How is Linda?'

'Well.'

'I'm glad.'

I turn to George. 'I'm in agreement to the change of days. Is there anything else to discuss?'

'My client wanted to talk about next summer,' Cat says.

'I want to take the girls to Disneyworld. You'll need to sign something to let me take them out of the country.'

I study Simon's face. It's something we'd always discussed doing as a family. He knows what he's doing. He's stealing my idea. The shit.

'Give me a note of the dates.'

George intervenes. 'Everything needs to be in writing Mr Chadwick and then it will be acknowledged by us. Miss De Vere can re-draw the custody arrangement and have it sent to our office so it's on record. When do you want this to start?'

'Is next week too soon?' asks Simon.

I shrug my shoulders. 'That's fine. So after we stick to our usual days this week, I'll see you next Tuesday.'

Lucy grins at me. I don't get it. Did Cat sip her water or something? George and Cat scribble away and Simon's phone suddenly rings. He leaves the room, retiring to the hallway to take the call. I keep an ear in out of habit.

'How is that possible when I ordered the MRI? Look at the notes. It's all on there.'

He paces the corridor. I bet it isn't, I think to myself. I know Simon professionally as we are both surgeons. We are different though. I hope I nurtured, whereas he has a touch of that stereotypical arrogance – he would never be told, was never at fault. *I am a surgeon, it's as close to godliness as you're ever going to meet.* I bet that instruction is nowhere near those notes and some junior doctor will get it in the neck as a result of his laziness.

'I have to leave now,' he says, returning to the room. 'Cat, we need to go.'

The fact that Cat obeys his command gives me every reason to think that they are having sex.

'I am sure we will stay in touch, Miss De Vere,' adds George.

'Naturally. Ms Callaghan. Thank you.' She emphasises the Mzzz to put me in my divorced spinster place.

'So, Simon… We'll see you next Tuesday,' Lucy says in a jovial tone, like she's telling a joke that I don't get. This is very like Lucy. She was out last night – it's very likely she might still be drunk. Simon and Cat don't get it either.

'Yes, next Tuesday.' Simon takes one last glance at the photo on the mantelpiece and turns to leave. He checks his own reflection in the mirror then studies the hallway walls. I had to repaint after I threw a bottle of Rioja at it. It was a bad January after he left and I'd found out the extent of his cheating. Waste of good wine that was.

We all stand around awkwardly. Cat and George shake hands and I am at least grateful that he has the sort of firm handshake that may have caused damage to her immaculate manicure. Simon and I face each other. This is always the bit that gets me. From the intimacy of marriage to looking at someone like you hardly know them, they are but somebody that you used to know. I don't think I could bear to hug him or even give him a polite peck on the cheek. To hold his hand in mine would feel foreign and cold.

'Ems.'

It almost feels wrong that he still abbreviates my name. He doesn't have the right to be personal with me anymore.

'Simon.'

'Lucy, always a pleasure.'

'Likewise. See you next Tuesday.'

Why does she keep saying it like that? I give her a confused look when his back is turned as she tries to keep the giggles in. As soon as they descend a few steps, he whispers something to Cat and she laughs. They're definitely at it. They can have each other. I close the door shut with a bit more force than is necessary. Breathe. I turn and barge Lucy with my arm.

'What the hell is wrong with you? It's like you're high.'

George's eyes widen, alarmed. If she's high then she definitely shouldn't be looking after children, never mind her not knowing first aid.

'You two are such squares. C… U… Next… Tuesday.' She shapes out letters with her hands like the YMCA dance.

'LUCY!' I gasp and laugh at the same time, holding my hand to my face.

George bursts into laughter. 'I like that one, I've not heard that before.' He returns to the living room to gather his belongings.

'If the bill fits… I will take great pleasure in using that for eternity from now on,' she says, giving me the biggest of hugs. She grasps me tightly to let me know he's not here anymore. He can't hurt me. 'I spat in her water.'

'I know you did. That's why I let you do the drinks.'

'Crapbag telling me I don't have first aid. He can bloody do one.'

'We had an au pair once who washed the girls' hair with washing up liquid so you're an improvement on her at least.'

She squeezes me a little too hard in jest.

'Can you try and at least be less combative when he's here? For the girls and the sake of keeping the peace?' I ask.

'Have we not met before?'

I smile. She's right. She was the mouthy Callaghan sister, heart on sleeve and gob without filter which is occasionally useful.

I go into the living room to see George. 'Are we OK, George? I'm so relieved it was nothing more.'

'I told you not to worry. I will get this all drawn up and couriered over for you to sign.' Maybe that was what was best about George; that kind of warm reassurance you get from a portly uncle. Maybe Grace the lawyer sister knew I didn't need fire and brimstone, I needed someone who was going to look after me.

'George, you do all this family law stuff… Is he the worst sort of lying shitface that you've ever met?' asks Lucy, coming into the room.

George doesn't even flinch. 'Miss Callaghan, Lucy – isn't it? I've been in family law for twenty-two years. I've seen it all. I once saw a woman throw an office chair at her husband. He needed twenty-three stitches. I've seen people fight over goldfish. I once saw a wife with video evidence of her husband shagging the neighbour and he denied it saying it was his long-lost twin.'

Lucy and I stand there enthralled. Me mainly, as George is normally quite beige.

'But yes,' he carries on. 'Simon rates up there in the top ten, maybe.'

Lucy looks vindicated.

'It's an ugly old business, divorce and broken hearts.'

'Then why be involved?' I ask.

'Beats property law. It at least feels useful. I'm helping people.' He smooths down the wrinkles in his shirt. He may have a lost a button near the waistband. 'Well, you know where I am if you need me?'

I smile and Lucy offers to show him out. I glance over at the glass of water on the coffee table and see a lipstick mark, showing that Cat took a sip. Well done, Luce. I look at where Simon was just sitting. I never changed the sofas. Maybe I should have done but there was no budget to do a complete overhaul. Today he took his normal seat, like he'd never been away. That part of the sofa was where he'd watch the cricket and sip his tea with the morning papers, dressing gown on but not done up. Bare feet.

*Breathe, Emma. Get to work. Let's not think about him.*

I turn to the mantelpiece to check the time and see the photo that sits there. Everyone who visits is always shocked to see it there. If Lucy could, she'd knock it over and use the glass from the frame to scratch his face out. It's a picture of Simon with the girls, on Godrevy beach in Cornwall. One of those glorious pictures framed in sunlight and blue skies. Iris had just lost her first tooth; their faces are dewy and golden. Why is it there? Because of my girls. He's still their father. Our daughters live here too and they should still have a relationship with Simon, no matter what's happened.

The picture once lived in the girls' room but Iris moved it here. I know why. She's little, she still lives in the hope that we'll get back together and the fairy tale will have a happier ending. *I tried girls. I hung around for as long as I could to make it work, for you, for us.* That guilt still penetrates so I leave the photo here, I try and block it out of my field of vision. Simon will have seen it now and I know what he would have thought. *She has a photo of me. She still loves me. I'm winning in these mind games.* Far from it. I study the picture, all the creases on his face and the broadness of his smile. I mouth the words softly to myself.

'See. You. Next. Tuesday.'

# Chapter Two

In the middle of my divorce proceedings, I got a letter from a nurse at Evelina London Children's Hospital where I work. Her name was Alice and she wanted, for the sake of her conscience and her career, to let me know that she'd slept with Simon on a number of occasions. She was contrite and she said if it was necessary, she could also list some others he'd slept with – she knew of at least two, including a patient's mother – and also provide pictures that he had sent to her including photos of his own penis. This letter got sent to my office. Maddie, my secretary, opens all my mail. She read it and hid it from me because I guess I didn't need salt rubbing in the already gaping wounds and to be fair, I knew what his penis looked like already. It was also around the time I lost a stone and would spend most of the time napping, crying and staring into the Thames from my office, surviving on bananas and cups of heavily sweetened tea. It's not a diet that I recommend as a human or medical professional. But Maddie took care of me in all respects. She was one of the people who saved me, that strong central beam in a house that was falling apart. She was the one who made me eat, kept me focussed on work and who went up to nurses called Alice in the cafeteria and gave them a piece of her mind. It was shepherd's pie day. Peas were flung, apparently.

'I got your text. I made you tea. Are you OK, love?' Maddie says, following me into my office. 'I got you snacks too. I know you won't have eaten. Clinic's in twenty. What is that sod up to now?'

Maddie does this, the words and tea flow fast. I put my hands up in the air so she can give me a minute, mainly because I also ran from Waterloo to make sure I was in time for clinic. I try to remember how to breathe. True enough, she's bought me some hummus and a set of mini cheeses from the supermarket, as well as some crackers and grapes. Little wedges of gouda and chickpea dip will fill in the cracks and soothe my soul. My snacks are propped up against the inspirational calendar she got me for Christmas. It's opened up on the right day and I'm being reminded, '*If you can dream it, you can do it.*' I often dream about killing Simon but I am sure that's deemed morally reprehensible.

I take off my coat and bag and try to wipe down the mist of sweat on my face. She squirrels around after me and takes a seat on my sofa. It was one of the things she first did when the divorce was going through: she got me this sofa. She had found me napping on the floor once between surgeries so she sweet-talked some porters into looking for any old sofas on the go and paid to have this one re-upholstered. She even bought me a fleece throw for it too. And because I needed all the inspirational words I could get, she also gifted me a mug that said, '*YOU GO GIRL!*' in pink cursive writing with a hint of glitter and a raving comedy unicorn.

'I'm fine,' I finally reply. 'Simon just wanted us to switch some of our days with the girls. I love cheese and I love you.'

She smiles. She's always been an ally; she felt my pain so empathically and tried to do everything she could to take it away. She's married to Mark, an extremely tall builder who was divorced himself so she also had some insight into how my world worked.

'Drink your tea, your first clinic appointment is soon. Lewis is back I'm afraid.'

I peruse some notes as she chats to me, nodding.

'Are you really OK?'

'Seriously, I'm OK. Not how you want to start any day really, having to spend time with that bellend, but I'm fine, really.'

She scans my face like she doesn't quite believe me. I used the word 'fine' a lot to define how I was feeling at the best of times. Throughout all of this, I was never outstanding, ten out of ten, fantastic, but I teetered at OK, fine, average where it could all have the potential to just nosedive off a cliff.

'That's a nice jumpsuit,' I gesture. She senses my need to change the subject.

'I've been experimenting. Bugger to go to the loo in though.' She sits on the sofa, large hooped earrings like curtain rings. Her round blue eyes that have always reminded me of a handsome cat still examine my face.

'Lucy told you to check in on me, didn't she?'

'She didn't, actually…'

People ask me a lot about my wellbeing these days. I appreciate the kindness but I know they conspire on occasion, forming a protective huddle around me. There was a time I needed it. Now sometimes I just need to feel the benefit of the doubt that I am healing and coping, just a bit.

'I'm sorry, you bought me little baby cheeses. I'm just annoyed I've missed a morning's paperwork.'

'You've been Simoned. It's fine. And you don't have stuff to do because I'm a really good secretary and I transcribed all those notes for you.'

'I don't deserve you.'

'Well, I prefaced everything with that because I also have something else for you…'

I hope it's salami to go with this cheese. She seems a bit more cautious now, like she may have done something she wasn't supposed to. She did this when I turned thirty, throwing a surprise party for me on one of the wards. She got a mariachi band in who wore tangerine ponchos, smelt of baked meat and had sinister facial hair. They got chased out by the nurses after they made the children cry.

'Don't be angry… so there was a gathering last night. Do you know Marshall in X-ray? The one who wears all white and then you can see his pants through his trousers?'

I will confess to have never studied any man's pants in that much detail but I nod and she continues.

'Well, it was his birthday and we all went out and it was a nice mix and there was a fab fab bloke there who I've known for a while.'

'Fab?'

'Like, so fab. He's very funny and you know how the other day you were talking about doctors in sports socks and moccasins and then you said the ideal shoe that a doctor should be wearing is—'

'Nike Air Max?'

'Yup, he had on these really cool Nikes in a vintage print and nice chinos rolled up. The man had some style about him. Oxford shirt, liked a glass of rosé.' Her face is animated as she describes him, like a tasty meal she ate once. 'And beautiful skin. I may have got drunk and stroked his face towards the end of the night.'

I turn away from my notes as she says this. 'Maddie, did you snog someone from X-ray? Because you liked his shoes?'

She laughs. 'No, silly. And he's not from X-ray, he's an anaesthetist. His name is Jag.'

'And?'

'I've set you two up on a date.'

I don't even register shock, more confusion.

'Maddie…?'

'Trust me on this. He won't be like that Tinder man who started crying. He's never been married. He has no baggage…' Her ocean-blue eyes are hopeful. That I won't fire her. This is why she bought me those mini cheeses.

'Then what's wrong with him if he's been single for so long? How old is he?'

'He's thirty. He had a long-term girlfriend who baked cakes for a living but it turns out she wasn't so great and dumped him on his actual birthday.'

'Who does that sort of thing?' I reply mockingly.

She throws a cushion at me. 'He drives a Kia.'

'Dull?'

'Economical.'

'He's five years younger than me.'

'Which means he has the advantage of youth and energy on his side.'

I love how she's trying to sell him to me based on the car he drives, his super-soft skin and his choice of footwear. I haven't been on a date since Phil the Crier over a year ago. Not that he had left me broken and scarred but because the experience was so incredibly petrifying. And tiring. I had taken a step in the right direction, out of the shadows of my former, broken self. But I'd been in a relationship for so long that it was all a bit much. It'd taken me two hours alone to get ready, flossing, rolling a lint roller over my tights and Lucy trying to teach me how to contour my face via FaceTime.

I was stepping out into a dating world that had changed beyond belief. Where people spoke in emojis and gin had become fashionable. The last time I had been single it was a different landscape. People were young, carefree and relationships were built on a pre-conceived notion of love. But these people were older now. Life had ground them down and changed (translate: destroyed) what they thought about love, fidelity and sex. I was one of those people.

'How did you sell me then to this Jag fella?' I ask.

'I said your name and he immediately knew who you were.'

I grimace. 'Because of the Simon thing?' I knew it was oft mentioned in these corridors and I hated that it was how people defined me.

'No, silly. You are also known for being a kick-ass doctor and get this, he said he was a "fan" and that he "liked your work".'

My brow reads furrowed and confused. Has he inspected my surgical skills?

'He's been in your theatre more than once. He said you have a lovely demeanour and everyone likes working under you. A lot of surgeons are wazzocks with egos and you're not one of them.'

'Oh OK, I'm glad.' But I'm still tentative. Maddie's the sort of person who'd already have booked a table and scheduled in a date for our engagement party.

'So, what do you say? I'll co-ordinate your schedules. You have some gaps in your diary over the next few weeks.'

'I was going to use that gap to sort out my garden.'

I wasn't lying. It was time to get my bulbs in and hose down the garden furniture. Maddie gives me a look. *You are swimming in your singledom, bobbing away in the ocean and I'm throwing you a life raft. Come on the boat. It's fun. If you don't like it, you can jump off again.*

'I guess I'll need to eat in between my weeding,' I mumble, hesitantly.

Maddie claps her hands together excitedly. 'I'll get it sorted. I feel positive about this one. He's a nice guy. He's so fab.'

I don't react. They all are fab on the outside. He could be someone who smacks his gums when he eats and leaves wet bath towels on the floor. I guess I'll be the judge of that when we meet and I can inspect him for myself.

'So back to today,' she carries on, 'clinic until 3 p.m. Scheduled PDA ligation in the laboratory for 4 p.m. and then evening rounds on the wards. Tomorrow is busier but we'll cross that bridge when we come to it.'

I nod and take it all in. 'One last thing…'

'Yes?'

'Did you know what "See you next Thursday" means?'

'You mean Tuesday? Are you calling me a "See You Next Tuesday"?'

I backtrack. 'No! Just a term I heard today…'

'You've got to get down with the kids, Doctor Callaghan.'

'Ain't it?'

'You mean, innit?' She smiles. 'Get to clinic, I'll put the cheese in the fridge for later.'


The Evelina is a second home of sorts to me. After my divorce, my career became my refuge, the one thing I knew I was getting right. Up to that point, Simon and I had been on the same paths. From medical school to choosing specialisms, we supported each other through stress, exams, long shifts and then into marriage. But then Simon veered off the path, into the bushes, as it were, so work saved me, kept me focussed. I specialise in paediatric cardiology. Yes, I fix hearts for a living. The irony is not lost on me. Neither is the fact that Simon fixes bones. When he's not being an arrogant prick then he's decent at what he does but I wouldn't let him near my bones now. That said, I don't think he'd let me hold a scalpel over his open heart either.

Of course, because we want kids not to freak out at being ill, children's hospitals are bright and primary coloured. The Evelina is no exception – it feels like it's been built out of Lego, we have slides, juice in small boxes, bins like red London buses and we like an under-the-sea motif so I spend a lot of time looking at comedy jellyfish. Paediatrics and poorly kids are sobering. It probably helped me a lot through my divorce as some sort of comparative exercise in who had it worse. The woman whose husband had multiple affairs or the six-year-old with heart disease who can't walk fifty yards without needing oxygen. The six-year-olds and their awe-inspiring resilience and faces like kittens always won. Knowing I could help fix them gave me purpose when it was all going to pot.

'Chadwick. How's life?'

Approaching the outpatient ward now, a voice booms from behind me. I won't lie. In medicine, you do meet a lot of self-important wankers. This is the worst sort, Dr Gargan, affectionately known as the Gargoyle. He's some antiquated dinosaur of medicine who has a non-PC anecdote for every situation and is fond of a double-pleated slack.

'Walter. Good, thanks. Yourself?'

'How's divorce treating you? Such a shame you let that fall apart. I thought you and Simon made a fantastic couple.'

I smile awkwardly at his brusqueness. I let it fall apart? What account of my divorce has he heard? The one where I was the career-driven bitch who threw Simon out on the street or the one where I had a breakdown? Small quarters like these means gossip can spread through here like a measles outbreak.

He gives me a look. 'I'm sure a lovely filly like you won't be on the market for long though.' And there's the non-PC part out of the way. 'Give Simon my regards when you see him next.'

'I think that's the point of divorce, I don't have to give him any of my regards, ever again.'

He replies with a look of confusion. There are just some men who'll never get it. I am lucky, therefore, to be saved by Rhonda.

'Dr Gargan. You are twenty minutes late. Your files are in your office and I suggest you make apologies to all your patients today.

Miss Callaghan. Always a pleasure.' Rhonda is a sister on the outpatient ward, a stern looking woman who wears the old-style uniforms
with thick woollen tights from the Florence Nightingale School
of Nursing. She has the type of hard face that you know enjoys a
strong cup of tea and has most likely never cried at someone's sob
story on reality TV. With such severity, she runs a tight ship but you
hope she has some affection in her life. Even if it's in the form of
a beloved houseplant. I love that she calls me by my maiden name
and gives cretins like Gargan what for. He skulks away, eyeballing
her for daring to call him out. I mean, he is a doctor and has a
penis, don't you know?

'Rhonda. Busy today?' I ask her, cheerily.

'Always. We had Mr Carver in this morning. He likes to talk.
About half an hour behind.' Dan Carver. Nice bloke, likes a comedy
tie, terrible name for a surgeon though.

'He always runs over. Don't mind me, I'll skip lunch and get
us back up to speed.'

'I'll make sure the girls bring you in some snacks. Your nurse
today is Marie . She's newly qualified, excellent manner, needs
instruction though,' Rhonda reports.

Marie is stood right next to her but looks too scared to be
offended. I smile to try and calm her fears that I won't shout and
expect perfect hospital corners.

The waiting room look on as I stand there. It's very open plan
here, a sea of noise, snacks and colouring pages, but there's always a
look of expectation, judgement on the faces of parents and guardians
when I walk in. They want to see if I'm old and qualified enough
to doctor their children. A Pixar film is singing at me from the

corner. There's always one child who has the whole family with them, grandparents and all, and at least one kid running circles around the seating – today he's a racing car. They all turn and face me. *Please let it be us next.*

I look down at my first chart and smile. 'Lewis Bromwich.'

A head peers up with some hesitation but as soon as he clocks it's me, he bounces off his chair. I've never owned a dog but I suspect and hope that if I did that it would hurl itself at me in the same way that Lewis would. I put an arm out hoping that he'll apply the brakes but no such luck and he bundles himself into my arms. I get a mouthful of curls in the process.

'Doctor C! I was worried!'

'You were worried, why?'

His parents follow closely carrying the usual coats and devices that people do when they know they're bound for a hospital waiting room. I go to shake their hands and see them into the examination room. I've known them now for seven years. Ever since Lewis's mum gave birth to this tiny human next door and his heart was literally broken. I have several patients and parents like this on my roster who almost feel like family. Ever since my early years of training, I've worked closely with them all; I've seen all their tears, watched over their children, they send me cards and wine, and despite all attempts to keep a professional distance, their kids do feel like my own.

His mum intervenes. 'The nurse said we were seeing a Miss Callaghan?'

'Oh, that's me. I've changed my name.'

Lewis looks at me confused. 'Because you didn't like Dr Chadwick?'

That's understating it a little, Lewis. 'I've gone back to my maiden name.'

'You were a maiden? Like in *Robin Hood*?'

His parents smile at me and urge him to sit down. 'We'll explain it to you later, Lewis,' says his dad. I notice his mother studying my face. For what, I'm not entirely sure but I am familiar with the attention. People expect you to look different in divorce. Sad, aged, the word branded into your forehead, maybe.

'Well, it's good I can still call you Doctor C because a name like Doctor W wouldn't sound as good.'

I smile broadly. 'That is true. And so tell me, how are you Lewis?'

He bounces off his chair to remove a dinosaur rucksack. 'I'm good. I drew you a picture. And I have half a Twix here. Do you want it?'

I always get an added bonus with Lewis in the form of a hand-drawn picture as recompense for having helped rebuild him from the inside out.

'I'm good for now. Keep that Twix for later on the Tube.'

'It's an octopus.'

I study the picture. I like that he's wearing a top hat and appears to also don a moustache and full beard. 'Did you give it eight legs?' I ask.

'Of course. Did you know octopuses have three hearts?' he tells me.

'I didn't know that. However, I do know that a blue whale has a heart the size of a small car.'

His eyes widen. 'Oh my god, that's mega!'

His parents smile and his dad strokes a hand through his curly mop of hair encouraging him to calm down.

'Do you think you could operate on a whale heart?' he asks me.

'I'd need a very big ladder. And a wetsuit. I'd give it a go though.'

He smiles a big toothy grin, tiny pea-green Converse swinging off his chair.

'So I hear we've had a touch of drama with you, young man. Can you tell me what happened?' I have it all in my notes but I like the way this kid tells a story.

'So… I was at school and we were doing PE and I wasn't really feeling it because it was cold and really we should have been inside but Mr Gray makes us go outside because he used to be in the Army apparently and he says we should get used to the cold but that's what they do in prisons.'

I smile. 'Go on.'

'And then my heart started running.'

'You mean racing?'

The three of them nod in unison. Racing isn't even the word. It sprinted to the finish like Bolt at 252 beats per minute, three times the speed it should.

'It felt like bubbles in my chest and then the school went crazy panicky and they called the ambulance and they brought me to hospital but not this one, it was another one and it wasn't as good because you weren't there and they had really bad biscuits.'

His mum intervenes. 'And they gave him some drugs to bring it back to a steady rhythm; they were close to shocking him.' Her voice trails off and both parents' faces look drawn and pale at remembering the incident.

Lewis looks completely unbothered by this. To be fair, we have put this boy through everything. We've cut his chest open more times than is necessary for someone so small, we hook him up to machines and put him on treadmills. His resilience and character amazes me but I can't imagine what it feels like to see your child so vulnerable and helpless, to be paralysed and weighed down with such worry.

'There was also a doctor who told me to try and fart to make my heart rate go down. Does that work?' Lewis tells me, cupping his hands to his face.

'Only if you've had beans for tea.' My lame joke eases his parents somewhat. 'So, little man, we need to make sure that your heart is working as it should. This is Marie. She is going to take you over for an ECG and we just need to make sure your tick tock is in good shape.'

He looks over at Marie. 'Are you new? You look new? How old are you?'

She seems shocked by all the questions.

'She's 105,' I tell him, studying my notes.

He laughs and jumps off his chair.

'Lewis, Daddy will go with you and Mummy will just stay here as I have some questions for Doctor C, is that alright?' He doesn't seem to mind. Over the years, both parents have always shown up for this kid and shared the responsibility and routine of having a chronically ill child. Dad stands up to salute us and offers his son a piggyback. Mum smiles. We hear Lewis offer that half of a Twix to Marie as they leave the room.

His mother turns to me as the door is closed, her shoulders relaxing, allowing herself to breathe.

I put a hand to her knee. 'And how are you?'

'You just think it's done and then something like that comes along to scare you.'

'Let's have these tests and then see if it's anything major to worry about. A child like him may have episodes of rapid heartbeat. We can look into drugs to remedy that.'

She smiles, nodding.

'Did you have any other questions for me?'

She studies my face for a moment too long. 'How long have you been divorced?' As soon as the words leave her mouth, she knows she's crossed a line. 'I'm sorry. You don't have to say if you don't want to. That was rude of me to pry.'

'About a year now. Officially. It just took me a while to change my name back. It felt strange not having the same name as my daughters,' I reply calmly.

She nods, her eyes glassing over. I hope not out of pity. A lot of it was because I didn't have the time and inclination to deal with the endless administration. 'Oh, I'm sorry.'

'Don't be. These things happen in life,' I say, cringing at my own platitude.

'I just… I mean it will show up in Lewis' records soon but my husband and I are… I mean, we're separated. We are going down that route.'

I pause for a moment. I can't quite compute the news as this is a couple I've known for the longest time. I've seen them at their lowest ebb, bound by friendship and their love for that boy so I feel sad. I feel disappointed they're joining my club.

'Why?' I mumble.

'It's been coming. I mean, it's completely amicable. He is an excellent father to Lewis and my best friend but we woke up one day and realised we'd become housemates. We were just stuck in the everyday. We'd fallen out of love.'

She realises she's said too much but there is comfort in her words, knowing she and her husband made this decision mutually. My divorce was swathed with such bad feeling that it's reassuring to hear how they've just uncoupled. How I wish Simon had done that, fallen out of love with me and moved away quietly rather than falling into someone else's knickers.

'We just… I mean we're still living together for now but both of us are terrified about telling Lewis…'

'He doesn't know?' I ask.

'We've tried. We really have but we're scared of breaking him. I mean, look at him. All of this stuff he's been through and he carries on like nothing has happened. We don't want to upset him, to take that away from him?'

I nod thoughtfully. I'm not sure how they've kept it from him but I guess I hid years of heartbreak from my own.

'You mentioned you have daughters?'

'I have two, they're eight and six.'

'How did you tell them?'

I pause for a moment. It was after I returned to our family home with our girls, weeks after that Christmas when I'd finally ended our marriage. Simon had left at that point; he'd taken his things and the coward that he was, he left me to sit down with our daughters to tell them that their father didn't live here anymore.

*Well, you're the one who wanted to end it, you tell them.* I remember sitting there, high off the emotion and not knowing how to do it at all. Every sentence sounded corny, clichéd and dishonest. So I did the only thing I could.

'I got us all into our pyjamas, brought all the duvets downstairs and I put on *Mrs Doubtfire.*'

Lewis' mum laughs under her breath. *Yes, I let Robin Williams assist.*

'And it came with a rambling commentary from me about what was going to happen.'

'How did they react?'

That evening still plays through my mind constantly. *I don't know what you mean? Where will Daddy live? Do you still love him? Did we do something wrong?* All the questions came from Iris. She was calm and thoughtful, she needed to know how this changed her every day. Violet just didn't get it. She thought Simon wanted to start wearing dresses. He'd have to shave his legs, she said. We giggled. I held them both tight. I had visions of standing over Simon with a razor, some hot wax. That would have been fun. I didn't say that out loud. *Do you hate Daddy?* The truth was I did. The hate felt like flames, it burned so bright. I wanted to turn Simon into a villain. To gather my girls under that duvet and tell them everything he'd done to break up our family. But I couldn't.

'It broke their hearts,' I say quietly.

She catches her breath. Naturally, a statement like that has different implications for her boy.

'Not like that,' I exclaim, backtracking immediately.

She smiles at me. It was my biggest hurt in all of this, I rewired two little hearts that night, forever. I couldn't see the damage, I didn't know if they'd recover. I don't know if they have recovered. I tear up.

'Oh dear, I'm sorry. I've said too much. I…' Lewis' mum mumbles, panicked.

I shake my head at her. 'I'm fine. Have that chat with him. The longer you leave it, the harder it will be. And it took a team of us the best part of six years to build Lewis' heart. There's a warranty on that workmanship. He'll be fine.' I'm realising I'm lying to her so I stand up and pull her in for a hug. 'It'll all be fine.'

# Chapter Three

It's ten o'clock when I get home that night. I approach the steps to the house and see the kitchen light on. Lucy better have food. And wine. I hope she did a white wash and didn't forget to pick up milk. Or the girls. Walking through the doors though, I hear a baby crying. The fatigue of the day makes me question which child this is. I don't have a baby. Do I? The last time I had sex was in 2017. Then a head pops out from around the corner.

'Yo, bitch,' comes a voice from the kitchen.

Beth. She's number three in our clan, the English teacher, the new Millennial mum and admittedly, our resident ditzy sister. I think Beth actually confessed to once leaving her baby in a Costa and only remembering once she got to a bus stop. Her little boy is Joe. As far as babies go, I think she has all of us beat. He seriously looks like a cartoon mouse with brown hair like waves of chocolate and hazel eyes, but then I am always biased when it comes to my nieces and nephew.

Beth will be the first to admit, motherhood wasn't planned for her. She was very much a happy, carefree Londoner who used to frequent festivals, take pictures of her flat whites and have weekend meditation breaks in Ibiza, making us all jealous with her Instagram posts. And then there was Joe. She's in leggings, a large T-shirt and

Converse today; battered and broken and that's just the shoes. The top is either covered in old milk stains or it's some strange avant-garde print thing. She carries Joe awkwardly like one would wear a rucksack in a crowded city when you're trying not to be pickpocketed. He cries lightly.

I head to the kitchen, dumping my bag on the counter and kicking off my heels. Lucy, who is propped up against said counter, knows to get a wine glass for me straight away. She then does something entirely unexpected and opens the oven door.

'You cooked?' I ask.

'Cottage pie.'

'Really?'

'Did I bollocks? I picked it up from that organic shop on the high street. Beth and I have been spending some quality sister time together over mash and minced beef.'

I shrug. It could be worse. For her first two weeks, my girls experienced a new dining adventure Lucy called 'freezer tapas'. She pours me a glass of wine. I head over and inspect Joe, urging Beth to hand him over.

'How are you? You look bloody knackered.'

'Why thank you. Why he no sleep?'

'Because he's a baby and he's excited to be in the world.' I settle him at my chest, holding him upright. The novelty of babies will never wear thin with me. I adored having my own, loving the warmth and fuzziness of a tiny baby head under my chin. I sway a little and he closes his eyes.

'He hates me,' she mutters, resigned.

'He doesn't. He just likes me better.'

Beth grabs a bench from the kitchen table and curls up in a ball. This may be her done for the night. Lucy looks over at me and mouths the word, *Will*. I pull a face. Will is Beth's other half. They never married so you never quite knew what direction their relationship was headed. Will is a nice enough bloke but both of them are struggling with first time parenthood, having trouble wrangling the new roles, the sleeplessness, the general void one falls into when a baby comes along and sucks the fun out of everything. She settles into a light snore and we leave her be. I take a seat, grateful for the warmth baby Joe seems to be offering.

'How was your day, dear sister of ours? Did you fix all the children?'

'All of them.'

'How are the girls?' I ask. 'How was gymnastics?'

'Excellent. Iris is officially my bendiest niece. We did cool hair stuff today too.'

'Please tell me you didn't dye their hair? I am pretty sure that's against the school rules.'

She gives my brown, poker straight bob the once over. I don't even experiment with layers as I worry it'll make me look like a spaniel.

'We did little plaits. We'll undo them in the morning and they'll look like little eighties rockstars.'

I don't reply because I'll eat my hat if she's up at 7.30 a.m. tomorrow, so it's something else to factor into the manic school morning routine.

'Some woman came up to me at the gate ranting about ponies and nuts? She looked me up and down and was talking slowly because I'm going to assume she thought I was a continental au pair?' Lucy carries on.

'Yeah…'

'Anyway, I played along and put on a Swedish accent.'

'Nice.'

'Made your girls giggle.'

I take a large gulp of wine and look over at Beth. 'What happened with Will?'

'I'm not quite sure. I think he's gone a bit MIA, always at work, still partying hard and they're not having sex. She hates how she looks. Just a new mum slump I think. She's laid down some timber for sure.'

I shake my head at her. 'Don't be a cow. It's what happens, she's breastfeeding, her leptin and ghrelin hormones are imbalanced. You wait till you get to your thirties and your metabolism gives up on you.'

'You're so medical and old, it's dull.'

I stick my middle finger up at her. She grins back at me.

'Anyway, I thought a good way to cheer her up might be to throw a party here for her birthday in a few weeks? We could theme it. It'd be good for you too, we could invite people and give you a chance to mingle.'

The thought alone is tiring. Plus with the sort of parties I know Lucy likes to throw, I fear for my carpets and soft furnishings.

'Who would be mingling?' I ask.

'I'd invite some of her teacher mates. I've met some cool people on my course too.'

'Students?'

Lucy was enrolled in a university course nearby in Roehampton in Dance Movement Psychotherapy. Her field of choice seemed to be in the arts but she had a hard time pinning down where she belonged in the field. After my marriage finally broke down, she used to have me in the living room trying to act out my feelings via the medium of contemporary dance. We'd both wear black. The last time we tried it out, her contemporary vision ended up in me voguing and laughing in her face. She then called me an emotionally-void bitch for not taking it seriously and then tried to wrestle me like we were children again.

'Are they clean students?' I ask.

'You're such a snob.'

I will be if some unwashed kids with skateboards show up and sit around lighting up spliffs. I look over at Beth who's drooling onto the oilcloth bench cover. She mumbles something in her sleepy delirium. Little B.

'Fine. Plan your party. But no shots in plastic glasses, no dance music that's all bass and no lyrics.'

She salutes me but has a look of mischief about her eyes that is always worrying. I know why Lucy is here. Six months after the Christmas Minge and Mince Pie debacle, she showed up with her bags on my front door. I'd stopped talking to everyone at that point. I'd had enough and knew I needed out of my marriage but it felt like too many people's opinions were in my head. I was grieving and I just wanted to focus on my girls. I watched a lot of box sets, long into the night, seeking solace from fictional characters and their messed-up lives. I mean Simon was bad but he wasn't Dexter who was an *actual* serial killer. And none of these TV companions spoke back to me in condescending clichés about moving on, keeping my chin up and finding myself in the next chapter of my life. I was told Lucy was at my door because her and Mum had had words. They had been having words since Lucy could learn to talk but I knew the real reason she turned up. She was here to look after me. I won't lie, I like having her around. She cheers me up with bags of penny sweets, she'd make me laugh until my stomach hurt. I wish she'd wipe down my splashbacks though.

'Are you OK from this morning?' She juggles with my oven and cuts me a large A4-sized piece of cottage pie. Her brief had obviously been to fatten me up for winter too.

'With See You Next Tuesday?' I reply.

'Ahhh, you get it now. You were staring at that photo, that's all.'

'I'm OK.'

'Can we move that picture?' she asks. 'Can we put it up in the bathroom so I have something to look at when I'm having a crap?'

'Nice… and no. Leave it there for now or you'll upset Iris.'

She scans my face. Through all of this I've always put the girls' needs before my own and she knows that. I hope she respects me for that much. I can't think about my idiot of an ex-husband any more, especially if I've got wine in hand as I run the risk of getting morose. Must change the subject.

'Maddie at work has set me up with someone.'

'Oooh, tell.' Lucy tosses the kitchen utensils in the sink and brings my food over, taking Joe and giving me a look that orders me to eat or she's going to tell our mother. Carbs. I don't care what anyone tells you but the true remedy to divorce is carbs. I trail my fork over the mashed potato to inspect that she's heated it up correctly.

'He's called Jag. He's an anaesthetist.'

'Here's hoping he doesn't make you fall asleep.' Lucy laughs at her own joke. 'Do we have a surname?' She gets her phone out and immediately goes to Facebook.

'No, what are you doing?'

'Doing what everyone does when they have a potential new date. You go through the internet and find out if they're legit?'

'Like stalking?'

'Like looking out for one's personal safety?'

'Did you stalk Phil the Crier?' I ask.

'No and that's where we went wrong because if we had then we would have known that he posts a lot of memes about love and being wronged and hasn't deleted all his wife's pictures yet. Found him!'

That literally took her a minute. This girl's talents are wasted.

'How?'

'You mentioned Maddie so I went on her friends list and he's quite easy to track down with a name like that. Would have been harder if he was a Tom or a Chris.'

She scrolls through his profile. I try to grab her phone but our baby nephew gets in the way. I eat my dinner sullenly as she gets her measure of him.

'I like this one Ems. He's a bit trendy.'

'Urgh, like skinny jeans?'

She puts the phone down on the table between us. Jag Kohli looks up at me. Maddie might be right, he has very clear skin. The profile picture seems to be one of him on a cliff admiring a view. He's wearing a helmet. His smile is wide and from initial impressions looks sincere.

'Why trendy?'

Lucy scrolls through some photos. He seems to spend his weekends on bikes but also in pubs with different arrays of acquaintances. He likes attending concerts of bands I've not heard of and enjoys a bowl of ramen. I guess trendy because there is evidence of bright, patterned trainers and the occasional beanie hat which I hope isn't hiding hair plugs or a perm.

'We're a bit opposite, aren't we?' I ask. I am safe when it comes to clothes. I like a shift silhouette, a medium indigo jean, a sensibly cut shirt that washes well. Lucy knows as much.

'I think he'd be a good influence on you. He's not too London try-hard, I've met plenty of those. He just has a style about him. He'd push you out of your comfort zone.'

'I like my comfort zone. What is an FKA Twigs? Is that an outdoorsy woodland thing?'

Lucy rolls her eyes at me. 'British singer. Very cool.'

I don't look convinced. I am many things in this world but cool is not a label you'd use when it comes to me and I've never really been that bothered about that.

'I could help? I mean I tried with the last date but you still went looking like a Greek widow. We could buy you some cool threads, it's all in the accessories.'

'You bought those weird knickers for my first date. I'm not sure I trust your judgement.'

She pulls a face at me. Lucy was on the different end of the scale when it came to cool. She has things pierced, tattoos spread around her person and a mid-twenties figure that can carry off cropped tops and dungarees as displayed this evening. If I dressed like that, I'd look like some middle-aged dairy farmer.

'I like the name too. It'd be an upgrade: Dr Emma Kohli. You'd sound worldly and global.'

I'm confused that she's got that far. I don't think I'll ever get married again after what I went through. I don't say that out loud though – she seems happy to imagine my future on my behalf.

'He looks like he'd be fun in bed too.'

She *always* goes there.

'Because he has nice trainers?'

'Because he looks like fun?'

She brings up sex a lot because she's Lucy: she's brash and has no conversational limits. I feel she thinks her purpose is to not only feed me but revive a pretty dead sex life too. She can sense I don't want to talk about such things but of course, that doesn't stop her.

'Did you reply to that man in Wandsworth?'

She's referring to Giovanni. You see Lucy had signed me up to Tinder in an attempt to pique my interest in men again. It was after a boozy Chinese takeaway a few months after the separation when I joked that a spring roll was the most phallic thing I'd had in my mouth since 2016. I remember a dumpling rolled out of Lucy's mouth in shock. It was, therefore, how I'd met Phil the Crier and look how well that went. Giovanni was her attempt to lure me back into online dating; he was a plumber from Wandsworth. He was lovely to look at but I was reticent to indulge in relations with a man who thought pictures of oiled abs and an erect penis could replace bad grammar.

'He couldn't string a sentence together, Luce.'

'But it was such a pretty willy, and those cheekbones. Don't have to talk to him, just fuck him.'

'You're so crass.'

She ignores my insult and continues to stalk Jag. Lucy thought that was the answer to all of this. Shag Simon out of mind. Replace him with sculpted plumbers from Wandsworth, heartbroken IT experts and soft-skinned anaesthetists with trendy shoes; their variety of penises healing my heartbreak. However, she forgets that sex was probably the reason I was alone. I'd often questioned whether it all ended with Simon because I was terrible in bed. Maybe I wasn't attractive enough. Maybe I didn't provide what he needed so he looked for it elsewhere. It's a thought that niggles. Of course, it really ended because Simon was a shit but it meant that my sexual urges had flatlined and I was reticent, if not terrified, to repeat the experience with another man.

The sleeping beast on the bench next to me suddenly twitches. 'Crapbags, did I fall asleep? How long was I asleep for?' Beth sits up and reaches out for a wedge of buttered bread, stuffing it straight in her mouth.

'Fifteen minutes tops?'

She reaches for her phone and seems to be searching for a text. 'What did I miss?' she asks, grateful that the baby is still asleep.

'Ems has been set up with an Asian dude with a cool name.' Lucy pushes her phone over to her to inspect.

Beth narrows her eyes. 'That's a good smile,' she notes.

'And we found her a fit Italian plumber in Wandsworth but Ems won't shag him.'

'Stop forcing Tinder on her. Have you not met Emma? She won't even buy things out of a catalogue because she doesn't trust the process,' Beth says, shaking her head.

'Sitting right here?' I say. I get my phone out to open Tinder and show Beth Giovanni's picture.

Beth's eyes widen. 'Geez, I'd have a go on him. What's wrong with you?'

'Honestly, I wouldn't know what to do with it.'

Beth giggles and places her head on my shoulder.

'The last time I had sex was nearly two years ago on Christmas Eve, girls. Do your maths, work it out.' The next day, my marriage collapsed.

Both of them huddle into me like penguins.

'Which is why you just need to get over yourself. Why don't you go and shag some randoms and remember what sex is like? It can be fun and make you feel good,' remarks Lucy.

'Because I'm not you?'

She shrugs her shoulders.

'And from all these men that you have me talking to, it would seem that sex has changed very much. I don't understand all these acronyms and everyone just wants to take me up the arse.'

Beth and Lucy erupt into cackles at hearing me in my white shirt buttoned up to the top speak so frankly. We'll thank the wine for that.

'What does VWE mean?' I ask.

'Very well-endowed. Show me this man immediately,' demands Lucy.

I shake my head, teasingly. 'Not that I'd know what to do with him either.'

Lucy looks concerned for me now. She knows that Meg, our eldest sister, and Beth were the London sorts who had partied hard and got their youth's worth of sexual experiences. She herself, still indulges in such escapades when the girls aren't here. The last was a young man called D'Sean who I met at 5 a.m. in his pants, rearranging his tackle by the light of the fridge and tucking into my Greek yoghurt. I just hadn't had those adventures. I'd studied. A lot. It wasn't because I didn't like sex. I guess it was because I'd always had a steady boyfriend who would become a husband who then became a cheater.

'You've had an orgasm, right?'

'LUCY!' exclaims Beth.

I've enough wine in my system to talk about this now. 'I have.' My response doesn't convince. As you can imagine with someone like Simon, my orgasms were always an afterthought.

'Where's the most interesting place you've had sex?' Lucy asks.

'York?'

Beth giggles. 'Nah, like in a car, outside?'

'We did it in the hospital once. In an on-call room.'

'In a bed?' asks Lucy.

Both sisters look a little disappointed. I don't want to know the ridiculous places these two have had intercourse, sullying the family name. Beth, at least, seems more sympathetic to my plight.

'Well, maybe the anaesthetist is a good idea. You can ease slowly into something, take your time?'

I grab her hand, she gets it. Lucy has taken to scrolling through my past conversations on Tinder.

'This man wanted to spit on you,' she says. 'Like in your mouth. That's even beyond what I'd do.'

I don't really want to know what Lucy would get up to.

Beth is horrified. 'That's how people get ill,' she comments.

'You see why I don't think it's the best platform to build up a dalliance?'

'Dalliance? Christ, you sound like Austen…' Lucy says, resigned. 'You don't have to court them and move to an estate in the country, just get your rocks off. Do what Simon did?'

As soon as she says the words, Beth grimaces. Oh, Lucy. We do love her for her front and audacity but sometimes the words echo with naivety, little one.

I take a large gulp of wine. 'Do what Simon did? Lie, cheat and hurt people? I do believe that's not my style.'

Lucy and Beth both sit there silently.

'I just…' starts Lucy. 'I hate to think that man has the upper hand. That he's going to hold you back forever. All those years you wasted on him.'

Beth looks like she doesn't have the energy to stop the fight that may be potentially unravelling here.

'Are you saying my girls were a waste of time?'

'You know what I mean.'

'I know I did everything wrong. I was stupid and wasted nearly a quarter of my life with him but I hope you look at those girls and know I tried to stick it out for them.'

Beth holds a hand in the air. 'You did nothing wrong.'

Lucy nods in agreement.

'I did. I ignored him and pretended it wasn't happening. I should have called him out far sooner. I guess I just wasn't brave enough.'

Lucy's face reads sadness. 'You cut out hearts of real people every day and save lives. You are the bravest person I know. I just won't let you self-flagellate over that man. You've made the break so now you find something for you. And it starts with some decent cock.'

'Luce, just leave her be. She'll have sex when she's ready, not as a way to get back at him.'

'Exactly.' I put a large dollop of dinner in my mouth. The fact is I'm not ready for random sex just yet; the thought of a real-life penis in front of me actually terrifies.

'I'm soz, Ems. I just want you to be happy,' confesses Lucy. She comes over to hug me in a baby Joe sandwich.

'You think lying there naked and being spat on by an accountant would make me happy?'

'Who knows? You might like it.'

Like I say, the girl has a way of making us all laugh.

'Pour me more wine, that would make me happy. And let's plan this party…'

'What party?' asks Beth.

'For you, you old slag. It's gonna kick off big style,' Lucy replies in some strange patois accent throwing up what looks like a London gang sign with her hands.

'I don't want a big—'

'Yes, you do,' Lucy continues. 'We all need a fuck-off big party to cheer us all up. Oooh, can I theme it? Can I make it a *Magic Mike* party?'

'You want a magician? At the party? She's a bit old for a magician?' I say.

Both sisters look at me strangely.

'I mean, how about some breaded prawns instead? Sausage rolls?'

# Chapter Four

628 days since Lucy threw Simon's phone out of a window, voiding his insurance

I awake to my phone ringing and the sunlight streaming through the cracks of my curtains. I don't like Saturdays like these. I'm not working and the girls are with Simon so everything feels quiet. It's the time I feel loneliness deep in my core. I miss the girls piling in here and us having cuddles and catch ups over the week just gone. I don't look at my phone before answering it so am shocked to hear the other voice on the end of the line.

'Ems, it's me.' He always says this. I know exactly who it is but the familiarity breeds contempt and a touch of morning bile.

'Simon.' I sit upright for a moment as I think why he would be calling. This could be about the girls, are they OK? But he once called me because he'd forgotten his banking password so I put little past him.

'I'm sorry to have to dump this on you but I'm ill. I think it's a virus, I've woken up with a temperature of 39.5. I've been feeling it in my throat all week. Mum is away. I can't look after the girls like this.'

He states everything in facts. There are no requests or questions or enquiries, just the plain assumption that I will have nothing else better to do with my time. He's not wrong. I was going to do laundry, iron and read but he still should have the courtesy to at least ask.

'There's some pony party too. I can't handle it. When can you come round?'

I pause so he can try and relay some sense of politeness in his manner. He doesn't, obviously.

'An hour? The party starts at ten from what I remember. Did you find the gift? It was in her backpack.'

'I'll look for it. It's number ten, you know where I am. I'll bleep you in.'

He hangs up. My bedroom door opens and Lucy appears dressed like Princess Jasmine from *Aladdin*.

'I thought I heard your voice. All OK?'

She sashays in to look at herself in my bedroom mirror then perches on my bed in her harem pants. This is Lucy's weekend job – she's employed by a kids' party company to appear as Disney princesses, unicorns and fairies and dole out two hours' worth of games, songs and dance. She's brilliant at it; kids loved her energy but she also told me it's a fantastic way to get numbers off fit single dads. Today, she's gone heavy on the winged eyeliner and shows off an enviably flat midriff. I quite like the pointy silver shoes though.

'Party?'

'No, Tesco. Obviously a party…'

'That was Simon. He's ill. I think I'll have to pick up the girls.'

'Oh, what about his mum?'

'She's away. It's fine. I had nothing planned really.'

'I'd help but I'm doing this party with Darren and I have to get there early.'

'Is he Aladdin? Do you have a rug? Are you going to find a whole new world?'

She pulls a face at my mocking. 'No, this lot wanted a genie so I have to go and do full blue body paint. Does this mean you'll have to…?'

'Go to his place, yup.'

She stands there, a little lost at what to do. 'I can ring Mum, she can go with you? Or Beth?'

I shake my head. 'Go, I'm fine.'

'One last thing…'

'Yes?'

'Can I borrow that giant tiger in the girls' room?'


We both describe the end of our marriage differently. Simon tells people I threw him out but really he left of his own volition. My family all ganged up on him that Christmas. The ongoing drama involved mince pie vomit, having to lock my eldest sister, Meg, in a bathroom so she wouldn't physically kill him and a visit to A&E with my mother. I didn't go home that evening and stayed at my mum's and then sister's until the New Year but when I ventured back into our family home, he had left. He had packed a bag of clothes and sent his mother over in mid-January to collect the rest. Apparently, to do that much was generous. It would have been the perfect time to have started a blazing bonfire of his belongings with an effigy of him in the middle according to Lucy.

Three months later, he started renting his flat in Kew that he eventually bought. The girls always made it sound so glamorous, the fact there was a lift and that you could put your rubbish down a communal chute but I'd never seen the place before. I hadn't had the need. We'd agreed to do all changeovers at our house and it's not like he was going to invite me around for dinner any time soon. *Come round for a coq au vin. We can talk about how you hate me and then I can die via indigestion.*

As I drive into the car park now, there's a mix of Audis and BMWs and I recognise his motor instantly with its personalised number plate: DR CHADZ 1. I remember when he came home with that car. I joked the number plate should have read TWAT100 instead. He responded that night by going out, shagging a random he picked up in a hotel bar and then letting me find out via our credit card bill. He could be cruel like that, to the point that he wanted me to react, to leave. It became a competition to see who'd be the first to break, who'd fail our children first. I didn't want it to be me.

I approach the front door with caution and key in 1 and 0 and wait for a response.

'Hello?' calls out a little voice.

'Iris? It's me, Mummy. Can you let me in?'

'Violet, it's Mama. She came!'

There's trepidation in her voice that I wouldn't have come which throws me a little. Simon always was a horrific patient; I wouldn't put the girls through that. She buzzes me in and I head towards the lifts. *Breathe, Emma.* As soon as the lift doors open, little faces are there to meet me and they throw themselves at me in a three-way cuddle. They seem anxious. Did they think I didn't want to be here? That I wouldn't come when my kids needed me? Relations between Simon and I had been civil in front of the girls, at least.

'You better come. We're really worried about Daddy.'

'How so?'

They hold my hand, leading me through the front door of the flat. 'I drew the curtains and made our beds,' says Iris as I scan the room slowly. There's a tremendous view over the Thames but the decor is pretty plain and I reckon came as standard with the flat. In fact that's what it feels like, a show flat. There are some dull prints on the wall, no photos, a palette of grey, stone and black. I'm not sure what I expected. When I heard that Simon had bought himself a bachelor pad, I assumed it would have a glow-up bar, a sex swing, and for it to be sheathed head to toe in leather.

I take my shoes off as that's what I always do and Violet pulls me towards their room. He's made an effort in here at least. It's a big room with a river view, there's a bunk bed draped in fairy lights, spotty purple wallpaper and angora soft furnishings.

I smile. 'Well done for tidying up. Have you got your rucksacks?'

I have the urge to grab and run but Iris seems more concerned than usual. 'Please can you check on Daddy? I got him a glass of water but he's really hot.'

'Maybe he just needs to sleep?'

'Please?'

Violet appears at my leg. 'We don't have to go to the party. We could all stay here and look after Daddy.'

I look at her little expectant face. There's no chance that I'm going to stay but the looks on their faces tell me what I need to do. Crap. I guess I did take an oath to do no harm. Taking a deep breath, I let Iris lead me to his room and I knock lightly on the door.

'Simon?'

When I enter, the curtains are closed and packets of ibuprofen and empty bottles of energy drinks litter the floor. He lies spread-eagled in the centre of the bed in just his pants. This is the first time I've seen him in such a state of undress since our split and it jolts the system. He moans lightly. Our daughters peer through the door with looks of distress.

'Is he dying?' asks Violet.

I can't answer this without sounding insincere, can I?

'Looks like he's got a bad cold or something. Was he really snotty yesterday?'

'He was coughing.'

As if by cue, he then hacks away like he's trying to bring up a lung. I'm not sure why but I lunge forward into action with a bin I grab from the corner of the room; force of habit as a parent and a doctor. He opens his eyes. 'Ems,' he whispers. I look down at the bin, seeing empty condom wrappers. I promptly put it down and stand over him. 'You came?'

'You told me to come and get the girls.' Against all better judgement, I put the back of my hand to his head. 'Do you have a thermometer here?'

'Somewhere.'

'And what are you using to bring the fever down? Just brufen?'

'I haven't got anything else.'

I reach into my handbag, rifle through a toiletry bag and find some paracetamol. 'Iris, honey. Go get Daddy some more water and does he have any food in his kitchen? Crackers, biscuits?'

'Yes, we've got some Rich Tea Fingers.'

'Get a big stack of them, put them on a plate. Violet, go and help, baby.' They scamper off. 'Simon, I'm leaving you some paracetamol. Make sure you eat before you take these. You know the drill.'

'I'm sorry about the girls.' He whimpers, curling up in pain.

I reach down and his feet are like ice. I do a quick scan for rashes, out of habit rather than concern. He seems to be fine. Rooting around a drawer, I find him a pair of socks and put them on him, trying to cover the rest of him with a light sheet. I then bend down and clear up some of the mess, shaking out old jumpers and shirts and laying them by the edge of the bed. A hair tie falls out on the floor. Possibly one of the girls'. Possibly not.

He coughs again, reaching over, and grabs my hand. 'Have you got a phone on you with a decent light? Can you check what's going on in my throat?'

I look over at him. 'You could do that yourself.'

'Please?'

'Open up.' He sits up and I flinch at his morning breath and the physical proximity. I cup his jaw and feel for his glands, prodding harder than I normally would. There are red patches at the back of his throat, tonsils are slightly inflamed.

'Tonsillitis at a guess? Keep a check, you may need antibiotics.'

'Thought as much.'

I look over at him. He knew exactly what was wrong but he wanted me to play the doting nurse. You tosser.

'Then again, it could be syphilis. You never know until you've had a proper swab.'

His face reads panic. Geez, Simon. Who have you been cavorting with now? You're supposed to be a doctor. I sit here for a moment too long. He touches my hand again.

'Thanks, Ems.'

That touch. He used to touch me all the time, in ways I didn't notice: a hand at a kitchen counter, the bathroom sink, over a duvet. But it feels different now. It annoys; there is no spark. It's all friction. My teeth clench.

'We got the biscuits, Mama.'

I turn and see two little people at the door watching. Both of them smile. I could smother Simon in his weakened state now. But I don't. I smile back.

I've never ridden a horse. In fact, I've never ridden an animal, not a donkey, camel or pony. When we used to visit the zoo or a farm as children, I always wigged out at the thought of relinquishing control to another sentient being whose mind you couldn't quite read. I felt it a recipe for disaster. As a doctor, I saw many injuries involving unpredictable animals, including one poor man who had to have a testicle removed after he was bucked by a donkey. Nothing is worth not having a vital reproductive organ.

Here the horses are all lined up and have names like Blossom and Twinkle. I can't quite read their expressions but I'm sure they wouldn't have chosen those names themselves. That one definitely looks like a Diego. Beside them is a line of squealing children set to torment them for the next hour as they ride in endless circles around this London horse riding studio, My Little Pony. I think about how much this party has cost and to that end, about these poor horses that will only be paid in apples.

We rushed here having left Simon's pretty quickly after he tried to fake some sort of impending death. I hope it's a virulent bacteria that's taken him over. Not something that would kill him obviously but maybe something that would cause temporary impotence or control of his sphincter in social situations. In any case, along with not being able to find parking and London traffic, we're a few minutes late and I know this will be all that anyone remembers about our attendance at this party.

'Emma and Violet! So lovely to have you here, we were expecting Simon I thought?'

'Oh, Simon is ill so I'm afraid you have little ol' me,' I reply.

Leah is Pippa's mum. She's the scanning sort who makes snap judgements just by giving you a quick glance up and down. It makes me want to kick her especially when she does it over a small child. Violet grabs my hand tightly. Leah studies her yellow Hunter wellies and leggings.

'I love those wellies.'

I look over at the children already lined up. It's a mixed affair of trainers, wellies and one lad who's wearing football boots but Pippa looks like she's about to compete in a serious equestrian event. She even has a riding crop. I think the horsiest thing we own is the sweatshirt Violet's wearing. I mean it has a unicorn on it but same gene pool, right? Violet stands slightly behind me which is standard, she's been using me as a shield since the first day of nursery. She's not her sister who throws herself into social situations, not giving me so much as a second glance.

'So, you're welcome to stay Emma and I don't know your name…' she gestures at Iris.

'My name is Iris.' Iris looks up at her disapprovingly as Leah's eldest, Jasper is in her class. She should know this information.

'Iris, lovely. I've laid on caps and croissants so you can just stay and watch. They are also taking photos so you can buy them afterwards if you want?'

Or take them on my own phone? I smile and see the assorted group of mums already convened in the café area. I know most of them from school events and the gate. They are the few I don't quite care for as they seem to talk in cliques and spend an eternity on the WhatsApp class chat debating the school lunch options. *I don't know if the salmon is breaded, Karen.* However, Violet's fingers are fully intertwined with mine. I get a sense of her reluctance. Have I passed over some inherent fear of live animals that one can ride?

'So, Violet… if you want to go with Matilda here who's one of the stable-hands and we can find you a helmet?'

Violet looks up at me and shakes her head. Leah doesn't look impressed. I bend down to Violet's level and tuck a strand of hair behind her ear.

'What's up, kiddo?'

'What if I fall off?' she whispers.

Iris rallies around and throws an arm around her sister.

'I don't think you're riding like in a race. I think someone is there all the time and holding the horse,' I tell her. 'Just listen to what they tell you and hold on tight?'

She won't let go of my hand. Leah hovers over us. She has obviously paid for this by the hour and didn't account for any of these kids potentially being scared of the pretty ponies.

'I can come with you?' says Iris.

Leah steps in. 'Oh, I didn't account for siblings.'

'I don't think Iris meant that. Maybe just for some reassurance?'

'Oh well, she'll miss the safety briefing then. We do need to get this thing started.'

'That's fine. Go ahead.'

'Well, maybe if you left then she wouldn't be so clingy?'

I glare at Leah. The 'throw them in the sea and watch them swim' approach to parenting.

'I'm not going to force her to do something she doesn't want to do.'

I stroke Violet's head as her eyes glaze over with tears. 'You not feeling it, V?'

'Can I watch for a bit?'

I nod my head. 'Sure thing.' I turn to Matilda. 'Could she maybe meet the ponies and get to know them first?'

'Sure, I have a pony that needs feeding and you can help me.'

'Can Iris come?' asks Violet. Matilda nods and Violet takes her sister's hand and they wander off. My heart crumbles seeing Iris resting her head on her sister's to reassure her.

I can hear Leah sighing behind me like I should have asked her permission first. 'I guess she can possibly join in later if the party technicians are OK with that?' she says.

Don't create a scene. Don't say a word.

I feel a hand on my shoulder. 'Has she been like that since the divorce?' Leah's words make my head swing around.

'Excuse me?'

'She was always such a bright little girl, so bubbly and now… a little different?'

I freeze, not knowing how to respond. How often does she see my daughter? For fifteen minutes each day? Have I dropped the ball somewhere between work and my divorce where I hadn't seen a change in my own daughter? My instinct is to take my girls and leave but that would just make it worse. Violet is just intimidated. She did the same at a party last year with the man dressed up as a low rent Captain America who lunged so hard clutching his shiny shield that he split his tights and we all saw far more than we needed to.

Leah gives me an awkward smile like she's trying to sympathise. It's a smile I get a lot in that school playground. *Oh, you're divorced. How sad. I'll pretend to know how that felt and how your life fell apart for a while.* Her words feel all at once rude and exposing. I do not want any part of her luxury coffees and pastries, despite a desperate need for caffeine.

I leave her to sort the children who have behaved as expected and I take myself away from the crowd. That barb, twinned with facing Simon this morning in his flat, half naked, means I can't catch a breath. I find a park bench overlooking the riding circle and sit. She's just one person, one opinion, I tell myself. It means nothing, but in the course of a divorce, those words all creep in somehow, they all meander through your consciousness, penetrate, burn and become an inescapable part of this new divorced reality. I watch as Leah returns to the mums in the café and I can sense she's reporting what's just happened. Shaming a six-year-old girl to a group of adults. I hope one of those horses launches a cannon of hot piss at her when she's stood near them.

'I see you've escaped the coven too?' It's a male voice. This man seems to be hiding behind a tree to escape the scene. I eye him curiously as he comes to sit down next to me. He's obviously smarter than me as he got his free cappuccino before fleeing. He looks familiar, definitely one of those cool dads. He has one of those designer beards complete with denim shorts, Caterpillar boots and a bright orange cagoule. Shorts in September means he at least deserves some respect.

'I'm Leo. I'm Freya's dad. I think you know my eldest too, Giles.'

I remember him from my school run the other morning.

'You're the parking rebel.'

He laughs. 'They've given me a nickname already?'

'I have, don't know about the others.'

'Is Violet OK?'

'I think she might be scared of horses. Which is always good to find out at a horse riding party… Leah's not impressed.'

'Is she ever impressed though? Really?'

I laugh as he glances over at her. She's gone to town in the café with the giant metallic helium balloons and what looks like a cake in the shape of a horse with liquorice for a tail. The party bags will be immense today. None of this sweet cone nonsense. I won't be surprised if we get a proper pony to take home. I hope mine comes house trained and with a Gucci saddle.

'I'll profess to not really knowing her that well so I can't really say…' I reply, admiring how polite I'm being.

'Well then you've lucked out. She's very good friends with my ex-wife.'

'Oh.' My ears prick up at the term ex-wife. We may be bonded by something in common.

'She's a judgemental old bint but hey, maybe one of the pros of being divorced is that I got rid of her too. So you are… Emma?' I nod. 'Dr Emma?'

'Is that my nickname?'

'Unfortunately, yes. You are handy though. When we had that chicken pox outbreak and you identified it on WhatsApp, it saved a lot of people a trip to the doctors.'

'Is that all I'm good for?'

'You're not the mum who makes the good chocolate brownies at the cake sales, are you?'

'No.'

'Then yeah.'

I smile. Leo is not my type at all but there's a conversation here that is, for once, not painful. The school gate is such a strange social scene and it feels nice to make an alliance instead of eking out small talk about the changing of the seasons and second-hand uniform sales.

'How long have you been divorced?' I ask.

'Decree absolute went through six months ago. World of joy ever since.'

'I bet.'

'I mean between kids, and sorting the house, it's drama after drama. I'm freelance too so can only take work around the children now and my ex is… what's the best way to describe the mother of my children, difficult?'

'Faith? She's your ex, right?'

When their divorce happened, Facebook told me she had an actual party in a bar. There were strippers and streamers and a cake involving a topper of a bride and groom, except the groom didn't have a head. I didn't go despite the open invitation. I always wondered how someone's heartbreak could end in a celebration especially when mine left me feeling like I'd been steamrollered into a bad wife pancake.

'The very one. And not because I'm prying but you are also divorced, I believe?'

'I am. Separated for almost two and divorced for a year now. My ex is Simon.'

'And you call me the parking rebel. He parks in the head teacher's space.'

'That I did not know.'

'I only try to annoy Hetty. She told everyone I had an affair and that's why Faith and I broke up. So when I see her in her hi-vis, it's like red to a bull.'

I smile politely. In divorce you need to reach for those small victories sometimes.

'How are things with you and Simon?'

'I haven't pushed him off a cliff yet...'

'Wow. That bad?'

'He has his moments. Can I ask what you heard happened between us?'

'I just heard you split up. But can I be honest?'

'I've just met you, why not?'

'He always came across as a bit of a...'

'Dickhead?'

'I don't need to be honest then.'

I smile. I think about a husband who used to show up to parents' evenings and sports days and walk around like people should have been bowing at his feet.

'He was a terrible husband. Serial cheat. I guess I finally found the balls to say enough was enough. I mean it took me years but hey…'

'Wow. That's bad. Worst thing he ever did?'

'I found a video of him in a threesome on our family computer.'

'Oh.' Leo's eyes dart around. That was the worst example to go with. Too much for the horses. He studies my face as I seem to project a certain calm about everything.

Last year, it had been a different story. Going through that awful phase of lawyers and financial arrangements… I would have hidden behind these trees from the fatigue, the shame. Now the shame is Simon's and it would seem I can talk about it plainly to people I've just met.

'Well, I've told you mine. What happened with you guys?' I ask.

He looks at me, wondering whether to invest his trust in me. I shrug my shoulders. I just told him about sex stuff and I'm here, not over there in the coven with the other mums. He takes a deep breath, his eyes seeming to change colour as he begins the story.

'We were best mates at one point but it just went to pot. Stresses of real life and money and kids. We had a lifestyle to upkeep and I couldn't give that to her so we fought all the time. Like, all the time. The turning point was when she went vegan and found reiki. She started talking in New Age riddles. I once brought a pint of milk into the house and she said I was shitting all over her energy.'

He looks over at Freya at this point, riding a pony at 0.5 miles per hour. The pony has an excellent fringe. He waves at her animatedly and throws a thumb up at her.

'For her it was all about appearances. I had nothing in common with her anymore. It turned into a really toxic environment for the kids too. I just felt like they were breathing it all in.'

We sit there for a moment, letting the information wash over us. I look across the way and see my girls brushing a horse's tail. Violet giggles as the horse sneezes and it vibrates through his whole body.

Leo's words haunt me. Maybe that was the best thing I did, taking the girls away from a family dynamic that was steeped in lies and insincerity. Even though, for the longest time, I thought the best thing was to keep our family glued together, I was wrong. Now was the chance to model something positive for them.

'How's his game?' Leo asks.

'His game?'

'Divorce was once described to me as tennis. Just back and forth, forever and a day. Sometimes they'll smash something right into your half, someone will drop the ball. But it's a game that will never stop.'

'That's depressing…'

'Faith is also the most competitive woman in the world – it's exhausting. So tell me of Simon's game.'

'We have a routine, we stick to it. I give good game face for the kids. I am civil.'

'I hate that word. The only time it's ever used is to describe a war.'

'Or a servant. It's occasionally a case of one-upmanship, he likes to peacock and pretend nothing happened but I try to not let that affect me.'

'Get that racquet up, deflect all those shots?'

'Or sometimes just lose, throw a point. Don't waste my energy on balls I can't return over the net?'

He's quiet. It seems like he may have spent a lot of time chasing balls, running himself ragged. There's a lot to be said for standing still sometimes.

'You're smart,' he says.

'Not that smart. I'm sat in the cold with you. We could be inside.'

'True but I've just told you what I think I was supposed to have told our marriage counsellor, that's interesting.'

'Why?'

'Because we paid that counsellor one hundred pounds per session and she didn't even provide drinks. Did you go down that route?'

I shake my head. The truth was it was beyond repair by that point. The wheels had fallen off the car, and whilst Simon was behind the driving seat, I was the mug behind it pushing its carcass towards some unknown destination. Uphill. In the rain. It had become tiring, humiliating.

I study Leo's face. He has that sallow look in his eyes where I can tell he's not slept much and is emotionally exhausted. I know that feeling. You feel drained and you don't know how the emotion will ever get topped up again.

'Have you sorted the school holiday childcare situation yet? Christmases? Birthdays? That's the fun bit. When you start bargaining and fighting over time. I've transplanted organs that require less logistical issues.'

'She'll cage fight me for Christmas. I know she will.'

'I'd pay to see that fight. Reserve me tickets.'

He laughs again and I like that feeling of rallying around him and being useful.

'Can I give you some advice?' I tell him.

'I am all ears.'

'I'm a bit further down this divorce journey than you. It is very overwhelming to start, like you're drowning in a river of all that grief, anger, disappointment. But don't drown. Just keep treading water. It does get better.'

'Tennis and rivers. We're killing it with the analogies, eh? I take it you've read all the self-help books too?'

'*I Do, I Did, I'm Done* was my favourite.'

'*How to Sleep Alone.*'

'That's the part I don't mind as much. I can sleep like a starfish now and build forts out of pillows.'

He laughs. 'Can I ask if you've heard anything about me at the school gate?' he asks. 'I think she's done a decent job vilifying me. The snarls some women give me.'

'I've heard nothing,' I reply. 'Unless you're the dad with the gambling problem?'

'No. I know him. He was addicted to online fruit machines, lost a whole term's school fees in three weeks. No doubt I've been painted as neglectful, always away on location, terribly unorganised and emotionally cut off.'

'I hope that's how you sell yourself on any new dating profiles?'

'Of course. The women flood to me now.' I laugh. 'It's been nice to chat to you, Emma, you should hang around the school gate more. We need more of your type.'

'Lonely divorcees who can offer medical advice?'

He chuckles. 'We need variety, normality.'

'I don't know if I'm ready to enter the fray, right now…'

'Well, you talked to me?' He gets out a roll of Fruit Pastilles from his rucksack and offers me one. I don't refuse. In his rucksack is a bike helmet, a stuffed zebra and a six pack of Pom Bears.

'Which is more than I've done with most, I guess,' I reply.

I chew on my lemon Fruit Pastille and look over the way. Leah keeps glancing at me and Leo and, no doubt, will report back to Faith that we had an intimate conversation on a bench sharing sweets and looking lovingly into each other's eyes while the ponies whinnied with their approval in the distance. I am tempted to touch his knee to add fuel to the fire but don't need the drama.

But then another thing catches my eye. Little Violet emerging from a courtyard on top of a horse, Iris beside her clapping and looking ecstatic. I can't read Violet's expression but it's somewhere between tears and looking like her teeth may shatter from the massive grin spread across her face. We're halfway through this party but hell, better late than never. I grab my phone and take a picture. The girl got on an actual horse. I pause. The first instinct would be to send this to Simon but I stop myself. Leo looks on at Violet and smiles.

'Can I friend you on Facebook, Emma? I only have one other parent on there. It feels good to have an ally. We could start a divorced parents' self-help book club.'

I look over to him. All my other male friends are doctors, relations, or the Ocado man who delivers my shopping every Thursday evening. His name is Ian. Maybe this is a step forward in the right direction.

'You can. I'm Emma Callaghan now.'

'You changed your name back?'

'Yes.'

'Good for you.'

# Chapter Five

637 days since Lucy caught Simon looking at
someone's lady bits on FaceTime

'Lucy, I'd look like a milkmaid.'

My sister is not listening to me but is sifting through my wardrobe looking for a jacket. She pulls a mustard polo neck jumper
out of my wardrobe.

'This is awful, can I burn it?'

'Luce, I think that's Burberry.'

'Doesn't make it any prettier, it's the colour of old sweetcorn.
You're not allowed to wear this anymore.'

I don't argue with her as I think that might be a gift that Simon
once gave me for Christmas. It wasn't me at all and I envisioned
that he just went into a shop, pointed to the first thing he saw and
handed over his credit card. I never wore it – next to all the black
I own it would have made me look like a wasp.

Lucy is in my bedroom like some very bad version of a TV stylist
except the criticism is personal and she's not listening to anything
I say. She holds up a polka dot Zara dress with Cardi B rapping in
the background, hoping that some of that cool may infuse into my

bones. The dress is a little floaty and not what I'd normally wear, and it's white which means I won't be able to drink red wine, surely.

'What you don't want is this cute anaesthetist to show up looking trendy and you just looking like you're there for a job interview.'

'It's smart casual.'

'It's boring as balls, that's what it is. I hadn't realised we had let you get this dull. At least try this on.'

I take my dressing gown off, standing in my pants, and she stares at them intently. They are flesh coloured and high waisted. The bra matches but is plain and functional.

'I don't get this underwear situation. Why don't you wear those knickers I got you for your first date?'

'The see-through ones without a gusset? No. These are comfortable and provide support.'

'Except when he has you naked and you look like a giant egg. They don't even have lace.'

I grab the dress from her and try it on. 'I look like a Dalmatian.'

'Then why don't you wear your black dress, with your black tights and carry your black bag?'

'You're mocking me.'

'It's my reason for living.'

It's a Monday evening and tonight is the night. My second date since my divorce except this one feels less a natural meeting of minds but more the biggest set-up in the history of dating. I can feel myself sweating through my actual bra; the balmy side of nervous. It's been a year since I last did this and look how well that turned out. I haven't even spoken to him and only know to look for the fab man who is five years younger than me with the good skin and shoes. Maddie told me he'll catch me at the South Bank at 8.30 p.m. after work. It feels late but maybe having a smaller window of time means there's less chance for things to go wrong. Maybe it mitigates the risk of him crying. I don't even know what he sounds like. Will he have an accent? What if he has a really high voice? Or a lisp? This could all go very wrong.

'Do you solely own blazers and suit jackets? Anything in denim or leather?'

'No. And these earrings hurt.' They look like chainmail and make bizarre clattering sounds like wind chimes.

'You can't just wear studs.'

Yes, I can. It's what I've been wearing for twenty-odd years. She pulls my waist in with a gold belt that looks like I'm about to fight for my heavyweight title. I shake my head at her. She throws it at the bed like she's done with me.

'By the way, did Meg ring you today?' I ask.

Lucy throws me a confused look. Meg was the eldest of the tribe but had moved up to the Lake District with her husband, Danny, living some country life idyll in wellies and North Face with their three daughters. Modern communications meant we were all in touch but it meant our ship no longer had a captain. I filled that position in her absence but we all miss her, she completes the jigsaw. She was the one who stood up to our mother, the one who could get us into parties because she was a cool journalist chick. I remember the time she got us into a *Glamour* magazine awards ceremony. It wasn't pretty, Grace got so drunk she threw up in her goodie bag and Lucy possibly copped off with a member of the Kaiser Chiefs in the loos but I loved how she would herd us like sheep and was always the one at the end of a night buying us chips and flashing the kebab man so he'd give us extra garlic mayo.

'I had a strange phone call from her before my last surgery,' I carry on. 'She thinks Danny might be cheating on her.'

Lucy stops accessorising to look up at me. 'What?' she says, already seething with anger. In our girl gang, Lucy was the wildcard, the likeliest one to carry a shank. In her mind, she's already halfway up the M6, drowning him in one of the Lakes when she gets there.

'I don't know. Apparently he had sex toys delivered to the house. She was a little vague. I think it might be a complete overreaction.'

Lucy's face turns to horror. 'What, Farmer Dan?' Danny wasn't a farmer at all but it was our nickname for him given he had that surly monosyllabic thing going on and occasionally wore a flat cap. I suspected that was also part of the attraction for Meg. Like a modern-day Poldark, without the six pack. 'Doesn't look the sort. What sort of sex toys? Like proper kink?'

I don't want to know what that entails and if she divulges it may taint the clear mind I'm planning to take into tonight's date.

'I didn't ask. Possibly a dildo.'

'Is she OK?' asks Lucy.

'I didn't pry. I told her to come back when she has concrete evidence. Maybe drop her a text later when I'm out.'

'Will do. Can I ring Danny and shout at him?'

'No.'

'Spoilsport. I am going to my room to find some jackets.'

She escapes for a moment and Violet enters wearing her nightie and giant rabbit slippers. The look of confusion is everything to me.

'It doesn't look right, does it V?'

'It's a pretty dress but you just don't look like my mummy.'

I smile. She climbs on to my bed and lies down on her front in a star shape, waving her limbs up and down like she's swimming. I replace the gold dangly earrings with a simple gold stud. It's a start.

'Where are you and Aunty Maddie going out for dinner?' she asks. I've not told the girls I'm going on a date. Both times I've met Maddie instead. 'You should go to Pizza Express. I like the dough balls there.'

I smile. It's not a bad shout but I suspect not cool enough for Lucy who would expect me to do something trendy and modern like Korean barbequing or hot potting, whatever that is.

'Or maybe you could go to McDonald's?'

Also not a terrible idea, we could cut this date back by an hour and I could have a McFlurry. The lighting would be the killer though. I smile as she sifts through the accessories on the bed and tries all of her aunt's vintage gothic rings on her little fingers. Lucy returns clutching a leather bomber jacket and a pair of gold Converse.

'Both, no.'

'You are soooo boring. At least one of them.' I grab the jacket and throw it on over the dress. It'll do but I don't think it'll provide much warmth nor protection should there be a light shower.

'I can wear those black Hobbs boots with the laces,' I say.

Lucy half smiles. 'Well, they look a little like Doc Martens so yes and what about a red bag?' She hands me something the size of a pencil case.

'No.'

'Why?'

'I'm not sure what I can fit in that? I'll need to take an umbrella for a start.' I open the red bag to find she's stuffed it with condoms. I throw it back to her in disgust. 'No.'

Grabbing a grey tote from my chair, I hang it over my shoulder. 'What do we think, Little V?' I do a circle and she giggles.

'It's funny seeing you in a dress, Mummy.'

'Not just any dress, it's bang on trend. It even has its own Instagram account,' Lucy says.

'But it doesn't have hands, how does it post its own pics?' I reply.

Lucy pulls a face, as if that was a terrible joke and I need to trust her. Does anyone trust Lucy, really? Before she came in here I had on black trousers and a white shirt. She told me I looked like I was going to dance with someone called Vincent Vega. Now I look a modern version of a milkmaid in a leather jacket. Worse, this has a hospital gown feel to it. He'll think that I mugged this off a patient. I stand in front of the mirror and Lucy drapes herself over me as we study my silhouette in the mirror. I can see her considering a velvet alice band whereas I am more concerned about visible panty lines.

A voice pipes up behind us. 'Last time I went to Pizza Express, I had a ham and mushroom pizza and Daddy shouted at the waiter because it came with olives but it was alright because Susie helped me pick them all off.'

Lucy's casual drape turns into a grip of my shoulders. We both pause for a moment. Mainly because we know Susie is not Simon's mum's name or that of any of his relatives. I stare straight into the mirror trying to forget what I just heard. Lucy won't leave it though.

'Who's Susie, V?'

'She's daddy's friend from work. We went to Pizza Express for dinner.'

Lucy goes quiet. I stare her out. I know what her next move will be. She wants to tell Violet that Mummy has friends too. Man friends and Mummy is going to go for dinner with them too, but now is not the time.

I exhale deeply. *You're allowed to go out with who you want, Simon. I am not your keeper but I am their mother, don't replace me just yet.* Lucy can tell this has shaken me and the anger which likes to vibrate through her bones comes to the fore.

'Does this Susie sleep over at Daddy's house?'

I shake my head at her. Not now in front of Violet who looks confused that the information has caused some upset. Was this something we should have discussed beforehand? He could shag who he wanted – he had done already, plenty of times – but when our girls are involved, then it's a game changer.

'Sometimes she stays at Daddy's flat.'

'Like a nanny?' Lucy asks. 'Do they hold hands? What does she look like?'

'Lucy, stop. Get out of here.'

'But Ems…'

I glare at her. *Don't you dare argue with me about this.* We can bicker over belts and earrings but not my kids and the state of my divorce. She leaves reluctantly, not closing the door so she can keep her ear in. I sit on the bed and gesture for Violet to put her head on my lap.

'I'm sorry. Did I say something bad?' she asks.

'No. Not at all.' I run my fingers through her brunette bob, smoothing the hair over her cheeks. That's the thing about kids post-divorce. You will love them completely and without measure, these little people that you've grown and nurtured, but you also have reminders of the person you made them with forever and a day. Look at those big hazel eyes, all him.

'Do they still have the dough balls in Pizza Express for pudding with the chocolate dip?' I ask.

'They do but Daddy said I couldn't have them as I had a lot of dough balls.'

'And you do love dough balls.' I smile thinking of a little V stuffing her face with them until she has cute comedy chipmunk cheeks.

'Susie's OK. She doesn't know how to do hair though.'

'Well, this is why we call Aunty Luce in so she can French plait the lot of us.'

'Do you want me to not like her?'

I hear Lucy cough outside the bedroom door. I ignore her. I can't play this game. I really can't. Yes, spy on that bitch and be completely awful and tantrummy and get on her phone and look for incriminating photos and send them to me. Wake her in the middle of the night and spoil every dinner and social occasion you can so she will leave Simon and deny him of the happiness because she can't deal with being your step-parent. But I can't.

'No. You keep being you.'

'Do you want to know more about her?'

I shake my head. Yes. But not from you.


'There's a Suzanne Donne but she's some battered old bird who lives in Hampshire. Looks about fifty-something.'

'That's his aunty. Look harder.'

'You're not talking to me while he's sitting there, are you?'

'No. But hurry up.'

I'm sat outside a bar on the South Bank clutching an overpriced tumbler of Prosecco in my hand. I know they don't give us a glass anymore because they don't want us to break anything, but now they give us plastic instead which I thought was bad for the environment. I'm waiting for the day when they ask us to bring our own glasses instead or allow us to join up those paper straws and drink the stuff straight out of the bottle.

I can hear Lucy humming on the other end of the phone. She's been given no other instruction today but to put the girls to sleep and not mention Susie's name in any way, shape or form. However, as soon as their heads hit the pillow she is to stalk that woman to the hilt.

This is not how this date should be starting. I am here twenty minutes early waiting on this anaesthetist and I should be having a drink, looking cool and trying to think of the best ways to project the best version of myself to someone new. Instead my hand shakes. Who are you, Susie? Reveal yourself to us.

'Found her.'

'Where?'

'Instagram. Susie Hunter but she's got a private account.'

'What does her profile picture look like?'

'Blonde, late twenties maybe. She likes a filter.'

'Could she just be a nanny?'

'Well, even then he's no doubt slept with her,' adds Lucy with substantial amount of spike in her tone. She's right. I veer between relief and worry. Would you take a nanny to Pizza Express? He'd tell me if he had a nanny. We used to take our au pairs out with us, not because we were lazy parents but we wanted to feed them and make them feel part of our family.

'Oh, balls. I'm looking at some tagged photos on Facebook. Definitely a nurse.'

'Oh. Is she pretty?'

Lucy is silent for a moment. 'She has a weak chin.'

If this is all there is to say about her then I'm a little worried. 'Does she have kids? Where does she live? What department does she work in?'

'I'm not the fricking FBI, hun. Give me a moment.'

'Look harder. Why hasn't he told me about her?'

'Because he's a prick. We've known this for years.'

'But the kids have met her? I don't get him. Why would he do that?'

Lucy is silent again. It's like we will always be completely dumbfounded by this man's level of selfishness. He should have said something. I down the rest of my pitifully small glass of Prosecco and feel it stick in my throat, burping quietly.

'Emma?' the voice comes from behind me. Oh, shit. He's early. Did he hear me burp? I hang up my phone and turn around. Try and blank it out of mind. Smile and breathe.

'Yes. You must be Jag?' For some reason, I have an empty glass in one hand and a phone in the other, so because I have no hands available to shake, I offer him a cheek. Confused, he rubs his own cheek next to mine and doesn't know where to put his hands so keeps them rigid, at right angles like a robot. It's the worst initial greeting ever. But he laughs as we part.

'I think it would have been better if I'd just tripped into you and landed in your lap,' he says.

I chuckle. 'Spilling this drink and making this dress completely see-through.'

This is the wrong thing to say as he scans the hospital/milkmaid dress. Maddie was right. His skin has a glowing quality that doesn't seem quite fair and when we are further into this, I may ask if he moisturises or uses masks or scrubs. He is trendy. I believe those are Vans trainers which I haven't seen since my teens but they pair nicely with his rucksack. He puts the bag down and opens it up.

'These are for you.'

I register complete surprise. It's a small bunch of flowers, wrapped in brown paper and twine, a sunflower in the centre. I smile, quite unexpectedly. People do flowers, still? And for a moment, I am grateful as the shock mellows my apprehension and lets me forget any people called Susie for a few seconds.

'Wow.'

'Too much?'

'Perfect, thank you. I got you nothing.'

'I wasn't expecting anything. I see you've started before me though.' He points to my empty glass.

'If you can call it that. It was like drinking out of a thimble.' I am conscious this makes me look like a cheap drunk but he laughs it off.

I like the way his face looks very joyous. There's a wide grin; I can't tell if it's natural or nerves. Is he one of those people who's always happy? I don't think I could do perma-happy. I am doubly conscious now that I look confused and critical in response, trying to figure him out.

'Can I at least buy you a drink to say thank you?'

He seems taken aback. I can't tell if he thinks it's because it's some feminist gesture but I hope it's showing that I'm just polite.

'I'm actually pacing myself tonight. It's just I have my car parked at the hospital so I'm driving home.'

'Safety first.' That didn't make me sound like some sort of sad case. 'So something soft? A juice? A…?' Force of habit makes me realise I almost asked this man if he wanted a Fruit Shoot.

'Well, we could stay here or there's a pub I quite like. We could just have a walk?'

This does not help my confused look. I came here on the presumption that things had been booked and plans had been made. I was ready to sit down somewhere. This is half the joy of having a secretary. I don't want to walk around London in circles with him. Or do I? Is that how people date now? What if you need the loo? Do you just pop in a public convenience in a park? Isn't that where doggers meet these days? He can sense I have many questions running through me, the most important of which is who the hell is Susie Hunter? It fuels some sense of panic that widens my eyes so I look like I haven't been able to handle that thimble of alcohol either. I go to stand up and stumble a little.

'Are you OK?' he asks me, chuckling.

'I am. I just… food. I think I'd quite like to get some food.'

'What do you feel like eating?'

I pause for a moment. What would I like to eat? I think about date nights after work when Simon would force me into some mid-priced European restaurant that would always have steak of some description on the menu. We'd eat in cold white open plan restaurants, dipping our bread into pools of olive oil, balsamic vinegar and sea salt, commercial jazz in our ears, glossing over everything that was inherently wrong with our marriage by chatting about surgeries and children. Being given a chance to choose a restaurant is a little different.

'Hummus,' I say.

He laughs, a little too hard.

'Is that funny?' I reply.

'No. It isn't. It's just Maddie told me that to get you onside I should get you hummus, avoid meringue and that you don't like sandwiches.'

'This is… true.' I think about how he could have replaced these flowers with a pot of hummus and it probably would have had the same effect.

'What else has Maddie told you?'

'She bigged you up. She said you were the most caring and honest person she knew, you're super low maintenance, that kindness and good manners impress you more than money. You also don't care about a person's height,' he says standing on his toes.

I laugh. 'Also, true. I know it's an issue for most women but I'm not preoccupied with size.'

He chuckles. I blush. Intensely.

'Then come with me and we shall find you hummus.'

'Really?'

He nods. We can't really fill up on hummus and I'm not sure it will soak up the many drinks I will probably consume but let's search it out. He adjusts his rucksack on his shoulders and starts walking. I follow with a little skip. Oh. I hope he isn't leading me to a Tesco Metro and we'll have to eat it on a street corner with some Cool Original Doritos. I don't think that's a date.

'So why no sandwiches?' he asks.

'I just have a problem with overfilling. Sandwiches fall apart. Parts of it end up on me. They're hard to eat attractively.'

'Even toasted sandwiches?' he asks.

'Yes. They're the worst because you bite into them and then squirt hot cheese over yourself.' I realise this sounds a bit wrong. 'I also don't eat blueberries, for future information,' I carry on.

'But blueberries are delicious?'

'My sister once told me they are Smurf testicles so I can't bring myself to eat them now.'

He roars with laughter. At me or with me, I'm not quite sure.

'Well, I'll remember this for future picnic situations.'

I grin. He really meant what he said. This is a walking date and I'm glad I didn't go for a heel but I wish I'd worn a scarf. Our first stop is a food festival where we find a stall specialising in all things Greek. He literally finds me vats of hummus sprinkled in herbs and spices and are beautiful variations of hummusy beige. He's not fazed by the hum of stalls as we stroll past. He seems to have a personal relationship with a man who sells Vietnamese rice bowls and smiles at a lady selling Portuguese custard tarts, instead of ignoring her as most would. He's very relaxed whereas I am tad more cautious, mainly because I usually don't do street food, not for a lack of adventure but due to a fear over food safety regulations. There are far too many pigeons flying around. However, his enthusiasm quells my uncertainty especially when he doesn't just buy me hummus, he goes all out with a slab of spanakopita, olives, dolmades and a variety of flatbreads. He tries some sample baklava and asks the vendor about which nuts they use. Walnuts make the difference apparently.

And then we walk. It's a wonder to me, all these bars, old storage container restaurants and skateboarders nestled in amongst the British Film Institute and Southbank Centre. Did I have a social life when I was married? I don't think I did. I worked and played mother and jumped on the trains and tubes between the two. I occasionally had drinks in the pub at Waterloo making myself cross-eyed by studying multiple train timetables. I would meet a sister occasionally or go out for a work thing but it was measured and uneventful. Glasses of wine while I clock-watched and wondered what the au pairs had given the girls for dinner. So, everything now feels bright and alien. There are lights, cameras and action and frozen yoghurt sold out of an old double-decker bus.

By the time we get to the Tate Modern, we find a bench and Jag opens up his rucksack to reveal two gin and tonics in tins. So maybe there was some forward planning here. It's sweet. And now I'm stuffing my face with really tasty hummus. It contains actual chickpeas unlike the wallpaper paste supermarket stuff I usually get. And so we sit here and we eat and drink and chat. And I will put this out there, I don't mind this at all.

Hello, Jag Kohli. You are thirty, five foot eight and you are an anaesthetist who trained in Manchester. You like Manchester but not enough to move there because London is in your bones and you now live in Brockley which still provides humour for you as you don't really like broccoli the vegetable that much as it gives you wind which wasn't something you thought you'd ever say on a first date. You have a sister who lives in Wolverhampton. You tap your feet a lot to a song that I can't hear and every so often in the conversation you dip into accents.

We both look out onto the river to take in the view of St Paul's.

'It really is quite a rubbish river, eh?' remarks Jag.

I smile. 'Most city rivers are really not hugely nice to look into. They're pretty filthy.' Case in point, as I squint and see some detritus in the moonlight that could be a floating rat or a large turd.

'The Seine is lovely.'

'But spoiled by all the tourist boats reversing up and down it.'

'True.'

'Amsterdam, nice waterway vibe there.'

'But spoiled by all the boobs and sex shops?'

'Again, true.'

He's so easy to talk to but I've kept it quite light. I'm not going to talk about Simon or my divorce. Let's just talk rivers and stuff our faces with extremely plump olives and not know where to throw the pips. What is most telling are the silences in between that feel neither awkward nor strange. And you're not crying which is a bonus.

'Is there anything else Maddie told you about me then?' I ask.

'Ah, lovely Maddie. She's your biggest fan, you know? She may as well sell T-shirts with your face on.'

'You don't have one of those yet?'

'Well, if they're there, I'll take a medium.' He laughs.

I glance over at him. It's a strange date as I seem to be seeing him a lot in profile: he has very long eyelashes for a man but I like the scattering of facial hair and the symmetry of his teeth. There's also such a relaxed vibe to him. It's like he wants to hang out as opposed to court me. Is this what being with him would entail? Park benches and convenient alcohol? Part of me is relieved. I don't think formality would have sat well with me today and this feels like a good way to get used to each other at least. I look at my phone. It's already ten thirty and a stroll back is needed so I can get on the right train home at a sensible time. That said, I stay where I am, for now. Then my phone rings. I glance at it. Balls, it's my mother. I put it on silent and ignore it.

'I do the same when I get a call from my mother,' he says.

'I bet your mother is not as bad as mine.'

'My mother is Indian and obsessed to an unnatural degree about my singledom.'

'Mine still buys me multipacks of full briefs.'

'So does mine. Perhaps they know each other?'

'Your mother buys you full briefs? I'd expect you don't need that much coverage.'

He laughs from the belly. I think I made a decent joke that I wish I'd recorded so I could send it to Lucy. Though I am conscious that I've referenced his undercarriage. Must change the subject.

'Your mother, why obsessed?' I ask.

'Well, she got the doctor son but now she needs to cap it off with making sure I marry a nice girl and give her some grandbabies. It's an Asian thing but mostly a generational mother thing too whereby she assumes ultimate happiness is being settled and having 2.4 children.'

I put my hand up in the air. 'Well, I am evidence that that is not always the case.'

He smiles but hesitates. No doubt, Maddie has briefed him over not going down that route of conversation. He's quick to swerve. 'There was a point where it was going that way. I had a fiancée. I liked her mostly because she made really good cake. In fact, she probably fooled everyone with the baking.'

'Was cake not enough then?' I ask.

'She dumped me. She hated my hours and she said there was an inevitability about us.'

'Wow. A little bit cruel, no?'

He glances over at me. I can't quite tell if he means it's because she wasn't or because he knows what I went through was far worse.

'How so?' he asks.

'It's just very negative. It sounds like she had something mapped out in which you didn't feature. I'm sorry if that sounds harsh.'

There is a look of recognition there. Is that sadness? I can't quite tell. Oops, I don't want to sour the mood. It looks like he's thinking the same so again moves the conversation on.

'It's quite late for a mother to call though. Is she with your girls?'

'No, they're with my sister.' I screw my face up as I realise he does have a point. This is late, even for my mother, on a school night. My first instinct is Dad. Is he OK? I grab my phone out of my bag. Two missed calls from her. I phone her back immediately and stand up from the bench. It takes her two rings to answer.

'Emma, I'm sorry. Were you in the middle of a surgery?'

I always like the way my mother assumes I keep myself wired to my phone when I'm operating on hearts.

'No. I'm out. What's wrong?'

'I've had a frantic call from Gill Morton.'

'Meg's mother-in-law?'

'Yes. Meg's hurt. She fell. We think she fell down the stairs. Blood everywhere, she's in the hospital. I am beside myself. Your father and I were thinking of driving up now.'

'Meg fell down the stairs?'

'She did, the idiot.'

Panic darts through me as I think about that phone call earlier on where a distraught Meg thought her husband was cheating on her. Is this related? Did he hurt her? I feel guilty that I'd ignored a plea for help. I also think about my elderly parents driving up in the middle of the night to the middle of nowhere. They have trouble getting out of multi-storey car parks. Plus, adding my mother to any drama that may be happening up north would add to Meg's worries as opposed to helping her.

'Look, don't get in the car. I'm in London and I can jump on a train. Is she in surgery? Is she conscious?'

'We don't know, Emma. Gill was very vague. Danny is with her.' I can hear her and my dad conferring in the background. 'Are you working? Can you go up there?'

'Well, if Meg is hurt then yeah, but the girls... can you go round and help Lucy out maybe?'

'You are the doctor.'

'I am. But when I say go and help Lucy out then don't go and wind her up.'

'I won't do anything of the sort. Please just make sure Meg is OK.'

'I'll ring you from the train, Mum.'

As I hang up, I turn round to see Jag packing up our little picnic. His face reads concern. 'If you weren't into me that's totally fine. You didn't need to get your sister to fall down the stairs.'

He can tell I don't quite get the joke. Meg? Meg was the one whom no one really worried about. Being the eldest means she is independent and fierce and we let her free into the wilds of the North knowing she'd be fine. You can die from falling down stairs. The thought of that makes the breath stick in my mouth. I start scrolling down my phone for train times.

'I am so sorry. I… seriously, this was lovely.'

'It was. Are you OK?'

'I just have people to ring and I don't know about trains. Maybe I should go home and change first and then drive up and then…'

'Where does your sister live?'

'The Lake District.'

'Oh. That's like six hours away.'

'It is.'

He looks at me for a moment, olives in one hand, feta in the other. This is weird. It really was lovely. Sitting with him by a river and taking in the air and the hummus. Being with someone of the opposite sex and not feeling it was about anything else but just being myself. He smiles.

'Then phone all those people from the car. I'm going to buy us some coffees and I'll drive you up. My car is literally down the road.'

I pause for a moment. 'Really? But we've been drinking?'

'We had one tin of G&T and that was seventy-five per cent sugar. Are you having fun?'

I pause. 'I am.'

'Latte with a hazelnut shot. One sugar.'

'How did you—?'

'Maddie.'

'You also like Maoams.'

'I do.'

# Chapter Six

638 days since Meg threatened to cut off
Simon's bollocks

'What the hell are you doing here?'

'Well, when you hear your sister's fallen down the stairs and there was blood everywhere then you make the effort to ensure she hasn't done herself any serious injuries. You numpty.'

It's 7.45 a.m. in the morning. I'm not sure how I'm still standing but I am here in my eldest sister's bedroom having travelled through the night to check in on her well-being. That said, my mother does have a flair for the melodramatic. The way she described it, I expected Meg to be lying here as an amputee. Instead she stands next to her wardrobe hobbling about, which lets me know this is just a bad sprain and that she's doing that Meg thing of not listening to advice. She should be lying down and that leg should be elevated.

I look around her bedroom with a strange sense of déjà vu. That Christmas when my marriage ended, Meg dragged me up here to get me and the girls out of London and away from Simon. Meg had always been like that, the protective mother hen sort who took it upon herself to give us all the guidance and support which my mother lacked. She relegated her husband Danny to the sofa and she would sleep beside me every night like we were kids in our shared room, spooning me while I cried myself to sleep. Her and Danny would take me on bracing walks up hills and she asked her mother-in-law to make me one of her famous trifles, which only I was allowed to eat. We saw in the New Year in their living room with a bottle of port, copious amounts of cheese and a log fire into which Meg threw a letter Simon had written to me trying to persuade me to give our marriage another chance.

I adore Meg, and hate her a tiny bit for not being in London anymore – we all blamed Danny for that really. As I look at her now, she still looks the same, if slightly broken and unwashed. She has always had this effortless style about her; she can wear a man's T-shirt and bundle her hair on top of her head and still look cool. Her and Lucy match in that sense, the way they can wear trainers with dresses and have more than two earrings per ear.

However, although usually bright and confident, today fatigue and emotion shine through. My instinct tells me this is not as bad as I thought. Still, what happened last night? There's no blood or evidence of her having fallen down the stairs but Danny was surly and non-conversational with me downstairs when I arrived. If Dan has hurt my sister then I will gut him – and I know how to do that. I always thought their marriage was strong and stable. It's the polar opposite of mine. There's love and true friendship. It always seemed so straightforward for them, but then I guess marriage rarely is. Also, what has happened to that chest of drawers? It lies in a heap in the corner.

Normally, I would launch myself at her with hugs but I'm clutching her youngest, Polly and her other daughters, Tess and Eve, are doing that for me. These girls are different to mine; I'm not sure if it's because they've been raised in the North but they're a little bouncier and carefree. Tess's wild blonde curls swing through the air as they engage with their mother while Polly, the baby, drools down this white dress that I'm still wearing. I make a note to tell Lucy that her youngest niece didn't approve.

'There's also a man called Jag who has Maoams in his pockets. He came with Aunty Ems. Can I go now?' chirps Tess.

Oh. Jag's name jolts me back to the present. Meg looks over at me. I look out the window clinging to Polly for dear life, pretending I need to study the drizzle outside. Tess and her sister vacate the room and I hope Meg might be in such a state of fatigue that she didn't hear the last bit of that sentence.

'So… all OK?' I ask.

'Jag?' She did hear that. I'm going to have to explain, aren't I? So yeah, I'm glad you're OK and still have a leg but me coming here prompted one of the most bizarre evenings of my life: a date in a Kia with a man called Jag who I literally met like twelve hours ago. I just got in a car with a mere stranger and did everything I was told not to do as a young girl. And it was all done in profile watching him drive up the M6. Taking breaks in deserted services with shiny floors and bad lighting where we had coffees and wandered around WHSmith bulk buying travel sweets. Bursts of conversation about hospitals and house prices. Taking it in turns to drive so the other could nap. The discovery that he snored lightly, the hope that I didn't. All his music being that sort of early noughties chillout stuff that Beth used to be into. But it's too early for that. Instead, I put Polly down to have a crawl and pretend to do my doctorly thing and examine her ankle. Definitely twisted. Her knickers are also on inside out but she doesn't need to know that.

'You'll have to shower with your leg in a bin bag. Any pain, warmth? And how did you fall?'

'None of the above and I didn't fall, Danny dropped me.'

I widen my eyes. *He did hurt you? Why was he carrying you? Like a fireman's lift? Or cradling you like a giant baby? Because you were drunk?* I think about what she confided in me earlier in the day. 'Because… you accused him of cheating on you?'

She sighs. 'Because we were having sex and it turns out he can't stand up and support the weight of big old heifer me.'

I can't quite take that last sentence in. Sheer panic that she may have been abused turns into relief, almost laughter. I am here because of a sex injury? This is incredibly funny, no? When can I tell the sisters? How do I tell our mother? They were standing up? We still do that at our age? What sort of sex are my sisters having that I seem to have missed out on?

'Right, which is why he had all the sex toys?' I ask, slightly horrified remembering her revelation that she'd also discovered he had some stash of sex toys. I think about the gruff flat-capped man stood in the hallway this morning and how he's possibly turned my sister into a deviant. I knew that's what they did up in these parts.

'No.'

She's about to divulge the truth when we are interrupted by someone at the door carrying tea. Darn it and you. Jag, this is a lovely gesture but you were supposed to stay downstairs chatting up Meg's mother-in-law because now she will direct all the questions at me.

He smiles on seeing me. Whereas my hair is frizzy and my lips dry and lizardy, his thick dark hair remains unchanged and his skin is extraordinarily bright.

'Oh, this is Jag.'

'A pleasure to meet you.' Meg looks at him curiously. Maybe I can palm him off as a very enthusiastic taxi driver.

'Hello? My daughter mentioned you but I thought…'

'Jag and I were having a drink when we got a call saying you'd fallen and yes, we are both here now.'

They engage in small talk and he's polite and all the types of things you want someone to be when meeting a relative for the first time. But then he looks over at me. And there's a moment. That was the strangest first date ever, no? And we spent most of it in silence and in the romantic surrounds of the M6 services. I can't even recall half the conversation now. I think we talked about quite liking Coldplay, trying to work out if that was fashionable or a guilty pleasure. And all that time, he never mentioned Simon once, speaking to me like a human whose past had not been tarnished by hurt and heartbreak.

Meg watches on and her mood softens. I wonder if Jag's knack for making people feel at ease is due to him being an anaesthetist. Maybe this is years of training from putting panicked people under. He leaves the room and winks at me. I attempt to wink back but look like I have a strange facial twitch.

'Follow him,' whispers Meg, angered by my hesitancy.

'But I was going to stay, I have some days off…'

'I mean to the door. He just drove six hours through the night to get you here. Go to him…'

She shoos me away like a pigeon. To be fair, it's not like he's driving away at this precise moment. I have time to hear the rest of her story with the sex toys. And I want details but not too many details if it involves bodily fluids and sex stuff I don't understand. But I will coax that story out of her later.

'Ungrateful cow.'

'You love me really.'

I do. And she's alive and intact which is important. I pick up Polly and head for the door as her phone rings.

'Mum,' she replies. I taunt her with widened eyes. 'Oh yeah, Emma is fine. Someone drove her up her… a friend… from the hospital. Oh, he's very handsome.'

I take it back about loving her. I shake my head at her. Revenge will come later when I can help shower her and misjudge the water temperature.

I escape into the hallway and spy the family pictures that line the walls including one of when Meg and Danny got married. Our weddings had been very different. It wasn't a competitive bridezilla situation – only to our mother as Meg had got married up here in a barn which Mum had hated. *Animals belong in barns, Meg. Why can't you have a wedding more like Emma's where all the dresses match and I don't have to wear wellington boots?* All I remember is her wedding being fun. We all got so drunk that Beth fell into a cowpat and had to be hosed down by a farmer. The groom didn't shag any of the wedding guests which is always a bonus too.

I study the picture for a moment. It feels strange to be here now. I mean, it's great to see Meg and the girls but this all feels so impromptu which is very unlike me. I don't even have a toothbrush or spare underwear and this dress is too thin to provide warmth up in these colder climes. I go through a list of everything I need to do today: I'll drop the girls to school, make sure Lucy knows to hand the girls over to Simon. I may have to go into town and buy some clothes, some first aid supplies. I need to sleep.

Polly looks up at me. *Christ, I don't half miss you tiny blonde one.* She barks at me and snot bubbles out of her nose. Yikes, that is some bad croup. We need to sort that today too, eh? I go into the bathroom on the hunt for a flannel or some tissues. But as I open the door, a person stands there in just their pants over the toilet, a long stream of wee emerging from them. Polly giggles.

'Oi oi!'

I knock my head back to avert my eyes and close the door on my face awkwardly. Polly laughs again.

'Ouch, yes, sorry…'

The person in their pants is Stuart, Danny's brother. One of those crossover relatives that I've met at weddings and such. The only other thing I know is that he travels a lot and I believe he has slept with Lucy at one point. He answered the door this morning when we arrived, dressed exactly as I find him now so if anything, I applaud his bravery given the temperature. I really twatted my forehead so stand there rubbing it.

'What did you do that for?'

'Well, you caught me by surprise?'

'Heard of knocking?'

'Heard of a bathroom lock?'

Stuart hasn't been particularly amused to see Jag and myself this morning and there's an antagonism there that I can't quite read.

'You're still here.'

'Why are you peeing for so long? That's not normal.'

I look at him at this point, which I shouldn't as one of his balls hangs out the side of his underpants. I cover Polly's eyes, fleeing the bathroom in shock. Even as a doctor, I don't see bollocks that often and they really aren't very pretty, are they? I take a deep breath in the upstairs hallway to steady myself but then hear two little girls laughing. Both Polly and I peer over the banister. Downstairs, Jag is surrounded by Tess and an Eve who appears to have a beard made solely of dark berry jam. He clocks me and smiles.

'We like him, Aunty Ems. Can he stay? What's Jag short for? It's a brilliant name,' asks Eve, her fondness of him obviously driven by the fact he's packing sweets. I descend the stairs as Polly checks him out.

'It's short for Jagpal,' he replies laughing. 'I mean I'd love to stay but I've just told your mum I've got to be back at work.'

Tess smiles at him. 'Are you a doctor too?' she asks.

'I am.'

'Are you Muslim?'

I panic at the forwardness of her suggestion. Twelve hours with this man and even I don't know that much.

'I am not,' he replies. I am grateful for the cheer in his reply.

'OK, because we have bacon today and that would have been awful if we couldn't have given you breakfast.'

He smiles at the invitation.

'Is he your new boyfriend?' asks Eve.

I grab a hairbrush from a shelf, and hand it to her so she knows hair is the priority at this moment, no more questions.

Luckily, Jag intervenes. 'We've only been on one date.'

'Well, I prefer you to Uncle Simon. Mummy calls him very bad names,' she continues, unabashedly.

'I can imagine,' I whisper.

'Now you've been on a date you can be boyfriend and girlfriend, you know? Charlie asked me in the playground to be his girlfriend and I said yes straightaway.'

Jag laughs, trying hard not to catch my eye. I pretend to wipe the snot from Polly's face.

'Why did you do that?' asks Tess.

'Because he's nice and he shares his raisins with me.'

'He sounds awesome,' says Jag.

'He is,' says Eve, glad to be vindicated. I love how this makes perfect sense to her and she sees relationships so clearly. There are calls from the kitchen that see Tess and Eve ushered in. It leaves Jag and I standing in that hallway, Polly watching us both curiously.

'I liked how your nieces mugged me for the rest of my Maoams.'

I laugh. 'And you thought South London was bad for crime.'

'I'm glad your sister is alright. I mean, that's a relief she still has a leg.'

'I feel stupid. I thought it was more serious.'

'Well, I'm glad your mother gave me an excuse to spend more time with you.'

I go quiet.

'That was too much. I was going to share my raisins with you next and then ask you to marry me.'

I am still quiet although glad he's able to joke to try and diffuse the tension.

He continues, 'I think my favourite part of the date was that second coffee in the services that had a name.'

'Richard… Charnock Richard.'

'Like James Bond. But not.'

I chuckle. 'I liked the first services with the soundtrack of the floor buffers and the scent of KFC in the air.'

'Eau de Hot Wings.'

'I don't know how to thank you.'

'No, thank you. I once had a date at a meat auction where a man elbowed me in the face for some prime rib so you've beaten that. And I go on far too many bad drinks and cinema outings.'

'Do you have to go?' As the words leave my mouth, I realise they sound needy and a little desperate. Please follow me around for a bit longer and keep me company. Except I don't know how to say it. *I've liked your company.*

He looks through the cracks of the door of the kitchen where little girls bounce off the counters. 'I'm going to grab a sandwich as Granny Morton looks like she fries that bacon until it's crispy. And I can help out for a bit but then I really should go so you can be with your family.'

His understanding makes my heart glow. Polly smiles at him and he gives her a baby high five. She studies his face and he looks her in the eye.

'Lord, you are cute. Can you tell your aunty something?'

Polly looks at him blankly. I don't actually talk much mate but I think I know where you're going here.

'Tell her that I had the best night and that she's amazing?'

Polly looks at him and smiles contentedly. *I think you just did that yourself.*

But then Jag leans into me, grazing my cheek with his and gives me a kiss. I can't. I step back. I freeze not knowing what to do. My heart. Why has my heart stopped working?

Oh.

# Chapter Seven

I can't really make out Lucy's words as she's busy laughing over FaceTime hearing how our eldest sister was dropped during sex. Beth is also in on this chat and baby Joe babbles away. It is a joy they've teamed up to help me out but I can see a stack of unwashed bowls next to my sink and I am wondering if it's rude to tell them they need to soak them first before they go in the dishwasher.

'Did the girls get to school alright? Did you remember to send Iris in with her lacrosse stick?'

'We did,' Beth replies. 'But we didn't know what one of those looked like so we had to google it.' Chances are they've sent her into school with a net we use for rockpooling. 'How is Meg?'

'She's fine, it'll just take a week or so for her to recover.'

'So Dan's not cheating?' asks Lucy.

I keep my voice down as the mother-in-law is still in the house getting the girls ready for bed. 'No, I think he was just trying to introduce new things to the bedroom and it freaked Meg out.'

'OMG, was he using the dildo on her and she got so shocked that she fell over?' asks Lucy.

'There was a dildo?' questions Beth.

I'm not sure what to tell them next as I know the actual truth. It turns out it was all a strange misunderstanding and Danny has found himself a new hobby which involves sex toys and being an erotic artist. Meg has just found out. She's not prudish about it but she's worried it was a secret in their marriage. A little pep talk from me made her realise that secrets in marriage can come in different shades of grey and if we were ever going to be playing that game then I would win, hands down, no contest.

It'll be weird to see Danny tonight though knowing he's very skilled at drawing penises. At least it makes him a touch more interesting. All his other pastimes involve hill walking with sticks, bedecked in muted khaki fleece. However, if I divulge this secret now then these sisters before me would not be discrete. They would blab to our mother, not now but somewhere down the line at a family gathering under the influence of alcohol. I'm going to have a hard-enough time making sure they don't tell the world that Meg was dropped during sex.

'Don't tell people Meg was dropped during sex,' I chide.

Their faces look riddled with guilt. I've seen these expressions before when they melted one of my doll's heads on a desk lamp by 'accident'.

'We told Gracie because it was too funny.'

'You've spoken to Gracie? Is she OK?'

Grace was sister number four and the one we all worried about the most as eighteen months ago, she became a widow. She was twenty-seven. For now, she was finding herself in every small corner of the world trying to get over the enormity of what had happened and we let her be. I envisioned her on hills, sobbing quietly into picturesque sunsets and pondering the meaning of life but Instagram also tells me this journey was also about getting drunk a lot, getting lost on Japanese trains and having her passport eaten by wildlife.

'Gracie's good,' replies Beth, smiling to reassure me.

'Did you mention the dildo?' I ask.

'Is it there? Have you seen it? I always knew Danny must have been kinky for Megs to follow him to the North,' says Lucy.

Beth cups her hands over Joe's ears.

'And what happened with Jag? Was he angry that you cut your date short?' asks Beth.

'Oh, Megs didn't tell you?'

'TELL US WHAT?!' they both scream in unison down the phone. I pause for a moment as I know the reaction that what I say next will elicit.

'Umm, he drove me up here. His car was at the hospital and he offered.'

An excited Lucy squeals down the phone at me. Even Magnum the cat on the counter heard it and he leaves for the next room. Beth's eyes smile knowing that it was a pretty perfect thing for someone to do. That's the sort of gesture you see in a Hollywood rom-com. The drive would be caught in a long sequence where the lights of the motorway would sparkle against the car windows and they'd play something by Adele to heighten the mood.

'Did you have sex in a Kia?' asks Lucy. Beth is in hysterics.

'I did not and it was actually very nice. We strolled along the South Bank and had hummus and this road trip up here peppered with midnight coffees and chat and Maddie was right, he's a very nice man.'

Beth smiles broadly whereas Lucy doesn't look so sure. 'He didn't even try and put the moves on you?'

Beth hits her across the back of her head. 'Look how happy she is. You're so coarse, Luce.'

'I guess that was a nice thing to do. Did you at least snog him?'

'No.'

I say that with some weight. I *think* he was trying to kiss me in that hallway. I wasn't sure why I didn't. It wasn't the perfect place for such things but it was the right time. Except I was conscious that I looked a mess and I hadn't brushed my teeth. I'm not sure if that's how he wanted to be paid for the gesture but I froze, almost pushing him away. He said nothing but his eyes read horror that maybe he'd been taken it too far. He hadn't. I just didn't know what to do. Even Polly looked at me strangely. *That was your moment, Aunty Ems.*

After that, the morning chaos in the house glossed over any awkwardness and he was the perfect impromptu house guest. He charmed Gill, did the washing up, texted Maddie to fill her in and accompanied me into town to help me buy emergency toiletries and clothes that weren't the white spotty dress. He even jokingly bought some mint cake as a souvenir. And then he left and I waved him off from the front doorstep like I was waving away an uncle. If it had been a scene from that rom-com I was talking about then I should have run after his car in the light drizzle with no shoes on and when his car stopped at the end of the road, I should have knocked on his window and served him a monologue about the whole last evening and morning being perfect and how he is perfect and I should have grabbed him by the lapels and kissed him perfectly. At that moment, an old couple would have walked past. The old man would have shaken his head in horror and the old lady would have stared a bit too long wondering about the last time she was kissed with such spontaneity. Cue strings and swirling emotional music on pianos and hell, let's bring in Adele again. But I didn't.

At this point, the kitchen door opens and in walks Stuart Morton. His face is sullen, like a moody, grounded teenager and it doesn't improve on seeing me. He's carrying a tray with an empty bowl that once housed an interesting soup that Gill made for dinner. Both my sisters notice him and Beth conveniently disappears from screen. Beth was there when Meg first met Danny and the story goes that she couldn't bear to sleep with Stuart because she was so drunk and may have actually thrown up on him. Lucy had her turn on him at Meg's wedding in the back of a car. It was a best man–bridesmaid situation that ended with my mother shouting at Lucy over a buffet breakfast that she had brought shame on the family as our Uncle Pete had seen everything from his hotel room window which really said more about Uncle Pete than anything. Is Stuart good-looking? He looks like he could have once been on *Neighbours.* There's a very bronzed and shaggy blonde thing going on. He's a perpetual traveller so looks a bit unwashed and he wears what looks like rows of crusty friendship bracelets on his wrist.

'OI! DICKHEAD!' shouts a voice from the screen.

Stuart looks over and laughs. 'There she is, the rabble coming in from the back.'

'I believe that was your move, mate.'

I really do hope Beth has removed Joe from the room.

'You bloody Callaghan sisters.'

'Are you going somewhere?' I ask him. He shrugs his shoulders and leaves the room again. Lucy widens her eyes at his frostiness.

'Stewie Morton. Blast from the past. Remind him he never called me back.'

'Do you want me to spit in his tea?' I ask. She smiles, knowing their moment was years ago, a distant teen sex memory.

'He was decent though. The kind of sex you think about when you're trying to get yourself off. You know?'

My expression doesn't read as such.

'Oh, I'm talking to the wrong sister.' I see her arch her neck to see if he may be in the room. 'Do you want to hear anything more about this Susie bird?'

And for a moment, I pause. For the last twenty-four hours, I hadn't thought about Susie at all. Jag and the invalid upstairs had made me forget. I shake my head and smile.

'I'm glad the date went well with Jag. I think it was the dress what did it.' She grins.

'Obviously all to do with that dress,' I say.

'Are you OK?'

I nod. 'Thanks for taking charge of my girlies. Love you.'

She throws a peace sign and hangs up. As my home screen returns to normal, I notice a WhatsApp message and open it.

*This place was a lot bleaker without you. Hope your sis is OK x*

It's a photo of a lone coffee cup in the Charnock Richard services, Jag's hand just in view. On his wrist, is a gold Casio watch that I joked about as I thought it was a bit bling. Turns out he'd got it for twenty pounds on eBay.

Meg and I dissected the Jag situation before. Why didn't I kiss him? He'd already seen me sleeping in his car and, knowing me, I'd have had my mouth wide open. He could probably tell me how many fillings I had. What if I've forgotten how to kiss someone? I wouldn't even know where to put my hands. Where does one put hands when they snog someone? On his arse? On his back? And so sheer panic followed that as lovely as he was and as much as that date meant so much, I did not know how to reciprocate any form of affection. Simon had ruined that much for me.

*Her foot fell off but I sewed it back on. Enjoy that coffee and again, thank you xx*

I debate the double kiss at the end of that message for a good fifteen minutes. Should I go with a smile emoji or the kissy emoji or make light and go with the monkey covering his face? Will he get the joke about me sewing on my sister's foot again? Does that make me look like I'm bragging about my skills as a surgeon? I look down at his profile picture. It's him in a festival field with coloured frame sunglasses. I haven't worn sunglasses like that since I was ten. I'm not cool enough for this man. I could text again to explain my previous text but then he'll think I'm weird.

I put my phone down and saunter through to the living room to see Stuart putting on his shoes in the living room. There is a large rucksack packed next to him.

'Where's next on your travels then?'

'Mates' house. By the way, I pee for that long because I drink a lot of water. I like to be hydrated.'

I don't respond as I had tried to wipe that from memory.

'You're still a doctor, right?'

'I am.'

'Well, can I ask your medical opinion on something?'

I nod cautiously. It was one of the lesser liked side effects of my job. People liked to show me parts of their body that they thought were falling off. Please don't show me your willy (again) or bumhole. I am worried as we were just talking about his urine. He sits down and puts a foot up on the sofa. I look down to see a big toe that's a little bloody and scabby. Lovely.

'Is that an ingrown nail, or something worse?' he asks.

'What did you do?'

'I think I stubbed it.'

'It looks like a blister, it's definitely infected. You've just been in Australia, no chance it's a bite?'

He looks a bit horrified.

'Because the poison can work into your system and cause paralysis.'

'How would that happen? How would I know?'

'Small twitch in your eye, involuntary shaking of the limbs, you'd lose all feeling in your genitals.'

He's lost for words. I smile broadly.

'That's for not calling Lucy back. It's an infected blister. Wear better fitting shoes, soak it in saltwater. Any warmth, or if it doesn't drain then get to a doctor. *Another* doctor.'

He laughs, a little surprised that I can do humour. 'You had me there.'

'Don't walk around barefoot either. Keep it dry and clean.'

He salutes me.

It's been a day, eh? You look knackered,' he informs me.

'I am.'

He looks at his watch. 'My mate can't give me a lift until 10 p.m., you fancy getting a jar?'

'Of jam?'

'Southerners. I mean a drink. I think we both deserve a drink.'

He's not half wrong.


'So you're divorced now, right?'

I don't know if it's a northern thing or a Morton thing but Stuart has put my glass of wine down on the table and cut straight to the chase. It's not just a glass either. He's bought the whole bottle as there seemed to be some sort of offer on. I had thought we'd be in a cosy Lakeland pub but the bar he's brought me to has a student union vibe about it. It's full of arty folk where the accents are broad and the ales are dark.

'I am divorced.'

'Sorry about that.'

'Not your fault.'

Maybe this was a bad idea. I needed a glass of wine to take the edge off but maybe I've chosen the wrong drinking partner. I down half my glass of wine to distract myself but given all I've had for dinner is soup and a bit of lumpy bread, I feel the effects immediately.

'Was he a complete shithead then? Think we met at Meg and Danny's nuptials?'

'Yes, you would have. And yes, complete and utter shithead.'

It's bizarre because last night, Jag and I did an awesome job of avoiding the subject of my divorce completely. I'm not sure what details Stuart needs to hear but then given he's had relations with both Lucy and Beth, I suspect him and my ex may be cut from the same cloth.

'He cheated on me a fair bit. Got around.'

'Better off without him then.'

'Yes.'

God, this is awful. He has a pint and seems to be one of those men who drinks beer like water. Medical school and general common sense assure me that's not a good way to hydrate oneself.

'How's Lucy? What's she up to these days?'

I don't quite know if he's being friendly or flirty. 'She's living with me, back at university and working.'

'She's a good laugh.'

'She is.'

I drink some more of my wine to escape the awkwardness and Stuart studies my face.

Do I ask him about what happened with my other sisters? Did Beth really throw up on him? I guess I should try and engage in chit-chat but I realise I'm not hugely bothered about knowing more about this one. Which is why the next question to come out of my mouth is quite strange. We'll blame the wine.

'Do you get around?'

He looks at me confused and laughs. 'That was out of nowhere.'

'I'm sorry. I'm just curious… it's just I know you've been with my sisters.'

'I have my fun.'

'How many people have you slept with?'

'Two hundred odd?'

I choke on a bit of wine. He reaches across and slaps my back.

'Really? Do you get tested regularly?' That's me talking with my doctor hat on.

'I do. How many have you slept with?'

I react like I'm appalled but I guess I started this line of questioning. 'Three?'

'Oh.'

Luke Travis, Ben Reid and Simon Chadwick. I know their dates of birth and where they all are now. I believe Luke works in graphics and has a dog called Toto. Ben is an accountant and had a wedding reception in rural Leicestershire that featured live swans. Simon lives twenty minutes away from me in London, we used to share a name, we still share two children.

'Why so many?' I ask him.

'It were there, eh? The opportunity. I keep figuring, I'm young and should just do it now. One day, I'll settle down and do the married thing but for now it's fun.'

I can't quite hide my judgement.

'Look, I'm nothing like your husband. I get around and I'm no angel but I definitely wouldn't screw up a marriage if there were kids involved.'

He looks slightly hurt that I would think him capable.

'It wasn't that. I guess I'm always still trying to figure out men and sex.'

'Some blokes are just dicks. High sex drives, they'll shag anything what moves. It's an arrogance thing. It's prefrontal cortex stuff.'

I am taken aback to hear him talk academically. He smiles.

'Just driven by something primal. Reason goes out the window.'

I am quiet at the thought and top up my glass of wine again. Have I drunk two glasses or three? Who knows?

'I'm sorry your ex did that to you. That he treated you so badly. That bloke this morning seemed a nice sort.'

'He is.'

'That got legs?'

'Possibly. I think I'm just out of practice.'

On all levels, really. I can hardly remember what it's like to be part of a relationship but also in terms of being intimate with someone again. What if I revealed everything to them, my whole true everyday self, and then the quality of the intimacy was deemed not good enough. Again. A second time would break me. There's a long pause.

'You know you're quite hot.'

'Excuse me?'

'Of all the sisters, you're top three.'

I cackle at the comment. He smiles broadly, revealing a chipped incisor that's a little crooked.

'You're the posh doctor one.'

'I am not posh.'

'It's what we call you. Danny doesn't do names so he's given you all nicknames. Posh Doc, Barf, Numbers and Cannon.'

'Cannon?'

'Luce cannon.'

I can't stop laughing, feeling slightly sad that Beth will be known as Barf until the end of time. Thank you, Stuart Morton. Are you a brother-in-law? Or are you once removed? Either way, I needed that laugh.

'Do you like sex?' he asks.

I stop chuckling. *Woah there, kid.*

'That is not appropriate.'

'You asked me how many people I'd slept with?'

'Not because I was propositioning you.'

'I'm doing nothing of the sort. I'm trying to carry on the conversation. Have you had sex since your divorce?'

'I… I don't…'

'I'll take that as a no.'

'I'm not ready.'

He laughs. It's like I'm in a swimming costume at the side of the pool, waiting. I don't know why I'm not getting in the pool. The temperature is wrong, there are too many people, I'm scared of jumping in and getting someone's old plaster in my face. I'm just going to stand here and watch for a bit.

'I'll repeat my first question. Do you like sex? Do you wank?'

I take a deep breath and nod, realising my face will now be the same colour as my wine.

'You're an attractive, thirty-something doctor. You could go on Tinder and find some sex with your first swipe.'

'I am on Tinder.'

'And?'

'They all want to do strange things to me.'

'And what do you want?'

I knock back the rest of my wine. Am I really going to tell him? I haven't even told Lucy.

'I need a taster session. Just straight out vanilla sex so I can remember what a penis feels like and what I need to do, where all the body parts and limbs go, you know? I do not need a new lovely man dumping me because I forgot how to have sex. I've literally forgotten everything.'

As I say it, I throw two hands over my mouth and giggle drunkenly. He smiles and then leans into me.

'You don't forget how to have sex,' he tells me.

'Don't tell me it's like riding a bike.'

'It's not but I see sex as a form of release. If I go at least a week without it then I'm bloody unbearable.'

'So you're telling me it's completely mechanical with you?'

'Not always. But it's allowing yourself to feel pleasure too. It's endorphins, chemicals and I don't suppose it's linked in with your psychology too.'

I didn't expect such gravity from this one.

'Maybe you need to allow yourself some pleasure.'

He looks me in the eye and I am little taken aback, mainly because of my physical response. I feel it deep inside a place I shouldn't. Up to this point, pleasure was eating hummus by a river, a cup of tea in my favourite mug and fresh sheets on a bed. He knows exactly what he's doing here too because he doesn't stop holding my gaze. He puts a hand on my knee. I catch my breath and I am really not very sure what happens next except that reason goes out the window completely. Lucy's words echo in my head that he's decent. Like, because of the size of him or the technique? Is this a signal? Is this the person to help me open me up to sex again? He's slept with one of my sisters; I think this might be incest. Is this incest? Am I doing this? Hell, I might be. I put my face near his and kiss him slowly on the lips. But then I completely pull back. Oh dear. He laughs. Kissing me was funny?

'I don't want to marry you or even date you and you don't need to follow up on this, at all. But yes, I think we should have sex. What sort of sex were you planning on?'

I just said that, didn't I? I asked for a description of what we might do next. This is what I ask students in theatres. How are you going to dissect that tumour? Why are you using that method? What tools do you have in mind? That is not sexy, is it? He leans into me and all the people in this bar disappear from consciousness. His voice drops in volume.

'Well, I know a spot out the back where I could perch you against a wall and you could unzip your jeans and I could slip my fingers into you. And then when you're really wet, I'd roll your knickers down and push your knees back and really slowly fuck you. Help you remember what it feels like again.'

I can't quite feel my face.

'Fancy a bit of that?'

I nod without saying a word.


It's 10.58 p.m. and I am sat on Meg's sofa bed in her pyjamas and I've just had sex with her brother-in-law. Lucy was not wrong. That boy knows what he's doing and if I had skills like that then

I'd probably share them with as many as I could too. It'd be like a public service. Simon did not have skills, despite all his infidelity, so I was always unsure about what he needed to share with people and what the appeal was. This time I had an orgasm, an actual penetrative orgasm. My knees high, his body gyrating against mine, that feeling of being taken, physically devoured by someone. I cup my mouth again and giggle. Am I still drunk? I'm not good on red wine. I take a large gulp of water sat here in fresh knickers and pyjamas fresh out of their packaging.

Then I panic. Jag. Was that cheating on him? I feel awful. Or not. Now if I choose to sleep with him, it won't be awful and awkward because I know how to do it. I remember how to kiss. Stuart was a good kisser. The stubble was a bit scratchy but there was a moment where he took my ear lobe in his mouth and then when he entered me. Christ. It's all playing back to me in flashbacks. I just had sex. Me, actual sex. Afterwards, he got on his knees and placed my knickers back and kissed my inner thigh. I hadn't even had a tidy down there. I thanked him and we shook hands. Is that weird? Did that make it like a business transaction? Then we waited until his lift arrived. And I looked at him again: scrappy blonde hair and blue eyes, seriously not my type at all with the big rucksack and the dishevelled T-shirt that looked like moths had attacked him. We laughed at what we had just done and he said something clichéd to me about self-worth and being pretty. And then we hugged and he disappeared. I've just had sex. With Meg's brother-in-law. She will kill me if she finds out. I can't stay here. I need to check train timetables. Oh my days, I've had sex with someone who's also had sex with Lucy. Condoms don't protect you from crabs either, do they?

# Chapter Eight

640 days since I realised Simon had cheated on me for the eighth time.

It had been Tuesday and I remember that day well: Violet was still only one but I was back at work and my brain was at capacity from dealing with teething babies, a busy three year old Iris who was an expert furniture climber, and trying to figure in work around motherhood. That day, I had forgotten my lunch so I made the brave decision to eat at the hospital cafeteria. It was chicken alfredo day. I remember a square container of pasta bedded together like nesting material in a pool of cloudy water. I had messaged Simon a few times that day as we had a new Australian au pair who had been very good at sending me photos of Violet, as if proving to us that she was still alive. I forwarded all the photos to him. He didn't reply. At that point, I hadn't thought much of it. I just assumed he was busy doctoring. Stood in the line of the hospital restaurant, a voice piped up next to me.

'Emma Chadwick, how the hell are you?'

The person behind me was Martin Nelson. He had been at medical school with myself and Simon and was an obstetrician now. He was one of those doctors from a long line of medical professionals who had a thing for double denim and who I believe may have once caught a baby that had flown out of its mother's nether regions in a lift, a move he'd always credited to his many years playing rugby. That day there was a long queue at the restaurant and talk naturally turned to Simon.

'How is he feeling?' he asked.

'About?'

'Oh, I thought he was ill. I was in theatre this morning and his surgeries had been rescheduled. A scrub nurse mentioned something about the flu. Tis that time of year, eh?'

'Really?'

I remembered at that time feeling concerned, a little panicked. Was this why he wasn't picking up his phone? But he was fine that morning. We left the house together, got on the same Tube and we spoke about a family holiday next spring to Ibiza. I joked the babies were a bit young for clubbing. He didn't get it. We went our separate ways at Westminster as he said he was meeting a colleague for a coffee. There was not so much as a sniffle from him.

I sat with Martin for the rest of our meal. He told me about a recent incident where a baby had been born with teeth and it smiled at him on delivery and he nearly dropped it. After lunch, I jumped in a taxi and went home. I turned my key in the door, entered the house and stood in the hallway for ten seconds to compose myself. I then found Simon giving our Australian nanny oral sex on the kitchen counter while our daughters napped upstairs. She was a heavily pierced young lady and when I came through the kitchen door, I remember the light reflecting off her piercings casting patterns on the ceiling. I stood there planted to the spot as they scrambled around with fumbled apologies, trying to retrieve their clothes.

I thought many things at the time. One, that was incredibly unhygienic to have your naked buttocks on the counter where I prepared food. Two, this was the fourth time I had caught him cheating on me Simon Chadwick. *Fourth* time. This time, I'd actually caught him as opposed to reading a text message or being faced with one of his many lies about where he was. One of those times, I was pregnant. And I think there's a typical way one should react in these circumstances. I should have reacted with wronged woman's rage and screamed and shouted and thrown things at him. I was in a kitchen, there were many things to hurt him within close vicinity: a Le Creuset casserole, a meat tenderiser, a watermelon. But I just stood there. I thought about my sleeping babies upstairs. I was very very quiet. If anything, I internalised it all and wondered what I had done to have this man treat me so badly. I didn't even cry. I closed the door behind me and went upstairs to check on my girls. Violet was fast asleep in her cot and Iris in her little bed, clutching her blanket. I lay down next to her, savouring the warmth of her body. Five minutes later, Simon appeared at the door. He watched us lying there.

'I'm sorry you had to see that, Emma. It just happened.'

Deep down I knew it hadn't. He would have got the train in with me and made a u-turn to go back to her. Where else had they had sex in this house? For how long? But I didn't say any of this out loud.

'She's been coming on to me for weeks. I was weak. It won't happen again, I promise. I'll ring the agency, we'll get her replaced,' he said.

I was tempted to say with a seventy-year-old severe-looking character who resembled Nanny McPhee but it was likely that Simon would have stuck his member in her too. I just held our little girl close to us and inhaled her.

'I should be back at the hospital. I'll catch a cab,' I whispered.

I stood up, smoothed down my blouse. He stared at me, longing me to talk. I had nothing to say. Women suffer all sorts in marriage, maybe this was just something I had to endure. It wasn't physical abuse and we had these small humans. I had literally just grown one and she was so very tiny. I had a responsibility to make this work for her.

'You know that you and the girls mean everything to me.'

This was his parting line. He whispered it as I walked past him and he tried to touch my hand. I moved it away as our fingers brushed.

'I do not want her here when I come back. Wipe down my kitchen counters please.'

And I left my child's fairy-themed bedroom and I went back to work. I was asked to scrub in on a young lady who had a hole in her heart. I stayed married to Simon for three years after that.

I'm brought back to the Australian nanny as I'm stood in front of three junior doctors hanging on to my every word. One, Alisha, has a collection of piercings that seem to have had a hypnotic effect in transporting me back in time. I use that story occasionally on my sisters to remind them of my stoic prowess when I was being wronged in my marriage. Naturally, they don't see it that way. They just saw it as me being a mug.

'I don't think that prescription is right so let's review that, get the parents to give me a call. Dylan Kelly, let's get that clinic date in before we discharge him and the little man in cubicle four; I want to keep him in for another night on observation.'

Alisha with the piercings nods. I like her but she lacks authority and I hope she can sort that out before the patriarchy swallows her up. I also want to ask about her piercings without sounding completely naive. Do they hurt? How pierced are you? Lucy apparently has a nipple pierced which I don't understand. Does it get caught on your bras? What if you plan on breastfeeding? Milk would pour out of those holes like a broken showerhead. She catches me studying her for a moment too long. Now she thinks I'm weird.

'Are you OK. Dr Callaghan?' she asks.

I smile. Christ, her gums are pierced. I'm too scared to go to the hygienist. Why would anyone put themselves through that type of pain? Oh.

I didn't miss any work after my brief trip to the Lake District. I simply jumped on a train home and got back to it. No one knows I've slept with Stuart Morton except me, and Stuart, obviously. Meg has a new sex toy angle with her marriage but is fine. I am fine. I have no idea what happened over these last few days but I will rely on work to provide distraction. I go through everything in my head that I need to do: eat, review three files about suitability for surgery, ensure I've signed the consent forms for Iris' school trip online, check in on Meg's leg. I go to my phone and there's a message there. Balls.

*Ems, I am at the house and the girls aren't here.*

Bloody Simon. It's been this way a lot recently. Since he last called me to tell me he was gravely ill (sadly the sore throat didn't cause his demise), we seem to communicate via the power of text. It is very flat and formal. I don't mind this in the least but I still hate how he abbreviates my name and doesn't ask questions but just state facts at me. The message was from ten minutes ago. I go to call Lucy.

'Yo,' she answers.

'Luce, where are you? I've got Simon messaging me telling me you're not at the house?'

'We're on the way back from swimming. Temporary traffic lights so the bus is stuck.'

I can hear the groans of the bus in the background and the crackle of crisp packets.

'He can piss off,' she exclaims. I wonder how many people on the 65 bus heard that, including my own kids.

'Or I can tell him why you're late? This would work if you had his number.'

'I refuse to taint my phone with it.'

'Well, when you get there, don't cause a scene.'

'Have we not met? Talking of scenes, some mum gave me something at the school gate and I may have kicked off.'

'Lucy!'

'Did you go to that riding party the other week?'

'Yes.'

'She said because V didn't ride for the full hour, she wants a partial refund.'

'She wants what…?'

'Coming at me with her Louis Vuitton satchel asking us for twenty quid.'

'How did you kick off, Lucy?' I stop for a moment in the corridor and rest my head against the wall. Will this mean I have to change the girls' school? Or change our family name?

'She still thinks I'm some Swedish au pair so I put on my accent and pretended to swear at her in another language. I mostly likely just reeled off items from the Ikea catalogue. It's part of my *Frozen* act when Darren has to be Sven the reindeer.'

I can't fathom if this is the best or worst thing she's ever done.

'Just get home. Text me when the girls have been handed over. Actually put them on. I want to hear them.'

'Mama?' It's a sound which always me smile.

'V. Is everything OK poppet?'

'Aunty Lucy got us the good seats on the bus, on the top and at the front.'

Little V living her best life on the buses. I try to think of a time when pleasures were that simple.

'Be good at Daddy's. I'll see you in a few days.' I hear the bus roll to a start and the phone go dead. I didn't get to speak to Iris. I stand here for a moment too long.

'Hello stranger.'

I look up. He smiles. I smile back.

'Jag.'

'Hi.'

I haven't really got in touch with Jag since I'd been back. I did send him a photo on a train though. It featured a cup of coffee purchased before my departure and sneakily included the lady opposite who was asleep.

*Poor company on the return leg. If I hadn't said it already, thank you x*

He responded with the kissing emoji which threw me a little. Was that to remind me I hadn't kissed him? Or there's a heart there, does that mean he loves me? I didn't reply. But I guess I also realised that in between everything, I'd gone and had sex with Stuart Morton. Was that wrong? It felt wrong; I was racked with guilt even though what happened with Stuart was nothing.

We stand here, exchanging smiles. He's in scrubs and his Nike Air Max trainers.

'How's Meg and her leg? When did you get back?'

'The leg is fine. I got back yesterday but I was busy sorting the girls and—'

'Don't worry. It's good to see you back on the manor though.'

I think about the number of times I may have walked past this man before in these corridors. Had he been checking me out? Had he smiled and I smiled back? How many surgeries had he been in when I'd spoken to him and heard him read out orders to me? I feel almost apologetic for not noticing him.

'Have I said thank you enough yet?'

'I think so. I just don't know how we'll top that date though?'

The indication that there will be a second date makes me smile.

'I have many sisters. I'll see who else can throw themselves into danger at a moment's notice.'

He laughs. 'So maybe we can grab a coffee in the week?'

I smile. That I can do. 'Keep in touch and we'll get something in the diary.'

I hope that doesn't make him sound like an appointment. I diarise everything, even my own menstruation.

'That sounds golden.'

'Like your Casio.'

He laughs and waves his wrist around. 'I'll see you around, Dr Callaghan.'

As he walks in the opposite direction, my phone bleeps.

*Lucy and the girls?*

Oh piss off, Simon.

*Stuck on the 65 bus at temporary traffic lights*, I reply. My finger hovers over whether to apologise but I didn't arrange to put those roadworks in.

*My girls are on a bus?*

He may as well have said: *my girls are on a peasant wagon?* I don't reply but text Lucy.

*Progress?*

*Five minutes away. Tell that shitfaced shit to chill his boots.*

I don't reply to that either. My brain feels stretched at feeling such a dichotomy of emotion. From the lovely warmth of seeing Jag to that feeling like I want to ring Simon up and scream at him. *I was your wife. You were in that room when I birthed our girls so speak to me with an ounce of decency.* And all at once that niggle about Susie comes to the fore. Is she a new girlfriend? Is she more? Tell me. Or don't.

'Are you OK?' When I get to my office, Maddie senses I am a bit frazzled. I saw her for a morning coffee earlier but for the rest of the day she was simply pointing me in the right direction. I curl into her and she gives me a hug.

'Simon – the girls are late back to the house. He's being a dick.'

Maddie pouts like this is information that she already knew.

'Well, there's little you can do from here. I've bought you a salmon salad for dinner and one of those green smoothie things you like. Eat it while you clear those files. I'll stick around.'

I hug her again. 'Is that OK? I don't want it to get in the way of home? The boys?'

'Oh, Mark has it covered. Anyway, we need to have a catch up. I talked to Jag.'

I laugh. I suspect the boys are not a priority given the large amounts of gossip in which we need to trade. We take a seat on the sofa where she sets everything up on my small coffee table. She's remembered napkins too and got me a Snickers for my pudding.

'I just saw him actually on my way here.'

Her shoulders are raised in anticipation.

'You told him I like hummus.'

'You bloody love hummus. I've seen you down a whole pot of it before.'

'Well, he bought me hummus.'

'Good boy. I like a man who knows how to take instruction.'

'And you are right, he is fab.'

She claps enthusiastically. I am conscious that now is probably not the time to also reveal that barely twenty-four hours later I slept with Stuart Morton. I open up my salad and pick on bits of cucumber as she pats herself on the back.

'I guess he told you about our road trip?' I enquire.

'He did. And I'm glad to hear Meg is alright. Do you want to know what he said?'

'Yes, unless it's awful.'

'It's not. He's totally intimidated by how amazing you are.'

That word again, amazing. It's lovely to hear but I'm not sure how much I believe it myself.

'That's not good, if he's scared of me?'

'No, I just think he always thought you were pretty untouchable but now he's spent some time with you and seen how down-to-earth you are and he's blown away by that.'

'I guess that's good? I take it you told him not to talk about my divorce...'

She nods and tucks into her sandwich. Through mouths of cheese and pickle, she continues, 'I just didn't want it to hang over you guys.'

I'm grateful. I know what she was trying to do.

'It nearly did though. Literally an hour before the date, Violet divulged that Simon's seeing someone.'

Maddie gurns. 'Really? Damn that man.'

'I mean he's allowed but the timing was off. Lucy has stalked her on Facebook; I've tried to not let it be a thing. We're divorced, he can date who he wants. Just a surprise to hear it from our daughter.'

'She's met the girls?'

I nod. She sucks some air in through her teeth.

'Name?'

'Susie Hunter.'

As soon as I say the name, she goes quiet. That's the thing about Maddie; she was there for all those years I tried to hide behind my sham of a marriage. She used to signpost incidents for me, willing for me to catch him and have the courage to finally confront him and leave. But I pretended to not see them. I'd change the subject and talk about my girls and she'd relent and realise that if I was ever going to leave him then I needed to do that on my own terms. Now, there's a look that says she can't hide what she knows. She knows who Susie Hunter is and I need to decide whether I need to know. I place half a boiled egg in my mouth. Not now, Maddie, not now. I open a file and change the subject before she has a chance to speak.

'I most likely will go on a second date with Jag though, so if you have any ideas then they would be most welcome.'

'Can you ice skate?'

'No.'

'What about a salsa dancing workshop?'

'Again, no.'

'Didn't I tell you he had nice skin?'

'It's genetics apparently. All inherited from his mum and he scrubs before every shave.'

'So… what did Lucy find out about Susie Hunter?'

I cast her a look. A lot has happened this week and I can't process anything too serious at the moment. I really can't. But she almost looks angry with me. *You went through the worst, Emma. And you are here and you can handle anything.* She thinks that the hardest thing was leaving him and moving on, deciding I wasn't going to stand for it any longer. She doesn't want me to skirt these issues again, like I did for so long.

'She's a nurse. She's blonde. Not a shock that Simon would go hunting within a hospital for his next prey.'

Maddie looks pensive. 'If it's the same Susie I know then she works next door at St Thomas'.'

I shrug my shoulders.

'And I think she might be pregnant.'

'Pregnant?'

I freeze. With a child? That's not even a new girlfriend or a new shag situation. That is a step-sibling in the making, a change of dynamic, a whole other group of people in my children's lives and thus in mine. I am still chewing the boiled egg that was in my mouth and the yolk tastes like balls of chalk cementing to my gums. Maddie hugs me.

'I'm sorry. I didn't want to upset you. I just don't want to hide things from you either. It could be a different Susie completely. I just saw something on Facebook and it rang a bell.'

I can't be angry with Maddie but I am silent. Simon and I are still stuck in the land of post-divorce games and despite my full body armour, this just feels like he's struck an arrow at me from a tremendous height. No warning. Nothing.

'And you have Jag now? And he's lovely. And… this could just repair all the damage that man did.'

'I've been on one date, Maddie. I don't know half of what I need to know about this man.'

'Is that important?'

'Yes. He could be a sociopath. He could have loans or webbed feet or questionable hygiene habits.'

Maddie looks confused. 'You have a new man checklist now?'

'There is no harm in being thorough.'

'Webbed feet would make him an amazing swimmer though.'

I laugh to mask my turmoil. Pregnant? Really? I see her go into stalk mode on her phone to check but her face tells me everything. My phone ringing interrupts her trying to launch into damage control. I'm not sad. I'm not emotional. I'm just confused. Lucy. I put her on speaker, glad for the interruption.

'Are you still on that bus?'

'Christ, no. We walked that last bit as Iris needed a wee. Girls are with their father.'

Her tone is frantic and worried. It's not normally how Lucy sounds so alarm bells ring.

'Luce, the girls… was everything OK? Did Simon kick off? Was he awful?'

'No but… are you en route? When will you get home?'

'Not for a while…'

'Oh.'

'Luce, you're worrying me.'

There's a silence and I can hear her go to the next room. She whispers down the phone. 'There's a kid here, I thought he was one of the girls' friends from school or a neighbour but he's on his own.'

'Kid?'

'Like I didn't know what to do. He's upset but he was so tiny, I couldn't just leave him on the doorstep?'

'Lucy, talk slower. Is he conscious? Is he hurt?'

Maddie stands up and runs to my office phone.

'His name is Lewis. Do you know him? He says he needs a doctor.'

# Chapter Nine

We're sat in Maddie's rusting Renault Clio trying to work out the best way to beat the South Circular. In my hands are files and numbers and Lucy on speaker. Lewis is at my house? On his own? He's seven. If he's upset and at my actual house then all manner of things could be going wrong. He could be hurt or need medical attention. And he's with my sister who I know is a hazard when it comes to emergencies. She's clumsy and reckless and without any first aid certification to her name. Maddie has called the police and his parents and sent them over to investigate while we peg it down there as quickly as we can. I say quickly, I forget that Maddie also drives like she's taking part in Le Mans. I'm a little worried that she doesn't seem to know what her indicators are for.

'Luce, are you still there?'

'Yes. We're having a cup of squash. I'm making some toast.'

'That's OK but is his skin a funny colour? Is he short of breath?'

Lucy's voice drops to a whisper. 'What? Is the little bugger dying?'

'No, and don't call him a bugger… Maybe take his pulse?'

'That's in his wrist, right?' She switches voices. 'What would you like on your toast, sweetie?'

'Just keep him safe and warm and occupied, keep your phone on so we can hear everything.'

The phone goes quiet.

'Wasn't he in recently? Was he OK?' asks Maddie.

'Episodes of SVT, we put him on beta blockers. He was fine.'

Maddie sees the worry in my face. Had I missed something? It wasn't hard. I should have looked closer at the ultrasound. Why isn't he in a hospital? Where are his parents? Are they hurt? Maddie switches lanes and I grab onto everything on my lap and reach out to steady myself on the dashboard.

'Who taught you to drive you absolute tool?' she shouts out.

I can hear the light patter of conversation on my phone in the background. She's all over the place is Lucy but she's warm and I can imagine she would have seen Lewis on my doorstep and not hesitated for a second in getting him through the door.

'Who lets a seven-year-old out of their sight? How does he know where you live?' says Maddie.

I am silent. Given the gravity of my work I'd always maintained a much-needed professional distance when it came to my patients but one Christmas I remember I gave the family my address so he could post me a card he'd made for me. He'd drawn me a bear in a hat. I don't divulge this to Maddie for fear of being told off.

I hear Lucy's laughter at the end of the phone. 'You are mental! Blackcurrant squash whips orange squash's ass!'

Maddie and I pause to take that in. *Language, Lucy.* And if you were a real parent you'd know you try and avoid the blackcurrant as it stains like a bastard. Just keep him talking.

I think back to two years ago when my daughters would have been at home with an au pair who spoke broken English and who wouldn't have known what to do with a random child showing up at the door. Worse, Simon may have been in and probably would have sent him away with twenty pence and a firm handshake. And then what would he have done, this poor kid, on his own? It doesn't bear thinking about.

'I love Billie Eilish,' Lucy says.

'Who is he?' I ask Maddie.

Maddie glances over. 'Billie is a girl. She's a pop singer.'

'Do you want anything else to eat? I have breadsticks? Vodka?'

'LUCY! LUCY! Don't give him alcohol!'

Maddie giggles overtaking a bus and almost ploughs into a Range Rover. We're two minutes away but less with the way she's driving. She thinks Lucy is joking about the alcohol but no doubt she's doing the shots herself. Don't get drunk with a minor in the house, dear sister. And that kid can't even have caffeine, his heart is that fragile. I think about his heart. I've held it my hands. He was born without all the things that help link it up and keep it beating. Oh, Lewis. Please be OK. Maddie screeches to a halt in front of my house and I jump out of the car, scrambling to get up the steps and my keys in the door.

'LUCY! LUCY! It's me! Where are you?'

I jog through the hallway, frantically opening doors and scanning the rooms. I see Lucy's hand behind my kitchen island rise slowly. I go over and the both of them are sat on the floor, Lucy's giant headphones nestled in his mop of curls. He has his head resting on her shoulder. I hope she's not playing him inappropriate gangsta rap. He catches me standing there and I put a hand up to wave to him. He jumps up at seeing me. Lucy looks confused. I get down to his level.

'Lewis, why are you here? Are you OK? Are you hurt?'

'I'm OK, Doctor C.'

I give him the once over. Maddie bursts through the door with my kit and a portable defibrillator, the police now hovering in my hallway.

'You had us worried?' There is a look in his eyes that I can't quite read. 'What's happened?'

'Mum and Dad are getting divorced.' I feel his words in my own heart as he says them, lip trembling. 'I didn't know what to do.'

He twists his lips, holding back the tears, and throws his arms around me. I have no choice but to hug him back.


Ten minutes later, we've put Lewis in an oversized hoodie and placated him with some chocolate shortbread until his parents get here. He studies my living room, his attention drawn to the picture of my girls on the mantelpiece and my tropical wallpaper, which I'll take as his mark of approval. He's taken a shine to Lucy who sits in with us.

'How did you get here? You live in Lewisham?'

'I used my pocket money and got an Uber?'

Lucy laughs at his sheer initiative.

'I used my dad's app and a man called Roy picked me up. I told him I was going to see my gran.'

'Roy could have been a bad person,' I tell him.

'He wasn't. He has grandkids and a labradoodle called Noodle. It rhymed.'

He sits there quietly knowing he's done wrong but I veer on that line of not knowing if I should be telling him off. I may leave that to the policeman chatting to Maddie in the kitchen. Or his parents. I doubt Iris or Violet would have the courage or know-how to pull a stunt like this but if they did, I'd be brimming with anger and disbelief.

'When did your mum and dad tell you then... about the divorce?'

'Yesterday. We were having dinner.'

'Oh,' I put my hand into his.

'It's why I'm here,' he says.

I am taken aback. He wants to move in? He wants advice?

'You're a doctor, you fix things. Maybe you could fix this.'

Lucy sighs and sticks out her bottom lip. I take my other hand and sandwich his in the middle. Oh, little man. I couldn't even fix my own marriage. He looks up at me, hopeful and so innocent. *I was there when we attached a mechanical valve to the inside of your heart to keep it beating but this isn't in my skill set I'm afraid.*

'Do you remember what I said in your last appointment about me changing my name?'

'Yes.'

'That's because I'm also divorced.'

His eyes widen. I guess all children assume families exist in some 2.4 traditional form. He looks over at the photo on the mantelpiece.

'Was he your husband?'

'He was. His name is Simon.'

'What's he like?'

I lightly grind my foot into Lucy's to stop her from talking.

'He's also a doctor.'

'Not as good as my sister, obviously,' Lucy interjects.

'And those are my girls, Iris and Violet.'

He looks at their pictures. 'How does it work, divorce? Do they still see their daddy?'

'All the time. They're with him now. We share them.' I've realised I've made my kids sound like a bag of crisps. 'Your mum and dad will work something out and I'm sure you'll see both of them, all the time. They are good people and they love you very much.'

'But you're a good person too.'

Lucy snuggles up to me to confirm this very fact.

'And I know it feels sad now but you're one of the brightest kids I know. Just talk to your mum and dad about how you feel. Divorce isn't easy at first but you just get used to it.'

'Like new pants?'

I scrunch my eyes up in confusion.

Lucy high fives him. 'Yes, like when you wear new pants, Ems… they're all uncomfortable and get wedged up your crack and then you get used to them,' Lucy adds, backing him up.

'Yes, just like that,' I say, unconvinced.

'I like your house, Doctor C.'

'I'm glad. Next time though, might be best to just call my secretary. We could have done this on the phone.'

'But then he'd never have met me…' Lucy adds, winking at him.

He smiles and comes over to hug me again, just as I hear two people burst through the door to steal him away from me.

'Oh my god, Lewis. You're safe, you're OK. Are you OK?' His dad grabs him tightly whilst Mum comes over to squeeze me in relief.

'We were out, my sister was babysitting, he was supposed to be asleep but he slipped out of the house and then his dad realised he didn't have his phone and then your secretary called and the police and…' Her face is flushed from tears and panic.

'He's fine,' I say trying to calm her down. 'He found his way here and you can thank my sister, she took him in.' Her hugs transfer over to a shocked Lucy.

'Lewis, you can't do that. You can't. If anything happened to you…'

He stares at both of them, not the normally verbose and confident child I see but pensive about what to say next. I know why. He looks up at me.

'I think Lewis was confused by what you told him yesterday. He came here because he thought that I could help fix it, being a doctor.'

Both of them are quiet. The last thing I wanted to do is shame them but their guilt and emotion is palpable. Lewis' mum starts to tear up. I put an arm around her.

'And so Lewis and I had a chat about my divorce. A brief one.'

'It's like new pants,' says Lewis.

I put my hand up to signal that I didn't come up with that analogy. His dad laughs, scooping him up and inhaling him closely. 'You can't run away, kid. You just can't do that. Mum nearly had a heart attack.'

'And it's my job to have the heart attacks,' he says trying to diffuse their sadness. We all laugh despite it being the horribly sad truth.

'We can talk at home. We can answer all your questions and we can try and work this out so it's not a bad thing,' says his dad.

He nods quietly to take it all in, leaning over to wipe the tears off his mum's face.

'Hun, I need to call my sister and your parents – everyone's beside themselves. I…' Lewis' mum turns to me. 'We don't know what to say…'

'Get him home,' I say. 'He's been on quite the adventure.'

Lewis smiles and nods. His dad puts a hand to my shoulder, 'Doctor C. How do we thank you?'

'I'll take another octopus picture?'

'An octopus in pants maybe?' says Lucy.

Lewis climbs down from his dad to come over and hug us again.

'Your husband was stupid to divorce you. You're one of my favourite people.'

We all stop for a moment to take that in. *Don't change, little one.* I hope this doesn't change him.

'Don't frighten us like that anymore, please,' I tell him.

'And make sure you give that Uber fella a decent rating,' Lucy says from beside me.

He gives her a cuddle too and then skips away to his dad. His mum turns to me.

'I really am sorry to have worried you with this. I swear that kid will turn me grey. How he managed to do this? Thank you…'

'He's safe. You found him. And you told him what's happening, it's a start…'

Her look back to me is filled with emotion. I don't know what to say. It's divorce. There are no rules with this game. I can't judge or advise or even let you know this will work out but he knows now. She takes my hand in hers before slipping away into the corridor and the police accompany them out of the house.

Maddie pops her head around the door. 'I guess we don't need the defib then?' she enquires.

'Only for me.' I collapse and perch myself on the coffee table.

Lucy holds a hand out and I grab it. 'I know grown adults who can't book Ubers,' she says.

'Well done, Luce.' I mumble.

'I thought you just sewed people up and fixed them.'

'Well, yeah... I do that too.'

'You're telling me.'

She comes to sit next to me, slinging an arm around me. I think that might have just been a compliment from my sister who only ever calls me boring and dull. I'll take that.

'The police will have a word with him but they won't do anything else. I persuaded them not to take it further with the parents. They've gone through enough,' Maddie adds. 'I'll get the tea on...' she says, escaping to the kitchen.

That vodka seems like a good option around now. I don't remember life being this eventful. I mean there was always a sense of bedlam with two kids and a busy work schedule but everything these days is steeped in drama and emotion. I hang on to Lucy for that bit longer.

'What a decent kid. What's up with him then?'

'Born with congenital heart disease.'

'Shit.'

'Mild understatement.'

'Do you think that's why they're splitting up?' asks Lucy.

'Who knows? We need to get you on a first aid course though. Who doesn't know how to take a pulse?'

'I knew really. I also know CPR from watching *Grey's Anatomy*.'

'I've seen *Game of Thrones*, it doesn't mean I know how to ride a dragon.'

She laughs but she looks at me through different eyes, her hug that much tighter. The moment is suddenly interrupted though by frantic knocking at the door. Is it Lewis again? The police? Lucy and I edge towards the front door and peer our heads into the hallway.

'EMMA! ARE YOU IN THERE?'

I roll my eyes at hearing his voice. What in the hell is Simon doing here?

'NO, SHE ISN'T! PISS OFF!' screams Lucy. *Oh Lucy, why?*

'It's my house too, Lucy.'

'Not anymore, I believe. And we've got a dog now, a huge dog and he hates wankers!'

I give Lucy a look. I hope she gets on all fours and barks through the letter box. He doesn't stop rapping at the door. If this is him coming over because he's forgotten a homework book or a pair of pyjamas then I will nut him.

'How did you leave it with him before?' I whisper to Lucy. 'When you were late?'

'He was a tit. I responded appropriately.'

'So this is about that?'

'EMMA!'

He rings the bell so its shrill tones echo through the house. Maddie comes out into the corridor to see what warrants all the noise. I answer the door, Lucy standing in a star shape like a rugby fullback trying to block the hallway.

'What on earth is going on, Emma?' he asks me.

'I'm fine, Simon. How are you?' I have no energy to deal with this intrusion.

'Mrs Phelps from across the road called me to say there are police here? Someone ran into the house with medical gear?'

'They've now gone.'

'Why were they here?'

'Why are you here?'

'Because you're my—'

'Ex-wife?'

Maddie and Lucy are strangely silent. It never used to be like this with Simon. I was quiet and subservient; now different emotions seep through my pores. I didn't have it in my bloodstream for all the years of our marriage, or when the divorce went through. Back then I would need troops and alcohol to prop me up.

'I was going to say you're the mother of my children.' His tone is softer, trying to fake that he's here out of concern.

'Like that's now important?'

'I was trying to be nice, look out for you.'

'Shame you never did that when you were spreading your man seed around.'

I said that, didn't I? Man seed? Seed sounds like such a nice word too. A seed is something that may grow into something fruitful.

What comes out of him, I'd liken to a bile-based manure. Lucy laughs and links arms with me.

Simon shakes his head at us. 'This is where my daughters live so I have every right to know why the police were visiting.'

'Our daughters,' I reply, correcting him.

He doesn't need to know, does he? Oh, just some kid patient popped around so I could counsel him about his parents' divorce. On his own. We've sent him on his way, this time with his parents and we also may have dressed him in one of your old university rowing hoodies that we found in the airing cupboard.

'Is there someone else here? Are you hiding someone?'

I laugh in shock. 'Who? A man? Yes, I'm harbouring a man in the kitchen. That's why the police were here,' I reply sardonically.

'I want to see for myself.'

'This is my house. No! This is none of your business. If you want to know, it was one of those door-to-door salesman types and he got a bit forceful. Lucy was very good and called the police.' It's the best I can come up with.

Maddie and Lucy are not very good at this game, both looking at different spots on the ceiling. He studies each and every one of us.

'You're many things Emma but I didn't take you for a liar.'

'No, that was always *you*.'

'Don't turn this on me.'

'Where are our girls now? Are they in the car?'

'They're at my flat.'

'With your *elderly* mother?'

He pauses for a moment. 'Yes.'

'Then maybe I'll ring Linda's mobile. It'd be nice to check up on them.'

He stares me out. Maddie shakes her head at me. Don't do this now, it's been a bugger of a day and you're full of emotion. Lucy looks confused as she doesn't know everything but you see her willing me on. *Embrace that fire, don't let this man have the better of you.*

'Or maybe they're with Susie?' I say calmly.

'Ooooh,' cries Lucy, jigging on the spot to hear that burn.

Simon rolls his tongue over his top row of teeth. 'The girls have obviously mentioned her then?'

'When were *you* going to?'

And that's when he breaks into the half smile he uses when he knows he has the better of me. He did this a lot when we were married. When I'd try to catch him out and ask him whose number was appearing on his mobile screen, he'd flash that smile and say it was the hospital, shrugging me off like I was imagining things.

'I thought I was the mother of your children. I have a right to know if they're spending time with someone that you have a relationship with.'

'It's not like that at all…'

'So you're not fucking her?'

Everyone freezes for a moment. I rarely swear but the word trips off my tongue with the hate that I thought I'd kept way down in the depths of my soul. Simon gives me that smile like I might be crazy again. He's probably spoken to the girls. *Is Mummy dating anyone? Have any men been in the house? Has she replaced me yet? I doubt she has.*

And I want to scream so the mirrors shatter and the paint peels off the very walls. *I can't stand you. I can't bear to look at you and have you within the space I call my home. I am dating an anaesthetist who has already proved himself to be a million times better than you. I shagged Meg's brother-in-law behind a pub. He made me come through my actual G-spot which I'm not sure you ever located with your sub-standard penis.*

'It's a yes or no question, Simon?' I'm almost laughing as I say it.

'It's just…'

'Because she's pregnant.'

Lucy's mouth widens like some cosmic black hole ready to swallow up the universe.

'And I do believe that's how people get pregnant. You should know, you're a doctor.'

# Chapter Ten

648 days since Beth caught me as I fell to the floor in shame and threw up a mince pie

I am stood in the en suite trying to work out this dress. Lucy's gone for the milkmaid theme again except this time I have a bonnet, a crook and an inflatable sheep. I'm not sure where this sheep is from but he also seems to have some sort of entry hole to its rear. I grab the disinfectant spray from under the kitchen sink and give him a spray and wipe down. I really hope no one has ejaculated in or around this sheep.

It's the evening of Beth's birthday party that we are hosting in my house, and Lucy went with a theme: we can dress as anything beginning with B. I am Bo Peep. I have lost my sheep except for this fella here who I prop up in my sink. Next door, Beth is on a FaceTime call with Meg and I can hear nieces and birthday songs being sung. *Breathe, Emma.* At least the dress is hooped and large so I can still wear flats under it. I hope I'm not expected to sing. The mention of my name next door catches my attention and I put my ear to the door.

'What do you mean, she's pregnant?' I hear Meg say.

'Simon's new girlfriend. Lucy was here and it all went down. She confronted him about it.'

'Emma stood up to him?'

'Lucy says she wished she'd filmed it.'

'How is she feeling?'

'Because of the baby or because she stood up to Simon?'

'Both?'

'Do you think that's maybe why she's not acting like herself?'

'How so?'

'Well, when she was up here…'

I swing the door open to the bathroom and Meg goes quiet. However, I also release a small laugh of shock. Lucy has really done a number on the costumes and seems to have raided her party princess stash. Beth is dressed up as Belle from *Beauty and the Beast* complete in gold-tiered dress and white gloves, her brown hair curled around her shoulders. Together, we look like we belong in some bizarre period drama which I hope is Lucy not passing comment on our collective ages.

'Is that Meg?'

'It is.'

A voice pipes up from the screen. 'What are you dressed as?'

'Bo Peep.' I can hear her laughing through the screen.

'What were you talking about when I was up there?'

'Well, I think you know Ems.'

Beth's eyes shuttle between us. 'Sisters, may I remind you it's my birthday and if you have gossip then you are legally obliged to share that with me.'

'Emma had sex with Stuart.'

Beth drops her phone to the bed and cups her hands to her face giving me the same horrified look as when Belle first met the Beast. All that's missing is the thunder and lightning effects.

'You did what? Not Stuart?' she sighs, disappointed. I glare at Meg through the screen.

'He told you?' I ask.

'He divulged. I can't believe you, Emma! Please get yourself tested.'

Beth is still silent mainly out of horror that he's managed to make his way around all us sisters with such ease.

'I don't get you. You're all telling me to get out there and have some fun and when I do, you're suddenly critical about who I do it with?'

'It was fun?' asks Beth.

'It was.'

'But Jag, you went up there with Jag. Jag is coming tonight,' Beth carries on.

Out of all us sisters, Beth felt the breakdown of my marriage the most. Meg and Lucy were so angry that I had been wronged but I had this feeling Beth looked up to me and when it all broke down, it shattered a lot of illusions for her about marriage. She had such a strong moral compass about what was right, about how she thought relationships should be. I sit down on the bed and hold her close.

'I'm taking my time with Jag. I don't want it to be about the sex. I want it to be about trust and getting to know someone again.'

'He drove with you all that way, he did such a nice thing for you.'

'So you're saying I should have repaid him with sex?'

'No, I'm saying you shouldn't have slept with Stuart.'

'But I did and I do feel bad about Jag and I'm sorry if you think that was wrong but you know what, at least it's out of the way.'

'What's out of the way?' asks Beth.

'The sex thing. At least I've had a taster session and know my vagina still works. I just needed to do that much.'

'Have you been drinking Ems?' asks Meg.

There's a look on both sisters' faces questioning my actions. This is not classic Emma. Classic Emma has sex in beds and wears matching white cotton underwear sets. This was the Emma they used to try and drag on nights out when we were in our twenties but they'd come to my flat and find me wearing pyjamas on a Friday night, hugging textbooks and drinking caffeine-free herbal teas. I can see that they think this may be symptomatic of some sort of mental breakdown.

'Can you both chill out? I am in no way interested in pursuing things with Stuart. I went on one date with Jag so please just calm down.'

'But you will still check your bits out, right?'

'You make him sound like an animal.'

'Who's an animal?'

*Lucy.* I open my eyes wide. I also feel weird about having shared a sex partner with Lucy so they better not tell this girl anything or I will disown both of them automatically. She comes sauntering into the room in a pink vinyl dress, with matching knee-high boots and her hair back-combed to perfection. Beth and I look her up and down.

'Excuse me,' asks Beth. 'How come we look like some *Little Women* tribute act and you get to be a Barbie doll?'

To be fair, I'm not sure I have the legs or the nerve to don that outfit but she has a point.

Meg laughs through the screen.

'You can laugh, she has me in pantaloons under this dress,' I say.

Meg smiles but also narrows her eyes, informing me her reprimand is far from over. I wave back at her mockingly.

'HAPPY BIRTHDAY BUMBLEBEE, WE LOVE YOU!' she shouts. Beth waves and blow kisses. Bumblebee was her nickname when she was growing up as she tended to bumble through life, buzzing here and there, bugging us older sisters. Why Lucy didn't think to make this her costume is beyond me.

'Who is an animal?' Lucy asks.

'Danny. She was complaining about something,' I say.

Beth shifts awkwardly on my bed. Lucy eyeballs us both and looks in my bedroom mirror to adjust her fake eyelashes. She bends over to reveal a matching thong. I hope that's not vinyl too. That can't be comfortable on the bits. It's only Beth's birthday but Lucy will do what she does and that's steal the show, grind in front of people and be her usual self. It's her way, as the youngest, to garner as much attention as possible so she's not the one on the end, totally forgotten. 'So Lucy, who's invited tonight?' I ask.

She sashays over to the mirror and turns to pose, looking at us.

'Well, all those people that were on the list. The teacher people and then your mates from school and then I've got some uni peeps coming… Maddie and you invited Jag and…'

I did invite Jag. I thought this was perfect second date material. There'd be enough people around in case things didn't go to plan and a chance for the sisters to see if he was up to scratch. However,

I'm doing bad maths in my head about whether everyone can fit in my living space and whether we have enough toilet rolls. There's a knock on my bedroom door. A head pops round. Will. He gives Lucy a curious look up and down which she returns.

'William, you could have made more of an effort.'

Will, Beth's long-term man love, is wearing his usual jeans and checked shirt but topped it with a builder's hat and hi-vis. In his arms is baby Joe in a bear sleepsuit. He's the honorary child at today's proceedings as the girls are with Simon though I have a strong wish to have them here right at this moment, if only to shield me. We could have dressed them as lambs but then that wouldn't have started with B and Lucy would have made a fuss.

Will is a strange creature. I don't dislike him but he always looks very tired and confused about life, like he's one of those student types that just needs to be shaken by the shoulders and told to grow up, face real life and stop acting like it's such a big surprise.

'I'm a builder.'

'Well, yeah… duh,' replies Lucy. She coos over Joe.

'I'm going to just settle him in the travel cot then?'

Beth nods. He stands there like he's awaiting instruction. Beth sits on the bed almost willing him to get that this is her party, she's off duty but he doesn't and she relents, standing up to leave the room. Naturally, Lucy doesn't sense what's happened there at all. She pulls her thong out of her arse. I look in the mirror. This is not a sexy outfit. I look like a virgin.

'Lucy, where is this sheep from?'

'It's from my *Toy Story* act. Darren dresses like Woody, I wear that and sometimes we get Big Lee along and he's Buzz Lightyear.'

'There's a hole at the back of this sheep.'

Lucy doesn't look shocked. 'The kids don't know what that's for. We stick the gummy sweets in there. Why do you think he looks so happy?'


Boris Johnson is at this party. He's sitting on the sofa opposite me and the way his mask is fixed, I can't quite tell if he's looking at me. I find it mildly strange that even though it's not actually him I still want to throw something at him in rage. I'm not sure what parties are supposed to be like but I think this one may be ticking over quite nicely and that may be because I'm three-quarters through a bottle of red. We have barbarians, basketball players, three Batmans, a ballerina, Bart Simpson and a Single Ladies era Beyoncé whom Lucy keeps scowling at as she's in a leotard and is *so* stealing some of her Barbie Girl thunder.

'Are you Emma?'

The man who has come to sit next to me has the most ludicrous black curly wig on and carries an inflatable guitar.

'Brian May?'

'YES! Thank god for that. Someone over there thought I was the bus driver from *The Simpsons* but he was like twelve. I'm Nick. I work with Beth.'

'So you're a teacher of...'

'Maths. Which is incredibly dull so we won't talk about that.'

'I like maths.'

'At least one person does. And this is your house?'

'It is.'

'It's wowsers. I still live in a flat share and I'm thirty.' He looks into the distance slightly forlorn that this is the state of his life. Even the end of his guitar droops slightly. I want to tell him that happiness and life satisfaction is relative. He may be in a flat share but he could be in a really stable and mutual loving relationship that involves regular orgasms, in a career that is gratifying and allows him to balance travel and a social life. Happiness is not a house. I don't get the vibe that he's hitting on me but do get the vibe that he's been at the punch. I didn't even know I had a punch bowl. I think it may have been a wedding present from an old aunt of Simon's. What sits in it now is a cranberry-coloured concoction that involves an entire bottle of rum.

A man comes down to sit next to Brian May dressed head to toe in brown, a clock drawn on his face. Oh, Big Ben. Bravo. Brian May's attention turns to him whilst I sit here cradling my glass of red wine. Boris still stares at me. He's engaged in conversation with a butterfly whose wings look like they're made out of drinking straws and old tights. Beth mingles and wraps her arms around everyone. She's introduced me to a few people and I'm polite back but tonight, I've mainly been involved in storing people's coats and looking after the presents. I'm literally herding which makes this costume all the more fitting.

'I thought that was you? How's it going Bo?'

Next to me, one of the Batmans appears and perches himself on the sofa arm. The three of them here today range in quality. This one is mid-range, he's not gone for the light grey body stocking sixties option that leaves a rather unfortunate moose knuckle situation. He pulls the mask back to reveal himself.

'It's me, Leo. From school?'

'Horse-riding Leo?'

'If that's what we're calling me.'

I laugh but my face says everything. Why are you here?

'Oh, it was Lucy who invited me. We've recently bonded as school gate renegades. I hope that's not weird, is it?'

'Well, at least it's someone I know. There are a lot of random faces here today.'

'Am I allowed to say there are some kids in your kitchen preparing Jägerbombs?'

'Like proper kids?'

'Like younger than me, which seems to be most people these days?'

I smile. He has a glass of punch in his hand and sways merrily to the party music.

'Anyways, I've had a shitty time with Faith recently. She's being a bitch, we're in mediation. I think Lucy invited me out of pity?'

'She does that, she likes her waifs and strays. I found out Simon has got another woman pregnant.'

'Ouch.'

'Not even from him.'

'Double ouch.'

There is a sense of camaraderie here; only Leo would know what it felt like to be in this situation. Everyone else's empathy always felt a little misplaced.

'I love our party talk – we always take it to such a positive place.'

He laughs a little uncontrollably at that comment – I credit the punch for this. It makes him fall into the sofa and drench me in the red stuff. I don't think I'm wholly bothered but this may not be good if Lucy needs this outfit in the next couple of days.

'Oh god, I am so sorry.'

Brian May turns to us and laughs. 'Christ, Batman, we can't take you anywhere…'

The men seem to strike up a drunken line of conversation so I stand up and leave them to their banter. I look like I've been stabbed. I head to my bathroom where the door is unlocked but a man dressed as a builder is on the phone.

'Will?'

'Sorry, Emma. I should have gone upstairs.'

'Is everything alright?'

'I just… I have to go.'

'Will, it's her birthday.'

'It's just… I can't. I have work. I really can't…'

I look at him and have an instant flashback to Simon. It was always work. He'd claim someone was dying and I wouldn't bat an eyelid. He'd leave children's birthday dinners, family picnics and walk out in the middle of films. How many times was it a broken bone or him fleeing to go get his rocks off? I have no reason to doubt Will but my silence speaks volumes.

'I love Beth… and Joe. You know that?'

Love. Simon used to talk of it every day. He'd drop it on to the end of texts like a way to say goodbye. It had no sincerity or meaning at all. He also said 'Ciao' which was one of those traits of his that made me want to throw things at his face.

'Then show her,' I say.

He's not sure what that comment means and he turns to the front door.

'You're not going to at least tell her?'

'She's fine. She's got so many friends here, you girls…'

He opens the door and slinks off as a few more guests filter in. *Will. Don't do this.* But he doesn't even look back.

Someone hands me a bottle bag. Who are you? Why have you brought crisps and are all in yellow jumpsuits? Is there a hazmat situation that I should know about? Are you minions?

I don't know whether to chase Will down the street but he's gone. I watch him take himself away from my house, away from this party.

'*Breaking Bad,*' says a voice trailing in from the rear. Jag. I smile. 'Clever. Maddie is parking the car. Where are your sheep?'

'I've literally lost them all. And you have come as?'

I look down, he's wearing quite a bog-standard suit. He reaches behind him and puts on a Barack Obama mask. I smile and pull him in for a hug. He stumbles a bit from the physical proximity but alcohol makes me brave.

'Go into the living room and give Boris a piece of your mind.'

Maddie comes shooting up the stairs covered head to toe in feathers and bright orange tights.

'Big Bird?'

'Yes! Where's the drink?'

'There's punch in the living room.'

'Come on Obama, let's get sloshed.'

Jag turns to look at me. *It's a party, it's mental. I'll find you later.* Through the kitchen door, I hear a roar of voices and think about

what Leo warned me about. I head there and true enough, a gang
of youths all stand around with plastic shot glasses and a bottle of
Jägermeister.

'Yo Bo!' one of them shouts. I salute them with my crook. They
seem to have turned up in their own clothes with an assortment
of animal masks. We have a bear, a baboon and a badger. But we
also have one poor lad who went the whole hog and has come as
school uniform Britney Spears. He's even donned the knee-high
socks. They're not particularly threatening but it's all so youthful
and screams of an experience I was supposed to have had many,
many years ago. Lord, that makes me feel ancient. I go to the sink
and try to exercise some damage control on Lucy's dress.

'Are you Lucy's sis?' asks one of them.

'I am. I'm Emma.' I wave to all the youngsters there.

'Always good to meet fam,' says one of them in a strong London
accent. I assume that to be me and nod.

'Nah man, she's the doctor sister, innit? This your gaff?' I nod
again hoping I've answered the question in that sentence. 'This is
niiiiice, man.'

'Why thank you.' To match my outfit, I curtsey to the room.

'Did you make the cake too? It is like proper legit,' says one of
them.

'Oh no, that was shop bought. I think her boyfriend's contribution.'

Will, at least, did that much. It's a two-tiered confection that is
covered in gold leaf and chocolate curls, dripping in fudge, from
some artisan bakery. It takes pride of place in the middle of my
kitchen island and I look upon it protectively as they all admire it.

A strange cocktail is pushed in front of me that seems to involve two glasses. I smile politely.

'I am sorry lads but my shot days are over. I'm on the red tonight.' I prove this by downing what's left in my glass. One of them laughs at me. 'Nah, we're not going until you have a Jägerbomb.' They all start clapping. I eyeball each and every one of them disapprovingly. But with a little bit of alcohol in my veins already and feeling totally lost at this party, this may be the answer. I down it all in one. Holy fire of balls.

'What the crap is in that?' I say as it rolls down my throat, tasting like cough syrup that's on fire.

'Red bull and Jäger, innit?'

'Innit.'

They all cheer and clap and start chanting, 'Bo! Bo! Bo!' I curtsey again but feel the effects in my eyeballs. Maybe I jumped the gun there. I don't know who these boys are. These drinks could be drugs. Mother of Moses, there could be Rohypnol in that drink. I may pass out soon. It could be liquid heroin. A song suddenly filters in from the next room and I hear it summon that group of boys over. They all disperse bar one who helps me tidy up. It's Britney, bitch.

'That costume is inspired by the way,' I say.

'They all fooled me and told me we were all going as Britney. I went on the Tube like this.'

He makes a very good Britney. He looks the sort who's never quite been able to grow facial hair so there is a wonderful youthful smoothness to his skin and he has very shapely calves. He is well house-trained and knows that the Red Bull tins go in the recycling and has the foresight to crush them first. I want to congratulate this boy's mother.

'And how do you know Lucy?'

'We all work for the party company. I'm Darren.'

'Oh, her partner in crime. You do a lot of parties together, don't you?'

'I love your sister to bits.'

He expects me to reply with the same response but I hear a bass get turned up next door and I fear for what the neighbours may think.

'Does she mention me at all?' he asks.

Oh. I look up for a moment at his face all shiny and hopeful. I can see the appeal with someone like Lucy. She is young and beautiful and she's the life and soul of a party but I wouldn't suggest he puts his eggs in her basket, not quite yet.

'She always talks about the parties you've worked on.'

He smiles back. He looks so innocent, so sweet. I remember being like that once; crushing on a handsome colleague on my course, thinking that I was special because he picked me over everyone else. Being young and hopeful. I don't want to take that away from him just yet.

'Are you really a doctor?'

'Yes.'

'Then can I ask you about a rash I have?'

This is what I need to make this party truly complete.

'Where's the rash?'

'Do you want to see it? It's on my thigh.' He pulls at the hem of his skirt.

'I'm good, thanks,' I say raising my crook slightly. 'Is it oozing?' I ask.

'Like how? Like pus?'

'Pus, fluid? Is it itchy?'

'Like you wouldn't believe. There are bumps.'

'I'm not a dermatologist but a lot of rashes are usually a reaction to something. Bites maybe? Any bumps anywhere else?'

'No. Is it like an STI?'

I smile at his innocence. 'On your thigh, then no. Unless you have these bumps on your penis?'

He blushes. 'No.' He then does a strange thing where he hugs me, taking my medical advice to mean he's not dying. *That said, it's just opinion. Definitely get it checked out.*

'Oh.' I look up from this strange embrace to see Maddie standing by the kitchen door with Beth. Britney stops hugging me, looking more guilty than he needs to. Maddie is in hysterics at seeing me being accosted by him but Beth gives me a funny look like she's interrupted something. I give her a look knowing that she's still carrying some judgement over Stuart Morton.

'Darren here has a contact rash. Try something medicated like Sudocrem and keep it clean and dry.' He nods, embarrassed, and scuttles off into the living room to rejoin his friends, his pigtails swinging in time with the bass of the music.

'Do you ever switch off, Dr C?' Maddie says.

'Never.'

'Have you seen Lucy? That punch could strip paint.' Beth tells me. 'And I haven't seen Will in an age either.'

I can't tell her. *Your boyfriend is a flake.* Maybe I should let her at least enjoy the cake first.

'I have some more juice in the utility room if we need to dilute it down.' I open the door and drop my crook. Seriously? Maddie giggles, seeing Barbie and second-rate Batman in an unexpected clinch. They part when they see me. I hope that's just the design of Batman's outfit and not an erection. I rub my forehead.

'Leo.'

'Emma.'

He takes his leave. How did that just happen? He was literally on my sofa ten minutes ago. Lucy emerges and adjusts her squeaky vinyl dress.

I roll my eyes and she reads it immediately. 'What was that, Ems?'

'Luce, he's a school run dad. What on earth?'

'Oh, stop being such a bloody prude. He's single now, it's a party.'

'She can talk, I just saw her touching up Britney Spears,' adds Beth. 'Darren?'

Maddie looks over at Beth like she's a little bit mad. Well, she's definitely quite drunk and that can help matters.

'He was asking for doctor's advice.'

'Sure he was,' replied Beth.

She gives me another look. I've gone down in her estimations again. *You're falling down some slippery slope, sister.*

'Woah, I don't need this. I've been swanning around your party trying to make this nice for you.'

'If it was such an inconvenience then we needn't have bothered.'

I raise my hands in shock. Well, we're all here now, some gratitude maybe?

Lucy glares at my chest. 'What have you done to my dress?'

'More like, what did Leo do to my dress? With that punch you're trying to kill people with? Why is he here? Why is my house full of random people?'

'I was trying to do everyone a favour. You two sad cows don't have a social life and I was trying to bring some of that here.'

'Did you put one of those open ads on Facebook?'

'I did not.'

'Can you two stop fighting please?' pleads Beth. She rubs her forehead, looking pained.

'You always do this. You always have to be the centre of bleeding attention,' I say.

'Seriously guys, stop it already,' says Beth. Maddie puts an arm around her. From the distance, we can hear a small baby cry.

Maddie tries to interrupt. 'Girls, you've all had a drink. Just calm down, yeah?' She waves her arms around and feathers fly through the air.

'I just can't believe she's gone after a school gate dad. It's like no one's off limits with you. That's about my girls.'

Lucy widens her eyes at me, trying to focus through all the booze but also at the lecture.

'Shag who you like but I need to show my face at the school and I don't want my daughters involved in any more school-gate gossip. Did you think about that at all?' I say.

Beth pipes in. 'Well, you can talk. I mean, you had a go on Stuart Morton last month.'

Lucy's head swings around. 'What happened with Stuart Morton?'

'She slept with him when she was up north.'

I swiftly glance around hoping Jag is not in the vicinity.

'You did WHAT?' shouts Lucy. 'And you didn't tell me? I've slept with him. Beth pretty much did the same.'

'I have not. I kissed him.'

'And touched his willy. Meg told me,' laughs Lucy. Beth looks like she could die of the shame.

Maddie looks confused. 'But… Jag went up north with you.'

I glare at Beth. There's this strange three-way fight happening in my very kitchen, around an island where we all look like cats ready to pounce. Come at me, Barbie, I have a bloody crook. I point a finger at both of them.

'Stop this. I don't need this today. I let you have your party and I look sodding ridiculous and now you're shagging people in my utility room…'

'We weren't shagging, just some light—'

'I don't need to know! And you're standing there all judgy about Stu Morton. Both of you went there with him so need to stop with all your presumption and bad advice. Ever since I got divorced, it's just all of you hovering over me and telling me what I should be doing. I should be dating, I should be having sex, I should be telling Simon to do one. I would never tell either of you how to live your lives.'

'We just care, Ems,' says Beth, a little tearfully.

'Well, maybe you should be looking after your boyfriend because he's not even here, he left—' As soon as the words leave my mouth, I see her tear up and I immediately feel regret deep in my core so my anger switches to Barbie Girl, in her stupid effing Barbie world, thinking she's so bloody fantastic. 'And instead of giving me your stupid outfits and creating all this drama, you should just piss off.'

And just like that Lucy picks up that birthday cake and missiles it at me like some Olympic shotput thrower. It hits me in my chest, an explosion of fondant and sisterly love, and I stumble back onto my kitchen counters. *You complete and utter cow.* Maddie covers her face whilst Beth looks on in complete resignation: *That was the only good bit of this party and my sister's wearing it down her front.*

I laugh and point down to my neck. 'You're such an idiot. I believe this is your dress that you've just ruined.'

I wear ganache like a face mask and feel some sort of liquid seep in between my breasts. I scoop a lump of chocolate off the front of the dress and sling it back at Lucy, only wishing it was a fresh turd. It catches her hair, which I know she would have spent ages getting just right. She shrieks, shrill like a harpy, looking for other things to throw at me.

'Go on then, little Lucy reacting by throwing her toys out of the pram again. You're such a spoilt brat!'

'Emma, don't goad her…' pleads Beth.

'Good job that dress is wipe down, eh? You can invite the next bloke along for a go? There are two other Batmans here tonight. I can go find them… '

She seethes with anger. 'Now we know why Simon cheated on you, maybe it's because you're such a bitch,' she says drunkenly. Picking up the next thing on that counter, a bottle of Jägermeister, she missiles it in my direction. I duck. The next person walking through the door gets hit square in the head and falls to the floor. Lucy cups her hands to her mouth. You didn't. You've just killed Barack Obama.

# Chapter Eleven

649 days since my mum told Simon she'd kill
him if she could get away it

It's 1 a.m. Lucy has thrown up five times since midnight and is currently asleep on my sofa wrapped in a kid's giraffe-print blanket. Beth marched upstairs after we threw her cake around and refused to talk to anyone. I don't sleep. I think it must have been that Red Bull shot so I eat all the canapés to sate my inevitable hangover and because I don't like to see things go to waste. In my kitchen, Barack Obama lies on one of the benches and his head is propped up on my lap. We didn't kill him but that bottle sent him flying and left a significant bump on the head.

Thinking she had killed him, Lucy flew into a panic and that was when she had her first spew, right into my kitchen sink, which then threw everyone else into a panic as it was bright red. Because of the punch naturally, but most presumed it to be blood. As you can imagine, that really put a dampener on a party so that was the point when people started to take their leave. Maddie escorted some of the stragglers but she didn't look too impressed with me. She didn't need words. *He drove you up north and you slept with someone else while you were up there. Pay your penance and look after this man, now.* Jag flits in and out of sleep. He occasionally looks up to study the underside of my jaw.

'Well, I'm going to go all out and say this was better than our first date.'

I laugh. 'I told you I'd get one of my sisters to help out.'

I uncover the tea towel stuffed with peas to see how that bump is progressing. Never mind that Lucy can sing and dance, she seems to have a hell of a left arm on her. Maybe she should be in cricket. I am reminded of a time at school when she hurled a can of Coke at a school bully and gave that girl a black eye. She was suspended for a week.

As I cradled her on the sofa, she thought she was dying and through tears apologised profusely that she called me a bitch and that was why Simon cheated on me. I stroked her hair and kissed her on the forehead. I also said I was sorry for calling her a slapper, telling her that she was much classier than the Beyoncé who'd been there that evening. I then let her pass out in my arms and put her in the recovery position so she wouldn't choke on her own vomit.

I put a hand to Jag's hair and he closes his eyes. 'Is it painful? Did you take those ibuprofen?'

'Just tender.'

I hold some fingers up. 'How many?'

'Four.'

I widen my eyes.

'Two, I'm just playing.'

I smile. I'm sat here in a dress smeared in red and brown like I've been stabbed and then defecated on, but he still chooses to rest his head here. I like the company, I like how easy it feels and that he's come into my home and has been physically attacked but it hasn't seemed to faze him. He feels close, physically closer than he's ever been to me but I don't mind. I'm not panicked. I stop stroking his hair in case it's coming across as pet-like and instead drape my other arm across his midriff. He goes to hold my hand.

'Are you OK?' he asks.

'Depends what you mean by OK? OK on a scale of one to ten sits at about a five. Like if I was rating food, this burger is not great, it's just OK.'

He smiles at me. 'Are you the burger?'

'Yes.'

'Like are you a traditional beef burger? How many patties? Are you in one of those newfangled brioche buns?'

'Oh, I'm quite traditional. The buns are a bit misshapen though.'

He laughs. I realise I've taken to innuendo here. Do I mention sauce? Being messy to eat?

'I like a traditional burger. Burgers comes with bells and whistles these days. It really is too much,' he says.

'But what if I said I'm not just a burger? I come as a meal deal. You can't just buy the burger.'

'Then I think that's a bonus?'

I look at his face to see if he's understood the analogy. I come with all the sides on the menu. Is that too much? Would he be willing to take it all on? It's too early to say it out loud. He may not understand this and still just be talking about food. He circles his thumb into my palm.

'I thought you got on with your sisters?' he asks.

I look over at Lucy. For the love of god girl, close your legs.

'I do but it's siblings, isn't it? It's that unique relationship where you'd stab someone for them but also have moments where you'd easily stab them yourself.'

He laughs. I hope that doesn't make me sound sinister. I reach over to the table and grab some cheese things wrapped in pastry. 'Do you want one?' He nods and I place it in his mouth, my fingers grazing his lips slightly. Crikey. That was a bit sexual for me. He kisses my finger and looks me straight in the eye. Not now. We're in costume. That's role play and I haven't done that before. The doorbell suddenly goes and he sits up, a little woozy.

'Shouldn't have done that.'

'Yes, lie back down and let me investigate.'

For some reason, I take my fake crook with me and head for the door. It's most likely someone who has forgotten something but then I think back to Mrs Phelps snitching to Simon the other day. This better not be him. Or is it the police? The music was quite loud, wasn't it? I open the door tentatively then swing it open fully to see who stands there.

'Mother?'

She stands there with my inflatable sheep and hands it to me. 'I found this in a planter in front of your house. It explains the bonnet.'

I put a hand to the top of my head. This whole time I left it on. 'It's one in the morning, mother. Did you come alone?'

She stands there shivering in the cold autumnal air. 'Well, yes. Why would I drag your father along too? You should take that dress off and let it soak at least. It looks like you massacred one of your poor sheep.'

I glance down. It's not a pretty sight. She walks in and gives me a half hug, surveying the damage. It wasn't a wild party but there seems to be a cup left on every flat surface and what looks like a sausage roll embedded into my hallway rug. She opens the door of the downstairs toilet and closes it again.

'We can tackle that in the morning. Lucy?'

I gesture into the living room. She takes off her parka and puts down her tote handbag to reveal a pyjama top underneath with bootcut jeans and the same Reebok Classics that she's worn since I was a child. As it seems to be my job today, I take said coat and place it on the bottom of the stairs. She heads into the living room picking up cups and cushions as she goes. When she sees Lucy, she sighs and rearranges my sister's legs and hair.

'I am going to assume that this was her idea?'

'Well, it certainly wasn't mine.'

'Your father was upset we weren't invited. He wanted to come as Björn Borg.'

'And you?'

'Barbara Cartland, obviously,' she replies a little deadpan. 'Don't enable this one. You know what she's like. Tell her to have her parties elsewhere. It's what I did for years and why we're banned from the community centre.'

'I think she thought she was doing something nice.'

Mum raises her eyebrows. She gets a shock for a moment spotting what she thinks is a live animal on the floor but is actually Brian May's wig. She stops when she sees Lucy's decorations – photos of Beth from through the years hanging around as bunting – and smiles at a favourite memory. She pauses when she sees a certain photo on my mantlepiece. She turns to look at me.

'Did Lucy throw up when she saw this picture?'

Out of all us Callaghans, my mother was on par with Lucy in how much she hated Simon. She proved it on that Christmas Day when Lucy outed him and Mum swung for him and dislocated a thumb. It was the beginning of the end. Her and Lucy had that much in common at least.

'It's for the girls.'

'Just a shame we all have to look at it. I heard he's impregnated one of his whores?'

'That's one way of putting it.'

'How old is she?'

'I haven't asked.'

'Have you warned her about Simon?'

'I have not. It's none of my business.'

She knows better than to start a fight so she gets the brush off my fireplace set and gathers crisp crumbs into a pile.

'Why are you here?'

'Beth called. I couldn't make head nor tail but she was in a bit of a state so I thought I'd double check she's fine and Joe is also upstairs so I thought a sober adult in the vicinity may be useful.'

'I'm sober,' someone pipes up from the doorway. Mum's head swings around to see Jag. He shouldn't really be standing or here at all, come to think of it. I should have ushered him into the garden. Darn it.

'I don't get the costume.' He holds his mask up to his face and she laughs. 'I like that. I'm Fi Callaghan.'

Jag tries his best to stand to attention.

Mum points to Lucy. 'Were you shagging this one in the utility room?'

'No, I believe that was Batman. I have a reputation to uphold as a former commander-in-chief.'

She pauses for a moment at his humour. Most men wouldn't dare, especially ones she's found in her daughter's house. The normal go-to stance is reverent and nervous.

'What happened to your head, Barack?' He points to Lucy. 'Oh, you're that one,' she replies, looking scornfully at her daughter as she still continues to snore peacefully. 'I apologise for that. She's always had a reactive streak. And you are here because...'

Jag looks at me. How are we playing this? There is no definition to what we have just yet and I hate to put it in strange youthful terms that one would find on a social media status.

'Jag is a colleague at the hospital, a friend. I told him to stay here for a while in case Lucy gave him a concussion.'

'That's good advice. Go and lie on the other sofa, Jag. Would you like a cup of tea?'

'I would and thank you. It's nice to meet you.'

'You too.'

Mum looks at me but doesn't say a word. She heads into the kitchen where she sees the remnants of thrown cake on the counter and the smell of Lucy's vomit taints the air. She sighs heavily, heading to the cupboard under the sink to find bleach and black bags. She fills the kettle and puts it on to boil.

'Why is your sink pink?'

'Lucy made a punch.'

'Of course she did. I can't believe you just left the cake here like this,' she says, as she stabs at bits of melted chocolate with a fork. 'Did you even get the chance to sing to her or make a fuss?'

'Umm, no. This isn't just us though. Will left the party early.'

'So I gathered. Still, both you and Lucy making a scene can't have helped. '

'It was Lucy's fault.'

'You are not six years old and fighting over toys, Emma. Beth didn't want a party. Did anyone ask her if she actually wanted a party?'

'Well, no but—'

'Where is she?'

'Upstairs. I haven't been up there.'

I let Beth storm upstairs after the cake and bottle slinging and haven't checked on her since mainly because I was trying to tend to the wounded and ensure that Lucy threw up in a receptacle as opposed to over any soft furnishings.

Mum doesn't respond to me but chucks half a bottle of bleach down my sink and proceeds to scrub away. It's very much my mother's way. All her words are cast in judgement, she always expects and wants better for us. There are a lot of 'shoulds' in her vernacular.

'Make some tea for your friend and for me too. Is Joe OK?'

'I think.'

'You think?'

I throw my hands up in the air.

'Why are you being like this?'

'Because Emma, it is fucking one o'clock in the morning.' I cringe. 'And I have five daughters over the age of twenty-six and

I am still out here in my pyjamas looking after all of you. Never mind the two who I can't keep track of because they moved away but you, Lucy and Beth… It was easier when you were all children.'

'I am sorry for the inconvenience,' I mutter under my breath. I'm under no doubt that Jag hears this all from my living room and is wondering whether the easier option is just to run into the night.

'You are all old enough to be making better choices. I have no idea what I did wrong here.'

'I'm sorry we've disappointed you with our string of failures as grown adults. Are you talking about Simon? I'm sorry I chose such a shitty person to be married to.'

She rolls her eyes at me. 'You know what I mean. You're a smart girl.'

'But obviously not *that* smart.'

I don't doubt that this was also a common thread of reasoning in my family; that I was clever and educated but chose to remain married to someone so venomous. It defied belief that I tried to flog my marriage for as long as I did. That I continue to self-flagellate beyond my divorce. Maybe the difference is that divorce wasn't medicine. There are no right answers or ways to do anything, there was no course to sign up to and ace the exams.

'Don't twist my words, Emma.'

I let her clean my kitchen and open the utility room door slowly, almost checking to see if Batman is still in there. He's not but I see a condom wrapper on the floor that luckily my mother doesn't clock. For lord's sake, Lucy. I'll have to rewash those hand towels on the side.

I finish making my tea and go to the living room to put a cup next to Jag, now soundly asleep. I check his pulse anyway in case Lucy hit him harder than we thought then cover him with a throw. I like that he's here. I like that he didn't come to this party as Boris Johnson. As I tuck him in, my mother gestures that I come upstairs with her. I do as I'm told.

Is it too early to make amends with Beth? I'm still a little bitter she outed me for sleeping with Stuart Morton but there is also a tiny baby upstairs whom I should check on. I notice my bedroom door wide open and see that the bed has possibly been slept in which means more washing for me. Did someone have sex in my bed? I don't even want to know.

I take off my dress and catch my reflection in the mirror, a thirty-five-year-old woman in flats, pantaloons, a Marks & Spencer bra and bonnet. It's certainly a picture. I finally relinquish the bonnet and throw a T-shirt on.

Mum pops her head into my room. 'Where's Beth? She's not in Lucy's room?'

'Tried the girls' room where Joe is?'

'Of course.'

We stand there for a moment. Did she actually leave? I'd have heard her go and she wouldn't have left her baby, no? We scramble around until I notice the bathroom door is locked. My mum takes action.

'Beth? Are you in there? It's me, Mum. I got your messages.'

'Mum? What did she actually say? Is she alright?' I whisper.

Mum isn't sure whether to divulge. 'She just sounded upset and half of the messages didn't make much sense but she said Will left.'

'He did.'

She looks at me and knocks again at the door. It's not a complicated locking device so I try to twist it open with the nail of my finger. We finally get in and there she's in the empty bathtub swathed in a nest of bath towels like the world's saddest sausage roll and hugging her phone and a bottle of children's bubble bath shaped like a sailor. It's how one would have found Belle had the Beast died at the end of that film. I immediately feel guilt. This is my fault. It was her birthday, and we just went ahead and had this stupid party and spoiled even that for her. Her eye make-up is halfway down her cheeks. I scan the floor and find tablets scattered across the floor like polka dots. Mum's face freezes as she sees them.

'Are they…?'

I quickly peel back the towels and get Beth to sit up. Beth? I climb in the bath to prop her up.

'Beth? Beth? Come on B…'

My sister opens her eyes but looks at us in confusion. Mum comes over and slaps at her cheeks with her hands which doesn't help.

'For fuck's sake Mum…' she mumbles.

'WHAT DID YOU TAKE?'

Panic strikes through me. The party wasn't that bad. Is something else going on here? Little Bumblebee. She used to follow me around at primary school and is one of the sweetest people I know. What has she done? She tries to curl around me and fall back asleep. We need to make her throw up. We need to call an ambulance.

'Oh, give over you two,' she says, tears welling up in her eyes. 'I was so fat and bloody clumsy, I fell into the bath and everything went flying. I think those are vitamins. I didn't take anything. I'm sorry I've made a big mess.'

'Then why are you in the bath?'

'Well, I found two teachers from my school in your bed for a start.'

I wrinkle my nose.

'And because I was drunk and I know what you would have been like if I threw up anywhere else...'

I hug her from behind. She knows me too well. 'I'm sorry B. I really am...'

But Mum knows. She cups Beth's face with her hand and Beth bursts into tears. 'Are you OK, love?' Mum asks.

'Where's Joe?' Beth says, tearfully.

'He's asleep.'

'He didn't come back?' Beth asks.

Mum shakes her head.

'Then he meant it,' says Beth. 'He's gone. He needs some space. On my birthday, on my actual birthday.'

'Beth?' I ask her. Mum can't quite bear to look her in the eye.

'He needs to work out what he wants in life. So he's moving out.'

He what? Will? Oh, Beth. I can't bear it, tears welling up in my eyes. *Not you as well.* I hug her tightly, feeling her body vibrate under mine. And all at once, I'm drawn back to our schooldays when Beth used to follow us around, copy our hairstyles, school bags and platform shoes. One night, I remember she followed us to a nightclub in Kingston, she was underage and she shouldn't have been there. I remember being in that club, telling her to leave.

*You don't belong in here. Get out.* I didn't want her to get hurt. And now, whatever I'm living, I don't want someone else I love to go through the same.

'Little bumblebee. I'm so sorry, I really am.'

# Chapter Twelve

653 days since Simon walked out of my parents'
house, his nose held together with tampons

It was 2014. We had just come off a private tour of St Catherine's
School where a woman called Irene had shown us round. It had
been unlike any school I'd ever seen, not just in terms of the facili-
ties and class sizes but simple things like patches of emerald-green
lawn that looked like they'd been cut with scissors. Simon did
what he normally did and strutted around the place in a shiny
blue suit, flirting casually with Irene by using her name a lot and
touching her forearm. You could tell Irene liked it from the colour
of her cheeks and the fluttery giggle.

'I think it's the school for Iris. Have you seen the results? They
speak for themselves,' he said.

I was sifting through the prospectus that was packed with pictures
of happy, culturally diverse children skipping along in their tartan
wear and monogrammed cardigans. I got to the page about fees.

'It's a lot of money. And then we'll have to factor in Violet too
in a couple of years.'

'Is this you going all socialist on me again?'

Simon said it so mockingly. He was from an affluent family: he'd been educated at the top-end toff palace that was Westminster and gone to a private prep school so education was nothing to him without a blazer and a debauched rugby tour.

'I'm thinking practically. The state system did alright by me and my sisters.'

He didn't respond. It was like he never heard me.

'It's not like we don't have the money, Emma.'

'Yes but I'm thinking ahead to university and how we invest for them.'

'Quite.'

'I just feel putting them here cuts them off from a whole section of society. I don't want them to grow up with a silver spoon in their mouths.'

'Like me then?'

The car went quiet. We had been having this discussion for months. Simon had visited local primaries and turned his nose up at sandpits and phonic boards. I had literally missiled a prospectus about boarding school across the kitchen.

'Well, we need to decide by the end of the week because that's how long they will hold the place for.'

I didn't reply. Our car was sat on Richmond Bridge in traffic and I watched as the lights danced along the river, a train darted past full of commuters. I wanted my girls to be like me. I didn't think that was a terrible thing. A terrible thing would have been if they turned into Simon. Even then I knew there were facets of his personality that I hoped they wouldn't inherit: the arrogance, the lying. But I didn't know how to say that out loud. I didn't know how to communicate anything to him. Simon was getting increasingly frustrated by the stationary cars on the bridge and hit his horn quite aggressively.

'That will help,' I said.

He looked aggrieved, like the traffic was suddenly my fault. 'Do we have any tablets in this car? I have a headache coming on.'

I rooted around in the glove compartment and my handbag. Nothing. I undid my seat belt and leant behind to check in the map pocket. As soon as my hand touched it, I knew. I pulled them out. Women's knickers. They weren't mine. I put them back. The next day I got them and threw them in the bin. I convinced myself they were never there. I said nothing. I also did nothing two weeks later when Simon told me he'd put down a deposit for that school. It was non-refundable. At least one of us had our girls' best interests at heart, he told me.


'But you're talking, that's a start?'

'He's not being completely shitty I guess,' answers Beth on the phone. I can tell she wants to bookend that sentence with 'not like Simon'.

Poor Beth. It turns out that a new baby was a game changer for her and Will's relationship and the pressures of work, real life and a whole lot of sleepless nights had turned things on their head. Will wasn't completely gone. He hovered in the distance and was staying with his brother. For now, the sisters and I all talk about him privately in slurs and anger. You don't do that to our Bumblebee. You hurt one, you hurt us all. Yet as I'm the only sister to have gone through something similar, I also prop her up.

'Why are your teeth chattering?' she asks me on the phone.

'Because I'm standing outside in the cold.'

'For shits and giggles?'

'I'm waiting for Simon. We're at a parents' evening.'

'Then wait in the school.'

'I can't because Simon wants it to appear like we've arrived together so I have to wait at the gate and then we can drive in the same car.'

'Then why couldn't he have picked you up from your house?' You can hear the confusion in Beth's voice.

'Because then I'd have had to sit in a car with him for half an hour and I don't think I'm capable of that.'

Beth doesn't have to say it. I've given him the power here. I'm the one stood in the cold. I could have been the one driving and he could be the one out here. I could have summoned up the strength and sat in that car with him but made it uncomfortable for him. But no. Instead I stand at the railings and every time a car rolls past, I hide in the trees so I don't look like I'm some strange straggler at the gates of a school. Beth's pause also reads relief that she's nowhere near anything this complicated with her Will just yet.

'Are you OK, B?' I ask her.

'Well, I got out of that bathtub. Each day at a time.'

'You'll be golden, kid. I need to go.'

She laughs. 'Golden?'

I smile as I realise it's something I've learnt off Jag. 'We are all golden. Love you, B.'

'Be strong, Ems.'

She hangs up. The sisters say this a lot to me. They send me emojis of the strong flexed arm. Do they want me to be emotionally strong? Or actually punch Simon one day? I assume the latter. Deep down, I know this is just a glitch for Beth. Like it was for Meg up north with her Danny, who've since resolved their sex toy drama. You're allowed the odd moment for dips in your relationship. It's good to expose them and question the stability of the foundations but I know those sisters will be fine. My foundations were always leaky to start, big crevices in them. I just pretended they weren't there. I moved the rug so no one would see them.

Simon's Range Rover doesn't even pull up to the curb. He literally stops in the middle of the road so I have to jog over in case he gets in the way of any traffic. I clamber in.

'Emma.'

'Simon.'

We haven't broached the subject of Susie and her impending pregnancy yet. When I confronted him, he walked away. It was none of my business apparently. But it was. This was a new sibling for my daughters, I had to gauge whether they were set to be replaced with a new family. Because it had taken Simon just over a year to replace me. Or maybe she'd always been there. I just didn't want that for my girls, best interests and all that.

He approaches the winding driveway up to the school and we sit in silence. Simon is fond of a valet so the car is always impeccable; mine is always the one littered in little girl shoes and sweet wrappers. He listens to some sporting event on Radio Five Live and when we finally stop to park, he keeps the engine running to hear the event's conclusion. I think it may be something to do with golf.

'Oh, by the way… Violet lost her first tooth?' he asks me.

'Yes?'

'Why did I hear about this from Facebook?'

'I need to tell you every time our daughter loses a tooth?'

'Yes. It'd be nice to be informed of milestones. I am her father.'

'Unfortunately, I'm all too aware of that fact.'

He glares over at me. *I could knock a few of your teeth out now if that would help.* We get out of the car and he gives me a once over to check I look presentable enough to be by his side. I've come straight from work so I'm in a sensible trouser with a kitten heel. He dons a shiny charcoal suit, one I actually bought him. The green tie, the colour of mushy peas, is a mistake but I don't say that out loud. We take the short walk to the school door and I watch him carefully. It's going to happen in a moment, isn't it? We see the headmistress, Mrs Buchanan at the door. And… action.

You see, Simon does a strange thing when we are in public, and that is to act like our divorce never happened. His body will relax and he'll move closer to me. Tonight, he's even put a hand to the small of my back. It's all part of the fun and games because he knows if he laid a hand on me otherwise then I would go completely ninja on his ass, body slam him and break his fingers. It's all about the show. *I'm not the bad guy here, I am such a nice bloke. How could she divorce someone who was so gentlemanly? And look at that soured snarl on this one's face. This was obviously all her doing.* I always act with bemusement at this character he puts on. He should've been an actor.

'Mrs Buchanan, always a pleasure!' He takes her hand, shakes it animatedly and looks at me to do the same, a fixed smug grin on his face.

'Mr and Mrs Chadwick, welcome.'

I think about correcting her now I've reverted back to Callaghan but that would just get us all off on the wrong foot.

'Busy evening?' I ask.

'Always, but such a wonderful opportunity to connect with our parents and build on the special relationships we have with our school community.'

Mrs Buchanan has big bushy red hair like Bonnie Tyler in the eighties and speaks like she's reading out of brochures.

'You are so right,' Simon replies attempting to be earnest. Christ, he's a cheese ball.

Two uniformed minions appear.

'Horatio, Yi Lin, please can you show the Chadwicks through to the drinks reception?'

They both nod in unison, the boy holding his arms out like a waiter showing us to our table. We follow them through the school's grand corridors to the main hall. It's the one thing I like about this place, the air of Hogwarts about it with its hefty engraved name boards and sepia photos of successful sports teams. In the hall, a throng of parents mill around waiting to see respective teachers. It's the same every year. We all dodge the people from the PTA trying to sell us quiz tickets, and the bowls of crisps out of hygiene concerns.

'Red or white?' asks a lady in an apron.

This here is the very reason I get through parents' evenings. From the look of the bottle, it's decent wine too so I can only think that's where a good proportion of our fees is going.

'Oh, I have a surgery tomorrow morning so I will just have OJ please,' says Simon.

The lady, who looks like her other job is in *Downton Abbey*, smiles. Oh, a surgeon and a dashing one at that. He had to drop that in, didn't he? He may as well have just got his penis out and whopped it on the serving table here.

'Red, please,' I say.

I take my glass and follow Simon to a corner of the hall. It's essentially a holding area without the background music. The idea is that all the parents will get on and create a party vibe but it just becomes a strange family gathering. As terrible as it sounds, it's sorted into cliques: parents who know each other via NCT groups, the international expat brigades who keep to themselves, the parents who've ostracised themselves by gossip, the ones who you know regularly brunch and ski together. There's a pat on my shoulder and I turn to see Leo. He seems sheepish and Simon looks upon him suspiciously.

'Leo.' I kiss him on the cheek as I know that will upset Simon further.

'This is Simon, my ex-husband. Leo is Freya's dad. Freya—'

'—is in Violet's class?' Simon finishes my sentence in patronising tones.

Leo's expression says it all. *I thought you were a dickhead and you are.*

'So, I just wanted to say I am so sorry about that party. I ruined your dress, I really didn't behave and I've squared it off with your sister but I didn't want you to think that—'

I can tell that Simon's ears have pricked up. He was unaware of any sort of social gathering and I was keen to keep that information from him. That said, it may be fun to keep him guessing.

'Don't. We were all drunk and did stuff we shouldn't have. It's fine.'

'I'm glad. I lost my mask by the way? It must be at yours.'

Simon looks mildly surprised now. *You had what sort of party involving masks?*

'Are you here alone?' I ask Leo.

'Oh, I'm not allowed to stand near her tonight.' He gestures over to his ex-wife, Faith, who is standing with Pony Party Leah. They pretend not to have been staring and look in other directions.

'Leo and his wife, Faith, are also divorced,' I inform Simon.

'Oh.'

I know Simon will hate that I've said the D-word out loud. 'That woman stood next to Faith. Do you know her, Emma?' Simon asks.

'Her name is Leah, why?'

For the love of god, he hasn't slept with her too, has he? I already know of him sleeping with one other mum. He'd met her at a sports day and they spent their time flirting over the free Pimms as we watched the foam javelins sail through the air. By the egg and spoon, they may as well have just mounted each other. Her husband stormed off in a rage. Two weeks later, said husband sent me pictures of both of them emerging from a Holiday Inn. That was a good day.

'She's the pony lady. She invoiced me for that party that Violet went to.'

This is new information to Leo. 'You were invoiced? For what?'

'Because Violet didn't ride for the fully allotted time,' replies Simon.

Leo looks aghast. 'That's disgraceful!'

'And she was pretty awful at that party too. She sent you that invoice too?' I ask. 'I thought Lucy told her to do one.'

Simon doesn't look surprised but he remains quiet and I know exactly what he's done.

'You paid her, didn't you?' I ask him.

'It was only twenty pounds.'

'I just wish you'd spoken to me about this first?'

'It's a small price to pay to avoid her causing added drama, no?'

I look at him as she shrugs at me. It's the principle of the whole affair. But then I'm talking to Simon; principles aren't his strong point. I shake my head while Leo surveys the awkwardness.

'Would it help if I said something awful that Faith has done this week…?' Leo mumbles.

'Be my guest.'

'She's made me take on all our credit card and loan debt because it was in my name.'

'Ouch.'

*'Let's put another holiday on the cards, Leo. We need it. We also need this copper-plated sink and hexagonal tiles in the downstairs bathroom.'*

'I'm sorry.'

'It is what it is. A man can live off rice and baked beans forever, right?'

He glances over at Faith. I know that look. It's pure exasperation that things are just so darned difficult. Why can't it be easier? I put a hand to his shoulder and Simon watches hesitantly.

Young Horatio suddenly appears in front of us. 'Mrs Westlake is ready for you now.'

'Good luck kids,' mumbles Leo and I grimace at him, gesturing that this whole evening is some self-imposed torture. I do have his mask. I'll return it in a school bag but maybe not via Lucy. I down my wine and pick up another glass on my way out. Just get this done. Violet's teacher first and then Iris' straight after. Smile and breathe.

Simon's act dips as we walk along the school's parquet floors. *Who is Leo? I didn't know that man. You had a party. And he was there in a mask.* I, meanwhile, can't believe he paid off that horrific school gate mum. I hope he slips on these floors and sprains an ankle or something. As predicted though, it doesn't take long for him to put on a show again.

'Mrs Westlake! We meet again!' he says, holding his arms aloft.

I have no qualms about Mrs Westlake. She's a seasoned teacher who likes a slack and sensible moccasin and we're familiar with her since she taught Iris two years previously. When we enter the classroom, Horatio bows in reverence, taking his leave and I wonder whether to tip him. I don't join in Simon's animated greeting but having a glass of red to keep me company means I toast her instead which I worry has hints of Cersei Lannister about it.

'You are looking so well,' Simon says.

I think I was a little bit sick in my mouth. I have no worries showing how unnerved I am, furthered when he decides to sit there and manspread himself on the plastic chair.

'It's always lovely to have another Chadwick girl in my classroom. Violet is a particular delight.'

We both smile.

'She talks a lot about you. She seems to have settled in well,' I say.

Simon nods. To his credit, I don't doubt that he still is a decent father and is proactive in his children's lives. I've seen his signature in the reading diary and his attempts at helping them with their homework. She opens up a couple of books and it's classic Violet. Iris is ordered and neat – if she makes a mistake then she deletes it completely and she underlines things with a ruler and listens to instruction carefully. Violet has more wild abandon about her; no rulers, she puts giant crosses through things that don't work and likes her bubble writing decorated with doodles of many, many cats.

I glance around the classroom as Mrs Westlake talks to us about standardised scores. The theme of the school is to show you how smart and educated these children are. Look at the copperplate handwriting, their reproductions of Van Gogh and our languages corner where they've all had a go at telling us what they like in French. I spy a contribution from my girl. *J'aime les chats et la glace au chocolat.* I hope that is useful to her one day if she ever visits Paris and is on a first date with a Frenchman.

'So to push Violet into those top scores then what do we need to do? Maybe tutoring?'

I've lost track of the conversation so try to catch up.

'For maths, perhaps, so she can grasp some of the concepts a little more tightly.'

I look over at Simon, a little confused.

'Umm, I don't think there's need, right? She is only six.'

Simon looks at me pointedly. *Put on a show, Emma.*

'We run an after-school tutoring club on Wednesdays that would help.'

Back when I was a youngster, clubs were fun endeavours that involved dancing, matching baseballs caps or were a chocolate biscuit that you had in your lunchbox. This was not a club.

'Is it free?' I ask. Simon physically baulks that I should ask this question.

'It's fifteen pounds per session.'

My point being this should be a parents' evening, not a sales session.

'Then it's something to think about. It could be that she catches up with people throughout the year,' I say.

'Possibly,' she replies. She goes into her folder and passes Simon a form. Sneaky.

'Violet has also shown great interest in languages and art. Her pictures have been a joy.' She goes to a file and pulls something out. It's a family portrait but one that involves quite a few people. Mrs Westlake takes a deep breath. 'I do understand that your family situation has evolved since I last taught Iris but this picture shows me that Violet's chosen to embrace any new changes.'

It is a bold statement to make and not one which Simon takes to well. *You are here to teach my daughter, not psychoanalyse her.* I am, however, a bit more grateful that she's looking after my daughter in a more global sense. It was what I worried about. How was she coping? Was any of this mess affecting her? I study the picture.

'Has she said much in school about it?' I ask tentatively. 'A parent mentioned something to me the other day and I got a little worried that maybe she was getting upset at school.'

'Which parent? You didn't mention anything?' asks Simon.

'That mum from the pony party,' I say bitingly. The one you paid off, like we were giving her licence to judge and belittle our little girl. Bravo.

Mrs Westlake looks at us. 'I can't really say. I've only known her a matter of months but I can ask around? In class, she's attentive, bright and very helpful. She's a credit to you both.'

Simon and I look at each other for a brief moment. We both tried to do right by those girls.

'And when family situations change then it's good for me to know so I can understand them. I hear names so I just try and piece it together. There is a mention of Aunty Lucy?'

I cringe, wondering how she may have come up in conversation.

'That's my sister. The one who draws all the smiley faces in their homework diaries. I am sorry about that.'

She smiles. 'And Mr Chadwick, they talk of your new partner and Oliver.'

Simon is visibly irked. They named the baby already? I've heard that some people do that but I've always been more cautious. As a medic I've seen how these things worked out so I wanted to meet my babies first. It intrigues me that Susie may be further along than I thought though. What do I do with this information? I can't believe the girls have already been talking about this at school? Will I now have to buy her a present? Simon can't seem to deal with the emotional honesty on show though. *Come on, Simon. Tell her it's none of her business like you did me.*

He is studying the picture in detail, his face a little pale. I glance down at it. It is a standard child piece of art. The grass and sky are strips of colour to the top and bottom and we are as tall as the broccoli style trees. Lucy is there dressed like a giant fairy and I am in that white and black dress that I wore on my first date with Jag. I smile at the fact it does indeed look like a hospital gown. We all stand in a long line between two houses. Does it hurt to look at this? Part of me thinks Mrs Westlake is right. The landscape has changed but there's no evidence of hate or sadness here. The most telling thing is that Simon, the girls and I are standing in the front and all the other people are on the periphery in separate homes. I notice a very pregnant Susie – poor woman looks like she's swallowed a basketball. And then a small little boy stood next to her.

'And I believe your son, Oliver will start here soon so that's lovely.'

*Who?* My chest rises and falls slowly. I take a large gulp of wine. I am pretty sure they don't take foetuses here unless that is some new pre-birth enrichment programme that I don't know about. Simon stares at me. Silently begging me to act this out.

'Remind me Simon, how old is Oliver again?' I ask.

'He's four,' he whispers.

I smile at Mrs Westlake. It's no different really. He kept things from me for years, in marriage, so no doubt he would do the same in divorce. But I wonder, when will this stop? When will he stop having this power over me? Who is this child? Who is he to him? Breathe, Emma.

'The only problem is that we can't pass all the girls' old uniform to him,' I add.

Simon laughs, a little too hard and looks me in the eye. *I acted for years and years, Chadwick.* He thinks he's good at this game, I'm better.

# Chapter Thirteen

659 days since my mum told Simon she wished
she'd broken his penis, not his nose

His name is Oliver Charles Chadwick. He takes his father's last and middle names, and he was born in 2015. That was two years before I finally decided to divorce Simon and however I do the maths, there is crossover. When my mum punched him on Christmas day 2017, when we were still married, he already had a son. That holy grail he had been searching for, someone to carry on the family name.

Simon loved his daughters but I always sensed he was after a boy, as if creating something else with a penis defined his own machismo. That son would have been two years old at that point. Was Oliver the result of a one-night stand? Did Simon go to them after mum punched him? When did he see this kid? Was he present at the birth? Did he know it was his?

I think about a mini version of Simon wandering around, a baby version in little chinos and brown suede shoes. Maybe this was my fault. I'd grown up with a massive family and understood what it was all about but to have matched my mother and had three more would be lunacy in this day and age. The water bills alone would bankrupt us. I was also keen to kick-start my career again so had held up my hand and said I wanted to stop. Simon who had been a single child, tried to convince me otherwise, every month, but I stood firm by my choice. Was this some failure of mine to bear further fruit?

I sit in my office and stare out on to the Thames. I've been to that flat of his – she certainly doesn't live with Simon, neither does young Oliver, so where are they? I turn to my desk. I may have gone a little overboard with my research. Social media queen Lucy helped but the person who really rolled their sleeves up was Maddie. She asked friends of friends and dug deep. She even managed to find out that Susie had given birth at St Thomas' next door. We found some evidence of Oliver on social media via relatives but he doesn't really feature on Susie's profiles making me think he's kept a secret. For that much alone, I feel nothing but true empathy for the poor kid.

'Have you eaten? Have a biscuit?' Maddie enters the room with freshly typed out notes and mugs of tea. I look over at her in my strange catatonic state. She sees the handouts on the desk, a weird mixture of photos and an article she found when Susie won a nursing prize in 2015 and looks at least six months gone in the pictures.

'Oh, love. Maybe put it away for a while? Have you thought about what you're going to do yet?' she asks.

I shake my head. Simon hasn't even told me to my face yet. After the parents' evening, I'd walked ahead of him in the corridor. I didn't want to get in his car nor wish him goodbye. It's one regret. I should have screamed *SEE YOU NEXT TUESDAY* loudly as I made my exit down the winding school drive. He didn't even message or call. I had to find this information out for myself. Again. I even had to ask my girls, as carefully as possible, *Have you met Oliver? Yes, he's Susie's little boy.* That's all they knew. Did he look like my girls? I mean this was hardly a surprise given Simon's track record but having to wade through his deceit and decipher all the layers was exhausting.

'He makes me feel like I'm being nosy, that it's none of my business. But it is, right?'

'Ems, this is classic Simon. He makes you think that you've done something wrong and gets you second guessing yourself. Of course this is your business, it's related to your girls and their living situation. The fact he hasn't introduced you to Susie is ludicrous.'

I shrug my shoulders.

'When I got together with Mark, the first thing he did was introduce me to his ex and we worked out the best way to raise his sons together.' She places some digestive biscuits in front of me. 'Please eat,' she says and goes back to sorting through her files on my sofa.

'Can I ask you a personal question?' I ask her. 'About Mark and his divorce.'

She stops filing to look up at me. She's given me snippets of their relationship but I've always just filled in the gaps.

'His ex-wife. Do you get on? What is she like?'

'Claire? She's… a character.'

'Like a good character?'

She grimaces. 'Like we all get on, really. But also like, say we were running away from a herd of zombies, I don't think she'd help me.'

'What would she do?'

'She's the sort who'd trip me up and use me as bait so she could get away faster.'

'Which is why Mark divorced her?'

She laughs. 'That and she was shagging a plumber called Jim.' She can see the cogs in my mind whirring. 'If you did ever meet Susie, she wouldn't have to be your best mate. Claire's certainly not mine but you just get to a point where this other person exists in your life, you keep it moving for the kids. And I love those kids like my own. They're my bonus humans. I'd do anything for them. Drink your tea.'

I do as I'm told and return to my desk thinking about a time when I would meet Susie. How would that happen? I am thinking a soft play centre may be best so there are squishy corners in case it comes to physical fighting. I could get Lucy to bury herself in the ball pool and ambush them if needed?

'Anyway, while I'm here… How are things with Jag?'

She raises an eyebrow at me. Since the party and her finding out about Stuart Morton, she's approached everything with a bit of caution. I guess she's the one who set us both up so feels a sense of duty that we both treat each other properly.

'Things are good.'

'And what happened up north with Meg's brother-in-law?'

'Was a glitch. Maybe I needed to get something out of my system, test the waters.'

She laughs. I think she knew deep down I wasn't doing ill by Jag.

'We went for coffee the other day. In the work cafeteria.'

'Romantic.'

'It was three in the morning, very romantic.'

Jag was someone I still kept in my periphery. I've questioned whether it's too soon to drag Jag into the giant ball of confusion that is my life. What I like about him is that he offers me a sense of reprieve from all of that. We meet for night-time coffees and they're quiet, serene – and backlit by the glow of the vending machines. He tells me everything about himself but I don't do the same from my end. I mean he's met my mother and slept on my sofa but I don't want to invite him in just yet. Maybe I'm just scared he'd see the mess and run away as quickly as those Nike Air Max would take him.

'Did he at least buy you some biscuits?'

'We shared a packet of Bourbons.'

She studies my face but I give little away.

'And when were you going to tell me that you're going to be his plus one at that wedding?'

She beams at me. Bloody Lucy.

'Maddie, I am going to be Jag's plus one at a family wedding.'

There is mild squealing and a seal clap. How has this news worked itself around my small network of people already?

'Lovely, that is pretty huge.'

'It's a giant family wedding at one of those London hotels overlooking Hyde Park. I'll be one of about a million people there so calm down.'

'I will not.'

'How did he ask you?'

'He said Emma, would you like to go to a wedding with me?'

She grins. The truth is that's not how it went down at all. Over our machine bought lattes he was telling me that he had a busy few weeks ahead as his sister was coming down and multiple cousins from all over the country and beyond. I asked him why and he said one of the cousins was getting married. I smiled and said how lovely. He said it was going to be one of those epic family get-togethers that was totally going to stress him out, mainly because of his mother who would use it as a way to emphasise how bloody single he still was. I asked him if there was any way I could help.

'Come with me, it'll be fun. If you like samosas and drumming and mammoth crowds of people.'

'Why not?' I said.

I don't know why I agreed but I thought at least if he got hit with a bottle this time round, it wouldn't be at the hands of my family.

'It's so romantic, being a wedding date,' Maddie says, excitedly.

'We're not the ones getting married, Maddie.'

'I know but I just have a feeling.' Which translates into her having already put an outfit together for our nuptials. I bet she's going with something coral with a statement earring.

She studies my face again. I am still grey with worry. 'Have a biccie before you do your last rounds…' she pleads.

I salute her.

'And promise me one thing,' she continues, 'don't allow that man to continue owning your headspace. You gave him back. He's not your problem anymore.'

I think that's the problem. Once I married Simon and had his children, he became part of my fabric and I don't know if and when I will ever be able to untangle him from my life. It's not as simple as returning him to a shop and getting a refund. *Here, take him. He's defective and not as described. I want all that time and my dignity back, please. Just bin him.* God, divorce would be so much easier that way.

I always do a final stroll of my wards to check all patients are accounted for and so I can double check orders and notes. Today, the ward soothes a broken soul and scattered thoughts. It provides distraction. I fill in some notes sat by reception and watch as a girl, who I could feasibly fit in my pocket, scoots past with a tiny golden Zimmer frame, literally learning to walk again after what looks like hip surgery. I smile.

'Doctor C!' I glance up and a familiar face looks up at me from a wheelchair. Lewis.

I panic for a second. 'Hello, there? All OK?'

'Yeah, I'm having an X-ray like you said?'

Panic turns into relief. I smile at his mum. 'I did say that. How are those drugs working out for you? More importantly, have you been riding in any more Ubers recently?'

He giggles. 'No. I got grounded. They took away my PS4.'

'I'm not surprised, kid.'

His mum intervenes. 'The drugs have calmed things down, no episodes recently.'

'Then that's good,' I reply.

Lewis studies my face. 'Do you want to come to X-ray with us?'

His mum shakes her head, laughing. 'Doctor C probably has things to do.'

I look up at the clock, I was supposed to leave an hour ago.

'Actually, yeah, why not? We can catch up. Actually, if your mum wants a break – maybe a coffee – I can take over?'

I see his mum exhale loudly at the offer. It's weird to see her here without her husband. He normally levels her out so the stress radiates off her today. I understand that completely. That feeling of solitude, of having to parent and do things solo is a novel and overwhelming experience. You have to exude calm for the kids but underneath the legs are kicking furiously. In those situations, even a machine-made filter coffee and half an hour to stare at her phone can help.

'If that's OK with you, Lewis? I mean I can come.'

'Could you go down to the shop and buy me Skittles?'

'I can,' she kisses him on the forehead and puts an arm to mine. 'Thank you.'

I stand and follow the porter out of the wards as Lewis puts an arm forward like he's charging the light brigade. The wheels squeak on the shiny floors.

'This is Godwin. He's from Nigeria.'

I smile at him, we are familiar with each other but I've never asked him about his heritage. I assume Lewis has all the answers though.

'He supports Spurs but we'll forgive him that.'

Godwin has a loud roaring laugh that bounces off the walls. We proceed to walk.

'And how are you Lewis? Last time we spoke, it was pretty…'

'Crazy?'

'For want of a better word.'

'I'm sorry I did that. I was confused. Dad's moved out now.'

His reaction to this is less emotional than last time. He still seems thoughtful but I guess the initial shock has subsided.

'He has a new house. He let me choose the carpet.'

'What colour did you go for?'

'Grey. The man in the shop said it was scotch-guarded and it was on offer.'

'How's your mum?' I ask him.

'She's sad. She cries a lot. She thinks I can't hear her in the shower but I can and she gets drunk with her friends in the kitchen and they talk about stuff.'

I think about all those private tears I shed through my divorce. The ones you hope are hidden and silent. I cried mine in my bed mostly, wearing my duvet like a shroud.

'Like?'

'Money, dating, her friend talks a lot about a man she's dating called Warren and he's into strange things in bed.' My eyes widen. 'I'm nearly eight, I'm not stupid.'

I smile. 'It'll be a lot for your mum to process. I'm glad she's got friends she can talk with.'

'Do you still get sad about your divorce?'

I am unsure how much to divulge here. Does he need to hear that I stopped eating, that I once cried in a Costa toilet, and once had to be fished out of a bath by Beth after I turned into a human prune? I was sad. I still wear that hat on occasion too.

'I do. It's the end of something, that's always sad.'

'It's not like you're dead,' he says, matter-of-factly. I have no choice but to laugh. 'Life goes on. I think dad is dating someone.

Maybe. He was talking to someone on the phone and I was listening behind the door.'

'You're a regular little house spy, eh?'

'Ninja skills.'

'And how do you feel about your dad dating again?'

He pauses. 'I don't know yet. As long as she's nice and doesn't put me under the stairs.'

'I'm sure she won't. In the attic maybe.'

Godwin laughs again as we wait for a lift.

'Isn't she funny, Godwin?'

'You both are funny.'

'Are you married, Godwin?' asks Lewis.

'I am. I've been married for thirty five years.'

My head swings around. 'Jesus Christ.' By the crucifix hung around his neck, this feels like the wrong expletive to use. 'I mean, you don't look old enough.'

'We were young,' he informs us. 'I am blessed. But she'd probably keep me in the attic some days too.'

Would I have kept Simon in the attic? Maybe six feet under my patio. Lewis presses the lift buttons again and the doors open. A few people filter out including one who captures Lewis's attention.

'Oh man, are those VaporMax?'

Are they the what? I look down at him, confused but then up at the person in the lift. I know that face. He steps forward to keep the doors from closing. Jag.

'Why thank you, Dr Kohli... How are you?'

'I am very well, Miss Callaghan. And yes, bud… These are indeed VaporMax,' he answers.

Lewis observes our interaction closely, with one keen eye still on the footwear.

'This is Lewis, routine X-ray.'

Jag goes to high five him. 'Doctor C helped replace two of my valves when I was born.'

'Doctor C, I like that. I'm Jag, good to meet you, Lewis.'

He releases the door and turns to salute me with one finger through the closing gap. I wave animatedly with two hands which is less cool. Godwin presses the buttons needed to get us to X-ray.

'Who's Jag?' asks Lewis.

'Just a doctor friend.'

'You're blushing. Wasn't she blushing, Godwin?'

Godwin smiles but doesn't reply.

'I am not.'

'Yes, you are,' he giggles.

'Do you like how I bigged you up and said you replaced my valves?'

'I noticed.'

'You like him, don't you?'

I look up at his expectant face. He processes life so well, so clearly. I credit this to his parents. Even the way they've chosen to end their marriage has been done so amicably and with the sole intent of making this boy a priority.

'Are you happy, Doctor C? I hope you're happy.'

I turn my head to look at this boy. He's such a tonic. I should have paid him to counsel me after my divorce – I could have paid him in Haribo.

'Jag seems nice.'

'Jag *is* nice.'

'He has cool trainers too. Those are VaporMax and they're like hundreds of pounds.'

'People are fixated on his shoes,' I tell him.

'Shoes are important. Like if he wore Crocs then I would tell you to kick him to the curb.'

He snaps his fingers and Godwin and I laugh deeply from our bellies.

'You should get together with Jag then. What are you worried about?'

'My heart?' I say quietly.

Godwin smiles at me through sympathetic eyes.

'But hearts are the strongest organs in the human body, Doctor C. They can go through anything,' Lewis tells me.

'And where did you get that information?' I ask.

'You!' He says laughing, the doors to the lift, decorated with three smiling octopuses, open. He did, didn't he?


It's seven o'clock and I am finished for the day. I went into X-ray myself and saw Lewis' valves are as they should be. I returned him to the ward and to his mother and I hugged her. She seemed surprised by the gesture but it was out of solidarity, knowing that sadness and how it penetrates so deeply. It too will pass and like your son just reminded me, it could be worse, we could be dead. Or wearing Crocs, so a lot worse. I smile, thinking of that boy as I exit the hospital and reach into my bag to find my ringing phone.

'You done, bitch?'

It's Lucy, obviously. Lucy and I have made amends after our party antics. News of secret children and Beth's relationship woes forced us back together but we also made a pact that I would replace her Bo Peep dress if she promised to keep school gate sexual relations to a minimum.

'Just walking out the hospital now. What's for dinner?'

'Ummm, nothing. We met Aunty Beth for tea and had a Subway.'

'Great. You didn't get me anything?'

'Were you looking for a foot long?' she guffaws at the end of the line.

'The girls? How are the girls?'

'Satan picked them up about an hour ago. I was very good. I said nothing but I may have hissed at him like an angry jungle cat.'

'Is that his new name then?'

'We could go with Shitbag, Wanker, Fuckwit, Bollockface...'

'Let's stick with Satan. Are you home? I guess I'm picking up my own dinner.'

I feel a tap on my shoulder.

'Nah, I'm taking you for a drink,' she says, hanging up her phone.

I grab her shoulders for a hug. 'You're here?'

'I am.'

'I don't want to get drunk. I'm not wearing the right shoes.'

She rolls her eyes at me. When everything first happened, her and Beth thought this was the way they could help me get over Simon. Pickle her, immerse her in alcohol and drag her on a dance floor so that she'll forget all the terrible things that have happened. Those nights would usually end up with me crying, once into the arms of a hirsute kebab shop owner called Hamid.

'One drink. Maybe.'

She studies my drawn and sallow face.

'Or we can raid an M&S, drink at the station and have a train picnic.'

I almost cry with relief at the suggestion.

'I'm too good to you.' She links arms with me and we head towards the station.

'You never come to the hospital?'

'Beth said to check in on you. You've been all morose since you found out about Simon's bastard.'

'He's a child, don't call him that.'

'Meg's a bastard. I call her that all the time. It's not bad if used in a factual sense.'

'It's always bad. That child is related to you in some way.'

'Will I have to buy it Christmas presents?'

'It's not an "it" either.'

She shrugs and drags me along the walkways to Waterloo, the winter breeze biting at our cheeks and whipping my hair into candy floss. I pull her into the M&S, dodging the marching commuters and grab a basket. I haven't really eaten all day so the whole place calls to me, the food almost asking for me to eat it. All. I start taking very random things off the shelves: a packet of raspberry iced buns. That'll do. I also take some hummus (obviously), some coleslaw, a family bag of salt and black pepper crisps and a trifle. I hope I don't bump into Maddie as this is not nutrition.

'I'll look for the wine. I want some sushi, none of that crap with the mayonnaise.' Lucy saunters off jigging to the music playing in the aisles.

Cheese twists, noodle salad, cocktail sausages. I then stop next to someone with a roll of yellow stickers in their back pocket. Hello there. Have I managed to find that sacred hour when all the food is being marked down? He labels some prawns with dip and even though I get a little squeamish about eating fish near its expiry date, I put it in my basket. I then follow him around the corner. Praise Odin, there are shelves of the stuff from cheese to pâté. This is dinner. I put all sorts of random foodstuffs in my basket and smile at the thought. It takes me a while though to notice that there is someone stood next to me. They are heavily pregnant but I don't think too much of it.

'They have some knockdown pizzas, I could get one of those? Have the girls eaten?' she says to someone on the phone.

There are pizzas? Maybe I could get a pizza. She reaches down and puts one in her basket. Only then do I look up at her face. Oh. She senses me staring, takes one look at me and stops talking to the person on the other line. Susie. She doesn't say a word to me, nor do I to her. *You are here, you are real and yes, you are indeed very pregnant.*

I guess this was always a possibility given we work in the same neighbourhood but I was never going to be ready. However, I can't read her. Is that anger? It feels like I'm something she just stepped in. She looks me up and down and turns her back to me. Excuse me? What have I done to her? I should be the angry one. As she goes to the tills, I hold back in shock around the reduced-price items. Simon won't eat that pizza. It has pineapple on it. How pregnant is she? *Tell me about Oliver. I'm Emma. I was his wife.* Say something. Go and talk to her, Emma. But I am mute.

'Look at you, yellow sticker bitch. Excellent work,' says Lucy, depositing two bottles of red in the basket. She turns to head for the tills.

I grab her arm. 'We can't.'

'Why?' She looks at me confused. I can't tell her. She'll go for her because she's Lucy. We'd start some middle-class bitch fight in this middle-class food hall, she'd pelt her with olives stuffed with anchovies and Percy Pigs and we'd be banned. I can't have that fight. I don't have that fight.

'I just…' I pull the already laden basket up to steady my shaking hands. 'Bread. We need bread.'

'We do? We've got plenty at home.'

'No, I ate that this morning.'

'It was a whole loaf? What's wrong with you?'

I shrug, silent. That's the thing, Luce. I don't quite know.

# Chapter Fourteen

665 days since I finally told Simon to go to hell
and my sisters cheered

*Why are you in the toilets?*

*It's not like I'm sat in a public loo. These are the toilets in The Dorchester. There's a sofa.*

*And? Go find the party? Go find the sodding bar.*

*I'm early. BTW, how on earth would I have needed ten condoms?*

*You found them. Well done. You never know ;) Which dress did you go for?*

*The black shimmery one.*

*Dull but predictable. Love you, have fun. Go get shitfaced, it's a wedding xxx*

I put my phone back in my handbag and look at myself again in the ornate mirror of The Dorchester loos where I've camped out due to nerves and paralytic fear. The black bejewelled dress I have on is courtesy of Lucy's mate, Siv, my overriding memory of whom was her ability, through school, to apply liquid eyeliner in the middle of a moving bus with expert precision. When we made the call that we needed eveningwear for an Indian wedding, she showed up half an hour later with twenty five outfits, from saris to trouser suits to dresses, and all worn once as she has thirty five cousins and her mother doesn't like the shame of repeated outfits in wedding photos.

I've played it safe in a black eveningwear number. The bodice is embroidered and sparkly in a way that doesn't look like I'm about to dance a foxtrot and it fits well and flows down to an acceptable length. I don't know what pretty or attractive looks like anymore because I'm stuck in that unfortunate habit of always questioning why I was never quite good enough for Simon. So it's a bloody shame I'm drawn back to a time when I last had on something similar. Simon and I were going to a medics' charity ball and I had bought a navy floor-length gown for the evening. It was hourglass shaped, boobsy and different to my usual shapeless shift dresses. I had spent a fortune on waxing and nails and asked the hairdresser to curl my hair in the fashion of some sultry nineteen-forties movie star. I rarely made an effort but it was two months after the Australian nanny. I remember standing in front of my bedroom mirror with fake eyelashes and elbow-length gloves and Simon barged past me, fresh from work. He saw nothing. He had a quick shower and put on a tux and told me to hurry as the traffic on the Hammersmith flyover would be a bastard this time of night. That night, he schmoozed his way around the room getting drunk on expensive bottles of whisky that he splashed out on in some sort of male pissing contest. He flirted with the waitress who brought our bread to the table. He bid on some framed print in an auction. *It's all for charity*, he said when he went on stage to collect it and people applauded and cheered him on. We didn't dance. I couldn't eat because my bodice was so tight so he lucked out by having two helpings of lamb shank. The nadir came at the end of that evening. I was stuck in conversation with a neurologist who was telling me about his research and had managed to sneak the word lobe into the conversation at least twenty-three times. I excused myself to go to the toilet. As I walked down the corridor towards the restrooms, Simon appeared out of an unmarked door. He asked me where I was going. To the toilet? Five seconds later, the waitress with the bread appeared, wiping her lip. I bowed my head. Simon shrugged and walked away like nothing had happened. *That's a really lovely dress*, the waitress said.

*Find the bar*, said Lucy. I don't know why I'm nervous and why I've been hiding in the loos. I guess on the way here I realised this was quite a big step as far as dates go. I could be in wedding photos that people will own for an eternity. I am going to meet family. What if they don't like me? They could hate me? I then saw shaped topiary as we pulled up and opened my clutch to pay the Uber driver and all of Lucy's planted condoms and sheer panic came flying out. Bar. Gin will help. A cocktail maybe? This looks like the sort of place that will have a bar with pristine square napkins and a gentleman playing classical piano in the corner. That's classy. I can do classy while I wait to gatecrash this wedding. And I am prepared for alcohol because Lucy told me to have toast before I left the house to line my stomach. She can be useful sometimes. I should have ditched these condoms in the loos. But that also feels wasteful.

'Evening madam, a table for you?' A waiter greets me at the door of the bar. I may bow back at him.

'I was just hoping to get a drink. I'm here for the wedding but I'm a bit early.'

'Ah yes, the wedding in The Ballroom. You're more than welcome.'

He leads me through and I try my best to take a seat on the stool without looking like I'm mounting it.

The bartender puts a napkin in front of me. 'Good evening, madam.' All this madam business is making me conscious that people assume me to be here as a prostitute looking for custom.

'Good evening. I was hoping for a gin and tonic.'

'Do you have a preference of gin?'

I look back at him blankly. The alcoholic type?

'We have over thirty-nine varieties. Maybe the lady would like to try something fruit-infused, or perhaps something spicy, dry? And do you have a preference for tonic?'

The gin and tonics I prepare at home are Schweppes and lemon slice based and sometimes drunk out of mugs. When did alcohol get so fancy?

'You know what? Surprise me.'

He grins at being given free licence. From beside me, a voice laughs.

'This is why I went for brandy.'

It's an older Asian gentleman in traditional dress. I don't want to assume he's here for the wedding too but he has kind eyes and a charming laugh, though that could be the brandy. He shakes my hand. 'My name is Arjun.'

'I am Emma.'

He gives me a second look and studies my face. 'This may be a strange question to ask a lady I've just met but...'

*Christ, please don't think I'm an escort.*

'Do you happen to be a heart surgeon?'

I narrow my eyes at his guesswork.

'I am?'

His laugh gets bigger. 'Then young sir behind the bar, this drink goes on my tab. I am Arjun Kohli, Jag's father.'

Never mind coming in here to calm my nerves. I've walked right into the lion's den. *You're Jag's father?* He says his son's name in a rich accent that makes it sound stately. I smile at him.

'I... then... I am very pleased to meet you, sir.'

'Please, not sir. I am not that old?'

'They've been calling me madam since I got here.'

'Ouch.'

We laugh. His study of my face becomes more intent and I await the inquisition. I should have prepared answers. I wonder what else Jag has said about me? Did he just sell me as the heart surgeon? What about my kids? Divorce? A glass slides in front of me garnished in citrus peel and cucumber.

'Thank you,' I gesture to both the bartender and Arjun and we clink glasses.

'I like how yours came with a side salad,' he jokes.

I grin broadly. 'All vitamins. So, how was the wedding ceremony?'

'My dear, it's been a long day. We've been here since nine this morning. The actual ceremony and prayers took over an hour because my brother likes a show, then there was lunch and now dinner in a moment and then dancing. Quite frankly, were it not for the fact I know how good these caterers are then I'd be ready for bed.'

I beam at hearing him talk so honestly. 'It must be lovely to see your niece get married though?'

'Oh, Meera is a darling girl but my first house was cheaper than this wedding."

I laugh. 'And her husband, what is he like?'

'Nice boy. A little bit of a square though. He normally wears glasses but Meera didn't want them in her photos so forced him to wear contact lenses for the first time. So the poor boy's eyes are bulging like his pants are too tight.'

I laugh straight from the belly and take a long sip of my drink, conscious he is staring.

'You're different to the girls Jag normally goes for.'

'Because I'm… '

'Normal?' he says roaring with laughter. I like that he assumes this so soon after meeting me.

'We were starting to question the boy's taste. I'll assume Jag has told you about the cake girl? His fiancée? Chay?'

'In passing.'

He leans into me. 'When she called off the engagement, we nearly threw a party. She is here today. She made the ridiculous cake in there. I swear, you could climb it and reach the moon.'

I laugh but try and steer him back.

'She's here?'

'With about five hundred others so I wouldn't worry. Look for the miserable one with the face like a codfish and a laugh like a dying parrot. She wasn't good for my Jag.' His attention is suddenly taken with someone behind me. 'Speak of the devil, why have you changed?'

I turn to see Jag approaching us, frustrated I didn't get to learn more about the mysterious Chay but also pleasantly distracted. I won't lie, usually I see Jag in scrubs and trainers so Jag in a dinner jacket is a good kind of different. He smiles but also looks similarly stressed that I seem to have entered into conversation with his father. Behind him is a younger woman dressed in a beautiful gold trouser suit, cradling a young child.

'I see you've met my father?' he says.

'Jag, that is no way to meet a beautiful young lady. Asha, tell him…'

'Dad, we've been looking for you everywhere.' She hits him playfully with her clutch then turns to me. 'I am the little sister, Emma. Lovely to meet you. And this is Zahra.' A little hand waves at me. Arjun giggles drunkenly but he's got brownie points from me for calling me young.

'Emma, you look stunning,' says Jag. 'Dad, you look drunk.' He slings an arm around his father's shoulder. 'You just disappeared from the room.'

'I'm preparing myself. I saw the table plan and they've got me next to your uncle's wife. I need the alcohol or I may have to drown myself in the dhal.'

Jag closes his eyes, slowly. I find it all incredibly endearing. His father rises from his stool and Asha steadies him.

'Jag, take Zahra and I'll take this old boozer.'

'Emma, it was my pleasure madam.' I giggle and he hugs me warmly. 'Asha, let's not cramp what little style he has. Where is your mother?' He links arms with his daughter and they totter towards the bar entrance.

'Is he alright?' I ask, watching as Zahra settles into his chest.

'Yes. I'm sorry. He's a character.'

'He was very charming.'

'It's just I'm ushering him around. I've also got two cousins who are at war with each other so I'm trying to separate them and Zahra isn't too well. It's all a little manic.'

I put a hand to the back of Zahra's neck, switching into doctor/parent mode. 'How old? She's a little warm.'

'She's three. Asha thinks it's teeth but she says her tummy hurts?'

I sit them down and hand Jag my drink. 'Down this.' He does as he's told. I grab his hand. 'Possibly the excitement of the day? She could just be overtired? We can keep an eye?'

He smiles knowing that my words have a calming effect. Seeing him in concerned cuddly uncle mode is also deeply adorable.

'Can you drown in dhal?' I ask.

'I guess if you were in a bathtub full of the stuff.'

'You're wearing a suit?'

'That I am. I was going to wear scrubs but Mum said it didn't go with the cake.'

'I've heard about this cake.'

He smiles at me and there's a moment between us, one that's becoming familiar. This feels like a date. We're all dressed up. No one's falling down stairs or throwing bottles around. There's even a man on the piano. Jag looks at me for a second longer.

'You really do look very beautiful,' he says.

'So do you. I mean handsome. Like nice to look at. You know?'

He laughs. 'Come on Doctor C, Little Z. Let's do this. You OK?'

I notice his black and gold brocade bow tie catching the light and I adjust it a little. 'We're golden,' I whisper.

'What was that?'

I shake my head. I put my hand out and he links his fingers into mine but then a cough. My eyes widen. It's deep, from the diaphragm. Zahra puts her hands over her mouth. I know this sound too well. A little person set to blow. I move my seat back so she'll aim for the floor but instead she turns from her uncle and throws up over most of my lap.

Jag's eyes read horror. I look up and laugh. 'And this is why we should wear scrubs, everywhere.'


'Are you alright my dear?' I'm stood in the bathroom of Jag's parents' room at The Dorchester. The taps are golden, literally, and the walls lined in marble. Now is the time for a selfie, a special one to send to Lucy as I am stood here in a crop top and petticoat about to be dressed in a sari. I've not had my belly button out since… never. While my sisters flaunted their stomachs in their teens and didn't mind a bikini, I was always the covered one-piece sister. But the only other option tonight was to wear my dress with a big giant circle of vomit in the middle, the shadow making it look like I'd wet myself. I'm not angry per se – kids choose their moments – but now I'm about to share an intimate moment with Jag's mother and sister which I really hadn't prepared myself for and this evening hasn't even started. I exit the bathroom quietly. Asha looks completely distraught.

'I am so so sorry. My husband is with the girls now in our room. I can't apologise enough. Here, I wore this earlier today. It's clean and non-vomity.'

I laugh it off. 'It's kind of an occupational hazard for me so please don't worry.'

Next to her is Jiya, Jag's mother, a vision in turquoise and silver. I see her give me the once over, holding a navy jewelled sari in her hands.

'Turn around for me my dear.' I don't really know what they're doing but they tuck material into the petticoat and encourage me to spin. I do as I'm told and see Jiya arrange pleats into the material and swathe lengths of it over my shoulder. She stands back to admire her work.

'That is a lovely colour on you,' she says.

I look in a mirror beside me, it's certainly different. 'I won't offend anyone dressed like this? Cultural appropriation and all?' I ask them.

Asha shakes her head. 'Nah, cultural appropriation would be if you went to a French wedding in a beret, holding a baguette. We're usually quite flattered when someone wants to play along. It's respectful. What do you think, Mum?'

Jiya eyes me curiously. 'Are you really a heart surgeon?' she asks.

'MUM!' replies Asha, aghast.

'I am.' I feel as if she is trying to catch me out. Would they have given their approval if I'd had another profession? What if he'd brought Lucy to this wedding?

'Please ignore my mother. She'd also like to know your monthly salary, your religious status and whether you're a virgin.'

Jiya hits her daughter around the head playfully.

'I am just curious. You're very young.'

'I'm thirty-five.'

Asha rolls her eyes. 'You're so nosey. The fact my daughter threw up on her and she's still here tells me everything I need to know.'

Jiya looks more thoughtful at this comment.

'Imagine if one of my girls threw up on Chay?'

Jiya laughs. 'She would have cried blue murder.'

That name, again. A knock on the door gets our attention and Asha goes to answer it. Jag stands there and steps back, a little bemused. He points at me.

'Are you OK?'

'Yes?' I reply.

'Mum, Asha – go, aunties are asking about us. I'll take it from here.'

They nod and take their leave while Jag and I stand here. He still looks confused.

'Was my mother alright? Was she horrendous?'

'She asked me about my intentions and showed me your naked baby pictures.'

'She did?'

'No.'

'You still look amazing.'

I blush. 'It's actually very comfortable.'

'I've heard that.'

He takes my hand, leads me out of the room and we walk along the elaborate, carpeted corridors to the lift.

'So how is this rating compared to our other dates?' he asks.

'I feel like our siblings are conspiring against us.'

He laughs nervously. It's a bright lift covered in etched mirrors and visions of us from every angle. I've not seen myself in such detail. I smile. He could bring me to the fanciest hotel in London or feed me hummus next to a river and I think I'd still get that same feeling standing next to him. There is silence as we think about what to say next to each other but he beats me to it.

'I need to do something because later won't be the right time…'

And that's when he leans over, cups my cheek and kisses me. And I'm not sure why but this time it feels right. I can't breathe for the intimacy, the feeling of his breath near mine, the gentle way with which his lips melt into mine. It's not a long, drawn out kiss. It's short but damn near perfect. The lift doors open. And it's a small magical moment as he takes my hand, the biggest of grins on his face and weaves his fingers into mine leading me through to the ballroom: a wondrous space of high ceilings, ornate decor, and sparkling floral arches. We hear drums and the loud blare of music. I stand there to soak it all in, silent. He just kissed me. On the lips. And this is unlike any wedding I've seen in my life. The hum and volume of guests in rainbow coloured saris. The tables laid out with towering centrepieces and fragrant curries. There are turbaned men carrying drums. And smoke. And a groom whose contacts do make him look like he has a thyroid condition. But I smile, broadly. In shock, in surprise? I don't really know anymore but Jag's father was right. That is one big fucking cake.

*

*Driver Confirmed and En Route*
*Malik 4.8\* Toyota Prius*

By the end of the evening, all that magic and drumming has taken its toll. I learned how to bhangra tonight. My frame of dance reference is tiny but there were lots of shoulders and joyous arms. I didn't quite get the rhythm so I was aware I looked like MC Hammer shimmying up and down like a crab but I didn't care. I absorbed all that joy, that exuberance and did what Lucy has been trying to get me to do for two years. However, it's quite evident my feet are not made for such levels of energetic dance so now I'm standing on the carpeted floor without any shoes on, ready to make my way home. Jag was a magnificent date but he's tasked with looking after older relatives so I won't draw this out. He didn't kiss me again after the lift. But we danced. We laughed over paneer, cake and sweets. I shimmied with his father who was keen on an underarm twirl and I danced randomly with an uncle. Was he an uncle? The term seemed to be bandied around for anyone over the age of fifty. I met at least twenty-two of them tonight, many of whom had questions about the health of their hearts.

I look at my phone and prop myself against a hidden alcove in the corridor. I take another selfie for Lucy who is ecstatic I am in a sari and shared the joy on our sister group chat. I have time to say my goodbyes and I think someone told me there are favours, which I anticipate will be huge given the general grandeur of the wedding.

'Did you bring her here to just embarrass me?'

The voice comes from halfway down the corridor. I glance out and see a light blue jewelled dress. I see Jag's figure next to her and take a step back.

'We're not even together, Chay.'

I am glued to the spot.

'Yeah but you knew I'd be here. It's disrespectful. It's all my mother can talk about. Jag's here with his new girlfriend. And she's white and she's a doctor.'

'Don't be a bitch.'

'I didn't realise you were in the market for old divorcees with kids.'

'Where is this coming from? You dumped me.'

'And, your point? Is she your girlfriend?'

'Well, no… but…'

And just like that, a heart which had previously been reset and glowing dims a little. All the arteries that were feeding it freeze. I know what's happening. I know without even having to look. But still, I peer around the corner. She's kissing him. I don't want to know what he's doing. Is he kissing her back? Is he drunk? Maybe that's why he kissed me.

A heart can beat millions and millions of times throughout your lifetime. Yet you can die from a broken heart. The symptoms are similar to a heart attack but it comes from a rush of emotion or hormone rushing through your bloodstream. But I won't allow mine to break. Not again. My feet still sore and aching from dancing, I grab my shoes and tiptoe towards a side door that leads to the foyer. I won't wait for Malik. A man in a hat opens the door for me.

'Evening madam. That's a really lovely dress.'

I don't reply. I just jump into a black cab and ask him to take me home.

# Chapter Fifteen

671 days since Lucy nearly pushed
Simon down a flight of stairs

*I tried looking for you but I couldn't find you after the wedding? Is everything alright?*

*Emma?*

*Did you make it home OK?*

*We have your dress. Asha got it dry cleaned.*

*Please could you just let me know you're safe.*

I study all my messages over my cup of tea. I haven't opened them for the last week. It was cruel perhaps but what I saw in that hotel corridor stirred up too much emotion. It was better to avoid it and not let it swell to the surface. It was the best sort of heart surgery, wrapping mine up so tightly that I couldn't break. I spoke to no one about it. Not a sister nor secretary. I concentrated on telling them the positives from that evening, I learned how to bhangra and I had the most amazing aubergine masala I ever tasted. Naturally, Lucy had to make a dick joke about that.

'When are Simon and the girls getting here?' Beth's head peeks around the corner along with little Joe. He wears one of those fluffy aviator hats that make me want to eat his gorgeous face. He's recently entered the world of child modelling which I am not surprised about. I like that it's given Beth a spring in her step and she gets nappies as payment. He giggles and I cave, pretending to eat one of his cheeks.

'Twenty minutes ago.' I tell Beth.

She pulls a face at me. It's been a weekend of logistical negotiations as I've allowed Simon to have the girls to attend his mother's birthday lunch. We play around with our allotted daughter time for special occasions and such but, as you can imagine, having to communicate the changes always adds stress to our already fraught relationship. He's late which means we'll have to dash for the Tube as we have plans to catch Lucy performing some gig in a London park as part of a *Frozen* Elsa competition. It's a big deal apparently, she can win money and a contract so we're going to show our support and cheer the loudest for her.

I didn't ask Simon about his lunch plans but I predict that he took them to a bistro. He'd have had a steak and his mother would have had some fish mornay dish. I remember those dinners well as I was always in charge of the cake. Linda didn't like chocolate. She liked a plain sponge with marzipan as thick as my thumb. We'd always give her bath salts and book tokens and Simon would write a card and sign it off with just his name. No kisses, no personal message, no hint of affection. I'd compensate by scribbling my name next to a message I didn't quite mean.

'Oh,' mumbles Beth, swaying with Joe in her arms as she looks out the window at the car pulling up. 'I've not seen her in a while.'

I stand up from my armchair, glancing at Simon's Range Rover parked outside and the girls sifting through his boot to get their belongings. Beside the car is Linda Chadwick, Simon's mother, glancing up at the house. She catches me at the window and waves. I haven't seen her for a while now either. I didn't get Christmas cards from her, or presents, and any communication was always made via the girls or Simon himself. She looks a slight figure standing there on the pavement, like she's lost weight, clutching her handbag tightly. I wave back.

'She's coming in, isn't she?'

'Yep. Grin and clench, girl,' Beth says.

I see the girls skip up the stairs and knock the door loudly. Iris' voice echoes down the letterbox.

'We're home!' I like that they still call this place their home. I answer it and the girls fall into my arms. They see Aunty Beth and go in to coo at their cousin. Simon stands there holding several bags, coats and what looks like a school sports kit he's expecting me to launder. The changeover period would be a lot easier if he just stuffed everything in one giant shopping bag but the joy of divorce is that I don't need to lecture him about his lack of domestic organisation.

'You had a baby?' he gestures to Beth.

'I did.' Beth is not Lucy or Meg, she's more civil to Simon but that's just her, she wouldn't say boo to a goose.

'Congratulations.'

His mother stands behind him, as if Simon is shielding her.

'Linda, it's been a while. Happy birthday.'

She barges past her son and embraces me tightly. 'Emma, you look well, really well.' I'm a little unnerved by the warm welcome but to be fair, this woman has always been nice to me. She's a good grandparent and I don't bear her ill will. But she looks like she wants to say something out loud. I need to gloss over this awkward silence.

'Did you have a nice meal?'

Violet skips up to me. 'We went for Chinese food. I ate four spring rolls.'

'Did you? That's exciting. Did Granny Linda have a birthday cake too?'

'Susie made a chocolate one.'

I smile to myself. Linda wouldn't have appreciated the cake or the Chinese either, she's a food xenophobe which drives Simon crazy but it made her easy to cook for. Roast dinners and sausage and mash all the way. I am strangely calm that Susie was there but the mention of her name seems to get Linda's heckles up.

'That is a bonny baby. Are you Meg?'

Beth looks concerned that she's been confused for a sister six years her senior.

'I'm Beth. Nice to see you again, Mrs Chadwick. I think the last time was Violet's christening?'

Linda nods and turns to my girls. 'Now Iris, Violet... come and give your granny big hugs and I'll see you very soon.' My daughters wrap themselves around her lower half and then head to their father.

'I'll see you next Tuesday,' I say to Simon, still smiling that he hasn't worked it out yet.

'Bye sweeties,' he says. They bundle themselves over into their father's arms and I see him close his eyes at saying goodbye. It may be the only time I ever see him express any form of tenderness but I never doubt its sincerity. Beth senses there is a conversation to follow and ushers the children through to the living room.

'I need to ask you a question, Emma,' says Linda. 'Have you met Susie?'

'Not officially.'

'And what about young—'

Simon interrupts. 'Mum, we really must be going.'

She looks shocked to have been interrupted.

'Oliver? I haven't met him either,' I say.

Linda appears startled that I know who he is. 'I met him today,' she says, aggrieved.

I look over at Simon. I can get why he didn't tell me but he didn't tell his own mother that she had another grandchild? That boy is four years old. Four years of life that she's missed out on. So he decided to wheel him out on Linda's birthday? Maybe he forgot to buy her a present.

'Are you implying that I should have told you?' I ask Linda, given that she's chosen to air her annoyance with me.

'No, I wanted to apologise to you in person.'

Simon shakes his head. 'Mum…'

She puts a finger up to him. 'You deserved better. I am sorry my son treated you so despicably.'

I freeze. Simon doesn't reply, turning and walking back to his car, the anger fuming off him. Linda must have been sat in a restaurant not of her choosing, being force-fed crispy duck, pancakes and revelations. Topped off with a birthday cake without marzipan. *This is my girlfriend, she is pregnant and this is my son who was born when I was still married to my ex-wife.* She would have sat there, trying to work out the timelines and unravel all his lies. *Happy birthday, Mum.*

'Linda, I don't know what to say. You didn't have to say that at all…'

'I did.'

'Do you want to come in for a cup of tea?'

Simon starts the engine of his car. She turns to glare at him.

'Maybe another time?'

'Do you still have my number? You can ring me any time you want.'

She nods, takes a deep breath and heads to the car. If he drives off now and leaves his own mother here then I will throw a brick through his window. I stand at the door and watch as Simon shouts at her as she enters the car and she replies with equal force and volume. He speeds off. I run into the living room where Joe is lying on a rug and Iris blows raspberries on to his stomach. Beth stands at the window looking concerned.

'Did you really go for a Chinese?'

Iris nods. 'I ate a whole plate of crispy seaweed, it all got stuck in my teeth.'

'Was it alright? With everyone there?'

Iris shrugs. 'I guess. Oliver was there too. Apparently, we need to call him our brother now…' Beth looks at me with wide eyes. '…which is weird because he's Susie's son and Susie is just Daddy's friend. Susie's pregnant as well, she's going to have a baby soon, Aunty Beth. But he won't be as cute as Joe,' Iris continues.

I pause for a moment to register this. This unborn baby is another boy. My girls have no idea about the parentage of these children. I have to ask. I take a deep breath.

'Who is Oliver's daddy?'

Violet looks up at me. 'We haven't met him yet.'

Beth looks over at me. All this drama, all these lies and loose threads. I have no idea what to do so I hold Violet close to me and watch as Joe's giggles fill the air. I should tell them. I don't want these girls to be fed the same lies that I have been. I want them to be raised with at least a modicum of honesty from my end. But maybe not now.

'Who wants to go watch Aunty Lucy be Elsa?' I say.

Everyone throws their hands up in the air.


What is the collective noun for a group of Elsas? I feel it should be snow-based: a flurry or an avalanche? I've never seen so much peroxide hair in one place. They all come in a variety of shapes, sizes, ages and heights. One looks like she's wearing a bejewelled net curtain and another has her own dry ice. We can't see Lucy but Joe is asleep in his pram and the girls are content in this play area that has face painters and soft play. Beth and I perch on a bench, slightly out of breath, truth be told, from having to carry the pram up and down flights of stairs on the Tube. We cradle overpriced hot chocolates and she rests her head on my shoulder.

'Is this my life now? Events like these?' she ponders, as we watch a dad walk past with his tantrumming son in a fireman's hold. Beth does this a lot, comparing her baby life to the one she had before.

Before Joe, she and Will would have been in this park at a gig, getting drunk and trading in hot beverages for cans of BrewDog.

'Kinda.'

'How bleak.'

'Charming.'

'How do you do it?'

'Always have change, baby wipes and then just fill them with sugar so they have enough energy to keep going.'

She laughs. A girl walks past with a giant cuddly Sven the reindeer that's bigger than her, the dusty pink glow of candy floss around her lips. Next to us, children charge around a light blue bouncy castle like they're maniacs in a padded cell.

'And avoid bouncy castles and trampolines. Our pelvic floors are not what they were. Meg once had to leave a barbeque because she peed herself on a trampoline. I didn't tell you that.'

She giggles. 'How are you about what happened earlier?'

'I have no idea. Those girls need to know who Susie is. But he's leaving me to have that conversation with them and that's not fair.'

Beth seems surprised. 'Good for you. Let him do his own dirty work. Do you think Linda is alright?'

'Who knows?' I have a fleeting moment thinking of them fighting in that car. I hope he wasn't a complete shit to her. 'And Will, how are things with Will?'

She takes a big sip of her hot chocolate and stares intently at Joe. 'He's still living with his brother.'

'And he's left you with Joe. I still don't think that's very fair.'

She pauses for a moment. 'It's more than that, Ems. He's really been suffering.'

I open my eyes in disbelief at the suggestion.

'I don't know. I think we talk about how hard motherhood is but actually with the pressure of being a father and the long hours at work, he's not been coping. He felt like he was failing us.'

'How?'

'We live in a two bedroom flat. It's London prices and job competition. I think we both thought this would be different. We'd be Instacool in matching clothes and have our shit together.'

'You do have your shit together.'

She gives me a look like I may be sugar coating the issue.

'You mean I look like shit, sis. I eat literally everything. I've gone up two dress sizes. I have no idea when and if I am going back to work. I don't even know if Joe likes me or not.'

'Of course he likes you. You're his mother.'

'Do you like our mother?' she asks.

'Are you nagging him about his life choices with rude and cutting remarks?'

She narrows her eyes at my sarcasm. Joe stirs. He smiles when he sees Beth.

'See? He does like you.' I don't add that I think that was just wind.

She pulls a face at him and digs through a change bag. It's a big mess of receipts, half-eaten snacks, toys and odd-sized nappies. It's like her school bag from her teenage years. She does have dark circles under her eyes, and her hair might not have been washed in a few days but you only have to look at the baby to see how happy and loved he is.

'So, what are you going to do?'

'Give Will some time, space to sort his head. It's all I can do really?'

I grip Beth's hand tightly. Most wouldn't have the faith or patience but maybe that's what separates her from the pack; she is quietly sensitive and places such value on loyalty to those she loves.

'Can I say something, B?'

She nods, using her sleeve to wipe at Joe's mouth when she can't find a muslin.

'At your party, the last thing Will said to me before he left was how much he loved you and Joe. I don't think he's a bad person. He's not a Simon at least.'

Beth looks at me. As the other sisters have been less kindly about Will's abandonment, it's as if she's waiting for the punch line.

'Give him until Christmas. But promise me you won't let him mess around with your feelings. This is about you, too. Let what I went through be an example to you, at least. Don't be a martyr for something not worth your salt.'

She throws an arm around me. 'Christmas. I promise. But I mean, look at you now. Even after all you went through, you have Jag? You never told us how that wedding went?'

I sip my hot chocolate so I don't have to answer.

'Lucy said you came home without your shoes on which is code for saying you slept with him and had to depart quietly so you wouldn't wake him.'

She's trying to goad me into revealing some details and I look over at her doleful expression. Joe was lucky to inherent her twinkling cat eyes. I almost feel a need to divulge so she doesn't feel like the odd sister out.

'I took my shoes off because they hurt,' I reply. 'And you're right, I didn't want to make a sound because I'd just caught Jag snogging his ex-girlfriend outside the wedding in a corridor.'

She cups her hands to her mouth. 'Oh Ems, why didn't you say?'

Because I didn't want to take that bath of shame again. Look at Emma, swan diving into new love dressed in an actual sari. And there she, is belly flopping into the depths yet again.

'I was humiliated… again. I went to a lot of trouble. I let his niece throw up on me. It felt special and then just like that, a punch to the gut.'

Beth grimaces. 'I'm sorry he wasn't who you thought he might be.'

I shrug my shoulders. 'Meh, he was younger than me, too trendy. Or maybe it's just me. Maybe I am the worst judge of character in the world.'

'Bullshit. You're great. His loss completely.'

'Back to being a single Pringle,' I say.

'Single Pringles together.'

We look into the distance and I let her rest her head on my shoulder as Joe watches us curiously. I have visions of sitting on the stairs at our family home, one step from the bottom and helping her do her laces. *I'm here, sis. Whatever happens.* This is when it pays to be the older sister. I think back to when Meg was worrying that her problems with Danny and her marriage were irreparable. I told her if that were the case, she could move back down south and I'd buy us a big mansion for us to all live together in like some sitcom family. Or convert my loft. I think about all the wine we could drink, the epic fights we would have over moisturiser and all our kids eating spaghetti around my dining table. Even though it's a got a cult commune feel to it, I don't think I'd mind.

In front of our bench, an Elsa walks past. Her dress is so sheer that she's unaware that all and sundry can see a black thong showing through. A voice booms through the PA above a stage in front of us. Small children run towards the front and my daughters filter back towards us. Violet's face is completely covered in silver glitter that will stick to my bathtub for days. Which of you Elsas are responsible for this? I will hunt you down.

'Are you ready, Dukes Meadow?!'

Beth and I look at each other in bemusement.

'Our finalists today have come from all over London for our *Frozen* Fiesta. They will be marked on costume, hair, song and dance. Won't you give them your warmest applause?'

My girls – who have already had hot chocolates, sweet cones and mini doughnuts – dance around and scream, a little deranged. Beth looks at them, confused. Dear sister, you thought teething and exploding nappies was bad; you have the next stage to look forward to.

'And our first Elsa today is Nadia and she is from Sutton.'

Beth and I clap as a girl skips on and throws handfuls of glitter over the stage. Nice try but her dress is completely the wrong colour. The second Elsa is obviously wearing a bad wig and number three is thong Elsa. The dads seem appreciative of her.

'And next we have Lucy from Richmond.'

My girls stand on the bench to get a better view and we cheer manically. Beth whistles. Lucy seems to have a partner. Oh, it's Darren from the party dressed as Olaf. I hope his rash cleared up. She pretends to pull his nose off and there's a cute role-play thing going on that makes everyone laugh. She does know how to work a crowd, eh? I chuckle under my breath and take some photos for the sister group chat. My daughters are entranced. *I save lives, kids. I can take an appendix out or insert a chest tube if needed but it means nothing.* Violet looks like she could explode from the pride at seeing her aunty up there. Lucy pirouettes and the chiffon of her dress swirls on the stage. Beth and I 'oooooh' in reply. She takes her leave stage right.

'Isn't that Britney Spears from the party?' Beth asks.

'Yes. And between you and me, I think he has a little crush on our sister.'

Beth and I look at each other and smile. Good luck with that Olaf.

'She has a flair for the dramatic, our sister… eh?' I say.

'But she does it so well. Where are the Annas?'

I look around. She's right. There are men as reindeer and in traditional looking Nordic outfits but no Anna, the other, arguably better, sister in that film.

'You mean the forgotten sister who's plucky and full of goodness but takes a back seat so her other sister can do cool things with the snow?' I say with wide eyes. Beth laughs heartily and buries her head into me again.

Now it's Elsa singing time. They've brought out thong Elsa and I know now why she's wearing a thong: to take away from the fact she sings like a deaf crow. Let it go, love.

'Oh, Emma? Fancy seeing you here?' I turn and next to me is Leo.

'Leo?' I go to kiss his cheek. 'You know Beth…'

He waves. The last time Beth saw Leo was as randy Batman so she looks upon him curiously.

'Lucy mentioned this at the school gate so I thought I'd bring the kids. She's definitely top three, right?'

'You haven't seen her dance yet,' Beth says.

'No, but she looks great and she has an Olaf.'

'But the one at the end with the dodgy plait has silly string shooters coming out of her hands. Marks for innovation?'

I'm not entirely sure why Leo is here but I like the effect Lucy has had on him. He seems more relaxed, like he may be enjoying life again. In the back of my mind, I know this probably means they're still shagging but I won't bring it up now.

Lucy steps forward to the microphone. Can Lucy hold a tune? Yes, but when you've heard someone holding a tune for most of your life, the novelty wears off. She's doing her drama school thing where she's over-enunciating all her vowels. *Don't overdo it, Lucy.* Leo watches in awe. She finishes and does a flourish of a bow and looks over at us, breaking character with a manic thumbs up. However, as she turns she slips on what looks like a bit of silly string that came from the Elsa with the shooter hands. She falls clumsily on Olaf, her skirt up over her head. And if you thought thong Elsa was bad then you were mistaken. Because this Elsa is not wearing any knickers. None at all. Complete nether regions on show.

The crowd gasp. Those dads who were here for thong Elsa shift their attentions elsewhere. Beth and I look at each other, neither shocked nor horrified. And just when you thought that was it, Lucy gets up and has a go at the Elsa with the silly string. Olaf tries to get in the middle but because his costume is bulky, he manoeuvres like a sumo wrestler into Elsa in the wig. The wig goes flying. Another Elsa who's obviously wearing something from a cheap supermarket range breaks down into tears. I'm not sure who throws the first punch after that but I sit quietly watching it unfold, children crying, parents shouting obscenities on to the stage, the whine and crackle of a microphone getting kicked across the stage, a mist of glitter and fake snow in the air. Beth puts her head on my shoulder and we watch Lucy pull someone's wig off and wave it in the air.

'Do you know that Elsa?' asks Beth.

'Never seen her before in my life.'


'Lucy, it was a children's event. Never mind that, you should generally always be wearing underwear.'

No one won the money and performance contract in the end after today's Frozen Fiesta Fracas. Probably rightly so. After a couple of men in Nordic dress split up the warring Elsas and the St John Ambulance tended to the cuts and bruises, the Elsas were called out onto the stage to apologise to the crowd and be told the prize money was being donated to charity. Lucy got a verbal caution from a policeman on duty there but also got two telephone numbers from audience members, so not a complete loss for her. She walks ahead of me now with the girls as we trek home. Naturally, she didn't bring a change of clothes so it also made for an entertaining ride home on the Tube.

'Isn't your foof cold if you don't wear pants?' asks Iris.

Beth nods and looks at Lucy. It's a valid question, no one likes a cold foof.

'I was in a rush this morning,' she explains.

'If you're in a rush, you forget your phone, not your pants,' my eldest explains and I laugh so hard that my breath fogs the air.

'Is Olaf OK?' I ask. 'We should have invited him round?'

'He's fine. He had another gig this evening. He's being Spiderman in Wandsworth.'

'He could have borrowed that girl's silly string.' Beth giggles.

Lucy gives her an evil. 'All tricks and gimmicks. And I know that Elsa, she doesn't just do kids' parties dressed like that if you know what I mean? She likes a bit of snow on her.'

Beth and I know exactly what she means, but I cock my head to one side to let her know she has my daughter's hands in hers.

'And Leo. You invited Leo today?'

'He was there?' she says, looking interested.

'I thought you told me you weren't going after school run dads anymore?'

'I like the school run dads. They're more grateful for the attention.'

'Why are you saying dads in plural?' Please don't be shagging multiple dads, Lucy.

Beth glances upon the two of us. Don't start again. Not in the cold when one of us isn't wearing knickers.

I suddenly bump into Iris, who stops in her tracks.

'Mummy, there's someone at our front door!' exclaims Violet.

Lucy is saved my lecture for now. All three of us sisters look up but the street light doesn't quite let us see this person's face. I jog up to greet them.

'Linda?'

I smile to see her, the girls running past me to say hello and into her arms.

'Granny Linda! Why are you here?' asks Violet.

'I thought you weren't in.'

Lucy catches up, looking suspiciously at her with a snarl. She looks back at Beth to join in so I'll have some girl gang muscle to prop me up. *You can ram her with the buggy and I'll summon up some snow.*

'We weren't. Why are you here?' Lucy asks. I put an arm to her to try and calm her down, realising she wasn't here this morning.

'You mentioned a cup of tea,' she tells me.

She looks at me with sad eyes. I go to approach her but Lucy is quick to get in between us. We don't fraternise with the enemy, sis. She turns her back to her.

'There's a perfectly good Costa five minutes down the road, she can get her tea there.'

But Beth rolls past us with Joe in his buggy and I see her studying Linda's face. It's often the way: Lucy gesticulating with wild anger in a corner but Beth is different in her approach, dripping in empathy, knowing when someone is hurt and withdrawn.

'You should come in, Linda,' she says. Lucy looks surprised. Beth turns to me. 'We haven't had dinner. She could join us for dinner?'

I can see Linda's eyes glazing over. I mean I was just up for tea but I see why Beth does this. It's her birthday for a start but there's something about Linda's expression that reads loneliness and Beth knows all too well how that feels at the minute. My heart hurts to see my sister respond so openly to her. I nod my head.

'Come in,' I say. I realise there's a conversation we need to finish having, the need to make some sort of amends. We all pile up the steps as Lucy glares at Beth who shakes her head at her.

'Come and see my science project, Granny... it's in the kitchen,' says Iris as she gets through the door, taking her hand and leading her through the house. I watch them tentatively. All the other girls (and Joe) are perched on the stairs, removing winter coats and shoes.

'That was the best day ever!' Violet proclaims. I worry if this means there was entertainment had from watching a real-life fight. 'Would you do my party, Aunty Lucy?'

'Anything for you, chicken nugget.'

She looks curiously at her. 'You and mummy like your food names.'

'We do. Anyway, talking of food, we all voted on the Tube and we all want Domino's for dinner, Mum,' Lucy says in my direction. Beth looks up and nods.

Violet giggles. 'She's not your mummy.'

'We wish she was… ' says Lucy.

I laugh. Violet scurries away to find her grandmother and I spy them hugging through the kitchen door. I hope Linda won't mind a stuffed crust.

'Is that a good idea?' Lucy asks Beth.

'You weren't here this morning, she was pretty cut up. Give her a break,' says Beth.

'I'll break her legs if she's here to cause a scene.'

'Lucy, she's like seventy,' Beth retorts in horror.

'Seventy three,' I add, horrified but secretly curious as to how Lucy would beat up an OAP in my house.

'Can I lick her garlic bread before I give it to her?'

'No, you can't,' I reply.

She pouts in disappointment, making Joe laugh.

'They like to spoil my fun, JoeJoe. You know I'm looking out for you both, right? You're both so civil and want to play nice but sometimes, you need someone with a bit of bitch fire for when it gets ugly. This is when I need Meg.'

I look through the kitchen door again to hear peals of laughter.

'And what sort of merry hell is Linda going to unleash on us?'

'I just don't trust someone who spawned something as horrific as Simon.'

'Mum spawned you. I trust her,' adds Beth.

'Such a cow,' she replies.

We turn to face Lucy, sat on the fifth step up. *Oh, Elsa. What a sister you are. The one we'd all call if we woke up next to a dead prostitute or got our tangas in a twist. But you're a very good Elsa. I'm also really glad I'm not your mother.* She sees us gazing and flashes us, laughing.

'Put your bloody minge away,' Beth pleads, shielding Joe's eyes.

'Never.'

'That's how you catch stuff,' I tell her.

'That's how you catch dick.'

'You're awful.'

'It's why you all love me.'

We don't reply.

# Chapter Sixteen

679 days since Meg told me
I was better than Simon/that wanker

'Well, the X-ray looks good, ECG readings are also stable. Drugs are working, let's see you in six months?'

Lewis sits in a chair opposite in an electric blue dinosaur hoodie but this isn't the lad who was huddled in the floor of my kitchen a month ago. He's back in the room with all the warmth and energy that I always associated with him. His parents are with him and there is something about them that makes me jealous, the ease with which they both sit here in each other's company without animosity or tension. I guess not all marriages fracture so violently. I feel like I need to ask them for tips. When the tide turned in my relationship, it felt like a tsunami completely submerging me.

'OK. How's Jag?' Lewis asks, hopefully.

His parents look confused.

'Last time Lewis was here, we bumped into a man I was dating…'

'Was? What happened? He seemed nice?' he enquires sadly.

'Lewis! We spoke about being nosey. I'm so sorry Doctor C,' exclaims his dad.

'It's fine. It just wasn't meant to be.'

'My dad has a brother who's single. He's a tree surgeon?'

I laugh, heartily to his parents' relief. I think about Lucy and all the tree-based sex jokes she could make about stumps and wood.

'You are sweet to think of me but I am going to stay single for a while.'

Lewis pouts for a moment. 'Well, his name is Adam and he's on Facebook, isn't he Dad?'

Mum shakes her head at me. 'We are so sorry.'

'Never apologise to me about this one. Get to reception and we'll book you in for that review.'

I'm rewarded with a Lewis hug.

*Look after yourself, kid.* I let them take their leave with a nurse and see Maddie stood at the door of the room. It's one of those days where paperwork has caught up on both of us so she's staying longer to assist.

'How is Lewis?' she asks.

'Cheeky as ever.'

'And all the stuff about his parents?'

'Sorted, I think. Or at least they've found a way for it to work. Look at them, you wouldn't know they're divorced, eh?'

I shake my head as we see them head for the main entrance, still a family, still connected, just people trying to get along. Can it really be that simple? Maddie and I head for a lift.

'It's just easier to be divorced these days,' Maddie adds. 'Only twenty years ago, it was a dirty word. Divorce was acrimonious and filled with hate. Now people are braver when they know their relationships aren't working. They don't stay in them, unhappy. They move on. Life is too short.'

I study Maddie's face. 'You sounded like Oprah there for a second.'

'That was actually off *Loose Women*.'

We both laugh. She grabs my arm and gives me a side hug.

'And why didn't you tell me about Jag?'

'Beth?'

'Lucy, who heard it from Beth.'

The protective huddle have all been chatting, I see.

'I mean I officially hate him now. If I see him in the cafeteria, I'll throw coffee at him,' she says.

'Don't do that. The burns unit is busy enough as it is.'

I see the guilt in her face. She set us up, she tried to make this happen but none of this is her fault. She was just trying to get me to dip my toes in the dating waters again. I hug her, letting her know none of this is on her. On paper, he was a safe bet. But then on paper I guess everyone is the best version of themselves. Nowhere on paper do I have to say that I'm a bit of a dweeb, have an irrational fear of pigeons and am wildly insecure.

When we get to the top floor of the hospital, there's a steely quiet punctuated by empty offices and the hum of everyone's computers on sleep mode. It's how Maddie and I like things. It's calm and we can get the best, non-stained mugs in the kitchen and scavenge the fridge for good snacks.

'Tea?' she asks.

'Always.'

I head for my office. Sometimes Dan Carver's wife makes cake and leaves it there for everyone to help themselves. I hope she's made cake. I better check in on the girls. And think about what train I should aim to get home. I turn the corner. But there's a figure stood by my door, silent. I look up. Oh. You.

'Emma?'

I nod. 'You're Susie.'

'I am.'

I have no reaction. I exhale deeply and just try and compose myself. This is how people get killed. Is she here to kill me? However, the expression on her face is different to the one I'd seen in the M&S Food Hall that day. None of that hatred but more a look of resignation, of fatigue.

'Were you just headed home?'

She's in light pink scrubs with a large padded coat over the top, a few lanyards around her neck, and her hair pulled back from her face. She's very pretty, dusky blonde hair, with clear skin and pale blue eyes. She leans against the door frame and instinct takes over.

'You look knackered. Come in. Have a seat.'

I'm not sure why I am encouraging her to stay, but she obviously came here for a reason and I think she may be too pregnant to actually kill me. I unlock the office door and she waddles in and sits in front of my desk where I normally consult patients.

'That day at the M&S, that was you, wasn't it?' she asks.

'It was.'

Was that all she wanted to know? Or maybe she's here to parade herself in front of me. Look at me carrying your ex-husband's baby. I'm going to be a stepmother to your girls and they will like me more.

'How far along are you?' I ask, not knowing what else to say.

'Thirty-six weeks. Today was my last day.'

'My girls tell me it's another boy.'

'It is.'

She carries her bump neatly to the front, not all around her hips and backside like I did. She adjusts herself in her seat.

'I'm sorry, Susie. I don't know why you're here… Did Simon send you?'

'Oh god, no. It's just…'

And that's when her eyes glaze over and she struggles to hold in the tears. I hand her the box of tissues from my desk and she takes one. She was sleeping with my husband when I was still married to him. I should feel nothing for her but spite. However, I also know that expression. That one where you realise you've been totally duped, of feeling lost and broken.

'You'll never guess what? Someone left some Hobnobs!' I look up as Maddie dances into my office, holding biscuits aloft. She spies Susie and then stops. 'Emma?' she asks. I look at her pleadingly. *The girl is broken. Give her a minute. I mean, leave the biscuits, but I'm OK.* I nod reassuringly to her as she puts a mug of tea down on my desk, eyeing Susie up.

'I'll just be outside if you need me.' She edges away but leaves the door open and I see her hovering. Susie obviously knows she's a marked woman and proceeds in whispers through her tears.

'In the past weeks, some things have unravelled. Things that Simon has said to me, about you, about your marriage. We had an epic row last night about it all, his mother hates me. So I guess I just needed to hear it from the horse's mouth.'

She's referred to me as a horse but I'll forgive her for the moment. I respond with a furrowed brow.

'When did you separate? Officially?' she asks.

'I asked him to leave on Christmas Day 2017.'

She catches her breath a little.

'He told me you weren't together at that point. That you were separated but living together for the sake of the girls.'

I laugh under my breath, she's right, technically, but it would have been nice to have been informed by Simon that that was the official arrangement while I was trying to flog our dying marriage.

'What else did he say?' I ask.

'He said that if you ever found out about Oliver then you'd ruin him and take his girls and all his money. He said you called my son a bastard.'

'I found out about Oliver at a parents' evening, about six weeks ago.'

Her tears flow freely now.

'Linda. When did Linda know about you?' I ask.

'I was introduced as a girlfriend right after your decree nisi went through. But we always kept Oliver from her.'

'Why?'

'Simon told me to. He said you had this fierce divorce lawyer who'd jeopardise access to your girls if anyone knew about him…'

The fiercest thing about George were the patterns in his knitwear.

'So you kept that poor boy a secret?'

I don't think my sanctimony sits well with her. I guess it's already dawned on her that she abetted the situation and allowed Simon to control what the world saw of this boy. Her face reads regret.

'He lied to both of us,' I say. We should sit here and possibly link hands that we are joined by this tragedy but I don't know what to say to her. Apologies feel a little misplaced.

'What did he say about our marriage then?'

'He said it was all for show. That you weren't sleeping together, that you'd fallen out of love.'

To hear those words out loud, even now, feels like a barb in my side. Were we ever in love? Maybe he never really loved me and needed something more. Something like the girl sat right in front of me. I can't respond to anything she's just said because we literally had sex the night before I kicked him out and she doesn't need to hear that. Even just piecing this all together is sad enough for her.

'Where are you living at the moment?'

'Ollie and I have a small house in Brentford. Simon's going to sell his flat and we'll look for somewhere together. I think…'

Is that what he told her? This girl is not me and her experience is not mine but every ounce of me wants me to tell her, *Run. Run as fast as you can from that man.*

'Is that what you want?'

'I can't process anything right now. I just can't believe he lied, to me, his mother. I'm so sorry because he made you out to be this horrible controlling bitch and all the while…'

'It was him?'

As awful as I feel, it dawns on me that all this time, she was the other woman. She lived off false promises and under some veil of secrecy. In the competition of who has it worse at the moment then I think she may just have inched it.

'Can I ask a question…? Has he proposed? What are your plans?'

'I don't know. He's not said much. I love him. I… I think he loves me too.'

'Is he faithful?' The words don't mean to slip out but it dawns on me that if things are unravelling then maybe we need to get that ball of string and just find the end bit, let her really work this out.

She looks horrified at me, standing up. 'Just because he was unfaithful to you, doesn't mean he'd do the same to me. He loves me.'

I let her think about those words. In just the last year of our relationship, I know of at least two other women Simon slept with who aren't Susie. One was a patient's family member. I'd put money on him currently shagging his lawyer. *If you're going to be cruel then I can lay out all those details for you here if you want and shatter all those illusions you have about this man.* But something holds me back. I'd just about freed myself from that man's quicksand, I don't need her dragging my ankles and pulling me down again.

'You should leave,' I tell her.

'I was going to.'

'Good luck.'

I don't want to be cruel and acerbic to a pregnant woman. Half of me is not shocked what Simon did. He blackened my name because it was the easier route. He didn't tell his mother because she would have hated him. He didn't tell Susie because he didn't want her to be the other woman. And I feel stupid, even more so than I ever did before because I helped him perpetuate that myth that he was this married surgeon with the perfect family.

Susie turns to leave, bending down to grab her bag. She rubs at the top corner of her bump and winces a bit. I pretend to pack my bag but watch her closely. She stops, using the back of a chair to steady herself. She drops her bag to the floor, her knuckles clenched white around the top of the seat. I rush over from behind my desk as she exhales loudly. Seriously?

'How long have you been having contractions?' I ask.

'Four hours,' she says, grabbing at my hand, her waters breaking all over my shoes.


'Yes, this is Dr Callaghan. I am up on Sky Level, I have a lady here in labour who needs transport over to St Thomas'.'

'Is she a child?' asks the voice on the phone.

'No, she's a pregnant woman.'

'I don't think I have a wheelchair big enough? Let me check.'

'She's not a whale, just bring what you have?'

The line goes quiet. I've moved Susie over to my sofa but she writhes around trying to get comfortable. Maddie is leaning over her and kneading her back. This man is never coming back. I hang up and try someone else.

'Who are you calling?' asks Susie.

'Simon?'

'NO! I don't want him here.'

My fingers hover over the phone. Simon could deal with this, he could take her away and leave me out of her drama but I see it in her eyes. She wants to get this baby out on her terms. She wants my help.

'Can you walk?' asks Maddie.

She screams as another contraction arrives.

'Deep breath in and slowly out the mouth, long exhalations,' I advise.

Susie gives me that look that I recognise all too well. *Don't be hitting me with your advice right now standing there pain-free.* I need to get her over the road and I sure as hell am not going to carry her there.

'Do you have any friends or colleagues that you want me to call?' Maddie asks. She can't answer. Maddie looks to me. 'Ring the ward, get them to send someone over.'

I ring a number, getting an engaged line. Maddie looks over at me, slightly horrified.

'Last time I checked,' says Susie through panicked breaths, 'you were a doctor.'

I give her a look. *You slept with my husband, you've ruined my suede shoes and now my sofa.* I know I took oaths and everything but she's very welcome to push that baby out on her own. I wind my mind back to the last time I delivered a baby. It was in medical school and it was done via caesarean section. All I have are blunt scissors and a stapler. Susie has turned around on the sofa, her arms clenched to the back cushions and her arse in the air. She bays in a low humming noise. Maddie doesn't know where to look.

'Emma, I think… I think I need to push…'

This is really happening, isn't it? I put the phone down and run to my sink to wash my hands.

'Maddie, just go downstairs and grab what you can. Gloves would be good, a nurse, towels?'

'Just hold it in, no? Until we can get someone here.'

We both look at her and I point towards the door.

'I'm sorry.' Susie is sobbing at this point. Fully sobbing. 'I shouldn't have come here.'

I go prop her up so she's sitting on the edge of the sofa. Taking off her trousers and underwear, I examine her. I don't usually swear but fuck, she's eight centimetres dilated.

'Well you're here now. It could be worse.'

'How could this be worse?'

'You could be on the Tube?'

She fake laughs.

'You don't need to push, one more contraction to dilate you fully. How did you not know you were in labour?'

'I was distracted with work. I thought it was Braxton Hicks? I'm not due for another month.'

She grabs on to my shoulders and sobs quietly into them.

'I really hate you,' she says through gritted teeth, almost laughing.

'The feeling is mutual?'

She hugs me tightly and bears down on me. I push back. It's kind of a strange wrestling move. I look down at my sofa, covered in patches of blood and fluid. She sobs gently.

'I can't do this on my own.'

'You're not on your own,' I whisper.

I cup her face in my hands and there's a look between us. What the hell is happening here? Two figures appear at the door and I swerve around to see Maddie marching into action, tearing open packets of paper sheets and to my surprise, Jag. This isn't weird. He also looks in total shock, as do I.

'Maddie saw me and dragged me up here. Jesus, Emma…'

'I said a nurse, Maddie… he's an anaesthetist.'

'It was him or Mira the cleaner,' says Maddie, frantic.

'Prop her up, Jag. Just support her from the back.'

Jag does as he's told, trying to smile at me. Given there's going to be a baby in the room very soon, I don't engage.

'This is Susie Hunter, she's eight centimetres dilated and—'

But before I can continue, another contraction arrives. Her legs straighten and the release of pain into her system sees her cry out into the room. I know that sound. It's pure human emotion yet her cries seem tinged with sadness. I glove up and examine her again.

'That may have done it, Susie. Are you ready to push?'

She looks me straight in the eye. *You are going to deliver my baby, aren't you?* Both of us don't really know who this humiliates more. But very soon another little person will be in this room who doesn't know a thing, who was just a product of this whole big mess. Let's just get him out safely. She nods quietly. She tenses all her muscles and Jag hooks himself under her arms so she can bear back on him. I instruct Maddie to push back on her legs. I think back to when I pushed Violet out, that surge of adrenalin in your system to push against the pain and free yourself of it. Violet. She flew into the world. I remember Simon being at the end of the bed, watching her crown. What an utter bastard for bringing these children into this world and letting them suffer from all his bad behaviour.

'I can feel the head, Susie. Just wait for the next contraction and then another big push.'

Jag looks at me. I can't quite tell if he's thrilled or scared but he grabs her hand and puts his face next to her ear. He whispers something that I can't quite make out but it slows her breathing down and makes her close her eyes. I see the pain swell in her again and she leans forward. I push her thighs back to allow her to make that final push, guiding the head and shoulders out so the rest of her baby boy can appear. And when he does, it really is like magic. One moment he wasn't here and the next, there's a whole other human in the room. I sigh in relief and Susie sobs quietly into Maddie.

'Is he OK? Is he safe?'

I hold him in a cradle pose. Jag scrambles around wiping at the baby's nose and mouth and he then lets out a huge cry, his skin pinking up. He's a little on the small side but he's definitely got lungs. He stops for five seconds to look at me. *Hi , welcome.* His eyes are blue but there's a look there that's familiar. *Poor little sod, you've got his chin.* He starts crying again.

'It's a boy and first glances tell me he is fine.'

I hand him over to Susie who holds him to her chest and Maddie covers him with blankets. The cry is like music to my ears; I let it drown out the white noise in my head. *What have we done, Susie Hunter? What have we let this man do to us?* She says nothing but tears well up in our eyes as we look down at this squashed baby face looking up at us.

'We were called about a woman in labour?' pipes in a voice from the corridor. A midwife appears with a porter and a wheelchair. We all help Susie to the wheelchair.

'I can accompany you back over to the main hospital,' says Maddie, putting her coat over her.

Susie sits there shell-shocked, mute, her eyes glazed over. I bend down to place a blanket over her knees and follow her to the lift. The midwife and Maddie chatter inanely about the excitement and how well she's done but she can't think what to say. As they go into the lift, I share a last glance with her before the doors close. I stand there for a moment, the cry of that baby echoing in my ears.

Back in the office, Jag stands there, cleaning up the worst of the sheets and paper towels lying around the place. I stand at the doorway, shell-shocked.

'Emma, you're shaking.' He pulls a chair over and I collapse onto it. 'Can I make you a cup of tea? What do you need?'

'I should call the cleaners and explain to them what happened,' I say blankly.

Jag looks worried. 'Emma, really… that can wait? Are you OK? That must have been a shock. I can go back and get Maddie?'

I can't reply. I look down at my trembling hands, and get up to go to the sink and scrub them clean. Jag watches me closely as I let the water get hotter. He comes over and switches it off.

'Emma, I'm worried. Who was she? Why was she in your office?'

I feel my shoulders suddenly collapse with emotion. Jag pulls me in closely and embraces me tightly. Maybe this was it. The final shot sent to kill me. Maybe Simon sent her to give birth here and humiliate me further. Because that's all that soars through me right now. I feel like guiding that baby out of my husband's mistress and holding his little vulnerable body in my hands was the last straw. I can't seem to stop crying.

'Why are you here? This is madness,' I say, almost laughing.

'You're telling me. I was eating an egg sandwich in the corridor and bumped into Maddie and she was hysterical. She said there was a baby coming. And then… I can't believe you just delivered a baby!'

He stands there, confused. I have no idea what to say to him. I've not seen him since he kissed his ex-girlfriend. I thought we were done. But there is a way in which he cares, shows concern, that makes me not want to send him away.

'She was hospital staff? Do you know her?'

The problem with Jag is that he doesn't know about any of this drama in my life. We've shared brief chats, moments and hummus. We never really talked about real life. I thought it was escapism but really it was just glossing over a truth that has just walked into my office and slapped me right in the face. I wasn't enough. How could I ever be enough for someone else? I look up at him. Time to strip back that gloss, for you to see how chipped and weathered I really am.

'She's my husband's girlfriend,' I say laughing, almost in disbelief.

Jag's eyes widen in horror.

'She came here to have it out with me as it turns out my ex-husband was lying to us both. They have another son together called Oliver who would have been born when I was still very much married.' My bottom lip trembles. 'The truth is my husband had multiple affairs when I was married to him,' I carry on. 'She was one of many and I put up with it for far too many years. So, now it seems I am living the ultimate humiliation which is to deliver their babies.'

I don't know how I expect Jag to react. Permission to leave, young man. He did well, a perfect birthing partner, but I do not expect him to wade through this crap with me. I am a mess. Just when I think I have rebuilt and I am ready to take on the world again, Simon pulls that rug out from right under my feet. However, Jag doesn't react as such. He pulls the hair back from my face. He wipes tears that are halfway down my cheeks.

'Shush now. I think you're pretty awesome for doing what you did. A lesser woman would have turned her away.'

'It's in my job description. I did what any person would have done.'

'Or not… I don't know how to deliver a baby?'

'What medical school did you go to?'

He laughs and I respond with a stream of emotion that involves me wiping tears and snot away with my sleeve.

He pauses for a moment. 'Are you OK, Emma? I don't know what happened with us or at that wedding but I do care about you. I miss you.'

I look him in the eye. If my time with Simon has taught me anything, it's that I now confront everything, head on.

'I saw a kiss between you and your ex. At the wedding.' He looks horrified. 'I just have enough drama in my life. I didn't need more.'

'Hang on, I thought you left because of the fight?'

'The fight?'

'I mean, Chay stuck her tongue down my throat and then I pushed her away because it was horrible. And then she started yelling, called me a loser and that I wasn't a real doctor and then my sister appeared. And my mum and then her mum and then well, I was so drunk I just stood there and cried which is why I thought you dumped me.'

'You cried?'

'I'm… sensitive. It was quite a fight. My sister gave her a good slapping. She lost an extension. We have a whole branch of the family who hate us. This is why Maddie hit me with the sheets in the lift, isn't it?'

'Possibly.'

I don't know how I feel about any of this. It seems to have turned into a day of shocks and revelations. I look down at a cold cup of tea on my desk then out to the twilight sky.

'It's all true. I can put Asha on the line now to confirm it all. You should have said something. I was so confused,' he says.

I smile in return. 'I had a husband who made a drama out of our marriage for almost ten years. I just wanted to back away quietly.'

He looks sad, apologetic.

'Emma, I am nothing like your husband. I'm sorry if there was a misunderstanding here but I would never hurt you like he did.'

I laugh quietly. Simon didn't hurt me, he carved my heart out while it was still beating.

'But, as you can see,' I say pointing to my wrecked sofa, 'that story's not finished. There is so much drama still here and you shouldn't have to take that on.'

He looks at me confused. 'And what if I do?'

'You want to take on my evil ex-husband who uses every opportunity to screw me over?'

'As long as you don't mind that I come with an evil ex-fiancée who makes giant cakes.'

I laugh through my tears.

'We all come with a story. Give me another chance. I like you, I really do. I think you and I could be golden.'

'Like your Casio.'

I look down at it. I think being a birth partner may have ruined it. I have no words left. He's here and he's showing care and authenticity in his words. He's held me and looked after me. He smiles and looks me in the eye.

'Maybe we need to start again.'

'How?'

He stands back from me. 'I'm Jag. Hi. I am thirty years old and didn't move out of my parents' house until I was twenty-six. I don't like Mexican food because I mean… fajitas, tacos. I don't trust food I have to construct myself. I was with my ex-fiancée for seven years and a couple of weeks ago she tried to kiss at me a wedding. Then, during the subsequent fight, she told the thirty-odd people present that she was glad she didn't marry me because I'm very hairy and she didn't want my furball babies. I am very hairy. My back needs regular mowing in the summer.'

I laugh.

'I'm Emma. I am thirty-five. I am divorced. My ex-husband had multiple affairs when we were married. In fact, I found out during my divorce proceedings that he shagged one of my wedding guests at our actual wedding. Like a mug, I stayed married to him because I like flogging dead horses. I don't eat sandwiches and I've only had sex with one person since my divorce and I only had sex with him to make sure I knew I could remember how to have sex. I don't like crying in front of people. I don't want to get married again.'

Was that a deal breaker I just added on to the end of that sentence? Also, I talked about sex quite openly there – we'll blame Lucy for that.

He looks at me and holds his hand out to shake it. 'It's nice to meet you, Emma. What are your thoughts on hummus?'

# Chapter Seventeen

692 days since we drove mum to A&E to X-ray
a dislocated thumb

'Christ alive. What on earth is that behind you?'

'It's a sex shop. That's the outline of a giant neon penis. Lucy is
quite at home here.'

I smile at the person on the screen. In amongst us sisters is
number four, Grace, the globetrotting Callaghan. At the moment,
she's holed up in Amsterdam visiting friends for a wedding and of
course, this gives Lucy the perfect opportunity to visit and pretend
she's checking in when really she's just there for the debauchery. If
there was a sister who was the other pea in my pod, it was Grace.
She was in finance and like me, understood the need for detail,
thoroughness and punctuality. Because of the tragic turn her life had
taken, we encouraged her to take the time and space to escape, to
heal, but I missed having someone who operated on my wavelength.

'Did we know Lucy snogged girls now?' she asks me.

'Meg mentioned something. Like kissing girls or sleeping with
them?'

'Who knows? A man has already approached her on the street
thinking she was on the game.'

I flare my nostrils in horror. 'What on earth was she wearing?'

'We were off to a BDSM night.'

'We?'

'Don't ask…' she says, laughing. It's so lovely to see her laugh. 'And Lucy told me about the latest instalment with Satan.'

'Is that what all you sisters are calling him now?'

'Yes. Have you told George?'

'No. Should I?'

'Most definitely. This changes everything from a legal standing.'

'How so?'

'If he has other dependants then it becomes an issue of finances. He's not married to this Susie but what happens if he died tomorrow?'

'You'd all throw a party.'

'Well, yes but it should be clear how assets would be divided and also what rights Oliver and this new baby would have. Does the new baby have a name?'

I pause before I say it. 'Louis.'

'Your middle name is Louise.' It was no coincidence. According to Maddie, Susie cried all the way to the wards and once she got there, the staff were a little worried she was suffering from some sort of post-partum breakdown. But then something changed. Simon tried to visit and she raised merry hell to make sure he couldn't get on the wards. It was quite a to-do apparently. My ex-husband threw all his weight around involving police and hospital board members but the ward supported and protected Susie all the way. That's nurse code for you. I got a card and flowers the week after thanking me and introducing me to my name sake.

Grace gives me a look that Beth, Lucy and my mother gave me. *Don't get involved.* It was gracious of me to help deliver the baby but that's as far as it should go.

'Get in touch with George,' she says. 'Document all the new information that you have because that should be on record. You know why he kept a lot of this from people right?'

'Because he's a twat and he's worried about how he'll look?'

'Hun, this is all legal collateral. If you wanted to fight for sole custody then you could drag him through the courts with this. You could argue he's reckless, a danger to your girls, a pathological liar. I bet if you looked through his finances, he's probably hiding earnings and assets from you. You could properly take him down with this if you wanted.'

That was never my intention. It took the sisters long enough to get me to leave him but I wanted to do it quietly and without the show and fireworks. I wanted my girls. I wanted this house. What she says makes perfect sense though. All at once, I miss the sister with the logical train of thought.

'Continue to protect yourself, get George on the case. Would you like me to talk to him?'

'On your holiday?'

'It's not a holiday though, is it?'

We pause for a moment. A voice pipes in from the background. 'Oi, London bitch!'

Grace turns around and rolls her eyes at our little sister.

'You should have come with, Ems. I could have brought you to a sex club…'

'Errrm, no. That's how you catch things.'

'Wouldn't have been anything worse than what you would have caught off Stuart Morton,' says Lucy.

Grace turns back to the screen and looks at me in horror. 'You slept with Meg's brother-in-law?'

'Yup, me and Ems are penis pals now.'

I say nothing but I do hope my youngest sister catches a dose of Dutch crabs for that revelation.

'I thought you were dating an Asian fella?'

'I am.'

It feels strange to say that out loud. Are we dating? Are we seeing each other? I feel too old to have a boyfriend but too square to have a lover. He shall be my man-friend.

Lucy eyes me curiously. 'Have you slept with him yet?

'Why are you so desperate for her to have sex?' asks Grace.

'Before Stuart Morton, she hadn't had sex in almost two years, Gracie. Your hymen can grow back after that long, you know?'

'It can't actually,' I say with some medical authority.

'At least prepare your bush for when the moment happens,' Lucy tells me.

'Yes, I shaved it all off this morning.'

'You did?'

'No, I have not.'

At that point, two little people run into the room and jump into my lap. 'What bush does mummy need to cut?' asks Violet, waving at the screen, Lucy blowing her all the kisses.

'There's a bush I've seen near your house, totally out of control,' says Lucy.

Grace tries hard not to break into laughter.

'You should have a tidy bush like that woman who lives across the road, she trims hers every day,' Violet continues.

'That's because her husband works and she stays at home so has time to do stuff like that.'

Lucy shakes her head at me.

'When are you coming back, Aunty Gracie?'

'Soon piglets.'

'We miss you.'

'I miss you too.'

Damn her being away, but it's something she has to do. I get that.

'Don't give her too much grief, Luce,' I say.

'*Moi*? Never.'

'Mum and the gang will be here soon for lunch, you want to say hello?' I ask them both. They shake their heads in unison and grin smugly.

'Good luck with that, tell them we said hi,' they chant in unison. '*Au revoir* London!'

You cows.

We all wave at the screen as it fades to black, the girls snuggled into me.

'Your lunch smells nice, Mummy,' V says, sitting on my lap, her palms covered in colouring pen.

'And why have you painted yourself?' I ask.

'So I can be Iron Man?' This makes perfect sense. I kiss her palms in the hope she won't kill me with her lasers. 'What time are Nanny and Pops coming round?' she continues.

'Soon. Did you make your beds?' Violet nods but I look to the ceiling and shake my head. 'I can see them from here…' Violet looks up. This will always be my best trick.

Iris knows better and giggles. 'You don't have X-ray eyes, Mama!'

'And how do you know this?' I joke.

'Because Daddy said so,' she says.

Damn him for stealing my best joke. She gives me the same look that Simon often used when I was attempting to be funny. How ridiculous that I can love these little girls so entirely even when they constantly remind me of someone who I hate with such bilious rage that I'd happily let him be eaten alive by rabid wolves. Iris comes over and we bury each other in a hug sandwich.

'Mummy, can we ask you a question?' asks Violet.

'Sure. What is it?'

Iris looks reticent but Violet doesn't seem to have that same filter. 'Can you ask Daddy what happened with Susie?'

I take a breath as her name is mentioned. I wasn't even sure if Simon knew that I helped deliver that baby. 'What did Daddy say happened?'

'He said that they weren't friends and we won't see her and Oliver anymore?'

Both of them look confused but sad by the revelation. 'And we don't even know if she had her baby. Daddy won't talk about it.'

Damn you, Simon. What has he told these girls? That him and Susie just met for play dates? That Oliver was just an occasional friend? This boy is a sibling. I look at the black screen where my siblings' faces once were. Iris and Violet link arms in front of me. They've always been close, I don't doubt for a second that's how they got through the last couple of years. I would hear their voices whispering in their bedroom at night and sometimes sit in the hallway hearing their chatter, their worries, their fears, sobbing quietly at their conversations.

'I'm not sure where Susie is,' I say unconvincingly, 'but maybe I can ask Daddy?'

'Can you?' asks Violet, hopefully. 'What do you think they called the baby? I said they should call it Juan.'

'That's an interesting name…' I say, smiling.

Iris looks at me confused. 'You'd really talk to Daddy?'

Iris has always observed the details of our divorce a little more intently. Every time I handed the girls over to him, she looked hopeful. Maybe we could just hug it out and her world would be just as it was again.

'He's your daddy, of course I will. Do you miss Susie? Oliver?' Violet nods, Iris looks like she doesn't want to upset me. 'She seemed nice?' I say.

'Was she Daddy's girlfriend?' asks Iris. Violet seems shocked by the revelation.

'I think she was.' Both of them are quiet. I hate this, fracturing their thoughts on the world and how the two people they love most are walking away from each other in different directions. Iris is quiet; I think that she always guessed that much, but you can see her trying to piece together parts of that puzzle, just like we all have. Damn you, Simon, for making our little girl do this. Violet is still bathing in the revelation.

'So that means they've broken up?' she asks.

'I guess so.'

They hold hands and I am suddenly cast back to a bench in a park a few weeks back where my little sister did the same to me. I think about two little brothers out there in London intrinsically linked to my girls through no fault of their own. I think about the four of them taking on the world. I click on the laptop and find an email from Susie. I open the photo attached.

'This is Louis, Susie's new baby.'

'She had the baby!' Violet squeals. 'He looks like a puppy!'

Probably not what anyone wants their baby to be compared to but I smile to see her excitement.

'Louis and Oliver are your brothers.'

Although this feels like quite the bombshell, they seem to quietly process the information. I hold them extra tightly.

'So our daddy is their daddy?' asks Iris. 'Then why did they tell us something else?'

They both look up at me and my instant thought is to cry for them. Your father told me something else for years. It's what he does. I am trying to fix that with some simple honesty.

'Our families were changing, I guess he didn't want it to upset you…' I say. 'You'd have to ask Daddy about that.'

I can't tell if Iris is angry or not. She's at that age when Father Christmas still exists but she knows the F-word and as simply as I relay the facts to her, I am not sure how she'll react.

'I hope that Daddy makes sure that you can spend some time with your brothers and get to know them though?'

Iris seems confused. 'Would that make you sad?'

'Oh love… not at all.' I curl her hair around her ear. 'Siblings are great. I have four of them and it's always a lot of fun.'

'Except when Aunty Lucy is being cheeky?' says Iris.

'Well, there is that but imagine having a little gang. You'd be the awesome foursome.' I can feel bad for how this little gang came to be but I can't feel bad about their future. 'What's Oliver like?' I ask.

'He doesn't like carrots, he really really hates them. He once threw some across a restaurant,' Violet says animatedly. Not important information but still. 'He's got blue eyes and likes dinosaurs. Does that make him your son too?'

I pause for a moment. 'No.' I guess he'll be in my periphery though. It makes me wonder whether for the sake of modern families they need to address some label of who he may be to me. A son of divorce, once removed? 'But I'd like to meet him one day.'

'Maybe we can go to Wagamama together?' suggests Iris. Violet nods. That was a lot of information there and a complete revelation of sorts but I suspect their way to process it for now is to try and con me out of some katsu and noodles.

'We can.'

They both high five. Iris looks me in the eye though. 'I mean, you'll always be our mama though, right? I won't call anyone else "Mama".'

Damn right. Amidst change and new people coming in on the scene, that will always be the truth. I nod and embrace them both tightly. *I'd fight people to the death for you two. Proper gladiatorial combat.* I study their faces. Has this changed their landscape further? Has this news hurt them? I'll never know but at least they can start to process it.

The doorbell suddenly rings and I watch their attentions shift as they rush into the hallway and meet my parents at the door. I hear the murmur of voices and walk over, sticking my head through the hallway. The girls hang off them excitedly.

'Emma, something smells nice,' says my mother. She's wearing a leopard print scarf which is very unlike her. She's been on the florals since the late nineties. She looks around the hallway for evidence of cobwebs and dust.

'Pork. You told me last time that chicken is too fiddly. Dad?'

Dad comes over and embraces me tightly. All you need to know about my father is that his beard is fluffy and most likely, he's bought his own slippers to change into today. He also spent thirty-odd years as husband to my mother and father to five daughters. He was outnumbered, he was overruled yet here he is, alive to tell the tale. All we really remember is that he acted as taxi service during our teens and he was always there to sit next to us on the sofa with a cup of tea and a Mars bar whenever exams had been failed, relationships had ended or he was trying to counterbalance my mother's melodrama.

'Emma.'

'You look well, Dad?'

'Your father has been singing this morning,' mentions Mum. 'He's joined a male choir. They think they're Westlife.' This is classic Mum. The girls giggle at the thought of beardy Pops being a pop star. Good for him if it gets him out the house. He nods and smiles at me. There's a commotion at the door and Iris goes to open it.

'Joe!' she squeals. Her little cousin hangs off Beth and there are hugs all round.

'Shouldn't he be wearing a hat?' says my mother.

I wink at Beth who goes to greet Mum with a hug and a kiss which is more than what I've been able to muster. Dad takes Joe who I feel will always be the favourite grandchild as he was the first to break the girl curse. Iris goes to close the door.

'Not yet, sweetie. What about, Will?' asks my dad.

I give him a strange look. 'But Will is living… '

'Living proof that someone can work too hard. He's at the office today, deadlines,' Beth says, looking at me with some urgency. You didn't tell Dad? Why the hell not? I'm going to have to lie to lovely Dad?

'That's a shame.'

'Yes, a real shame,' says my mother through gritted teeth. Beth looks at me. This is going to be quite painful, isn't it? Wine, I hope one of you brought sodding wine.

The roast became a tradition that my mother started when we all left home. The idea was that any sister who was left in London would convene every two or three months for a family meal. We'd all take it in turns to host or meet out if needed. Of course, we don't always have a roast but the name stuck given it was also a chance for our mother to check in on us and tell us how she disapproved of all our life decisions. Meg conveniently missed most of them now but Beth and I were the usual regulars. This month, Lucy was going as far as Amsterdam to sit this one out. I just wish that my mother could make these occasions more bearable. I look at her through the kitchen door, where she sits at my dining room table pretending to colour in with Violet but really glares at the picture of Simon on my mantelpiece.

'You didn't tell, Dad,' I tell Beth.

'No, Mum said don't because she's worried about his diabetes.'

'How would him knowing affect his diabetes?'

'Hell if I know. Maybe it will make him comfort eat but now he's asking me lots of questions about him and now I want to drink. I've bought wine, much wine,' she says, searching for glasses.

'You were also in charge of pudding,' I tell her.

'Yup, done that too. You got a dish I can put this pie on so it looks like I made it?'

'Bottom left cupboard. Kitchen foil in the drawer above if you want to look proper authentic.'

She winks and does a shooting hand at me. It's exactly what I'll be doing with the Yorkshire puddings later so I do not judge. She unpacks the pie, hides the packaging under a few layers of recycling then pours both of us a large glass of white.

'Am I allowed to ask about Will?'

'He came round the other day.'

'That's good.'

'To get a hoodie.'

'Oh.'

I look at her face, lost and forlorn. Any kindness I am supposed to show that man is shrouded by an intense desire to also attack him with a chair, in the face, like a wrestler. I pull her in for a hug, an extra toasty one given I'm wearing oven gloves. Mum interrupts us by walking into the kitchen and looks at the pie. 'That looks... interesting?' she comments.

Beth and I smile as we know exactly what this word means. She uses it to describe new haircuts, a bright winter coat, an interior design choice that confuses her, a baking project that hasn't quite risen. It's her go to word when there are no negatives left. You can imagine that Lucy is her most *interesting* child.

'It's peach.'

'Did you use tinned peaches or fresh?'

'Fresh, naturally.'

She nods and looks at my Yorkshire pudding packet on the counter. I've been caught out. Dammit.

'You should have said, those are so easy to knock up. I could have brought some batter.'

I smile in return as she gets a wine glass out and then studies the label on the wine that Beth brought along.

'Have you heard from Will yet? About when he might be back?'

I turn to Beth again, her face scrunched up with anxiety. I am supposing she's told Mum something different too. Whether he would return or not was so up in the air. However, she also knew that Mum's reactions would be full of fire so I don't suppose she also does this to protect Will. I mean, she dislocated a thumb that Christmas and I had to take her to A&E where we had to sit next to a man who had tried to insert a Christmas bauble up his bum.

'He just needs to work some things out, Mum,' I say.

'Is it a money thing? We can always lend you money,' she digs further. 'I just think it's terrible that he's basically abandoned my daughter and grandson.'

Beth looks alarmed that her voice may carry through to Dad. I am more alarmed that she will cause a scene and people will leave. There is a whole loin of pork resting on the counter that needs eating.

'He didn't abandon me. He's just having a time out. He…' Beth takes a large gulp of wine. She looks at me for help. We know Mum too well. Soon she'll start with the catty comments about his ability as a father and partner that will cut and penetrate because essentially it's a reflection on choices we made. I'm all too familiar with this. We used to stand in this kitchen and have the same conversations about Simon all the time. *He's working? On a Sunday? He's cheated? Again?*

'Let's just have a nice lunch. Mum, could you get my big serving bowl out?' I ask, trying to diffuse her line of interrogation.

Beth exhales loudly as our mother roots around in the cupboards.

'I believe this is my dish, Emma.' Mum gets the dish out and places it on the counter. It's not the prettiest, there's a seventies sunflower vibe going on but it cooks a good crumble. I always thought it was a rite of passage that we should at least inherit one thing from the family home kitchen. I can hear my oven door has been opened and turn to see Mum peeking to no doubt check whether the roast potatoes are up to standard.

'I mean he better be in his son's life for Christmas or I'll be having words with him myself… ' Mum says, adamantly. 'Do I have to get him a present?'

'Mum, don't be like that,' I tell her.

'Please, Mum…' pleads Beth.

But then at that precise moment, a figure walks through the door. It's Dad. It's a classic Dad move; he almost has a sixth sense when there's trouble brewing. 'Fiona, the girls are upstairs and wanted to show you something, some sort of fashion show?'

It's clever because granddaughters trump daughters every time so she takes her leave, but not before her final stab. 'Those potatoes are looking quite brown. Your dad's dentures might not be able to take them too crispy, Emma.'

I salute her as she closes the kitchen door and Dad chuckles to himself.

'What can I do?' he asks, grinning. We both smile back at him.

'You could drain my green beans?' I stand over the joint of meat at the counter and get carving. The joy of being a surgeon was that this was the task that I inherited in the family. You should see me with a turkey at Christmas, I can remove legs like a pro.

'Did I walk in on something?'

Beth shakes her head.

He looks over at her warmly. 'She's just worried about what's happening with you, Beth. You know that, right?'

We both look over at him strangely and he smiles.

'Have you ever met Lucy before? Gob like a black hole?'

'Lucy told you... about Will?' I ask.

He nods. Beth goes over to embrace him.

'I sometimes like your mother thinking I don't know everything, it makes her think she has the upper hand.'

Beth chuckles in reply. 'I should have told you. I'm sorry, Dad.'

'Not your fault. How are you? Do you need anything?'

She shrugs her shoulders. 'I'm surviving. Just help me deal with Mum's comments today.' Beth looks fraught and he hugs her again.

'She cares, you know. Your mum.'

Beth and I look at him curiously. It's been like this since we were little. As a mother of daughters, I got it completely. You want your girls to find their place in life, smash the patriarchy and rule the world but she always held us to impossible standards as a consequence. I respected and feared her for it in equal measure.

'She'd move mountains for each of you. I think that's all she's done since Meg was born but she's protective too. That's the lioness in her.'

'I was thinking more dragon,' says Beth laughing.

'Then don't confuse her fire,' he replies sagely.

I laugh under my breath but Beth and I look at each other and know exactly what he means. It's all some outward expression of love and care. It's at times blistering and we feel the effects of those flames but they've never really been directed at us. He smiles. I never got Dad's opinion on what happened with Simon. He was consolatory and kind but never had the same fire that Mum had. I don't know if that was a good thing or not but at least it balances out my dear mother.

'And don't listen to her. The potatoes are perfect, cookie.'

I pause for a moment. Smart cookie was his nickname for me growing up. Pickle, peanut, chicken and bean. That's where the food theme came from. I side hug dad without him really knowing why.

'LUNCH!' I shout as Beth and I get the last of the dishes and we hear the flutter of people on the steps. To be fair, there is a warm glow about having everyone near, to see my girls embedded in all of this love and commotion. I take the roast out to the table and move the apple sauce away from my mother as even though I've spooned it out into a bowl, she'll see it's not got lumps and know I've got it out of a jar.

'This looks delish, Ems. Thank you so much,' Beth says as she straps Joe into his highchair.

My mum silently rakes through the vegetables. It's a difficult balance with her. She's either saying too much or nothing at all. At least congratulate me on the pork as I don't think I've completely killed this.

'So Beth, why don't you tell everyone about Joe. Mum, Dad… He's been on a few modelling shoots.'

Dad sits up in his chair as he serves himself some broccoli.

'Well, obviously he got my good looks.' The girls giggle.

My mum looks over. 'Is that how you're going to earn money now? It doesn't seem very reliable?'

*Mum. Rein it in. Say something nice, even if you don't quite mean it. You know she needs it more than ever now.*

'Are they keeping your teaching job? You were such a good teacher.'

Beth has taken to flooding her plate with gravy. *Don't eat the stress away, sis.* I look over at her. There is the need to FaceTime all the other sisters immediately so they can share in this awkwardness.

A little voice pipes in. 'She is a good teacher,' says Iris through a mouthful of stuffing.

Beth pauses. 'What was that, hun?'

'Granny used the past tense. Aunty Beth *is* a brilliant teacher. You taught me about adverbs the other day. And you're a great aunty. I don't know why Uncle Will left you but he's a prize idiot.'

I drop my carving knife so it clatters on the floor and luckily doesn't slice off my toes. Beth brings Iris in for a side hug while my mum and dad sit there, open mouthed.

'Dad knows, Mum,' I announce.

They both glare at each other. They can thrash that out in the car later but for now, I smile at my Iris for knowing or at least appreciating the wonder in her aunt Beth. She who counteracts the madness of Lucy, who doesn't hate anyone – not even that bloody ex-husband of mine, not even the boyfriend who left her.

'I didn't mean that, Iris,' replies my mother. 'I know Beth is brilliant. She's my daughter. All my daughters are brilliant and they deserve the world because they are a fucking marvel.'

And we all freeze. Violet drops a fork at hearing the swearing. Beth's eyes glaze over and we look at each other. Those words will never leave her mouth again. At least not in the next decade but we were the privileged two who got to hear them. This has made today worth it. Dad beams broadly as if to say he told us so.

'Even Aunty Lucy?' asks Violet.

'I'm sorry I swore. Yes, even your aunt Lucy.'

'Because she showed her foof to the entire park the other day.'


'Is that a Yorkshire pudding under your pillow?' I ask Violet.

'Yes, I may get hungry in the night.'

'Unless a mouse finds it first and eats its way through your face to get to it,' says Iris.

Violet looks horrified and I cast Iris a look as I am pretty sure her sister will never sleep again now. I gesture for her to hand over her contraband but am mildly amused that she hides savoury baked goods instead of sweets and thought to wrap it in a napkin first.

The meal went well after my mother's shock announcement that she was quite fond of her daughters though we may need to prepare Lucy for the onslaught of reprimand she'll receive after Iris and Violet outlined the whole Elsa in the park incident. *She smacked one right in the gob and called her a peroxide titface. Really, Granny. It was brilliant!*

Beth lingers downstairs to watch television as my set is bigger and my sofas are comfier whilst Mum and Dad have returned home with some pie – which Mum 'loved'. Beth nailed the pastry, she said, which is probably the first time my mother has ever lied but I think she wanted to continue in some theme of kindness and raising her daughters up for one small moment.

'When will Aunty Lucy come back?' asks Iris.

'She and Aunty Gracie have just been to a wedding and then she's back on Tuesday.'

'Freya's mum is getting married,' Violet pipes in. I realise who this is. It's Faith, Leo's ex. She's getting re-married already? I'll text him and make sure he's alright. 'Freya said they're getting married on a beach and no one will wear shoes? Can you get married without shoes?'

'I guess.'

'Did you wear shoes at your wedding?' asks Violet. Iris glances over at her.

'It's OK,' I reassure her, 'I wore white high heels and they got ruined because there was a lot of grass so by the end of the day, they were light green.'

'Like the Hulk?'

'Exactly.'

Iris eyes me curiously. 'Do you think you'll ever get married again, Mummy?'

'I don't know. It'd be a lot of fuss.'

'You could have an office wedding?' says Violet.

'You mean a registry office wedding?' I grin imagining an actual office wedding backlit by the glow of a photocopier.

Iris is quiet and I beckon her over so we can have a squish and a hug altogether.

'Are you OK, little potato?'

I know she feels this all a lot more than her sister.

'There's just a lot of people to think about now. You spoke about the awesome foursome before and that made me sad.'

'Why?' I ask.

'Because that's what Daddy used to call us.'

I hear sadness in her voice. I hadn't even pegged where I'd heard that term before.

'And sometimes I just miss it when it was the four of us.'

The emotion is a little unbearable and a tear trails down my cheek. Violet looks petrified.

'Don't be sad, Mummy.'

'I'm not sad. I'm just sorry Daddy and I couldn't make it work. You know how much we love you though. And how I'll always love him really for giving me you two little pumpkins.'

'You're calling us food again.'

'Because you're both delicious.'

'That's called cannibalism,' says Iris.

'Do you have a new boyfriend?' Violet asks.

I pause. Do I do this here? Now? Do they meet him first? Do I show them a picture of him?

'I've been on a few dates with a man called Jag.'

They both giggle.

'What's so funny?' I ask.

'That's a silly name, like a Jaguar?'

'He's Asian.'

'Is he nice to you?' asks Violet.

'He buys me hummus.'

'And you love hummus,' says Violet, rearranging her pillow. 'Does he have kids? Would we have more brothers and sisters? Then we'd have to buy a bus.'

I smile at hearing her talk so plainly. She thinks it's a chance to make new friends and have a party on a bus. When did this one grow such a big heart?

'Jag has no kids and he's also a doctor.'

'And you love doctors,' says Iris, jokingly. I narrow my eyes at her cheekiness. Suddenly, my phone rings from over on the dresser and I peel myself off the floor to go answer it. Speaking of doctors I've once loved...

'Simon?'

The girls sit up in their beds. 'Is it Daddy, can we say goodnight to him?'

However, the voice on the end of the line is hushed, the breathing is in short gasps. Oh my god, has he sex dialled me? But something's not quite right.

'Girls, time to sleep.' I give them swift kisses on the tops of their heads and vacate the room quickly.

'Simon, what's wrong? Are you crying?'

'Ems.' He can hardly catch his breath.

'Is it Susie? Your boys?'

This feels different. Even when we divorced, I never heard him like this.

'It's my mum. They've just wheeled her into surgery for a blood clot…'

I sit down on my bed to steady myself. 'Oh Si… is she OK?'

'Can you get here? Can you come down?'

I pause for a moment. I am sitting here in a room that once belonged to us, in a house with our girls. A court of law has said I don't have to be his wife anymore. But I hear his voice, that panic and my heart aches and I am not sure why.

'Tell me where you are.'

# Chapter Eighteen

If you had to say there's a noise that marks out the soundtrack of my life, it's probably that of a heart monitor. The bouncing sound is a comfort to me – it means someone is alive and their heart working. But the droning sound of when a heart stopped, dragged and prolonged, haunts me. When a heart dies, a monitor detects a complete lack of electrical activity within the muscle. It stops beating. It's still. I often think of waves on an ocean rippling to a halt, leaving just a wake of still water.

I haven't been in a hospital as a visitor since last year when Grace's husband died. His name was Tom and it was all so very tragic. One moment, they were this young beautiful couple with everything at their feet and the next, Tom was given a diagnosis which changed the landscape forever. He was gone within a month. I was there when he passed and Grace collapsed to the floor because his body stopped working. I held her. I felt the immense pain that tore through her and it diminished everything that I had been going through. Those were not fractures that would just heal over in time, it was a heart crushed into nothing.

'Are you family?' the lady on reception asks.

I pause for a moment. 'I am, Emma Chadwick. I'm her daughter-in-law.'

The ward on this hospital glows quiet; the lights have been turned off. A strained voice comes from a ward behind me and a nurse walks in to placate them. It's a symphony of monitors and a creaking trolley that delivers charts and medicines. Geriatric medicine was like this, there was a serenity to it but I found it all exceptionally sad – people saying goodbye to loved ones they'd known for years, some dying alone, others who'd lost all reason and understanding as their minds faded.

The receptionist looks at her computer. 'She's still in surgery.'

'Her son was with her, is he about?'

'Tall, good hair?'

'I guess…?'

'He's waiting in her room. Room 4 to the left.'

She smiles in the way I've seen a thousand times before and I walk over to the room and stare at the door. Why am I here? I knock lightly.

'Come in?'

When I walk in, Simon's figure stands by the window. He wears a navy pea coat and I know that coat well as it's the one I gave him for Christmas on the very day I decided to leave him. Shadows mask his face but I can tell that he's been crying. Simon never cried – not when our daughters were born, when he lost patients, when we divorced. After our breakup I often wondered if this made him some form of sociopath. Now he wipes tears from his eyes then moves towards me cautiously. I am not that much of a monster so open my arms out to offer my condolences. His body curls into mine and I feel the shudders from his sobbing.

'Thank you for coming.'

He realises he's shown a moment of weakness and we part. I retrieve some tissues from the bedside table and he goes back to stand at the window. It had been just Linda and Simon growing up. His father had left them when he was five so he had no siblings and few relatives to speak of.

'What's happening?'

'Stroke.'

'Oh, Simon. Were you with her?'

'Yes. Emma, what if she dies?'

He pulls a chair out to sit down, bowing his head and crying quietly. I put my bag down to go over to his side of the bed, holding a hand to his back.

'Was there anything to pre-empt this? I always thought she was in good health?'

'She was. She always kept herself well.'

'Then you know as well as I that she should handle any surgery really well… Did you get her in quickly?'

'I did.'

'Did they scan? Is it ischaemic? What are they doing?'

I sit on the bed in front of him. He doesn't reply and I assume the worst. I deal in hearts and all those connected areas. As hardy as they are, they're also unpredictable. I guess he needs reassurances that hers is maybe different.

'Did she still do her morning walks around the park?'

'Yes. Decked out in lavender fleece, every morning. She used to take the girls too.'

'Stop talking in the past tense. I'm sure it'll be fine.'

We stand, feeling a little helpless. Kingston Hospital is beyond our remit but I don't doubt that Simon most likely swanned in here with his credentials and good hair and got his mum the private room.

'Did you really go to a Chinese for her birthday?' I ask.

Simon laughs under his breath to hear me change the subject. 'God, she hated it. You know how she is with food. And then the cake and… Oh god, I fucked up, Ems.'

I don't know if this is a general statement so I stay quiet.

'That was just the beginning of everything going wrong. The last weeks all we've been doing is fighting. This is all my fault.'

I am not awful enough to confirm the fact he gave his own mother a stroke but I can see the guilt raging through him in this rare show of emotion. I almost feel jealous I never saw this much when we were married. I stand back from him.

'I was cruel. You know the last thing she said to me before she collapsed? That I'd turned into my father. A man who walked out on us for another woman.'

I turn to the window. She wasn't wrong and I'd sensed this, that despite his father not even being a part of his life, despite me never even meeting him, that the worst parts of him were in his biology. His dad was the worst sort. He kept his distance, he threw money at them, pretending that he was involved. But to confirm or rebut anything feels insincere at a time like this.

'She came to see me. A few weeks ago. After that morning in my house. We invited her in for dinner.'

He turns like he's waiting for the punch line.

'What did you tell her?'

I don't reply.

'You should have said something?'

'Your mother came round for some garlic dippers. She had a nice evening with her granddaughters. My sisters were there, we cracked open a Merlot. To be fair, we hardly talked, I sensed she just wanted… '

'Answers?'

'Company. It was her birthday. And I felt like she wanted to clear the air… Redeem her son's mistakes?'

Was that cruel? Who knows anymore?

'Do you need anything?' I ask him.

'I screwed things up with Susie too. She's not letting me see the baby or Oliver anymore.'

'I was thinking more a cup of tea? Do you want me to check on progress?'

He looks at me like these are nonsensical details. I came here to try and be helpful, be kind. I don't want a heart-to-heart and most certainly not in this room, right now.

'Do you want me to call Susie?' I ask.

'I tried, she wouldn't take my call.'

'So you called me instead?' Always the second choice.

'I actually called you first.'

'Why?'

'You're at the top of my contacts.'

'Why?'

'I never changed it. I actually think you're still my next of kin.'

I don't reply. Next of kin was the first thing I had changed when we separated. I trust Lucy more now with decisions about my life and that's saying something.

'Did I turn into my father, Ems?'

'I never met your father.'

'Mum was furious about the Susie thing anyway. Then I told her she'd had the baby and that we couldn't see him and then…'

'The truth trickled out.'

He doesn't reply.

'The baby has a name. He's called Louis.' He looks up at me, confused.

'Susie came round to my office to confront me and she went into labour. I delivered your baby on my office floor.'

He swings his head around, shock embedded into his face. 'You did what?'

'She went into labour crying about you.'

'You delivered our baby?'

'I believe we're both qualified to do that?'

'How was he? Was he OK?'

'He has your chin. But yes, when he left me, he was well.'

'And you didn't tell me?'

'Tell you what? Your mistress came to see me? I helped bring her baby into the world? No. Our doorstep never felt like the right place to bring it up.'

'We'd agreed on calling him Harry.'

I am silent. Harry was on our list when I was pregnant. We never found out the sex of ours but it was always there in reserve so this feels slightly cruel.

'Louis feels a little common.'

Now that's cruel.

'I think it's from Louise, my middle name.'

'Oh.'

'I told the girls too.'

'Our girls?'

'They'd been fed a few lies about these boys. I thought it was important they knew who their brothers were.'

He pauses in disbelief. 'I'm not sure that was your responsibility?'

'I'm only their mother, Simon. I didn't want them lied to anymore.'

He rubs at his temples. The bags under his eyes weigh his face down; a normally clear complexion is faded and ashen. I don't know how I should be feeling at this moment. I don't want to stand here and preach that the pain he feels is deserved or wallow in his suffering but I can't generate any form of sympathy either.

'We need to tell them about this too.'

'Can you?'

'We'll do it together.'

'I can't… I have to sort work, I have to…'

'FOR FUCK'S SAKE, SIMON!'

He jolts at hearing me shout. I rarely did it. Had I been scared of him? Even in the worst parts of our divorce, my anger was sublimated by my sadness. He gives me a look like I have to be nice to him, given his mother is downstairs being operated on.

'I am so sorry about your mother. No one deserves this. But I won't lie to those girls anymore and I won't do your job for you. You left me to tell them about our marriage ending. And I was the one who told them about their brothers. Have the decency and the balls to sit down with them and explain to them that their grandmother is poorly.'

'And that it was my fault?' He sobs quietly. 'I don't want them to think badly of me.'

'But in the end, they will if you're not honest with them.'

There is silence as he blows his nose, wiping his eyes. Where were these tears two years ago? I hate to say it but they summon an unexpected jealousy in me. At least I know he cares enough for his mother that his heart is not completely missing.

'Did Linda have high blood pressure? Maybe something was just missed?'

'You think I missed something? That I'm a doctor, I should have noticed?'

'Don't put words in my mouth.'

'If I hadn't cheated on you and not met Susie, had Oliver or Louis, as he's now called, then my mother wouldn't have got so emotionally stressed and most likely wouldn't have stroked out.'

'Correction, if you hadn't lied – about any of it.'

He is quiet.

'When your mother showed up on my doorstep, it was because she was so sad that you weren't the man she thought you were, that you'd lied to her all that time. It's just been a cycle of lies and you not taking responsibility for anything.'

'Wow, Ems. Just say it like it is, why don't you?'

I really don't know why I'm here. But I didn't come here to be an emotional punchbag, to be someone he could deflect his grief off. *Emma, she'll put up with my crap, I'll invite her along.* I turn to pick up my bag.

'I'm so sorry, Emma. Please stay. I really have no one else.'

'Friends?'

He laughs under his breath. I join him by the window and we stand overlooking the car park, gazing at the cars driving in circles, searching for spaces. A man with a giant bouquet of flowers walks past, his helium balloons dancing in the breeze.

'You were my only friend,' he says.

'I was your wife, Chadwick.'

'You were. You haven't called me Chadwick in years, not since medical school.'

I flash back to a simpler time when we had matching university hoodies and we'd test each other on the parts of a kidney whilst walking into lectures, sitting next to each other, sharing pens and cans of Lilt.

'Well, I became a Chadwick too. It would have been confusing.'

He laughs under his breath. 'Can I ask you a question?'

'Sure.'

'Am I bad person?'

I try to find the right words. 'Not… bad. Damaged maybe. You are a good father. Our girls adore you but you were a shit husband.'

'I'll take that. Why… why damaged?'

'It's not my job to work you out anymore.'

'Did I do anything right as a husband?'

'It's a small list.'

He cared about dental hygiene, he loaded the dishwasher correctly and he was excellent at spelling. That's all I have but I won't say it out loud. He looks out to the car park again studying the cars circling for days, looking for spaces.

'How do I fix this, Emma?'

'You? How do we fix you? Therapy? Counselling?'

'Shouldn't *we* have done that? Together.'

'I did that on my own.'

'You did?'

'You thought I just split up with you and got on with real life?'

'It certainly felt that way.'

'You broke me, Simon. I needed to speak to someone about it who wasn't my mother or—'

'One of the sisters. You think the counselling worked?'

'I said what I needed without judgement, she listened. I worked out my issues.'

'Which were?'

'Where do I start? Self-esteem, my hurt and worry about the girls, trying to figure things out. Speaking about it gave me clarity. Made me realise that despite my best efforts, it was unsalvageable.'

'You told her everything?'

'It's a confidential service in case you're worried?'

'Well, what did you say?'

'I spoke about the time with the nannies. The French one and the Australian one.'

'That wasn't my fault.'

'See? *Nothing to do with me, I'm just a slave to a high sex drive.* A reaction like you didn't really care, complete apathy.'

'I did have a high sex drive. You knew that.'

'Then watch some porn, wank into your hand? You used it as an excuse. You made me out to be the problem.'

'You weren't.'

'Good to know now, I guess.'

'You were a good wife.'

'Why do I feel like you're going to pat me on the head?'

He laughs under his breath.

'Can I ask you a question?' I take a deep breath. 'How did you meet Susie?'

'Through the hospital. It was a one-night stand and I was careless and she got pregnant with Oliver.'

I take pause to hear him talking of his son as a careless mistake.

'And you've been together since Oliver was born?'

'We kept in touch, I gave her a deposit for her house. Made sure she was looked after. When we finally split, we became a couple.'

It seems trivial to query where the finances came from but I ask the question that I desperately want answered.

'Do you love her?'

'I think I do.'

'You think? Have you been faithful to her?'

'I've made sure that her and that boy were looked after.'

'You didn't answer my question. Why did you keep them a secret, from everyone? Even your mother?'

'I don't need sanctimony now. They're still my sons. I have a right to them.'

'Well, I'm not a lawyer. Cat De Vere can help you with that.' I smile, knowingly.

'You know I've slept with her, don't you?'

'We were together for well over a decade, Simon. After a while, you became a little predictable. I'll assume Susie doesn't know.'

'No.'

'Lucy spotted it a mile off too.'

'Well, if there were four other people who hated me more than you did, it was probably them.'

'Five, you forgot my mother.'

'How is Fiona?'

'She has a business selling voodoo dolls of you. She's made a fortune.'

Simon smiles momentarily then looks out again into the night sky. He touches his nose. Lucy obviously got her left arm from our mother as he had to have surgeries on it to correct the damage she'd inflicted. He's snored ever since and his nose still curves slightly to the left.

'And I didn't hate you.' I'm not sure why I add that aside.

He pauses. 'I didn't hate you either.'

'It sometimes felt that way. It certainly didn't feel like respect. Or love.'

'Of course I did. You know that, right? I cared for you greatly. I had such admiration for your intelligence and the way you gave me our girls. I think there was love there.'

'You think? Well, if it made a difference, I loved you.'

Balls. To say those words out loud, admit that to him feels like a moment of weakness. My thumb runs at a part of my finger where a ring used to be.

'I am sorry, Emma. I really am.'

As the words leave his mouth, I exhale, my shoulders relax. Maybe that's all I ever wanted, for him to take responsibility for everything. 'I think that's the first time I've ever heard you say those words.'

And for the first time, I see something drawn on his face that I've never seen before. Guilt? Repentance? My gut tells me not to trust it. He'd always been so smug, such a complete dick.

'I can't explain it, Emma. Maybe I was like my father, I wanted to self-destruct. I didn't understand what it was to be part of this family that I had had no experience of.'

I still can't work out where this depth and clarity has suddenly surfaced from.

'It wasn't all you, though. I also enabled you to cheat. I didn't call you out on it.'

'You didn't. I never worked out why?'

'Did you expect me to beat you up?'

'Well, no but I expected anger.'

'It was there. I imagined and wished horrible things for you at times.'

'Like?'

'A plague of horrors to affect your genitals, really…'

He laughs, surprised at my attempts at humour at least.

'You never challenged me? Even when you knew what was going on?'

'I swept it under the carpet because I didn't want you to get the better of me. Pride, maybe? And we had the girls. I did it for them. I couldn't bear for them to feel the extremes of my hurt. I thought I was protecting them. So I carried on like nothing was happening.'

'When really…'

'It was like a punch to the guts each time. The tears I have cried over you. The moments I was paralysed, broken over how deeply I felt that pain. How it grew inside of me and just tore me down.' I can feel myself welling up but compose myself.

'It wasn't all horrific though. Those years we were together? I wouldn't have survived med school without you.'

'True. And we had our moments. We have our girls.'

'Those girls.'

'I know, right?'

We pause, letting that sink in. In all this mess, they were and remain everything, some symbol of our marriage not being a complete disaster.

'That photo you have in your living room... Why?'

'Iris likes it. I don't have the heart to take it away from her. That cream tea we had on the beach. Christ, they were tiny.'

'You could fit them in your pocket. I can't believe Iris is going to be nine. When did she get so tall?'

'You're six foot two, it was inevitable they'd inherit that much.'

'Well, I'm glad they inherited all the good stuff from you.'

'I think that was a compliment.'

'I am capable of them.'

'Iris said something before... She sometimes gets sad that it's not just the four of us anymore.'

'I get what she means... Things were simpler back then. What did you say to her?'

'I said I was sorry things couldn't work out between me and you. I told her I'd always be connected to you because you gave me my daughters.'

'That's good of you.'

'Those girls have to believe they were born out of love. That's the one thing I need out of all of this.'

He nods. There was love. There were moments. The point was that for all the ways I can describe how awfully Simon behaved, it was made all the worse because it felt like he took a dump over all my love I felt for him, our family. I can't help it by this point. I cry. Tears flow as much as I try to hold them back. All this honesty from him better not be a sham or I will cut him. He's crying too. This is painful, embarrassing.

'Oh, Ems.'

He puts his hand in mine and brings me in for a hug. I don't know how this feels. It doesn't feel right but maybe this is part of the process. I hate this but can't seem to unlock myself from him. But then I see a shadow of his face, it comes towards me.

He kisses me. I push him away with some force.

'No.'

'I didn't mean to do that.'

'Story of your life.'

'I'm confused. My mother—'

'Don't you dare use that here.'

'I have no one now. Literally no one. Susie won't even talk to me. You and the girls are all I have.'

'Your mother's not dead, Simon.'

'But I need—'

'You'll need help to look after your sick mother? So you come to me? I'm not yours anymore.'

'But Emma, all those years. We can fix it, we can go back and see where it all went wrong and we can—'

'Do nothing, Simon.' I can't believe I'm hearing this.

'But the girls, we could be a family again. The four of us. I love you?'

I laugh. He phrased that as a question? What on earth is he doing?

'Emma?'

'Seriously, stop.'

And then I see a boy in a bar in a Hackett top with his floppy hair and swagger, charming everyone with his eloquence and there was a time, years ago, when he once chose me. I fell at his feet. I adored him. He made me feel like the only girl in the room. But something happened. He realised the power of his charm and instead of staying in that room with just me, the girl he chose first, he invited others in. It inflated his ego, his narcissism and he covered it all with his charisma and lies. He thought he was untouchable. Until it got to a point where I chose to leave and suddenly, I was the one who walked out on our marriage. I can't believe he's trying to get me back in that room. I can't believe I even set foot in it again.

A knock on the door interrupts our conversation.

'Mr Chadwick?' a young surgeon pops his head around the door with a nurse. I recognise that look of fatigue and relief. He looks at me and comes to shake my hand.

'You are?'

'Miss Callaghan,' I reply pointedly in Simon's direction. He is quiet.

'Your mother is doing well, she'll come up from recovery in a while.'

'Did you have to go in cranially?' I ask.

The young surgeon shakes his head. 'It was a minor attack. We weren't worried. Small procedure and drugs should do the rest.'

I nod as he says it. 'Thank you for your efforts.'

He takes his leave and I watch as Simon collapses to a chair. He exhales, sighing with relief. I am relieved too but also still hurting from him trying to kiss me, attempting to give our marriage another bash. Let's resurrect something that was very, very dead and wear it again like an ugly hat. But I watch him and it's comforting to know that my heart isn't completely dead. I am here. I don't want him. But I do care about what happens to him. I need him to be around for our daughters and for this to function in some bearable type of arrangement.

'I might go, Simon.'

'Where?'

'Home. Your mum is alright. You'll be OK?'

'Will I?'

'I don't want to be here when they bring her up but call me if you need anything?'

'Seriously?'

I shrug and grab my bag.

'Emma… I'm sorry.'

'Twice in one evening. I feel spoiled.'

He laughs. I put a hand to his arm.

'Try not to worry too much. I'm working tomorrow but I can drop by with things if you need them. If you have to spend some time here and it's hard to juggle the girls then let me know, but in the meanwhile, I'll see you next… in the week?'

He nods in reply.

# Chapter Nineteen

710 days since Lucy called Simon an
embarrassment to all men, everywhere

'I bought wine. Was I supposed to bring wine? At our school,
we're told to bring our own.'

Maddie hasn't just brought wine, she's bought three bottles,
hiding them in her handbag exceptionally well.

'Meg said that up north they had mulled wine and it made the
parents turn on each other, they had to call the police,' replies Beth.

'That's the sort of school you want to send your kids too, eh?'
Maddie replies.

It's the annual St Catherine's Christmas Quiz night where I was
duped into buying tickets by my eight-year-old daughter, handing
over money thinking it was for the raffle instead. So I called in
the troops and before me sits a strange array of people that may
either just use this opportunity to get absolutely hammered or take
everyone down in this room with their general knowledge. We
won't need Maddie's wine as my ticket money has already paid for
a couple of bottles, pizza and some decent pens. You know you're

in a school with money when you get a fancy rollerball and some red onion and goat's cheese on a sourdough base.

'Who has the best handwriting then?' asks Jag, presiding over the stationery. I smile because this is also a date and an important one as Jag gets to be in the vicinity of my sisters, who hopefully won't attack him with a bottle of alcohol this time. I give everything to Maddie whose shorthand is superb and watch as her Mark rolls up his sleeves, knowing he's here to drink, answer questions and help us out with anything football related.

'They won't accept my quiz team name,' pipes in a voice approaching the table.

'Lucy, what did you tell them?' I ask.

'We Like To Come From Behind,' she says sulkily. Jag blushes, Mark is in absolute hysterics. 'Apparently, it needs to be Christmas-themed... anyway, I also found us a straggler.'

Behind her stands Leo looking a little lost in a Christmas hat. I've not seen him since I heard that his wife was soon to be re-married and I reach over and give him a hug. I still can't quite work out how this man is in shorts though in December.

'I'm sorry to gatecrash. I was going to be on a team with some of the dads but then politics, and Faith is here with her new bloke and she's not shy in letting people know.'

'Mate, more the merrier, I'm Jag.' Jag pulls up a chair while there are brief introductions and I do the right thing by pouring him a glass of wine.

'I can't believe she brought him here. He's like a foetus, he's so bloody young,' says Leo.

We all turn to glance at their table.

'Don't all look at once,' says Maddie.

We all turn back again. Leo sits there and half the table, who have no idea who he is, await the story.

'That's Faith, she's my ex-wife and that is her fiancé, Brandon and he's some online entrepreneur start-up kid who drives a Tesla and he's completely plant-based, even his shoes, the children tell me.'

Lucy puts a reassuring arm around him. I look at the body language closely to work out if they're still at it.

'I'm Leo. I'm old as balls. I like leather shoes and I drive a Skoda.'

'Mate, I'm Mark. I drive a white van so please don't worry yourself. I came up the drive to the school and they thought I was here doing a delivery.'

'Kia,' says Jag with his hand in the air. 'Everyone laughs but the mileage I get is amazing.'

Leo smiles faintly.

'Specialist topic?' I ask him.

'Britpop.' he replies.

Beth high fives him. It's a mixed bag around this table but at least we'll be fun. I sit down next to Leo and encourage him to have a sip of wine.

'Are you really OK?' I ask him.

'They're getting married next year in Devon in some eco-sustainable bio dome thing. She's plastering it all over social media, she's having a fun old time letting me know every bloody detail. It just feels cruel. It feels rushed. But I have no say.'

'Not even when it comes to your kids?'

'She's made that very clear. A child is going to be raising my children but it's nothing to do with me.'

'How old is he?'

'Twenty-six. He looks like he should be in a boy band.'

Lucy looks over at him, scanning down from hair to shoes. 'Wankers like that are usually shit in bed. Vegans usually are because they don't understand meat.' A bit of pizza shoots out of Jag's mouth in laughter. 'Come on, you,' she adds, 'we could have some fun and flirt all night? Not like we haven't done it already. And I'm younger so I have him beat. I can get my boobs out?'

I think all of us around the table blush at hearing that. Oh, Lucy. I feel the shame but also applaud the fact she wants to help. Leo shrugs. I guess he's past caring. If it distracts the other teams so we win this quiz then I'm all for it.

'Pizza for you, Miss Callaghan?' Jag offers with a smile. I like having him here and I like how he fits into this dynamic so well. If we became a thing would he start coming to these school events with me? Our conversations mention the kids more now and we talk openly about my divorce and all those things we avoided before. He listens. I hold his hand under the table and give it a squeeze.

'Oh, flaps.' Beth who sits opposite me with a mouthful of pizza suddenly stops. Her eyes stare at someone who's just entered the room behind me. I pause and turn to see who it is then quickly twist back. Lucy and Maddie see him too, their expressions horrified. *Really?*

'Isn't that…?' asks Mark. Maddie gives him a swift elbow to the ribs.

I need to tell Jag. Or not? But he senses the tension and turns around to see Simon stood there, right behind him. I haven't seen my ex-husband since I walked out of his mother's hospital room. To be honest, I am not entirely sure what happened that night but I made sure the girls wrote cards to their grandmother and we sent her flowers. That was the most time we'd ever spent talking honestly about our relationship. There was something about it that cleared some of the mud out of view. The problem was I hadn't told anyone about it. When I left Beth that night to watch the girls, I told her there was a problem at the hospital. I was too worried about the fact that when that man came crying to me, I was there for him. People wouldn't have understood. Why is he here though? I certainly didn't buy him a ticket.

'Callaghans, Maddie…'

'Simon,' Maddie replies.

Something clicks in Jag's brain and he stands up. 'Hi. I'm Jag.'

Simon shakes his hand but is typically inattentive. Simon studies the people around the table.

'Our team is full now,' says Lucy bluntly.

'Oh no, I was asked by Freya's mum to join their team. I bumped into her at gymnastics and I thought why not? Good to give back to the school.'

He looks me in the eye as he says it. We're all dressed in casual festive partywear but he's in a suit and that navy pea coat, straight from work, still wearing his ID to ensure everyone knows that he's a doctor.

'Where are our daughters?' he asks.

'They're waiting in the car for us,' adds Lucy, sarcastically. 'They're smoking skunk and getting tats from my mate, Tank.'

She has a mate called Tank?

'My mum has all the grandkids this evening,' I reply, unsure why I have to explain this to him.

'Jag is Emma's boyfriend,' adds Lucy. Jag widens his eyes. I am not sure that needed to be announced but so as not to make him feel too uncomfortable, I link arms with him. It's worked. I can sense Simon's discomfort.

'Remember that quiz we did when we first joined the school, Emma? Between us we could name all the English counties. We were quite the dream team.'

Simon said that out loud, didn't he? It wasn't just us. It was two school governors and another couple – he shagged the wife and they've since taken their kids out of the school because of it.

'I believe I named all the counties because all you knew were Surrey, Hampshire and Kent,' I reply.

Lucy and Beth cackle behind me.

'And what do you do Jag?'

'I work at the Evelina.'

'As a surgeon? I don't believe we've crossed paths before?'

'Not unless you've needed a paediatric anaesthetist?'

'Oh.' I immediately want to punch the man I divorced. Jag beats him on every level, from better facial hair down to his shoes. But Jag doesn't seem threatened or bothered. I guess he knows enough about Simon to realise that he has little to be worried about.

'Anyone got a ruler so Simon can actually measure the size of his cock this evening?' asks Lucy.

Maddie and Mark can't hide their giggles. Beth pretends to root around in her handbag.

'Oh, Lucy. Always good to see you keeping it classy.'

'Someone has to…'

'Oh… and I hear someone's back on the singles market, Beth?'

Beth sits there in shock. Lucy stands up from her chair looking territorial. 'How is that any of your business?' she asks.

'The girls told me,' Simon replies, deadpan, 'such a shame with the little one being so young. What is his name, Jamie?'

'Joe. You have a couple of sons, don't you? Remind us of their names? Isn't one of them named after my sister?' adds Lucy.

Oh, hell. My sisters are intent on throwing petrol on this bonfire tonight.

'Yes. Well, good luck today, all. And Emma, I meant to thank you for coming to the hospital the other day when my mother was ill. For being there for me, it meant a lot.'

There is a moment of silence as Lucy and Beth look over disapprovingly. *You did what, big sister?* I grab Jag's arm a little tighter.

'I did it for the girls, their grandmother. Not for you.'

He replies with a shrug and a smirk before walking away to his table clutching a bottle of his favourite Rioja. All of our eyes follow him across that school hall.

'You went to which hospital?' asks Lucy.

'When you were in Amsterdam and everyone came round for lunch, he rang and told me his mother collapsed, she had a stroke.' I reply.

'And you…?' Maddie asks.

'I went to him. Whatever's happened between us, she was once my mother-in-law, she's the girls' grandmother.'

There is silence as I rush through my explanation, embarrassed. Why is he here? He hated these school events and often told me he'd rather just write out a cheque to these people than have to spend time with them. He goes over to his table, air kisses everyone and shakes hands amidst roaring laughter and conversation. If looks could kill, our table would win that competition hands down.

'We're so ripping that team a new one, right?' asks Mark.

We all nod. There's a little tap on the microphone.

'Can the captain of the Ho Ho Hos make themselves known please?'

Lucy puts her hand in the air.


'Wrong book, that's *Sense and Sensibility*,' whispers Beth. Maddie crosses out the answer and scribbles in the right one but she's had a fair bit to drink so her writing is off the chart. 'I am certain of this. I taught it at A-level.'

The joys of having an English teacher on the team whose knowledge of Austen goes beyond Colin Firth and Kate Winslet. Beth has killed the literature round whereas Leo nailed the music of Fleetwood Mac, Mark aced sports as predicted and Jag was king of world capitals. I have nailed the wine. I'm very drunk and I'm not sure why. It could be because Lucy is here and she has that unfortunate habit of topping up everyone's glass when they're not looking. This is evident from the bottles below our table which make us look like a recycling point. But I also drink to try and blot out the fact that Simon is here, making a spectacle of himself and trying to piss over this occasion for me. So far, he's already bid £500 on a weekend break in someone's cottage in Suffolk, gone to the stage to receive it and hug Mrs Buchanan. He's taken off his tie, he's loud and shouting out asides about the easiness of the questions. He's tactile with Leo's ex-wife and another woman on the table who I feel I should warn. Lucy has one leg draped over Leo and has occasionally flashed her knickers to the room so I worry for my reputation within these four walls. That said, she's wearing knickers so it could be much worse. I down what's left of my glass and glance casually over at their table.

'Leo, how does Faith know Simon?'

'Beats me. Knowing her she's using him for his brains. That dad over there is an MP, that mum is a lawyer and I think she was on *University Challenge* ten years ago. A doctor just completes the group. She's a cow and a competitive one at that.'

I look at the blackboard on the stage where one of the secretaries has been keeping tally. Simon's team is the Noel It Alls which speaks for itself but they're in first place. We're in third behind the Jingle Ladies who are all staff members and will most likely win this as they are staying professional, sipping at cranberry juice so all their faculties are in place. The scoreboard gets updated. We've moved up to second and I double high five Beth in a moment of drunken exuberance.

'YES! You fucking clever bitch, you!'

Maddie bursts into laughter at me swearing. Jag pulls me back down to my chair.

'Alright there Callaghan?' he asks.

'We've got to beat them, we have to. For Leo, for me, and for little baby Jesus.'

Lucy cackles. 'When do I get my boobs out?'

Leo smiles and Beth shakes her head.

'We can do this. We are clart, smever people,' she mutters.

Maddie takes her glass from her. Never mind winning this quiz, I just hope we can get out conscious and not have to carry anyone home. Jag laughs at all three sisters and cosies into me while we wait for the last round.

'I like being here. This has been fun.'

'I'm sorry about Simon being here and spoiling things…'

'Actually, it's been good. To confirm what a dick he is.'

'Isn't he just?' interjects Lucy. 'Like the most colossal of dickheads. Like a nuclear style dickhead. Mass weapon of dickheadedness.'

Leo thinks this hilarious and we leave them to continue in what is quite an open display of flirting.

'I knew anyway. I'd seen him around the hospital, his reputation preceded him.'

'And I guess you're thinking how could anyone be so stupid as to have married him?'

'No. I'm thinking he took advantage of your good nature, that's all.'

We smile at each other.

'So what number date is this?' I ask.

'Do we count the cafeteria coffees?' he says.

'Or the hour-long conversations on WhatsApp?'

Maddie has her ear in and I can see her smiling to herself.

'I'm counting this as official date seven,' I say. 'And I'm waiting for what's in store.'

I realise this sounds vaguely sexual so panic a little but he laughs and plants a kiss on my forehead.

'So, the final round to decide who the winners will be tonight is on the human body.'

Lucy shrieks and does a fist pump. 'We've so got this.'

Her and Beth bare their teeth in quite a show of aggression and even Maddie grasps at her pen knowing that we have a trump card here. I glance over Beth's shoulder to see someone looking over at our table. He catches my eye and I bow my head to him to initiate the start of combat. A lady comes over with a quiz sheet and gives it to Maddie.

'Fuuuuuckk…' she says.

I grab the sheet from her. It's a diagram of a skeleton asking you to label bones, Simon's specialism. He probably slept with someone to plant this as the last round. I watch as he rolls up his sleeves, announcing the cavalry has arrived.

'Cranium, mandible, clavicle, humerus, radius, ulna, pelvic girdle, coccyx, tibia, and metatarsals,' I say almost robotically. My shoulders drop. We may have lost this and it all feels a little rigged. Maddie frantically fills in the sheet and I watch as they do the same across the room. On a table next to us are The Wise Men whom Leo was supposed to have joined and I tell them the answers too as I'm really not bothered now who wins. We hand in our papers and I wait for the horrific show of smugness that will be the winners' celebration. I may have to actually leave. I watch the teachers on the stage discuss the papers.

'So, in the first ever time of our Christmas quiz, we actually have a tie break situation.'

My head looks up. Simon looks confused and holds his hand in the air.

'We were ahead though? How has that changed?' he asks.

'Your team got one answer wrong in the last round.'

I stand up and may put my hands to my mouth. Please say that again out loud for us all to hear and so I can record it, play it back for all in the medical community and have it as my ringtone.

'Really?' he exclaims.

'Well, yes.'

'Which answer would that be then?'

'You put skull when the correct answer we were looking for was cranium.'

Beth and Lucy cannot hide their glee and the heckling is both petty and loud. Jag has the broadest smile on his face.

'The diagram was not clear.'

'My sister got it right,' announces Lucy to the room.

A few of the teams stop to observe the drama about to unfold. It's why we're all here really, never mind the school's fundraising efforts. We're here to gawk and find out whose marriage is best, who's had the most convincing plastic surgery, whose child is Grade 8 oboe and who had the best holiday in Dubai this year. Simon glares at me. *You should know that, Simon. Bones are your thing.* I only deal in hearts and cut through the occasional rib.

'So please could a representative from the Ho Ho Hos and the Noel It Alls come to the front of the room. We have a tie break question and whoever answers first will win.'

'And the subject…?' asks Faith on Simon's team.

'It's another question on the human body.'

'I got this!'

I stand up from my chair and make my way to the front of the hall as people clap and Lucy and Beth cheer me on drunkenly. I stand with Simon and wait. Mrs Buchanan knows exactly what she's doing and I don't doubt that this is for her entertainment too but I know what I have to do. Simon stands in front of me and I think about a time when his back was turned and I was always behind him, watching, following, letting him take the lead, never believing I was good enough. His stare is both conniving and different to me now. I'm not intimidated by it. It doesn't dictate my self-worth. I look right through it and wonder what I ever loved about it.

'So, for the prize tonight. The first person to put up their hand and give me the right answer is the winner today. Ladies and gentlemen, some quiet please.'

Please know this, please know this. Let's take this bugger down.

'What are the names of the three bones…'

'I know!' I shout, my hand raised in the air.

Crap. She didn't finish the question, did she? I went too soon. Three bones. Which three bones is she talking about? It's either arm or ear. But the arm was part of the diagram. So was the leg. I need to take a risk. I don't like risks. Unless she's talking about the torso. Ear. There are three bones in the ear. I have to get this right.

'Malleus, incus and stapes, also known as the hammer, anvil and stirrup.'

The whole room is quiet. Then Mrs Buchanan smiles and nods. A corner of the school hall erupts so much that Beth falls off a chair. Leo waves over at his wife. Maddie points to me with both hands and Mark tries unsuccessfully to start a chant in my honour. Other less inebriated teams look on confused and I realise we may have given ourselves quite the reputation. I'd like to say Simon is gracious in defeat but he goes over to challenge Mrs Buchanan.

'It was not pointed out that we could answer at any time. I think you should do that tie break again,' he states plainly.

'Oh, suck it up Chadwick. We won.'

'Mature.'

'Just better.'

'Touché,' he says, and then goes to shake my hand.

He can't take this away from me. I know we're in a school hall swathed in holly with parquet floors, and it's just £100 shared prize money, and a resin trophy shaped like a brain but this moment belongs to me and I'll take this over all those other moments where he humiliated me and made me feel like I was nothing. I beat him in a contest in his own specialism.

Mrs Buchanan laughs under her breath as I take the envelope and trophy from her hands and hold it above my head, jiggling it lightly. I think Mark may have just thrown up in his wife's handbag but this moment is mine and it's really very very sweet.


Later that evening we all part ways. Maddie gives me the biggest hug and tells me she is going to share our victory all over Facebook. Beth has gone on a mission to find food. Jag and Lucy wait outside the school booking Ubers whilst I try to level my reputation out by helping stack some chairs in the school hall.

'Well done,' a voice pipes up behind me.

It's Faith, Leo's wife. I've not really engaged much with her over our shared time at this school – I knew we were levels apart when I saw she wore Balenciaga trainers on the school run.

'Strange to bring a nanny to a quiz night? Is she your nanny?'

I know exactly what she's doing here. She's trying to work out who the young girl was who was sat in her ex-husband's lap. I need to do something for Leo in some sort of divorced club solidarity. The alcohol in my bloodstream will no doubt help things along.

'She is. Her name is Elsa. She's twenty-six.'

'That's interesting.'

'Not as interesting as the sex I hear they're having.'

Her face drops. I say drops. She's had a fair bit of Botox from the looks of it so I think that vacant expression may be shock.

'In your house?'

'Oh no, Leo and I have become friends. We talk. It's nice to hear that he's happy.'

She tries to stare me out. I don't know how to extend this lie to make it not sound ludicrous. Do I say 'Elsa' is a part-time actress? Or that she's part of Swedish royalty? Either way, it pains me to see her so angry that her husband may actually be moving on, just like she has. That it's a race to see who reclaims their happiness the quickest.

'Well, divorce is a funny game as you very well know,' she retorts.

Can you kill someone with a resin trophy? She wanders off to find her young entrepreneur fiancé man and I stare at her wondering to what capacity divorce can just transform you into such a bitch. Maybe she was always one. Well done Leo for getting away from that when you did.

I collect my bags to leave, Mrs Buchanan waving at me as I do. I think she likes me now. I then make my way out to go find my Uber buddies through the school's winding parquet corridors. I hope Beth has sourced chips. A sound grabs my attention though.

A jarring crash to the floor. I tiptoe over to see the source and find Simon, sat on the floor of a darkened hallway, outside a classroom lined with Santas made out of paper plates and cotton wool. In front of him are the remnants of a smashed phone. I think about a similar phone on my mother's patio two years ago.

'I hope that's insured.'

'Look, it's Mastermind herself. Nice work, Callaghan.'

I gather bits of shattered screen into my palms, thinking about young children walking along here tomorrow morning.

'Thank you. You never come to these things, why are you here?'

'Truth?'

'For a change?'

'I thought Susie might be here. She had bought tickets at an open evening for Oliver.'

'She's got a pretty small baby, chances are she'd give it a miss.'

'True.' He rubs at his temples. 'I think I fucked up there. I don't think she'll take me back.'

'Well, she's a wiser woman than me. Have you met the baby yet?'

'No.'

He sits there quiet. It's a rare thing to see him so still, processing his emotion rather than just acting on it. He was not usually so big on thought.

'How could you label it a skull? I feel embarrassed for you.'

'I'll take that, the shame. Or maybe I let you win?'

'You're the most competitive man I know so that's a lie. How's your mum?'

'Getting there. Thanks for asking.'

I turn to walk away.

'I'm sorry I tried to kiss you in that hospital room.'

I'm silent and stop. There's a tone that I can't quite read.

'Are you OK, Simon?'

He catches my eye to check for any hint of sarcasm.

'It's a bit of a mess, Ems. I don't know how to make this right... what do I do now?'

I look at him. Is that what I wanted? Defeat? Him lying on the battlefield, bloodied and broken, my leg cocked on his body whilst I wave a flag of victory for all the wronged women out there?

I take a deep breath. 'I'll see you tomorrow, the girls are looking forward to seeing you.'

He nods and I take my leave. Outside, Jag and Lucy are in hysterics recalling the events of the evening.

'Hold that trophy up. Let's get a picture of you,' says Lucy.

'That was a pretty crazy night. Well done you,' Jag says, locking arms with me.

'Was the dance too much? In front of everyone?'

'I believe Maddie filmed that...' Lucy informs me.

'She did?'

'I've just seen it as an Instagram Story.'

'We're going to get banned from the next one, eh?'

'I thought we were great value. Did you see the team to the far left? The Silent Knights? I've seen cadavers with more character,' Jag jokes.

His phone rings and he breaks off to speak to a lost Uber driver while Lucy smiles broadly. *I like this one*, she mouths at me. Behind us, the school door opens and Simon walks out. Jag and Lucy say nothing but roll their eyes when he's out of view. I watch him grapple with his keys to escape into the car. But before he opens the door, he holds my gaze and salutes me. *It was just a game, Simon.* But maybe it's time to just stop playing.

# Chapter Twenty

'Oh no, I think you'll find the big seventies bush is coming back into fashion. I don't know why but I've had a lot of men ask me to grow mine out, like down the creases of my thighs.'

We all sit around my dining room table enthralled by Lucy's latest revelation about her love life, while I'm slightly worried about what constitutes a lot of men. We've extended quiz night to pile back to mine and give my sisters the chance to get to know Jag further. It also feels like something I should have done during my marriage. Informal takeaway nights in the comfort of my own home, involving alcohol, chat and people I liked instead of surgeons and people whom Simon was trying to impress. Beth had drunk too much of the quiz night wine to buy food sanely so before us are the remnants of a KFC bargain bucket, a selection of Thai food, a giant bag of chips and some battered sausages. I bite into a spicy fishcake to hide my horror at learning about my sister's body hair situation.

'Leo was all about the hair.'

'What's the deal there? You're still seeing Leo?' I ask, curious.

'Kinda. He's a nice guy. He doesn't want to marry me. It's very lustful. I think I'm a distraction, I make him feel better about himself. I feel like I'm offering him a service.'

'You make yourself sound like a prostitute,' adds Beth.

'A kind one with a heart of gold. I make him tea and let him jizz on my boobs. He's got a decent willy.'

'LUCY!' shrieks Beth.

I seek safety in chips, Jag looks over in complete shock. It's not like I didn't tell him about this sister before.

'Leo doesn't even want me to shave my pits.'

'I don't shave my pits,' mentions Beth. I want to add that I don't either unless necessary but don't want to scare Jag away.

'Yeah, but that's not a fetish thing,' adds Lucy. 'That's a lazy comfort thing. You shave them in the summer when they're out?'

Jag laughs. 'Like my back. I only shave it when I have to, it's a tiring endeavour otherwise.'

'How do you shave your own back?' Lucy asks.

This naturally piques my interest as I am sure that unless he's a contortionist then it's impossible. I also realise this is something that he may require me to do moving forward if this became serious.

'This is embarrassing. I ask my mum.'

Lucy and Beth roar with laughter while I sit there wondering when talk turned to body hair. There was me thinking we'd at least attempt to have civilised conversation about politics and the state of the environment.

'And with that revelation, I am going to the loo to die of shame.'

He gets up and grazes my hand as he does. This doesn't go unnoticed by Beth. They wait until he's locked the door of my downstairs cloakroom before they say anything.

'Like how hairy are we talking? *Planet of the Apes*?'

'Lucy! I haven't seen it yet.'

'But how?'

'Because I haven't slept with him yet?'

'But you've been on dates and stuff?' asks Lucy.

'Well, we kissed but we're taking it slowly.'

'Shit! Tonight then? You could shag him tonight.'

'I haven't thought that far ahead,' I explain.

'Beth and I can piss off out and then…' She does a strange rave-style dance as she thinks of her plan coming together.

Beth looks worried. 'Do you want to sleep with him?' she asks.

'What do you think of him?'

'Honestly?' replies Beth.

'Of course.'

'He fits in the jigsaw. Will always says we're a hard outfit to infiltrate. Ask Danny up north, Tom when he was here, maybe even Simon… You don't enter into a relationship with one Callaghan sister, you get a whole gaggle of them. He's coping remarkably well considering.'

'Did Simon fit in the jigsaw?' I ask her, laughing.

'Maybe he was that annoying rogue piece that was a bit misshapen. We forced him to fit in when really—'

'We should have just thrown him in the fucking bin,' adds Lucy.

'He seems like a good man, Emma,' says Beth, hurt still haunting her eyes from Will's absence. I grab her hand. Jag returns from the toilet and Lucy jiggles in her seat. *Don't you bloody dare sister.*

'We were just saying Jag…'

'Were you still talking about my back?'

'No, but we need wine. There is not enough wine and we thought you could walk down to the corner shop and get some?'

Beth and I wonder what she's up to.

'Yeah, I could get wine. Any other requests?'

If she tells him to get condoms in then I will skewer her with a chopstick.

'Anything you might fancy or need?'

She's walking an incredibly thin, thin line.

He gets up to retrieve his coat and I offer to give him money but he refuses. I hand him my keys and he heads for the front door. Beth stares Lucy out.

'Seriously?' she says.

'We need to prepare you if you're going to sleep with him.'

'Like mentally?' I ask.

'Like have you had a tidy?'

'You just said men like seventies bush,' interrupts Beth.

'Yes but I do it as a request. First time, I've always at least tidied up the flaps and done a bit of topiary.'

Who is this woman? How can you raise five girls in exactly the same house and come up with such a random entity?

She stands up and heads for my kitchen drawers, rifling around until she pulls out a pair of scissors. 'Show me your bush,' she orders.

'Lucy! I prepare food with those scissors.'

'And we'll wash them?'

Beth is in hysterics as she sees this scene unfolding in front of us.

'I'm not getting my bush out in my kitchen.'

'You're so dull. I'm trying to help. What are your pits like? Shame there's no time to tackle your upper lip.'

I put my hand over it instinctively. 'I have a moustache?'

'Well, you're not Tom Selleck but it could do with a bleach.'

'You're being cruel now, Luce,' says Beth. 'But I think we do need the comedy of seeing Lucy trimming your bush in the kitchen.'

I stand up reluctantly and unbutton my jeans.

'Ha!' exclaims Lucy. 'You're wearing nice pants, you knew this was going to happen. Just peel them back and let me have a look.' I let her have a glance and she tuts loudly.

'Be quick for god's sake. This is something that no one needs to see.'

'Do you want a shape?'

'Like a heart? No!'

'You're a heart surgeon, it'd be cute!'

'No!'

'I'll trim the length then. Beth, put your hand out…'

'Do I have to?'

'Don't you love your sister to at least hold her pubes?'

I don't know what's happening here. One sister is very close to my private regions with a sharp object and I hear the creak of metal as she shears away. The other collects the trimmings in a napkin in her palm. This feels like an opportune moment to ring Meg and Grace and start a FaceTime chat. That time we all took one for the team so Emma could reclaim her sex life.

'Thank you, Lucy.'

'You don't say this enough I feel.'

'We don't,' says Beth.

'You want me to look at yours, B?'

'I'm good.'

'What if he's into weird stuff?' I ask.

'Like?'

'I am very vanilla. I think I've only done sex in five positions.'

'Well, no one breaks out all the moves on their first time,' says Beth. Lucy gives us a look like she begs to differ.

'And he can't cum in me. I'm not on anything. I might get pregnant.'

'That's what condoms are for?' says Beth.

They both give me a look that says I am the doctor and I should have an inkling about how reproduction works and the preventative measures that I can put in place to stop myself getting pregnant. I think back to a time about when I had sex with Stuart Morton. I've forgotten everything, again.

'How do I initiate it?'

'Well, you could dance for him?' says Lucy, mockingly. 'You've both had a drink, let it just happen. Planned sex is the worst kind of sex.'

'I planned nothing. You're the one who's got the kitchen scissors next to my vag.'

'I'm done, anyway. Not my finest work but then at least he'll be able to find it?'

Beth rolls her eyes and goes to the bin with her napkin of pubes. I do my jeans up and sit at the table, downing what's left in my glass. What if he doesn't fancy me? What if he can't get it up? Or worse, he takes one look at my boobs and shrugs and says they're not for him. I have modest boobs. They wouldn't win any competitions. What if he wants better boobs?

'You're overthinking,' says Beth.

'I don't have condoms.'

'I put some in your bedside cabinet.'

How far ahead has Lucy planned this?

'Meg also sent me a vibrator for you but we thought against it.'

'Because I'm so sexually closed off?'

'Because I kept it for myself; it'd be wasted on you,' she replies.

'This is why Simon slept with other people, didn't he?'

'Woah there,' says Lucy holding out her hand. 'Simon was a dick, get him out of your brain. There is no comparison here. Look, tonight, just get naked with the fella, assess the back situation, have some bloody fun. Enjoy yourself.'

The problem may be that I don't know what fun is anymore. Am I fun?

I hear the key go in the latch of the front door. That was quick. Christ. Jag enters the kitchen with two bottles of red that I immediately feel guilty about as I have a rack of it in the utility room. He also carries a few packs of crisps and takes the kitchen scissors that were on my table, covered in small shards of hair, and goes to cut them open.

'Crisps?'

'Ooh, you went for something spicy. You like a spicy crisp, Ems.'

Beth and Lucy descend into giggles. I hate you both.


'It's a party in Brixton. A mutual mate's birthday, totally forgot…' says Lucy unconvincingly, pretending to check train times.

I feel awful. I'm sending the sisters back out into the cold so Jag and I can have the house to ourselves. Lucy keeps winking at me which is more down to the fact that she's had at least two bottles of wine to herself. Jag stands at the kitchen door while I wave everyone off. I can't do this. I don't want to look him in the eye because I can feel myself blushing and I am conscious that I may die from my face overheating.

'Have fun, kids!' chants Lucy as she shepherds Beth away from the house. I shut the door.

And then there were two. I turn and Jag is no longer at the doorway. I tiptoe into the kitchen to find him stacking plates. He goes to put the kitchen scissors back in the drawer.

'Oh, those need to be washed.'

He smiles at me and then puts them in the sink.

'Shall we tidy up now?'

'It can wait?'

'OK.'

He smiles that magnificent smile at me from across the room and I feel relaxed but also on the faint side of nauseated. It's first time nerves. Is it weird that I am also thinking about the cleanliness of my bedroom? Did I pick up yesterday's pants from the corner of my room? Do I remember how to give a blow job? He starts to pour the last of the wine out.

'Stop.'

'Hammer time?'

'Say what?'

'I was just trying to be funny.'

I fake a laugh, walking over to the countertops where he stands. I grab a glass and take a large sip to steady myself.

'Last time I was in this kitchen, you were nursing me back to health.'

'After Lucy threw that bottle at you?'

He smiles a little nervously. 'Can I say something? I think I need to tell you this before it happens.' Here it is. The sex talk. Is he pre-empting the back thing? 'It's just, I don't want you to see it and freak out.'

It's either his back or his penis. There is something wrong with his penis. I can't seem to reply.

'I got you something for Christmas. And I normally wouldn't spend so much on someone but it was on offer and now I feel like I overstepped and you'll think I'm a stalker or something.'

I'm still speechless.

'I got you a new sofa. For your office. Because the new girlfriend covered yours in amniotic fluid and stuff.'

'You did what?'

'I told Maddie and she cried. And now I think I've gone over-board but it's from Ikea. Don't get too excited. I don't think you have to build it yourself but—'

And in that moment, I grab him by the collar and kiss him. He stumbles a little but then lets his body fold into mine. I can do this. Crap. He's lifting me up. He sits me on the counter and I'd like to say the moment overtakes but there's red wine inches from my arse so I move the glass with my hand whilst still kissing him. We're kissing. He's good at this. His lips. It's pleasant. I feel his hands in the small of my back and then he lifts my jumper over my head. I'm in my bra. Don't overthink it. Oh, the bra is off. My nipples are out in the kitchen. He's kissing my nipples. Oh. Do I mention the condoms now? I realise my nipples are hard because someone bought me a sofa.

'So not too much?'

'I haven't got you anything?'

'This is perfect,' he whispers. He looks me in the eye and brushes the hair from my face. 'Not that I'm saying you have to pay me in sex. God, that's not what I meant at all.'

I smile and kiss him back, feeling his erection pressed up against me. 'I would like to give you the sex?' I blurt out.

He laughs, 'The sex?'

'The sex.'

'I mean, I don't want to assume but now you've asked and… I haven't shaved my back so I'm going to warn you in advance.'

'My sister literally just trimmed my pubes for me.'

We both laugh, though he does look slightly confused.

'Are you sure this is what you want?' he asks me.

I nod. I can see the soft beat of his jugular through his skin, a pulse dancing underneath, and I put my own hand to my chest, almost to feel my heart open again, blood rushing to parts of me, giving me permission to feel something again. You bought me a sofa.

'Yes. The sex. Please.'

# Chapter Twenty-One

713 days since Grace told Simon to get a
lawyer. A really fucking good lawyer

'Soooo… you've been very quiet about it. What was his cock like?'

I pretend to stare intently, looking for parking spaces trying to maintain my dignity and grace, compared to Lucy who sits there sprawled in my passenger seat in a onesie, Uggs, a parka and sunglasses. I think the onesie even has ears. It's been a few days since I slept with Jag. Was it a passionate display of lovemaking on my kitchen like one would see in a French New Wave film? No. We re-located to the sofa. It was first time sex: I laughed as he struggled to take off his jeans, he got incredibly sweaty, we headbutted each other and I got cramp in my right foot. But there was something incredibly real and honest about it. He was so sweet, attentive and complimentary and it just felt right. Lucy texted me the day after with rows of sexual emojis from baguettes to water droplets to avocados. I ignored her.

'You've said nothing. I tell you everything,' she complains.

'And that's how we're different. It was very pleasant.'

'Walks in the park are pleasant. Did he make you come? Was the back like a rug?'

I stare back at her and smile and she pouts sullenly. We're here this morning on a retrieval mission. One of the advantages of being a doctor is that my body clock is completely buggered. It's not ideal but it means I am your go-to person when you need to chat to someone in the middle of the night or require a pick-up from an airport. So when Grace messaged to tell us her flight was getting in at 6 a.m., I was nominated. In any case, I didn't mind at all. I haven't seen her in forever and I'm desperate to hug her and have another sister back with the clan. Naturally though, I also dragged Lucy out for the adventure. Her body clock is governed by all those sozzled nights out so she's like a human owl. I reverse my car into a space.

'At least tell me what you were working with? He looks the sort to have some girth?'

'It was a very pleasant penis.'

'You are so dull. Grace has better stories than you and she's a widow.'

I cast Lucy a look. It feels strange to use that word to describe our sister. She's still so young that it just doesn't seem real.

'What stories would that be then?'

'She went to a warehouse rave in Brooklyn and slept with a man called Z.'

'He only had a single letter for a name?'

'That's all you got from that?'

'Yes.'

It's hard to imagine my fellow straight sister doing such a thing but maybe that's what we've both got out of the last two years: we'd peeked over the line and dared to do something off the beaten track.

'It's so shitting cold, Ems.'

'That's because it's December. What have you got on under that onesie?'

'Nothing.'

'Not even a bra? What happens when you need a wee? You'd be sat in a cubicle with your boobs out.'

'I love that's what you worry about. You know what would warm me up though, Mum? A coffee…'

She links arms with me as we try to find the terminal entrance. She's taken to calling me Mum a lot recently which makes me feel aged but it's usually a ploy to make me pay for stuff. I look like I've been accompanied here by a giant child. We find the arrivals gate and make our way through the sea of assorted drivers, holiday package operators and relatives towards a Starbucks. A person behind the till baulks at seeing Lucy approaching but they're wearing Christmas antlers so they can hardly talk.

'Hello, what's the largest size of coffee you do?' says Lucy.

'Like the Venti?'

'Yeah whatever that is. Americano, double shot it or whatever you can do to make it strong as tits.'

There's a pause while the person behind the till tries to find the 'strong as tits' option on the ordering screen.

'And just a regular cappuccino please.'

'Name?'

'Catwoman.'

I look at her strangely while I pay for them.

'And why?'

'It's funny? Another bitch called Lucy stole my latte once so I do these things to protect my caffeine and amuse myself. Do we have a flight number or anything?' Lucy asks.

I glance over at the screens. I actually don't but Grace has been in Amsterdam so I'm sure we can pick something out. All we've been given is a terminal and a time. I check my phone again and scan the screens. There's a flight coming in from N'Djamena? Havana? Lucy perches on a table and we watch as people filter in and out. Christmas means relatives are returning or visiting and files of grandparents trot out merrily to be met by little people with homemade banners. A kid obviously back from travelling hugs her father dearly who doesn't let go. Behind them I see a happy reunion of a couple, engaging in a long drawn out kiss. There is a glow between them despite the hour. Lucy deposits three sachets of sugar into her coffee. She spies the reunion of the happy couple.

'I don't think I could love anyone enough to pick them up from an airport at six in the fucking morning.' She takes a large sip of her coffee and makes fake retching sounds.

'You're here now?'

'It's Gracie. That's not romantic love. That's a love forged in stone. I'd chop my limbs off for my sisters.'

I like the grand admission in that statement. I'm not sure I'd do something so wildly impressive. I'd certainly negotiate other avenues first before losing all my limbs.

'Maybe the right person hasn't come along. One day you might meet someone you'd go to the ends of the world for? Maybe she was desperate to see him after some time apart.'

'Fairy-tale bullshit. Maybe he's a lazy cheap shit who didn't want to waste money on an Uber.'

We look over at them again. He pushes the hair back from her face. She's made an effort with some make-up so obviously had to rise half an hour earlier to make herself presentable.

'Or maybe they're having an affair. Maybe he's a French business-man called Thierry and she is his British bit on the side. He's told his wife he has to come to London for an important trip but really, he's gonna take this bird down some airport hotel and they're going to get shagging. Fiver says she's not wearing knickers.'

I look over at her confused as one, she said most of that in forced French tones, and two, there's also something that makes me wonder when she became so jaded about love.

'One day you will end up in love, falling for all those grand gestures you speak of so cynically and I will laugh.'

'It'll never happen. The greatest thing I've learnt about being the youngest? I've got to see all of you and your experiences and it's made me realise it's not worth the hassle or the heartbreak.'

'So you're saying I've put you off love?'

'Nah, I'm saying Meg got it sorted. I'd rather Meggy was closer but then you married Simon, Beth and Will are still in relation-ship limbo and well… Tom died.' We both go a little quiet. She continues, 'So, that's four sisters: only one of whom has done alright out of love whilst the others have demonstrated the potential for things to go very wrong. Those are not good averages.'

'But I found love again?'

'So you love Jag?' she replies excitedly.

'I mean, my divorce was not the end.'

'True. But the more I see of relationships, the more I just don't like the risk involved.'

'Says the biggest risk taker of us all.'

'I have hidden depths, dear sister. I'm a sensitive sort with a fragile heart really.'

'And I've heard you're snogging girls too now?'

'On occasion.'

'So you're bisexual?'

'I don't put a tag on it. If I fancy someone, I go for it. With penis or without. It's all good fun and experience.'

'And what if you want children down the line?'

She looks at me like I might be crazy.

'Do I look like a mother?'

'No one looks like a mother.'

'You forget I work with children. There is far too high a risk of me ending up with a duffer that eats its own hair. Essentially, you sisters did all the hard work for me. My nieces and nephew are bloody wonders. You made the loves of my life for me.'

I smile broadly knowing her love for all our kids has always been the loudest, the most colourful. They will need a fun aunty Lucy to take them cool places and buy them the stuff that I'm far too un-streetwise and responsible to know about.

'Plus I like my vag too much to put it through that. I heard Beth's birth story.'

She winces, holding her crotch. I pull a face in resigned confusion.

'Can I get a muffin or something?'

I sigh and nod, delving through my handbag looking for coins. She stands up but takes pause for a moment as three people head towards us. Lucy has the biggest smile on her face but I stand here, confused.

'Gracie!' screams Lucy, launching herself at Grace. It takes me a little longer to react.

I move from my chair but bend down to the tiny person beside Grace, a small child who hides behind her leg. She has a gorgeous mop of black hair and big brown eyes like chocolate buttons. She looks sleepy, dishevelled, and carries a purple rabbit toy under her arm.

'This is Cleo.'

'Grace?' I say, looking up at her.

Lucy coos over the baby in the pram next to her.

'And this is Maya.'

I can't seem to process the words.

'I guess you're aunties. Again?' Lucy does a celebratory dance.

Grace smiles, tearing up and I can't quite help but do the same. I hold my hand out to Cleo.

'Hi, I'm Emma.' She smiles and gives me her rabbit, my heart expanding beyond a size I knew feasible.


Back in the safety of my house, Grace sits curled up in one of my living room armchairs. Maya is asleep in her arms whilst Lucy entertains Cleo on the rug. Lucy will want to assert her domain as the fun aunt from the outset. Grace watches on and smiles serenely.

'How old then?'

'Cleo is three and Maya is one.'

'And how?'

'I visited the orphanage and school in Vietnam where Tom used to work. He spent months down there helping them build it and he was like some local hero. I was there for about eight weeks. These girls had recently lost their mother and I guess something clicked. Bonded through loss perhaps.'

I don't mention Tom yet but I can see what she's done here is invest her love in something bigger than her. She looks completely enamoured. From talking to those girls in the back of the car and the way she keeps kissing Maya on the forehead, there is a heart-warming connection. I've always loved this sister of mine but the way she accepts this role of mother without question or doubt fills me with such pride.

'We thought you were in Amsterdam?'

'I flew to Vietnam a week ago to get the paperwork done, jumping through rings to get things sorted so I could bring them back.' There is a look in her that reads sheer joy and relief that she is embarking upon a new chapter.

'Is your house sorted?'

'Two weeks left before I can get back in but I was going to stay with Mum for a bit. Spring this on her and Dad.'

'You've mean you haven't told anyone?'

'Not a peep. Paperwork was literally signed forty-eight hours ago then there was a mad scramble to head to Singapore to get gear for the girls and flights back here. I wanted to be sure.'

'You should have said. One of us could have flown out to help you?'

'It's done. I'm here.'

'This is huge, Gracie?'

'I know.'

'And the trip? So many questions.'

'I have ones too. How's Jag?'

'Lucy told you?'

'Of course.'

'I can't wait for you to meet him. And for the girls to meet their new cousins.'

'And you? How are you?'

'Alive.' She says the word slowly, with meaning.

I smile over at her. 'You're back.'

'That I am.'

We look over at Lucy tickling little Cleo, making her giggle. Grace knew these girls would have aunties, grandparents, all sorts of cousins to be a part of our clan. And for a small moment, I think about two little boys out there, Oliver and Louis. Boys who are not part of my biology but now are part of this wider thing I call family. I think about a sister here who has opened her heart up to love kids who need her. I am in awe. And shock.

'And how are things with Simon? Did you talk to George?'

'I did.'

'And? What are we doing there? Did he get forensic accountants out? Are we going to take him for every penny he has?'

I smile. Grace is serene but she also has the sister fire.

'I haven't decided yet. I have some communication with Susie, the other woman, and we'll see what happens.'

She looks at me intently. 'You seem different, Ems. I like it.'

'Different?'

'Happier?'

'Then, I'd say so do you.'

She grabs my hand from across the way.

What a couple of years we've had, kid. I'm glad we're both here to tell our tales.

'I need tea. Proper builder's strong as tits tea.'

I laugh and get up to make her a cup.

'No, take Maya. I need to get up or the jet lag will kill me.' She puts the baby in my arms and stretches her arms out. 'Cleo, let's see what Aunty Emma has in her cupboards? She always has biscuits.'

Maya's warm body curls into mine and a head of black curls nestles next to my chest. Oh my days, I have literally only just met you but I am going to love you forever, little one. As long as you don't mind my big rather mental family then, welcome. I look over at Grace, my sister who was on the floor two years ago, not just broken but bruised and angry. Super Gracie is back, her heart refilled and replenished. I look down at Maya again. That warmth is a full nappy, isn't it? I got this.

# Chapter Twenty-Two

723 days since Dad told Simon to get out of his fucking house and my Dad never swears. Not even at Lucy.

'Mummy, why is his willy so tiny?' asks Violet.

'Well, babies can't be born with normal-sized willies, can they?' Iris replies, rolling her eyes in embarrassment.

I look down as Susie changes Louis and the girls look on. What is a normal-sized willy then? I am glad I didn't have sons; the changing situation looks different. I hope this one doesn't projectile urine over my rug. I watch as Louis' little fist grabs on to Violet's finger and she coos over his tiny babyness. Iris hands Susie wet wipes and I stand and watch it all. Is this weird? Louis is in my house and so is Oliver who's kneeling at my kitchen table and demolishing the crisps I've left out, leaving speckles of potato crumb all over his face and hair. George, our lawyer, watches him curiously. I think he may have found his spirit animal.

It's a strange day. In the last fortnight, Grace has been back with us and I've seen a lot of my new nieces. They've hung out with their cousins, they've learned the joy of CBeebies and are partial to Kit

Kats. They are a delight. Maybe it was down to meeting them or seeing Grace back, so serene having survived such heartbreak, that I felt inspired to do something I hadn't been sure I was capable of doing. I've invited over Susie so I can meet her sons and they can meet their sisters. I didn't know how today would pan out but this feels like a step in the right direction. That said, I've also bought in a Christmas quiche in case it all goes to pot.

Susie and I still can't define our relationship. She is neither friend nor foe at this point but I have a feeling that I will always need her onside. I see her pack her change mat away and I hand her the wipes and muslins she's pulled out of the bag. How do you start a conversation with your ex-husband's new ex-woman? Do you completely avoid asking about him? Do you joke about how he used to clip his toenails in bed? Or about the incomprehensible way he liked to watch action movies from the nineties? Lucy is not much better. She watches her quietly from the kitchen, still assuming Susie might be here with an agenda.

'Can I carry him, Susie?' asks Iris.

Susie nods. 'Of course you can. Make sure you support his head.'

I watch as Iris cradles him tight and my heart skips in different directions. This was never what I wanted when I married Simon but what I see in front of me is perfect. It's my girl connecting with someone who should be part of her life forever. I hope that happens. I hope he's a Beth because I suspect the crisp gobbler at the table will be her Lucy. The kid's not giving up until he eats that whole bowl. Lucy comes out with the cup of tea that was promised and gives Susie the eye. Her brief was to be civil and I hope she's managed that much. I check the surface of the tea for foam.

'Can I see you in the kitchen, Ems? I don't know what to do with this quiche?' Lucy says casually. I leave my girls and follow her through the door. Inside, she's all arms and whispers as she glares at Susie through the crack in the door. 'I hate her.'

'We don't hate anything, Lucy. We say we're not keen.'

She laughs. Those were my mother's words when we grew up. Broccoli didn't deserve to be hated, it had done nothing to you to deserve such words.

'I don't get you being so kind. She screwed you over, she knew exactly what she was doing. I couldn't forgive that.'

'Yeah… but look at the girls. It's more than forgiveness. I don't even know the word for it anymore.'

She sees her nieces interacting with the boys and looks at me. 'It's called having a big heart. You really are better than me, eh?'

'That's stating the obvious really.'

'I'm not available for any of her parties though. I still want to be the one who reminds her that what she did was wrong.'

'Just civil, yes?'

'Whatever that means. When is Satan getting here? And seriously, I thought we could just eat the quiche like this?'

'Soon. Oven, 180, fifteen minutes and get some forks out.'

She makes a face, realising she's eaten cold quiche her whole life. I walk over to the dining room to chat to George who has all his paperwork out, paper clipped and an expensive fountain pen cued up next to some cough lozenges and a handkerchief. I like that this is how he conducts serious business.

'I hear Grace is back. That must be a relief?'

'Less a relief, more a joy. She's doing well.'

'Glad to hear.'

He catches me looking over to the living room where Violet sits in Susie's lap. I don't know how I feel about that but he gets an idea and tries to distract me.

'So, since our last meeting, we have a new joke in our office,' he explains.

'Oh…' I suspect this won't be as funny as I think it will be.

'Well, occasionally we have a person in a divorce proceeding who is really quite awful. They may cheat or hide money and behave pretty despicably and now we have a code for them based on what your sister said last time?'

'Lucy?'

'We refer to them as the Tuesdays. It works particularly well.'

I laugh.

'Is Simon in that club then?'

'Oh, he's the chairman.' Another joke, you're on a roll, George. 'Having spoken to Miss Hunter in depth, it's been very interesting to find out how he's manipulated you both – whether it's financially or emotionally, everything he's done has been to serve his self-interest.'

It's not a surprise but maybe it's a good thing that Susie knows everything. I look down, where there is a letter for Susie marked with a red stamp. I know that stamp as it's an invoice for fees.

'Give that to me, I'll handle it.'

'You will? But—'

I shrug my shoulders. She's just had a baby and a large legal bill is probably not what she needs right now. I put my finger to my lips urging him to keep it a secret. Maybe if this is going to start on the right foot then I need to put that foot forward.

George smiles and the doorbell rings. I see Susie freeze for a moment. We're really doing this, aren't we? I go into the corridor and see his figure at the front door. Breathe Emma, breathe.

'Daddddyyyyyy!' squeals Violet as I open the door. She jumps into his arms.

Behind him stands the well-groomed Miss De Vere who is a vision in camel. I pray that a child here attacks her with Ribena. I lead them through to the living room where Iris stands holding Louis, and Oliver plays with a car on the floor. Where the hell is Susie? I scan the room to see George at the end holding his hands up in the air. Seriously? Simon stops at seeing his son and smiles at Iris.

'Is this…?'

'This is Louis, Daddy.'

He cradles the baby in one arm and is silent as he looks at his face for the very first time. 'Hello there, little man.'

I don't say a word. I've seen that hold, that face before. Simon was many things but I don't deny he is a good father. He's attentive, involved, and our girls adore him. He would love this boy. He loves him already. I see Oliver curl around his leg and this little team of children surrounding him and I'm stunned into quiet.

'Where's Suse?' he asks.

Suse and Ems: he refers to us so casually like we're some sort of pop duo.

'She's helping Lucy in the kitchen,' George answers.

She legged it. Did she run out the back door?

Lucy enters the room, shaking her head. 'He's like a cuter version of you, Simon.'

'Lucy.'

She eyeballs me. 'Your quiche is burning, Em.'

'Then why didn't you take it out of the oven?'

'The other quiche.' *Oh.* 'I'll stay here and keep watch. Now kids, do any of you know what the three smallest bones are in the human body?' She grins as Simon pretends to ignore her.

In the kitchen, a pale, limp quiche lies on the counter and the utility room door is ajar. I go inside and see a pair of legs hanging out of the coat rack.

'Remind me never to have you on my team for hide and seek.'

She doesn't reply. I close the door and lean against the countertop, looking down to see a tub full of Lucy's used knickers. I shake my head and throw them in the washing machine with a tablet. Susie peers through to see what I'm doing.

'I'm sorry. I just heard his voice and I couldn't bear to see him.'

'I get it. You're not sure if you'll just burst into tears or—'

'Stove his face in?'

'Exactly. So you left Louis with Iris and ran in here?'

'That was bad form, sorry.'

I don't respond. I put my hand in the tub of laundry next to me and start to fold some school uniforms. I always tell Lucy to do this as soon as it comes out of the dryer. Does she listen? No. Like she doesn't listen when I tell her not to toss her dirty knickers in the sink. Susie emerges to give me a hand.

'Is that a mermaid outfit?' she looks at me confused, as I certainly don't look the sort.

'It's my sister's. She does kids' parties at the weekend. This is her Ariel look. She has a wig and travels with a man who dresses like a crab.'

She laughs quietly. I don't think that costume was machine washable but she came back covered in some sticky substance that she said was ice cream. One never knows with Lucy. We come to the giant pile of tights and cardigans that the girls get through in the week.

'I haven't bought the uniform for Oliver yet? For St Catherine's. Is it a lot?'

'There's a stupid amount that you have to buy but we have some bits we can pass on. They have a second-hand sale day too. We could go together.'

'Thank you.'

I bury through a pile of socks and she hands me one so I can create a matching pair. She looks slightly murderous and I hope and pray she doesn't take it out on me. Could she kill me with a mop?

'How do you do it?'

'Do what?'

'You see him all the time, twice a week and you just get on with it. You don't want to throttle him? I just don't know what I'll do when I'm out there. I don't trust myself.'

'How would you kill him?' She looks at me curiously. 'I have fantasies about gutting him, a slow knife to the stomach and then watching him bleed out,' I reply. That could have been too honest and I'm conscious that we are not quite on the level of friends yet. I hope she doesn't report me to the board.

'I was thinking something even more drawn out. Poisoning. Every night in his dinner. Some poison that would maybe cause alopecia. Because we know how much he likes his hair.'

I smile at her. She's at that point of the separation. The angry, enraged part where it just feels like every one of your cells is fizzing with emotion.

'I fantasised about hiring a hit man once. I wasn't sure how I'd have found one though?' I say.

'Phone box, no?'

'Twitter, I thought. I imagined the ways I could have made it an accident. How I would have sat at his funeral. I even wrote him a eulogy. Is this weird?'

'No. In my fantasy, it ends with me walking across a London bridge in the black dress I wore to his funeral and throwing something he'd given me in the river.'

I laugh and look at her. Would I ever really hurt him? No. Sometimes the emotion felt that way, it was so raw, simmering inside me and turning me inside out. But after all that hate boiled away into nothing, these little people were still here and the world kept turning.

'You know he's done it again?' I say, my hands smoothing over the creases of a school cardigan.

'Done what?'

'He's out there with all our babies and we've been relegated to a glorified store cupboard.'

Susie is quiet and tackles the impossible task of trying to pair all the dark socks. I think about the scene that's probably outside this sanctuary of ours: Lucy sitting there with a string of snide comments to Simon and his lawyer. The kids running riot. George sat at my kitchen table fiddling with his paper clips and eating the last of the snacks.

'We need to be out there.'

'I can't.'

'But isn't the idea that we do this together? Strength in numbers?'

'There's only two of us.'

'And one of him? If you go for the nuts, I'll take his eyes.'

She smiles.

'What was he like with Oliver? Did they get on?' I ask.

'He's very good with him.'

'Maybe focus on the very few positives. My girls adore him. He does right by them. If he ever treated them in the same way that he did me then I'd floor him. I'd literally run him over and reverse back over him several times.'

'I'd act as your alibi. '

'It's OK, I have four sisters for that.'

'You don't think he's evil then?'

'Define evil. Like Hitler? No, he's screwed up in plenty ways. He is selfish and a liar and plenty of narcissism sits in his soul. I just have to make sure my daughters never see any of that. I need to make this whole situation less awful for them.'

'What if his lawyer comes at us with something today? What if he tries to take my boys?'

'Then I'll attack him with that quiche.'

'I need to say something to you,' she says.

'You do?'

'I'm sorry. I don't think anyone sets out to be the other woman. My own mother hates me for being that much.'

'We were all other women.'

She picks up a pair of knickers that are literally just pieces of string bound together by seams.

'Those are my sister's,' I blurt out.

She doesn't look convinced.

'Seriously, that looks like it would garrotte my lady parts.'

She chokes a little on her own breath. 'I hate him.'

'Reserve your hate for people who really need it.'

'Like?'

'You'll be joining the school gate soon. Trust me.'

It's strange. Little fibres are starting to poke out of the fabric and connect us to each other. We are suddenly a family of some description. I think of sisters who I never chose, whom occasionally, I don't quite get on with, but who are part of me. Who am I to say what a family looks like? But Susie and I are bonded by a sisterhood of being wronged by the same man. Maybe that's how it should be. I open the door to the utility room.

'Please, before Lucy actually kills him.'

She stands rooted to the spot.

'For the four of them in that front room. We get this sorted and then we can move on.'

'Move on to where?'

'I can't answer that for you. But just out of my utility room for a start.'

'Miss Hunter can't afford those fees on her own but she is happy to pay for a small part.'

'Mr Chadwick does not contest this. He is happy to pay for tuition if she can pay for uniform and sundry items.'

'Define sundry items?'

'Clubs, trips, equipment and scholastic items.'

Susie nods at George. She hasn't dared looked at Simon through the whole debacle. When she went into my living room, the tension in the air was viscous. I was unsure whether she was going to launch herself at him like a wildcat, swoon into his arms or fall to the floor in a flood of emotion. She stood glued to my side watching as Simon did what he does best. He laid on the charm to the kids, he made the baby smile. Those sorts of small actions used to make me ache with confusion. I hoped Susie wouldn't fall for it. Their greeting was muted as soon as she saw Cat too. I should have warned her about her.

Upstairs, Lucy sits with all these children. I've paid her ten pounds and the promise of my house for a social gathering so she can entertain them. I don't know what she's doing but I can hear the faint bass of some song from *Moana* kick into action and I text her from under my kitchen table to turn it down.

It's a strange arrangement in here. Susie, George and I sit to one side of the table and Cat and Simon to the other. In better circumstances, we'd be playing Monopoly and I'd be putting hotels on Mayfair and slaying Simon financially.

'And Miss Hunter's current abode? The house in Brentford. Miss Hunter has accrued some funds where she'd like to take over the mortgage on that property. She wants some reassurances that the house will remain in her name.'

'Funds?' asks Simon.

'My mum. She's going to move in with us.'

He stares back over at her to check if she's lying, shrugging his shoulders.

'So, now talk of custody and visiting arrangements…' mentions Cat. She's excelled herself today. The dress is clingy and the eyeliner winged and threatening. 'Mr Chadwick would argue that you are keeping him from seeing his sons.'

'For good reason,' interrupts Susie. I grab her elbow next to me. Reason over emotion, Susie.

'Yes, if I was a danger to those boys but Emma would tell you that I've never been a threat to my own children.'

You clever one you, dragging me into this.

'I am willing to take this higher so I can have at least visitation rights.'

Bring out the trump card, George.

'Well, yes… you are not a threat but Miss Callaghan and Miss Hunter want to ensure that you develop healthy and appropriate relationships with your children.'

Simon eyeballs me.

'And it has also come to their notice that both these sisters and brothers need to bond as siblings,' George continues. 'So Miss Callaghan and Miss Hunter have come to a mutual decision that they would like the children to spend some time together in the week. Naturally, this can be done under your custody or in moments in the week that are mutually convenient.'

Simon seems taken aback at the news.

'I don't have space for four children.'

'But seemingly you had the time to bring them into this world,' I tell him. 'We can help, we want them to see your mum too. We just want what's best for them.' We can all hear the scamper of little feet upstairs and what sounds like Lucy letting them jump off beds.

'And another condition too,' George adds, 'we are under no doubt that Mr Chadwick is an excellent father but he has led us to believe that he has facets to his character that worry us.'

'How so?' asks Simon.

'Hints of addictive behaviour, emotional manipulation. Misses Hunter and Callaghan do not appreciate being used against each other either.'

'How on earth have I done that?'

'You told me she was a bitch looking to get sole custody,' adds Susie. 'You made me hide Oliver like a dirty little secret.'

'I was trying to do what was best. I didn't want anyone to get hurt.'

'You were doing what was best for you.'

It feels all at once sad yet satisfying to catch him out. His blank expression tells us we've achieved that much.

'I'm sorry, Susie. Is there any way I can make this up to you?'

There's a look between them both. I wonder if she's falling for it but then her eyes mist over and I see some other emotion there. I assume it to be self-respect. She looks at me.

'I want those boys to have a father. I want them to know their sisters. Let's make that work.'

He nods.

'I don't want any communication from you. Any hint of midnight sexting or anything provocative then I review this. Know the boundaries.'

'I was drunk when I sent those...' says Simon trying to cover his tracks.

'You sent some last week. I had to block you.'

George slides some print outs to the other side of the table of screen grabs that Susie must have taken. Simon's face drops. I don't even flinch. I've seen that penis from all angles. He used to love taking pictures of it for others. He was so proud of it; look at my willy, isn't it great? Cat looks like she could stab Simon with a biro.

'Exactly,' comments George. 'This is not the behaviour of someone these women want to have around their children. There is potential for it to be toxic and unhealthy so we want conditions in place.'

'Conditions?'

'Weekly visits to a therapist or counsellor when you can review your behaviour.'

'That's all?' he says surprised.

'Yes,' George concludes. 'You were expecting more?'

'Yes, quite frankly, I thought you two were going to take me to the cleaners. You're seriously saying that I go see a shrink and I can start seeing those boys?' he asks.

'We want proof of appointments and then we can work on a timetable that is suitable to everyone.'

Cat is still lingering on Susie's admission and she pushes her chair back from the table. I see her note the dates and times on the messages. Then she calmly puts her stuff back in her bag and slaps Simon sharply across the face. He doesn't react but Susie may let out a laugh.

'Are you alright, Miss De Vere?' asks George.

'George, send through all the paperwork to the firm and we will get it sorted. Mr Chadwick, a new solicitor will be appointed to you moving forward.'

Susie's face reads relief but also vindication. She glares at Cat telling her to run. Cat doesn't need any persuasion and storms out the room, Simon in close pursuit. I follow them to ensure she is alright but I won't lie, this is worth me having a snoop. The front door opens and there is animated chat at the foot of the stairs, Cat points a finger in his face and actually tells him that he is a See You Next Tuesday, before making quite a stylish strutting exit away from my house. *Wow, good for you, Cat.*

And then there he is, out on the street, on his own. He follows Cat's figure but then looks up into the sky. This is the bit where you're supposed to cry and fall to your knees, Simon. It should rain at this point too.

'Chadwick?'

He looks over at me. The thing is he's not alone really, is he? He looks up at me. I take a seat on the steps, urging him to sit beside me. He comes over and does just that. And all at once, there's a strange feeling of déjà vu. These steps witnessed a lot of our marriage. We liked to sit out here in the summer. When we first moved in, we sat out here with beers, sleeves rolled up, boxes stacked into Jenga-style columns. We don't say a word to each other for a moment.

'Well played, Callaghan,' he whispers. He puts his hands to his face and presses his fingers into his forehead.

I am generous in response. 'No, you also had good game.'

'Why?'

'Those girls. Have you seen them? They have brothers. They're beyond thrilled.'

He still seems confused that I don't seem to have too much anger about this.

'It's certainly a crowd.'

'I grew up with a crowd. It's worth it.'

'Did you persuade Susie to let me see my boys?'

I pause. 'I did. I persuaded her that you were human. That we needed a chance to make this work.'

Whatever I thought of him and whatever he did to me, it's time to move on. All that hatred, doubt and emotion was like a cancer eating away at me. He did a bad thing but it was tiring trying to vilify him constantly.

'You are human, aren't you?' I ask him.

'I think so.'

'Go for the counselling. Fix yourself.'

'I will.'

'And I want us to stop dancing around each other.'

'How so?'

'You are inevitably going to be a part of my life forever. I don't love you but I don't want to hate you either. No more games…'

'Unless they're school quizzes, of course.'

'Well obviously. I'm up for a rematch next year so I can defend my title.'

'You're on.'

'Then we try and make this work? All these children, let's do the right thing by them.'

'It takes a village and all that.'

'Something like that.'

'Am I the village idiot?'

'Why, of course. Can I buy stocks?'

'Deal.'

There is silence. A quiet hum of traffic in the distance, puffs of breath cloud the air making me think we should both be wearing coats. I spy Mrs Phelps, her tree is up and she stands beside it, trying to hide her figure in the curtains. Christmas is nearly here. Nearly two years since I decided to divorce him. Yet here we are.

'I do have a new boyfriend by the way. The Asian fella from the quiz. His name is Jag.'

'I figured. He seemed alright. Have the girls met him yet?'

'Soon. We're going to the circus together.'

'OK. Was Cat your girlfriend?'

'Not really. Going forward, do you want to know who I'm seeing?'

'Unless they're meeting my girls then no.'

'How much does Susie hate me?'

'As much as I hated you two Christmases ago. Give her time.'

We sit quietly in each other's company.

'Are we friends yet, Emma?'

'No. Maybe one day. But we're something, I just don't have the word for it yet.'

'Mrs Phelps is watching us from behind her curtain.'

'I know. Probably because Cat called you a See You Next Tuesday quite loudly in the street.'

Simon stops for a moment.

'That's what that means! I thought your sister was overly fond of saying it.'

'Well, you are one…'

'I'll take that.'

The front door opens and two little faces pop out from behind it.

'What are you doing? It's freezing!' shouts Iris.

'Well then come here and give me cuddles and warm me up,' says Simon.

I see Lucy watching us from the living room window. She gestures that now is the perfect time to push him down those steps. I don't. Simon and I take a girl each. I take Violet and let her entangle her legs in mine, cradling herself into the hook of my arm. Her hair smells of coconut and Play-Doh. Iris uses Simon like a climbing frame. He bops her on the nose as he has done since she was a baby. It never stops being hilarious to her. The sky starts to dim, trees casting shadows onto the pavement. A house down the road has some festive lights that switch on and flicker on and off in strange syncopated patterns.

That Christmas day it all happened, I remember being perched here watching the girls ride scooters up and down the street. Simon and I were both in pyjamas and slippers sipping coffees out of matching mugs. My heart aches. Our marriage was peppered with vignettes like that, moments that made sense, that made me want to prolong what we had in some vain hope that it could all be that perfect. But it wasn't. And for once that sits fine with my soul.

'Mama, why are you both sitting in the street?' asks Violet.

'Technically, it's not the street. It's still our own house,' I tell her.

'Aren't you cold?' she asks. 'What is frostbite?'

'It's when your extremities get very cold and turn blue, why?' I explain.

'Aunty Lucy said something about daddy getting it in his willy.'

'She did now, did she?' says Simon. He turns to the window but Lucy is quick to hide from view. Iris nestles her head into Simon's chest, in the shallows of his neck.

'I can hear your heartbeat,' Iris comments.

It's reassuring to know there's something in there.

'Ba-boom-ba-boom-ba-boom… why does it beat like that?'

'Ask your mother. She knows hearts.'

I smile.

'I know. She's also a better doctor than you too. Aunty Lucy said that.'

He laughs under his breath.

'Let's get these girls into the warm, Simon.'

He nods. 'Sure thing, Emma.'

# Epilogue

## The day I gave my husband back

'Are you calling my turkey dry?'

I look over at Meg in the corner of our family kitchen wondering where on earth she had the courage to come out with a comment like that. Even Danny stops washing up to absorb what his wife just said to our mother. I mean, you think it, but you just douse it in gravy and make do. Such is the joy of a white chalky meat like turkey. Why do this now? Now she'll harp on about the bacon she puts on the breasts and all the goose fat. But it's Meg. She likes the challenge. I secretly think the only way she believes she can have a relationship with our mother is to spar with her regularly so they at least have one line of communication.

'It was a lovely dinner, Mum. Did you make the mince pies?' Meg winks at me.

*You know very well she didn't.* I shake my head at her and bring the plate of mince pies through to the living room. Amidst my mother's wreaths and tinsel wrapped around the lampshades, it's a familiar tableau: Dad asleep in the armchair in the corner, a holly green paper hat covering his eyes. Small children crawl on the floor and make angel shapes with their bodies amidst remnants of old glittery wrapping paper. I hope Mum's made trifle. Beth and Will snooze on a neighbouring sofa, still nursing London hangovers from last night where they partied in some neon warehouse bar in Hoxton. I like this part of Christmas where bits of old crackers litter the floor and twilight takes over.

I take a mince pie and escape to the last vacant spot on the sofa. Four-year-old Violet rests her head on my knees. 'What you eating, Mama?' I like how she calls me Mama. It's ever so slightly continental. I look down at her big hazel eyes and wonder how she can still be hungry as she must be ninety per cent roast potato.

'A mince pie.'

'With cow mince?'

'No, like fruity bits.' I pick out said fruity bits and drop them into her mouth like a baby bird. She pulls a face, tasting it, and then rolls away.

Will very possibly farts next to me but I ignore him. Him and Beth are wrapped around each other. Actually, that may be the smell of weed. Stoned and drunk and full to the brim with sprouts. That may be medically quite dangerous. Time to bring on the better alcohol, kids. Make wishes for a better year. I scratch at my neck. Simon gifted me a very mustard jumper that is soft and cashmere but has made me break out into hives around my neck. It also isn't red and that has upset my mother's colour palette for her photos. Where is Simon? Is it bad that I ask this question a lot? Is it bad that all I wanted to say was sod the jumper, some assurances that you'd stop putting it about would be a much better Christmas present? He could hand that to me as voucher, maybe frame it.

'Pass us a mince pie, Emma,' asks Will as he sifts through the TV schedule to look for a film for the little ones. Dad wakes from his slumber and smiles at me.

'All good, Ems?' he asks.

I smile and nod. It's a stock response these days. I could be sick, my girls could be ill, I could be in a war zone or homeless or without anyone in this room. It could be worse. But everyone knows about Simon so I get this question a lot. They question my judgement and my sanity. One of the sisters will occasionally get drunk and tell me I'm an idiot and acting like I'm some wife from the fifties but none of them have been able to tear me away from him. None of them understand my fear, my anxiety over being divorced. I'd be alone. I would be thirty-three and on my own with young children and a career. Every time I've even imagined some alternative future where Simon isn't there, the future is muddied and unclear. I would be lost. I would be broken. And I would hate that very personal feeling of failure. So I stay where I am. I feel the better option is the one you know, even if it does involve ritual humiliation.

Tom is on the floor with four nieces sat on his back while he colours in with them. He's the fun uncle whom they all love because he's got a skill for origami and animal noises. Grace comes over, plonking herself atop my lap and gives me a huge bear hug. Someone has been at the sherry.

'Emsy Ems. Love you. Thank you for my slipper socks.'

'And thank you for my chocolates and wine. You always say you have cold feet. I was trying to be functional.'

'They are very useful. More useful than the rude coasters that Lucy got me.'

'What's on yours?' she asks.

'Mine are inscribed with *Use A Fucking Coaster*,' I whisper given the children in proximity.

'I got actual penises, in graphic tiled print.'

We both laugh and she downs the rest of her drink, watching Tom intently. Those two have been together since university, they're an unlikely couple in a relationship that's run quite the emotional gamut but their wedding last year seemed to quieten all the doubters. Except we don't talk about the cake. A cake made of cheese was not a way to cement a relationship, my mother said.

'And how are you?' she asks.

'I am well, I may need more alcohol though.'

'Meg told me about the parent from school who Simon—'

I put my finger hand to my mouth to encourage her to be quiet around the girls.

'I told her not to say anything,' I say. Grace gives me a look. When have any of us ever kept quiet about anything? You tell one sister and it trickles down the grapevine. The other parent was also married and from what I hear, she's now separated. The kids got taken out of the school in quite an acrimonious split. I quizzed Simon about everything and he denied it but I knew. Of course I knew. Did I want the same to happen to our girls? That upheaval and distress? So I let it go. Like all the other times.

'He tells me it's over.'

'Ems…'

'Don't. It's Christmas.'

In an uncharacteristic move, she cradles my head and strokes my hair.

'Ems, can I ask you a weird question?'

'Sure.'

'When should you worry about lumps on bollocks?'

'What sort of lumps?'

'Like they're not his bollocks but there's something there. Tom won't see a doctor. I just keep telling him but he keeps swerving. Would Simon have a look? Or you?'

'Kid, I love your husband but see a specialist. It's probably nothing. I'll text you some numbers.'

'Sure. I've drunk too much. I can't feel my face.'

'Keep drinking, will make it easier to beat you at Scrabble later.'

'You wish…'

It's then we hear it. It's not like we've not heard this noise before in this very house but we hear the sound of Lucy screeching from in the hallway. Knowing her, she's having a fight with someone or opened a good present or is just being Lucy. But I hear Simon's voice too. I hear her run around upstairs and then a scuffle. We look out to the patio as something falls onto the slabs. The children run and press their faces against the window.

'It's a phone. A phone has fallen out of the sky,' says Iris.

We all stand to attention in that room. Tom springs into action.

'Girlies, who wants to watch some television with Uncle Tom?'

Iris, Violet, Tess and Eve all climb on top of him and I watch Meg make her move, her gallop echoing on the stairs. Dad closes the living room door to drown out the noise from upstairs. Mum and Grace soon follow but I just stand still because I know what this is about. *Christmas Day, Simon? You have truly excelled yourself.*

I take a slow walk up the stairs of my parents' house to see all four Callaghan girls and my mother taking him on.

'He literally was in the spare room talking to some girl about all the things he wanted to do to her. I heard every word,' shrieks Lucy.

'I was talking about a procedure at the hospital!' he protests.

'Involving licking someone's clit?' Lucy retorts. Grace, Meg and Beth shake their heads silently.

'And then your sister threw my phone out of the window!' explains Simon.

'You're lucky I didn't throw your lying arse out that window.'

Meg comes over to back Lucy up. 'What the hell, Simon? What the actual hell? Your kids are downstairs! Your daughters!' she shouts.

'Emma, it really is not what you think.'

'Then what is it?' I ask.

He looks at me like he always does. *You know what this is about. You'll never leave me.* I stand back from the melee.

'He had some tart on FaceTime and she literally had her gash on show.'

'Lucy, if you could be slightly less vulgar,' requests my mother.

'Me? He's here doing what he's done for years. You are such a complete bellend. Please Emma, have some fucking sense for once.' She slurs her words as she's been on the sherry too but she looks me in the eye. Stop doing this to yourself, Ems. Stop this now. Grace holds my hand tightly. Meg points at him and I see her fury, how much emotion this dredges up in her.

'I literally want to rip off your cock.'

'Meg, please,' I whisper.

Beth fumes silently, crying next to me at seeing this unfold. And my heart aches. It was broken anyway. I was broken. But I always thought there was no way it'd ever repair itself. Today tells me differently. Today reveals all these people to me who are bigger than my marriage. In some rare cosmic occurrence, all five Callaghan sisters are together. No one is at the in-laws, no one is working a shift or travelling. We are here in force. My marriage was so insular before, I always thought it was about me and him but really what I went through was felt by others too; people who would love you whatever the storm, who'd guide you through it, who wouldn't ever allow you to drown. I see tears. I see fury. I see heart.

'Who is she? Just some slapper? How old was she? Does she know you're married?'

'Ems? Ems?'

'Keep the girls downstairs, David. Play something on the piano!'

'I needed that phone for work.'

'You're a shitty human being.'

'This is my marriage and nothing to do with you.'

'Emma, you are better than this wanker!'

'I'm begging you. Don't let him keep doing this to you.'

'Get out of my goddamn house, before I throw you out.'

'Takes a slut to know one…'

'You better find yourself a fucking good lawyer.'

I don't know who's saying the words now but I just stand here trying to work out where to go next. I see the fist flying and make contact with Simon's nose. I see blood. I hear Lucy cheer and Grace catch my mother as she falls from the sheer force. She did *what*? Mum? Beth's hands cover her mouth in shock. Meg is laying into

Simon that he's lucky that's all he gets. Someone locks her in the bathroom. Blood. Everywhere. Pumping out of his veins and his slightly crooked nose. She's broken that. I throw up. All I can smell is mince pie and blood and I prop myself against a wall, Beth holds me up and wraps her body around mine. I realise it's all very much over, this marriage of mine. This is the point I finish it. Where I give you back. This is where I start again.

(It's never) THE END

# A Letter from Kristen

Dear Reader,

You're bloody marvellous! You're back again (or maybe you're new?) Either way, it's lovely to meet you and thank you from the bottom of my heart for reading my book. I hope that you've cried, cheered and laughed with Emma and enjoyed her story. If you are new to my writing then go find *Has Anyone Seen My Sex Life?* which is all about Meg, Emma's older sister. And if you liked Beth, Grace and Lucy then their stories will be coming to you in the very near future – keep up to date with when they're released by signing up at the following link. Your email address will never be shared and you can unsubscribe at any time.

*www.bookouture.com/kristen-bailey*

I love Emma (like a sister, one would say) but I was never sure how I was going to write a book about divorce. My marriage is far from perfect but I quite like my husband so I looked at it from the flip side, as a surviving child of divorce. My own parents split when I was twenty-one in possibly the most amicable split in history. They still go on holiday together and buy each other Christmas presents. So from their story and observing divorce amongst my friends and acquaintances, it inspired me to write about divorce from a different angle, focussing on the multitude of ways in which relationships, families and love exist in the aftermath. Divorce can spike so many emotions – we hear a lot about the sadness, the conflict and the pain but when the dust settles, it also can lead people to better places, happier times and ask them to be kinder humans. I'd love for the hope and forgiveness in this book to shine through or, at least, that Emma's story makes you obsess over hummus, the shaping of your own pubic hair and Nike Air Max.

I'd be thrilled to hear from any of my readers, whether it be with reviews, questions or just to say hello. If you like retweets of videos of dancing pandas then follow me on Twitter. Have a gander at Instagram, my Facebook author page and website too for updates, ramblings and to learn more about me. Like, share and follow away – it'd be much appreciated.

And if you enjoyed *Can I Give My Husband Back?* then I would be overjoyed if you could leave me a review on either Amazon or Goodreads to let people know. It's a brilliant way to reach out to new readers. And don't just stop there, tell everyone you know, send to all on your contacts list, announce it on WhatsApp groups. It also makes a wonderful gift. Not to your own husband, of course.

With much love and gratitude,
Kristen
xx

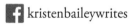 kristenbaileywrites

 kristenbaileywrites

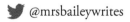 @mrsbaileywrites

🌐 www.kristenbaileywrites.com

# Acknowledgements

Bookouture! You're just a bloody marvellous thing and as a publisher, you've provided me with so much support, love and camaraderie. You are book FAMILY and I can't think of a better place for my books to be. To the many who bring my books to life, my sincerest love and thanks. And Christina, you're still the proper bestest editor there is, thank you for helping me find my funny and for your overwhelming enthusiasm in all that you do.

My husband, Nick, never fairs well from the titles of my books so a thank you to him for enduring. I've often thought of exchanging you for Idris Elba but truth is I know he wouldn't be as good a tea boy as you. So yes, I never want to give you back. You're stuck with me. The kids like you better anyway.

This book is, in part, about sisters and I have the best sister in the world. Her name is Leanne and she's the same height as Kylie. We went ice skating one year and we recreated Torvill and Dean's 'Boléro', we even sang the music. The rest of the family pretended not to know us. No doubt, you are the best sibling of the three of us (we don't count the brother because he smells) and all the funniest lines in this book are probably something you've said to me at some point in our sisterhood so thank you for a lifetime of material.

The heart element of this book was inspired by my own daughter's adventures in SVT and a person actually called Lewis. Both of them re-define bravery for me so a special shout-out to both of them and the amazing NHS that has kept them both alive.

Here's a list of random names of people who are friends and save me from a solitary writing existence. Whether you've let me nick your name and style, lead your lives by example, retweeted the hell out of things, proofread, fed me wine, sent me playlists or let me talk at you for hours on the phone, my love and eternal gratitude to you all for your physical and emotional support: Emma Harris, Dan Turkington, Leo Williams, Morgan Hamer, Anna Le Jeune, Sara Hafeez, Graham Price, Joe Rigby and Jag Sanghera.

And finally... I hated writing the character of Simon mainly because he reminded me so much of a lot of tossers I know and have heard about in my lifetime, just really appalling examples of husbands. Despite the inspiration you gave me, thanks don't seem appropriate so instead a message to any woman who has a feeling she is still married to a Simon. Bin him, give him back, start again, you deserve better, make you and your happiness the priority.

Printed in Great Britain
by Amazon